Dancing with Shadows

Dancing with Shadows

Shiraz Pradhan

PARTRIDGE

To order additional copies of this book, contact
Partridge India
000 800 10062 62
orders.india@partridgepublishing.com

www.partridgepublishing.com/india

Web Conversations...

I'm currently reading your book 'Dancing with Shadows' and enjoying it very much. Some parts of the book reminds me of R.K.Narayan's **'Malgudi Days'** series of books. And, of course, it reminds me of Bollywood cinema in Uganda. It takes me back to my youth! *Naziara Ismail-Kaye, UK*

Just finished reading Dancing with Shadows and am now at a loss as to how I can live without my daily visits to Jerusha and the incredible exploits of our hero and his friends. I was really riveted from start to finish and honestly only put it down very reluctantly between reads. A mammoth achievement combining so much of life, love, romance, music, poetry, science and philosophy. A helter skelter ride through the intense experiences of youth trying to crystalize into a full grown compassionate human being. Our hero manages it well despite so much intrigue, death, injustice and repression in the society that surrounds him. We can draw little comfort from the fact of this setting taken place in a turbulent African country torn apart by tribal war and conflict, many aspects of the human condition portrayed are universal and only too familiar to us all. We suffer with those who find themselves in excruciating circumstances, we find joy, hope and love with those who have come to an acceptance and understanding of life without loss of their humanity. The author brings into focus the question of how real is our reality. A truly remarkable piece of inspired writing. *Ormond Noonan, Teddington Literary Circle. UK*

"Shiraz's latest work is a book that is hard to put away once you start reading. Intrigue and fascination, keeps you in anticipation of what lays ahead. The backdrop to the storyline is exotic, mysterious and unfamiliar to most westerners and therefore very interesting...Shiraz uses science, philosophy, psychology, religion and spiritualism to embellish his thoughts while drawing from the Indian poetry form of Ghazal, thus keeping the subject matter fundamentally romantic. The language he uses is reminiscent of the Anglo-Indian-African era of the time, almost Victorian in fabric. **Shabir Dhanani, Vancouver, BC**

Pradhan's *Dancing with Shadows reminds me of Huckleberry Fin...fascinating.* **Taveesub Nagamkam, Thailand.**

Very Interesting...reminds me of my time in the sixties in Kampala. Looking forward to reading your book. **Rashida, facebook.com/indiawellnesstour**

Your book has been a wonderful source of bring back wonderful memories, thanks Shiraz. **Ashwin Raichura, UK**

For a debut author Shiraz Pradhan has a gripping story that touches every aspect of life. **Venu Nair, India**

If you can't smell the fragrance
Don't come into the garden of Love
If you are unwilling to undress
Don't come in the stream of Truth

(Rumi)

Acknowledgements

M y thanks to Shabir Dhanani, Khatoon Noonan, Saroj D. Ellis and Roshan Hussein for their editorial comments. I have consulted Wikipedia during the formative stage of the book for ideas on various subjects including Urdu Poetry, *Gazals*, Hindu Trinity, and Krishna. For concept of *Udhric,* I have consulted *The Passion of al Hallaj* by Louis Massignon, Princeton University Press. The quotation of Rumi is taken from an Internet site 'Write Spirit Sharing – Ancient Wisdom and Modern Inspirations'. The poem by Amir Khusro is a free translation of the original recited to me by Ashraf Kabuli many years ago. The image used in the cover design is an adaptatio in the public domain and/or meet the US Fair Use definition per US Copy Right and Wikipedia web sites. To my wife Mariam and my daughters Shainila and Yasmin go my thanks for their critical assessments of my work which encouraged me to try and excel.

Shiraz Pradhan was born in Uganda and attended universities in Kenya and USA attaining graduate degrees in Engineering and Mechanics. He is a practicing professional engineer and had resided in Canada, USA, Japan, Singapore and Europe and is currently living in London, UK, with his family. Shiraz's writing career stretches back twenty years. He has published several essays on philosophy and mysticism and has been a regular contributor to technical publications. His second book, King's Peacock, in the genre of the Alchemist and Children of the Alley, is currently going through final editing and will be published in 2017. He has two other projects, Saving Love and Judgement at Baghdad in their final phases and will also be ready for final editing in 2018. Dancing with Shadows is his debut novel.

Circles of Life

Rehmat rises first, even before the sun is up, to cook breakfast. At this early hour, the granite rocks at the back of the garden are dark patches, standing as sentries to Suwakaki Forest which is still a solid wall of black. 'Wake up brother,' Henna's voice pulls me up from deep sleep. As she rushes off for a shower before anyone else, she says, 'You had asked me to wake you up.' Henna hates wet floor in the bath room. I stumble out of bed and come to the breakfast room. The bay window is glimmering with shafts of orange and pink from the eastern horizon. Suwakaki is abuzz with a cacophony of bird songs. Appetizing aroma of frying omelettes fills the house. Jeff is sitting by the old Phillips radio, which is crackling with news commentary from BBC World Service. He is oblivious of me, chewing on his lower lip, shuffling through an old copy of *The Telegraph.* All at once, he drops the paper, rushes out through the patio door and sprinkles birdfeed by the garden shed. Droves of bees are buzzing around the blooms of African tulips and hibiscus near the garden shed, adding to the hiss from Jeff's radio and the hum of bicycles of workers rushing to work on Zanzibar Road. The huge tropical African sun is above the horizon by now. Jeff then disappears behind the granite rocks which are covered by deep red and violet bougainvillea. A squadron of birds swoop in for the bird feed. A pair of ducks, the newest residents of our garden, quack across the lawn to get their share of morning feed. Henna, a walking Encyclopaedia, had said that these were falcated ducks from India, migrating to South Africa.

Their green necks indicted to me that these were more like Canadian than Indian ducks but I did not argue with Henna. Wherever they had come from, the ducks are now a permanent feature of our garden and it does not appear that they are leaving for South Africa anytime soon, which is fine with Rehmat. She had asked me to erect a nylon net around the pond to ward off any predators. I did so, but had cautioned her, 'Ma, the way Simba is chasing them, they might be his evening meal one of these days.' This had petrified Rehmat. 'Good lord, he dare not,' she had declared with the forcefulness of Pope Urban and had put the monkey on my back. 'From now on, it is your responsibility to keep Simba out of mischief.'

The ducks waddle across the lawn with Simba, the crazy Alsatian, in hot pursuit. I run out, catch Simba and chain him by the doghouse. This distresses him. He whimpers an apology, licking my leg. 'Then be good,' I say and release him and return to the breakfast room, startling Azul at the table. 'Son, why are you up early?' he asks.

'Oh, don't you know, Daddy? Today is the event of the century. So exciting. Anytime soon NASA's Mercury will blast off for module tests in space and man will be on the moon in one year.' Just then Jeff walks in. 'What is he on about, Daddy?' he asks. Azul repeats my answer. Jeff waves his hand in the air, 'On the moon within a year! I told you Daddy, he imagines these things.'

'No, Jeff, he has researched it well,' Azul defends me, boosting my ego. Jeff and I are like cats and dogs. Ordinarily, I would have reacted angrily to Jeff's innuendo. Lately, he had been propagating this myth about me being delusional. I remain calm. 'Jeff, if you don't stop name-calling, I will return the favour.' My cool reaction confuses him. I add more punch to my attack. 'The only person delusional is you. My information is from the United States Information Service (USIS).' Jeff backs off. 'Okay,' he says, 'don't take it so seriously.' Azul gulps his tea, stands up and says, 'I have to be in Pala soon. Son, keep me informed about the Mercury Mission.'

Extreme heat or cold change our mental perceptions. An intense heat wave that gripped Jerusha one time severely tested my mental faculties, blurring the line between reality and delusion. Such was the intensity of heat that tar on roads began to run like black lava. To escape the searing heat I made my way to a gurgling brook close to a fig tree in Suwakaki. I dipped my feet in the gently flowing waters of the brook and sat watching the kaleidoscopic dance of sunlight filtering through the towering leaf canopy of Suwakaki, lighting up a clearing to my right like a stage. I was overcome by heat exhaustion and felt drowsy. Suddenly I heard a jingling of anklets, humming of a haunting tune and a girl dancing in the clearing bathed by sunlight where a few seconds ago, there was no one. I sat up straight. The shafts of sunlight gave her a magical aura. Her sudden appearance seemed out of this world. 'Good gosh, where did you come from?' I asked. The girl continued dancing and humming the tune which was very familiar and which stirred up strange emotions. In my confused state I could not recall the lyrics to the tune. My mind drew a blank on any memories associated with it, and emotions without associated memories were deeply disturbing.

'What are you humming?' I asked. The girl stopped dancing. 'Dear Goldie Locks,' I pleaded, 'lift these locks from your face and tell me.' I was getting desperate by the second. 'I am not telling,' she teased me and lifted her hand with air of a royalty and moved the locks covering her face. Her elegant move was deliberate. A beautiful, moonlike face emerged from behind the clouds. The tune that she had hummed had invaded the recesses of my heart like a sweet poison, and knowing what song it was, was the only antidote that would cure me. 'What song is it?' I asked in desperation.

'What will you give me if I sing the words?'

'Anything you want,' I replied. She moved closer and pointed at my neck. 'That chain and the pendant.' I was intoxicated by my desire. A bargain was a bargain. I reluctantly unclasped the chain and gave it to her. She took it gracefully, examined it, then turned and ran. 'Come find me if you can,' she yelled. I was frozen. In the flash of a moment, she disappeared in the thick of Suwakaki, only the echoes of her laughter lingered.

I traced my steps back to our garden, startling Henna who was skipping under the mango tree. Someone had told her that skipping was the best way to maintain a trim figure. She stopped skipping. 'Henna, did you see a girl run out of the forest?' I asked.

'What?' Henna immediately rushed and felt my forehead. 'Do you have a heat stroke?'

'No,' I replied. She embarrassed me by saying, 'Silly boy, what girl are you dreaming of?' Despite the oppressive heat, I hid in the garden shed for the rest of the afternoon. Towards the evening, sky became crowded with dark clouds. Thunder and lightning followed. During dinner, it began to rain. Henna jumped up and clapped. 'Hooray, Ma, can I go dancing in the rain?' Rehmat had to curb her zeal. 'Henna, sit and eat. Dancing in the rain . . . are you crazy?' I was continually putting my hand to my collar and pulling it up. Rehmat noticed this and came and examined my neck. 'Where is your chain?' she asked.

'Ehm . . . Ma, I think I lost it.'

'Lost it? You careless boy, do you know what you lost? It was a family heirloom.' She turned to Azul and asked in exasperation, 'What am I to do with your son?' Azul continued to eat in silence, which incensed her more. 'Spoil him.' Jeff looked at me disdainfully, Henna made a dismissive hand gesture, while, Salim, my younger brother, clapped gleefully. Henna rubbed salt in my wound, 'Ma, this afternoon he ran out of Suwakaki, talking about some girl.' Jeff added insult to injury, 'Isn't it too soon to dream about girls? I told you, Daddy, he is always dreaming.' Azul maintained his composure, 'Let him eat in peace. You all are overwhelming him.'

I lumped my dinner as best as I could and returned to my annex which I had named *Uhuru*, a word which in our part of the world had gained coinage as a paradisiacal state of freedom from the tyranny of the British Rule. *Uhuru* connected to our house through a vestibule lined with pots of orchids and overgrown lime and rubber plants interlaced with morning glories. During the day, sunshine, filtering through the latticed panes above, made the vestibule look like an enchanted garden. At night, it assumed a sombre appearance. This dramatic contrast gave flight to my imagination.

When I came into *Uhuru* after dinner, a rain-laden wind was howling in through an open window, which was banging against the wall. In the orange glow of the street lamps filtering in through dancing branches of the trees, the garden was like a grand cathedral celebrating midnight mass on Christmas Eve, with gusts of wind singing hymns through the trees and a wind chime ringing somewhere in the darkness. I stretched out to close the window, relishing the cool rain spray in my face when I saw Simba shivering by his flooded doghouse. I put on my raincoat, grabbed a towel and guided him to the garden shed and dried him. He sat down on a dry rag and rested his head between his legs. As I left, he barked, thanking me.

The rain continued to pelt down with fury, and would continue to do so for the next two days, causing the flash flood of Jerusha, which affected the area around the Town Hall. Later I would find that the aftermath of this flood was interwoven with my life.

I returned to *Uhuru*, dried myself, and lay down in my bed. Sleep eluded me. I thought about the girl in the Suwakaki. Who was she? What melody was she humming?

Music has the magic of creating sweetness in the soul. Before we had electricity in the house I used to watch Jeff perform the ritual of lighting the Petromax every evening. As the menthol of the Petromax became incandescent, by magic, "there was light" and the world became translucent silver. This miracle never ceased to amaze me. Jeff then hung the Petromax like a chandelier in the dining room. Dinner was enjoyed in regal fashion under this blazing light. Once dinner was concluded, the Petromax was extinguished, and we sat talking in the glow of a kerosene lantern, while Jeff tuned his battery-powered Phillips to the All India Radio's "music hour" during which, on the canvass of the night, enlivened by the orange glow of the lantern, Lata Mangeshkar, the nightingale of Bollywood, weaved an enchanting garland of Bollywood film songs, until I felt as if I saw music. Its sweet wavelets floated in my mind like little fairies and then a carriage drawn by colourful butterflies delivered me to the bosom of sleep. Some nights I fell asleep to BBC's classical hour. Radio became a powerful tool that connected me to this magical world. In those early, lantern-lighted nights, I thought that a man wearing a Turkish fez in a poster hanging above the radio had something to do with music. I had seen his lips move. When I told Jeff about it, he laughed. 'Silly boy, you are dreaming. He is just advertising Clipper cigarettes.' It was from this time Jeff thought I was delusional.

Years later, in my limited understanding of reality, it dawned on me that events did not happen in isolation. There was a connectedness to them. There was a method to the madness and that my early ideas of music were building blocks of what was to come. The Universe was about to take this confused jumble of events and assemble it into an intricate mosaic that would change the very fabric of my inner life. A year before my encounter with the mysterious girl in Suwakaki, during the year-end school Variety Show, an event happened that had a great deal to do with the mysterious girl and the unknown melody she had hummed. Towards the very end of the Show, a girl by the name of Ratan came on stage. After the razzmatazz of the earlier performances, which were vibrant with colourful costumes and energy, plain Ratan did not arouse much interest from the audience. However, a kind of mysterious magnetism radiated from her. She stood in the centre of the stage, with a white flowery pin in her hair. Without much fuss, she came closer to the microphone, raised one of her hands to her ears as if in prayer, and started humming a tune in lower octaves. Everyone sat down, and the murmur died down. Then suddenly, as if driven by some mysterious power, Ratan progressed from low octave humming to what in Indian Classical singing is called, *gayaki*, singing in words, on a sweet note that was four octaves higher. The auditorium shook with the energy of her melody which was from the soundtrack of a romantic Bollywood picture and number one on Radio Ceylon's Hit Parade.

What realm is this, O beloved magician?

Beyond stars, what dreamy world are you

Leading me to . . .

Ratan's singing lifted me to the world of dreams that she was singing about. That such pure magic could flow from the voice of a diminutive girl amazed me. Later, when I told Henna that Ratan had opened up a seam of treasure in my heart, she laughed. 'My gullible brother, what treasure seam? If you are not careful, people will take advantage of such sentimentality.'

The connectedness of events did not stop with Ratan. Echoes of infinity had a way of reinforcing the theme. I had been begging Azul for months to take me with him to our coffee estate. He always resisted it. 'Son, it is just a jungle and mountain villages.'

'Daddy, I still want to see it.' During school holidays, he surprised me by inviting me to join him to the coffee plantation. 'Really, Daddy?' I asked.

We spent a week on the plantation. The terraces of coffee shrubs nestled on the slope of forested Nirambeya Mountain astounded me. 'Daddy, this is fantastic,' I said as we roamed the paths between rows of coffee shrubs. 'It is the cool mountain air which gives our coffee an edge,' Azul explained. 'A day's delay in harvesting and the berries' aroma and the magic are lost.' It was the best biology lesson I ever had. We walked up to the summit of Nirambeya to an exclusive section of the plantation. 'This section has export-grade coffee,' Azul explained. 'Like a Shiraz wine it has a wild tropical scent that sets it apart from other coffee and it is very popular in London.' On our way down, we stopped by our coffee grading station where Azul showed me the tricks of coffee grading.

One night, we sat around a log fire and ate boiled groundnuts, the first crop of the season. They melted in the mouth and were unlike anything I had tasted. 'Daddy, these are so sweet and different,' I commented. He explained, 'These are a local, purple variety. They only grow on this mountain.' We talked about many different subjects as we savoured boiled groundnuts and enjoyed fresh coffee boiled with cloves and cinnamon. I asked Azul about religion. He laughed and said that Karl Marx had said that religion was opium of the masses. I asked. 'Does God exist?' He fell silent. After a while he said, 'When Einstein was asked the same question, he reflected on it for a long time and then said, "There is something out there".'

'So what is your answer, Daddy?' I asked. He chuckled and said, 'There is something out there. But, son, how could mind which is created understand that which is uncreated?' We fell silent. The jungle around us pulsed with strange noises. I continued to open groundnut pods for Azul. The sky above was studded with stars. Azul pointed to a cluster of stars. 'That is Orion. When the Egyptian pharaohs were anointed as kings, they were drugged and were hypnotized to believe that they were from Orion which was home of Osiris, their ruling god.'

'Seriously, Daddy?'

'Yes, the Egyptian king-making ceremony was very cleverly done and that is how the myth of Son of Osiris perpetuated.' In the dancing flames of the log fire Azul looked like a sage. I handed him a fresh mug of coffee and a plate of peeled groundnuts. He took it, but his eyes were riveted to the sky, as if looking for something special. Then he turned 180 degrees. 'Ah, there it is! That bright one is Venus. Do you know, son, when God first put the spheres in motion and they danced in their orbits, they produced a Celestial Symphony.' This powerful statement had immediate resonance in my heart.

'Really, Daddy, a Celestial Symphony, God's Music?'

'Yes, that is what the ancient Greeks told us.'

'Daddy, is it still playing?' I asked. He smiled, 'Yes, if you become one with nature, you can hear it, even now. May be then you will know about existence of God.' My mind immediately reeled back to the time when Ratan had sung her classical song and the girl in Suwakaki had hummed the mysterious melody. All at once, everything seemed to fall into place. My Aristotelian mind went into an overdrive and the magic quadrilateral of logic was complete. The garland of music that Lata had weaved during those lantern-lit nights, Ratan's dream song that taken me to the height of ecstasy, the tune the mysterious girl had hummed in Suwakaki, and Azul's powerful statement about Celestial Symphony were all connected. Sitting on the slope of Nirambeya, with my back cold and my front hot from the log fire, with a mug of fresh, spiced coffee in my hand and the sweet taste of purple groundnuts in my mouth, the inspiration and enlightenment came. What I had heard the mysterious girl hum in Suwakaki was God's Symphony. And the mysterious girl was no other than a divine nymph. I had seen a picture of a painting titled "Nymph on the Seashore". I felt sure that the mysterious girl was this nymph. The locks of curly hair, the enchanting smile and lips like rose buds, the resemblance, between the two, I felt was uncanny. The very next minute, my Aristotelian mind took a sharp turn. What if I was under narcotic influence of fresh coffee and purple groundnuts? How could I be so blessed that divine nymph came down to reveal to me God's own Symphony? But, there it was. A conclusion was reached, and it was not possible to reverse it. I questioned and debated it many times, but the premise stood intact.

In the days that followed, the conclusion that I had reached on the slope of Nirambeya began to grow like a pearl in the oyster of my heart. I began to look for clues and facts that supported my conclusion. I searched our local library, and in one of the volumes of *Collections of Great Paintings*, I found the painting of the "Nymph on the Seashore" (which I learnt was housed in a Madrid museum) and re-examined her face. It reinforced my conviction that it resembled the mysterious girl in Suwakaki. In looking for other clues, the depth of my perception became even deeper. I had a realization that I had stumbled upon a fourth dimension and there after I became aware of "circles" that ruled life.

It was natural that anything to do with music captivated me. One Friday evening, I heard music wafting from Majnun Hall which is close to Picture House, opposite Kabir Mosque. I stepped into its atrium and was about to enter the Hall when a bearded man barred my path, 'You are not allowed. This is not for children.'

'Sir, I am not a child,' I replied. He laughed and felt my face. 'Child, your beard is some springs away, and your pubic hair is waiting for fertiliser. Come when they are in bloom.' The musical manner and rhyming tone in which he said this did not offend me. He turned and walked away. My unbound curiosity anchored me to the atrium. I hung around, listening to excellent lyrics to the accompaniment of harmonium and tabla coming from the hall. I did not fully understand all the verses, which were recited in Urdu, but the few that I understood were enough to hook me to this genre of music. After a long time, the bearded man came out for a smoke, and seeing me, he rebuked me, 'Are you deaf? I told you to leave and you are still sitting here. It is late. Go home.' I was not prepared to leave, so I argued, 'You told me that this is for adults. There is nothing adult about it. It is crying about love.'

'You won't understand it. What do you know about heartbreak?'

'Do you suffer heartbreak?' I asked.

'*Le . . .*,' the man thundered, 'silly boy, now you are becoming personal. Leave now!' As I climbed down the steps, I asked, 'What music is this?'

'It is *ghazal*. It is not for children. *Chalo futo*, come on, get lost.'

'I am leaving now. But I will come back next week to see your bleeding, broken heart,' I threatened him. He took a deep drag on his cigarette, its scarlet circle becoming a red-hot star. Puffing out the smoke, he said, '*Sala haramzada*, bastard, arguing.' This was my introduction to the first of the Circles of Life in Jerusha, the Music Circle.

In fact, the Circle of Music, I found, had two more circles within it. On Saturday nights, the suburban African township of Gembe became a Mecca for revellers. Scattered among its narrow streets were three clubs where they played African Jazz, the soul of Africa. It was interesting, how jazz which took birth in America from the pain and humiliation of homesick slaves, was exported back to Africa and found expression in old African ballads to the accompaniment of hand piano, guitar, trombone, and cow skin drums. And in Gembe, it was rendered with authentic elegance; Gembe was not a venue for the faint of heart. Here African jazz mingled with *Ngulie*, a potent concoction brewed from millet, reached a high level of frenzy. Despite the fear of reprimand from Azul, I ventured to Gembe one evening and stealthily entered one of the clubs on South Africa Street. It was a tiny room, packed with people, wall to wall. It reeked of intoxicating fumes of *Ngulie*. The jazz musicians sat on a raised stage under a light bulb that cast ghostly orange shadows on the brown mud walls. As the music progressed in intensity the crowd began to sway with potent energy. I was squeezed between several tall men, high on *Ngulie*, who swayed in synchronised rhythm to the beat of the drums. They had in their hands long bamboo straws and sucked from a large pot of *Ngulie* in the middle of the room. All at once, the man to my right thrust his bamboo straw to me. 'Drink and be merry,' he screamed. I was scared. I refused to take the straw. He felt insulted and grabbed my shoulder. 'Why, you think my mouth stinks? You rascal, drink.' I held the straw in my hand. The man shouted, 'Suck.' I put the straw to my mouth and felt revulsion and began to pass out. I steadied myself, had a gulp of *Ngulie,* and wriggled out of the club with difficulty. As soon as I was on the street, the gulp which I had held in my mouth, ejected like a ballistic missile. A passer-by shouted, 'You filthy young drunkard, if you can't stomach it, why do you come here?' I knew there and then that the ABC of mastering the second Circle of Music, the Jazz Circle, was not easy.

With my bad experience at Gembe, I thought that perhaps the jazz at the crazy Flamingo Bar along Boja Road was a safer bet. But like Gembe, Flamingo was not a place to hang around for long. Besides, despite my bad experience, the little jazz that I heard at South Africa Club was riveting and had a quality and energy that was missing elsewhere. The jazz at Flamingo, although good, was an imitation of American jazz, without a soul.

My sobering conclusion was that Majnun Hall was safer to progress my knowledge of God's Symphony. The next time I went there, the bearded man was reconciliatory. 'Ah, it is my young friend, who wanted to see my bleeding, broken heart,' he commented. I apologised to him for my insolence. 'Listen,' he said, 'sit out here and no one will disturb you. If I see you touch Scotch, I will box your ears,' he warned. Gradually, I introduced my friends to the delight of *ghazals* and we made a habit of hanging around Majnun Hall on Saturday nights.

After my momentous conclusion that divine nymph had come down to guide me to God's Symphony, I took all signals and signs that I came across, however trivial, very seriously. Hence, I took keen interest in *ghazal* and found that it had its origin from the royal courts of Persia but was influenced by Indian and Pakistani music. This *Ghazal* Circle, I found, was an exclusive retreat for the heartbroken and the unrequited lovers, where they expressed their laments in lyrics which could be recited as poetry or could be sung, *gayaki*, accompanied by harmonium and tabla. In some of the lyrics the poet complained directly to the Architect of the Universe about his misfortune in love. This, I thought was religious.

The bearded man became friendly. One evening, in a light-hearted mood, he explained to us the protocol of the *Ghazal* Evening. If the audience found the recited lyrics reflect their inner pain and sadness, they burst out with accolades of '*vha vha*'. It was from this quarter that I developed love of this form of Urdu poetry:

> I am reduced to ashes in your futile love,
> Blow not hot air of passion to re-flame me.

I also found that these recital nights were strenuous for the attendees, because both the reciter and the listener were emotionally drained by their secret pining for their beloveds. To recharge them, there was a free flow of Scotch and soda, although at the end of the evening, sodas were left untouched, most of the dejected lovers preferred to drink neat Scotch, for this seemed to heal their wounds better. When the heart searing lyrics and Scotch had worked their healing wonder, late at night, succulent *biryani* was served to console the broken-hearted and to strengthen their saddened souls to enable them to endure another week of living in a bad world, which had robbed their pleasure of love. Some nights, the bearded man arose above his love-grief and brought us plates of *biryani* and goblets of sweet, *falooda,* a concoction of milk, rose water, vermicelli, and ice cream.

My introduction to *Ghazal* Circle I thought was my giant step towards God's Symphony. However, something else waited for me around the corner. I felt that I was flying a rocket homing towards a loftier destination. The target I was approaching was from the minds of gods and hence more close to God's Symphony, at least that was what I was told. Like a time-traveller, I was approaching the target of my destiny at breakneck speed and there was always a chance of overshooting the target or a crash landing.

However, Brother Jeff was unaware of all of this music mumbo-jumbo and even if he knew, he would not care. His immediate concern was my "Friend Circle". Honestly, I had never known Jeff to be so boorish and stiff. He was not always like that. There were times when he was fun to be with. I used to run like a puppy behind Jeff and his friends when they used to raid Riyama Orchard for jackfruits and papaya. They used to post me as lookout at the fence. The real trouble started after Jeff got married and crossed over into the "Married Circle". As a result, his own "Friend Circle" changed, and he started mixing with other like-minded married couples and felt compelled to become an adult. I was certain these "adults" must have applied peer pressure on him and forced him to adhere to their rules and customs. And this is how he morphed into a personality with four faces.

However, as they say, "shit happens" and my use of this very slang was pounced on by Jeff that led to a fracture of my relation with Azul. But, long before that, he told me, 'I do not like your "Friend Circle." You should not be friends with that fellow with spiked hair, Joger.'

'What is wrong with him?' I asked. Jeff rolled his eyes and said, 'It is not a question of what is wrong with him but what is right for you. A man is known by the company he keeps. Running around with a boy wearing those striped T-shirts like thugs from Bollywood cinema does no good for you. I've heard that he will soon be expelled from school, having failed his exams for two years.' I was tired and beyond rage and saw no point in arguing. Jeff was a blue-blooded Tory, or at least that is what he believed. During his school years, he served as the editor of the school newsletter and wrote his right-wing editorials under the pen name of "Jeff" instead of his given name Jaffer. That is how his name morphed to Jeff. Now, as you well know, Tories are usually punch-drunk in their ideology, and I concluded that it was better, in general interest of democracy, to let them be caged in their glasshouses of exclusivity and myopic ideas of equality because democracy requires an opposition and if the likes of Jeff and his Tory friends gave up their ideology, lord only knew what other ideology they would adopt. I had seen Jeff reading a book with a picture of Hitler on the cover.

The truth was that I liked Joger the way he was. However, a bonfire behind the Moon Bakery changed Joger, and Jeff had his wish. Joger withdrew into a shell like a tortoise. His shiny, bulging eyes developed a shade of grey, and he shunned friends for a long time. I hardly ever saw him. Only lately he had started to peek out of his shell. I remember a comment he made one warm evening, long before the Moon Bakery bonfire that silenced him which made me emotional. He and I sat in the patio of Paan Cafe, which was where Jerusha folks gathered in the evenings for beetle nut *paans*, sodas, ice cream, and people watching. We were sharing a Pepsi Cola and munching cassava chips when he turned to me and recited a couplet from Ghalib that we had heard at the Majnun Hall:

If you must cry, cry on the shoulder of a friend.
In your final journey, let those shoulders be your pall bearer.

Joger's recital did not surprise me; it was normal for us to sprinkle our conversations with such couplets. However, his choice surprised me. 'Joger, why this sad couplet?'

'Oh, Junior, I just thought of our friendship, and it came to my mind,' he replied, taking a swig of the Pepsi Cola. Sometimes hard-shelled exterior hides a sentimental heart.

Just at the time when I realised I was riding a rocket towards a loftier and much higher "Circle of Music", I had an absurd realisation that I was riding yet one more rocket, whose trajectory was leading me towards a "Circle of Life", which was unique and totally unlike any Circle I had encountered thus far. Like the hidden roots of trees which anchor them, this Circle that my second rocket was homing towards was the root Circle, hidden from public eye, seldom talked about, but nonetheless very much in public consciousness. It was a forbidden Circle, whirling in an invisible orbit and influencing lives in untold ways. The delicate veins of my heart stretch to a breakpoint when I mention this Circle. I had no knowledge of the middle ground of this Circle because I was like a blindfolded initiate in a Freemason Temple, guided like a puppet by a mysterious voice. How then to describe the Temple? It would give me a very severe migraine if I tried to explain the half-understood, inner workings and taboos of this Circle. Looking at the time horizon, in not too distant a future, the bluish vapours of this Circle would turn crimson red, not once but twice.

Garrison Hill

A distant barrage of gunfire on Garrison Hill reels me back to reality. Soon we are to enter a war zone. I increase my pace on a soggy forest path to catch up with Joger, my Martian friend. Ahead of him walks another companion, Luke Gaitano, who, like a machine, is hacking a path through thick forest ahead of us. At one time, this patch of forest, which surrounds Garrison Hill, was part of the greater Suwakaki. The construction of Churchill Highway which finally connected Railway Roundabout with Riyama Dam, divided it. On hot afternoons, in this isolated swath of forest, we had played dangerous games which only youth and ignorance could conceive. Today, the forest is no longer a playground – far from it.

Luke comes to a stop at a barbed wire fence, which has a rusty, foreboding sign of a man pointing a gun, and a caption "Keep Out, Military Property." Ahead of us looms ghost-like peak of Garrison Hill, the home of the African Rifles. The rattle of gunfire recommences. 'The fighting is much closer,' Joger comments. Never in my wildest dream would I have ever thought that fate would bring me to this point. I am using the word "fate" loosely. I have wavered in believing in it. However, as they say, "shit happens."

Luke ducks under the barbed wire and wiggles his way into the forbidden territory. Joger follows him. I follow next. Joger stands tall above me, watching me. My jeans get tangled in the jagged barbs. He kneels down to help me. In that instant, the Ghalib couplet that he had recited to me at Paan Cafe comes to my mind. This is what friendship boils down to: standing by a friend through thick and thin.

Suwakaki reverberates with another barrage of gunfire. My past folly has put lives in danger, and I am dragging my friends into this quagmire to save those innocent lives. I mumble an apology to Joger. He looks at me with his bulging eyes and says, 'Junior, stupidity is stupidity. We can't change that. Mind your gun.' He turns around, and follows Luke. I clutch my Lee Simpson. Its steely coldness unnerves me. I say "my" Lee Simpson, but nothing could be further from the truth. It is a borrowed weapon. Neither Joger nor I are soldiers. We have strayed far from our knitting. Our dream is to one day make a "picture" in the city they call Bombay. In the universe of picture-making, nothing glitters as bright as Bombay with its giant picture studios of Raj Kapoor, Mehboob, and larger than life heroes, who churn out melodramas of love, tears, and sacrifices that have been my cultural staple from the age of five when I was dragged to tear jerker ladies' matinees with Rehmat. 'Ma, these pictures make me cry,' I used to complain. But she would have none of it and would promise me chocolates and off we would go to the *Zanana*, exclusive show for the ladies, with Rehmat and Henna.

With only one cinema in town, Hollywood and "English" pictures were screened only on Friday and Saturday nights, and these foreign pictures did not exude as much raw emotions as did our crying, crooning heroes from the Bollywood black and white celluloid blockbusters such as *Baiju Bawra* and *Awaara*. Yes, we understood tears, sacrifices, and love or lack of it, and this is what Joger and I wanted to weave into our "picture". But it hardly matters. Dreams are dreams, and when the curtain of sleep lifts, nothing remains. Our iconic history master Mr Roy had once said that one must not stray too far from one's back-garden, referring to Emperor Napoleon's folly of venturing into unknown Russia and his subsequent crushing defeat. It seems today, the curtain of innocence has lifted, dreams have evaporated, and we are straying far from our back-garden into the unknown. With my co-dreamer brandishing a loaded Colt and me brandishing a Lee Simpson, I see with utter clarity the truism of Mr Roy's "play in one's back-garden" analogy and the looming catastrophe. This term "back-garden" has strange connotations in my mind. Once I had a difference of opinion with Joger on the theme of our future "picture". He suggested that it must be a murder mystery with love as a side plot. 'Joger, you don't understand. Filming a murder picture is very difficult. We have to decide if it is a premeditated murder or an act of passion. If you just show a stabbing, it has no impact. You have to build up the scenes leading to it. And then we have to solve the mystery. On the other hand, a love story is natural. It just flows. There are conversations, songs, and dance to support the story. We must stay in our back-garden and do what we are familiar with.'

Joger's zeal for murder mysteries was due to Alfred Hitchcock's *Strangers on a Train* we had watched at the British Council's Film Club in Pala. Being unfamiliar with Alfred Hitchcock's pictures, when I saw the poster of a steaming train with an attractive couple beside it, my mind weaved all kinds of romantic ideas. However, during the picture, the bizarre murder plots unnerved me.

Just as the murder theme is not our back-garden in picture-making sense, tropical Suwakaki, which surrounds my home and is practically our back-garden, is in reality not our back-garden. It is a strange place. It hides secrets. Under its green canopy, there are footsteps that lead to forbidden patches. Azul has forbidden me to venture into it. It has this invisible sign: Keep away. This is not your back-garden.

A week ago, when I sat with Henna and Salim in our garden patio, relishing savouries, I had to curb their zeal for an outing to Suwakaki. 'Take us to that small stream at least,' Henna begged. 'Henna, if Daddy or Jeff found out I will be in trouble.'

I clutch my Lee Simpson and I mumbled an apology to Joger who pays no attention to me and follows Luke, who is forging ahead, wielding a machete and cutting a path through the underbelly of Suwakaki. From time to time, he stops and glances back to ensure we are following him.

Luke Gaitano is a different kind of a comrade. He is a Christian and I am a Muslim. One afternoon, he had taught me the art of looking beneath the surface of water, and we had read the Bible together. In his heart, he had a secret, and he knew much more than just looking under the surface of water, a lot more for a boy of his age. The memory of the passages from the Bible that I had read to him is seared hot in my heart. These passages were the key to the secret in his heart. I have often heard knowledgeable people say the true meaning of scriptures is not the literal meaning but the hidden meaning, and Luke taught me this.

A light drizzle blankets Suwakaki, and the gun battle on Garrison Hill eases. The gentle murmur of the drizzle lulls me into a false sense of security. Joger and I walk around a rock and join Luke. He points to a small dark patch behind a web of bush and climbers. 'The tunnel,' he whispers. We enter the steamy vestibule in silence and crawl towards an ochre glow at its exit. We stop and huddle together. 'When is the bugle call?' Luke asks.

'At five,' I reply. The Garrison compound comes alive with a ferocious rattle of guns. We hear muffled voices and shouts. Smoky carbine smell mixed with the rancid stench from a rotting trash beyond the tunnel opening pervades the air. A delayed fear claws deep into my heart. Beads of perspiration run down my forehead. I clutch Joger's arm. The battle dies down. In the excruciating wait in the tunnel, memories flood my mind.

Fate: Not in my Scientific Dictionary

In the morning, when I boarded the 6.35 am Dakota turboprop from Nairobi to Jerusha, the stewardess sensed my nervousness and brought me sweets, 'These will calm you down.' It was my first aeroplane journey. As the plane gathered speed for take-off, lurching forward and sideways, I clutched my armrest and closed my eyes, reciting the name of Imam Ali. Once in the air, I relaxed. It was only a short flight. During the descent to Jerusha the plane levelled off over Peace Lake and ahead of us a Van Gogh landscape of contrasting colours came into view. The turquoise waters of Peace Lake lapped Jerusha Pier. To its right stood the hills of Riya, Gama and Murima which rolled gently to the lake. A carpet of green from the Pier led to the urban sprawl of Jerusha, crowded with rows of houses in all colours of the rainbow. The crisscrossing streets dotted with palms, mahogany and mango trees ended abruptly at the tangled web of green of Suwakaki, To the left, the vast expanse of Peace Lake narrowed into a channel from where fell the mighty Riyama at the milky white cascades of Thomson Falls. Beyond the falls, turbulent Riyama made its way north through the equatorial jungles.

On our final descent, I had a glimpse of my home, shining like a pearl in the middle of Suwakaki. I imagined I saw our garden pond and the scaffold on which hung my punching bag. Mind has a way of filling the gaps in the holes of reality. On the left sprawled Commander Leman's homestead where one afternoon, Luke and I had helped him with a barbecue and he had taught me how to use a semi-automatic weapon, much to Rehmat's dismay. That night, Rehmat had castigated Azul, 'You should have stopped Leman from corrupting my boy with dangerous weapons.' Azul, as usual, remained calm.

I was happy to be returning home. I was home sick after only three days in Nairobi. However, at the same time I had a sense that fate awaited me like the taxman. I must say that this "fate" business is against my scientific belief. My friend Nash would vouch for it.

Garrison Hill

A volley of gunfire jolts me back to reality. Joger is patting his thigh with his Colt. He whispers in my ear, 'It was Professor Pinto and his mumbo-jumbo physics that turned your world upside down. He influenced you the most in the class. And you, Junior, took science to be gospel. And look where it has brought you.'

'Professor taught what was in the textbooks. Interpretations were my own,' I reply. A creature hisses and scurries along in the dark tunnel behind us. It could be a snake. We all look back. I have bigger fears than snakes, not for myself, but for people whose lives I have endangered. Joger continues to whisper, 'People use science as a horse, to make it work for them. You took science as religion. You became its slave.' I sit motionless. His words mutilate my heart. Had I really become a science slave? Maybe he is right. Maybe I had put too much faith in physics and its theories, but I cannot deny that fate had also played a role in shaping the events of my life.

Luke strikes a match and its amber glow dances around us. Joger looks at my worried face. 'Junior, I know you have had a rough week, don't lose hope.'

Stupidity of Juniors: Bang of KMLs

A strange mental condition possessed me. In my subconscious, many strange images whirled and danced. They bubbled up from a mysterious source. Some were fleeting and disappeared like ripples on a lake. Others were enduring and, due to their enigmatic nature, stood out like Mona Lisa at the Louvre. I was not given to hallucinations but I dreamt. My dreams were made of strange stuff. In it were burning infernos, violence, and blood that pulverised my soul. Then there were soothing images of diamond-studded palaces, larger than life cinemas, and a mysterious cat that jumped in and out.

Reeling from the vertigo of these dreams, one evening, I declined to join my family for the premier of Shakespeare's *Taming of the Shrew* by a travelling theatre company from Rhodesia. Its all-white cast was renowned in our part of the world for its superb staging of English and American plays. Rehmat felt my forehead to make sure I had no tropical fever. 'Come, join us, you jewel of my eye,' she said lovingly, hoping that I would change my mind. When I declined, she grudgingly agreed to let me stay back. Jeff in his cynicism parted with words like, "only you know what you do". After the family parted, I sat at the dining table sipping tea. Strange ideas began to bubble up in my mind. An unknown force pulled me up to our roof terrace. The sun which was a huge orb on the horizon set rapidly with a brilliant display of colours and suddenly a pall of darkness stretched over Suwakaki and millions of stars crowded the vast African sky. The silence of the night talked to me. Azul's words came to my mind, 'If you be one with nature, you can hear God's Symphony'. The melody the mysterious girl had hummed in Suwakaki surfaced in my mind. The starry sky above kindled a desire in my heart to hear God's Symphony. I spread a mat on the floor and lay down facing the sky. The tall chimney of the copper smelter on the Murima at the edge of my vision intruded in this otherwise perfect vista. Silence of the universe sang in my ear. I lay still, feeling the rotation of the earth. Alas, God's Symphony eluded me. In its place, bright Venus mesmerised me. My mind played tricks, and I saw pulsing stars around Venus conjure up the face of a girl with arched eyebrows. She had an inviting, mischievous smile which invoked sweet memories of love, first love. I felt a deep longing for her. I had met her some months ago. Driven by these inner tugging of the heart, I got up and pulled out Salim's harmonium from the steel cabinet by the stairway. Salim had a way with music. He had a divine voice. My singing was like the crowing of a crow. Yet overcome by my craving for music, I played the harmonium and sang many songs until someone from the neighbourhood shouted, 'Shut up. Give it a rest.' I hung my head in silence and fell asleep by the harmonium.

Towards dawn, our neighbour, Mr Hukum Singh's sonorous hymn singing woke me up. Anyone who has a Sikh neighbour will know that at dawn he will commence a ritual of kirtan, hymn singing. At first you find it irritating, but after a few weeks it becomes like a lullaby.

A faint shaft of greyish orange was spreading from the east. A cockerel crowed from our hen house. Sweet musk of ylang-ylang hung in the air. A bugle played the First Post from Garrison Hill. Having eaten only leftovers for dinner, I felt hungry. I tiptoed down to our lobby in the dark, stumbling on Henna's shoes. She had this habit of kicking off her shoes by the front door. One time I had told her. 'For heaven's sake, Henna, put them away properly.' She had pulled my cheek and replied, 'Dear brother, I will do what I like.'

'Henna, I wish mother would marry you off, and I would not even cry to see you go.'

'And I will not miss you either,' she had replied.

I opened the front door and rode out on my bicycle on Zanzibar Road towards Moidin which was an African version of an American doughnut shop. Moidin who had gone to Baton Rouge to get an engineering degree ended up marching for the Civil Rights Movement in New Orleans. Facing racist bullets during the marches and subsequently expelled from the school for engaging in political activities, he was forced to work as a waiter at a coffee and beignet shop in the French Quarters of New Orleans from where he learnt the art of making beignets. Disillusioned with the rest of his American experience, he returned to Jerusha and set about perfecting the lowly *mandazi,* African doughnut, by applying his beignet making expertise to it. Sprinkling it with caster sugar was literally "icing on the cake". Africans loved his version of *mandazi* and his coffee shop and its addictive, syrupy concoction "Chino", a corruption of Cappuccino, became very popular.

Zanzibar Road which would normally be crowded with influx of workers on their bicycles and motorcycles riding to work was quiet. Caltex Junction at Africa Street which on a normal working dawn would be a hive of taxis and buses was deserted. Street decorations hanging from lampposts reminded me that it was a national holiday to welcome the Israelis, who would land at Jerusha Aerodrome in a few hours.

At Moidin, I propped my bicycle against a lamppost, close to its open-air kitchen. In the greyish light, a man stood stirring a *deg,* a large pan of boiling Chino on a charcoal stove. Rivulets of perspiration flowed from his forehead. Ever since I remember, I had seen Suleman standing like a sentry, day and night, stirring his coffee concoction and continually emptying packets of Nescafe, jugs of water and condensed milk, and other secret addictive ingredients to the *deg,* as waiters scooped jugs of the boiling syrup from it. The only time Suleman left his post was when he came to

JCB (Jerusha Café and Bar), sat in a corner in Blue Room for a beer, and chatted with Azul about old times.

'*Salaam,* Suleman,' I greeted him. He looked up. In the bright red of the glowing stove charcoals, his face had the sad dazzle of an inspired prophet. A weak smile played on his face. I asked him, 'Suleman, do you ever sleep?'

'Mock me not, you young fool,' he replied. 'When I was younger, women robbed my sleep. I had two in my home and one at Gembe. Try juggling three women, and then you'll know about sleep. Now old age robs my sleep.'

'Suleman, three women, really?'

'Aye, now would I lie to you?' he asked, as a smile spread on his face from memories of his youth. I pulled out my sketchbook to make a sketch of him. 'What in the name of black crow are you writing in your little book?' he asked, looking me up and down with piercing eyes. I replied, 'I am sketching you to remind me to include the scene in my picture.'

'As father as son. Azul was a dreamer like you, wanted to conquer Japan. Rascal had skeletons in the closet,' Suleman commented. My curiosity barometer zoomed high, 'Skeletons, really, Suleman? What skeletons?'

'You inquisitive fool, some other time. When I am at JCB, buy me a beer and I will sit with your daddy and tell you all about it. I knew your daddy before he bought JCB. Let me get on with my work. Truckloads of soldiers will come for Chino before they go to the aerodrome to welcome the Jews.' I put the sketchbook in my pocket, picked up a thin, two-page holiday edition of newspaper from the rack, and sat at a table by the door. Simisu, my favourite waiter, poured me a cup of Chino, pushed a plate of *mandazi* to me and asked, 'Are you going to the aerodrome?' I ignored his question and continued reading the lead story in the paper: 'Welcome Israel. The arrival of Israeli military advisers will usher a new era in our nationhood.'

Our national Independence when it came was greeted with jubilation. Ghana was the first African Nation to achieve independence. Since then twenty-three African countries had joined Ghana. But soon tribal factions in our military began to wrangle for power and then all the freedom euphoria died. The pending collaboration with the Israelis kindled hope that things would get better. We waited eagerly for the arrival of the Israelis at Jerusha aerodrome.

The drone of a plane caused a stir in the crowd. Our prime minister accompanied by General Kikuna and Commander Leman, the two arch rivals who shared the joint command of our military, prepared to receive the Israelis. The El Al plane, bearing the Star of David, made a perfect landing and the military band master barked, 'The Israelis have landed.' The band played a fitting tune as Israeli officials and military personnel disembarked from the plane with the air of gods from outer space. I stood with Nash and other classmates from Jerusha Secondary, waving flags to welcome them. No sooner were the ceremonies over, Nash tugged at my arm, 'Einstein, let us join the procession up to the Garrison Gate.'

'Nash, we look stupid waving flags like children. Let's go swimming with Joger and Billy.'

'Don't be stupid. You know where we have to be at twelve,' he whispered. I did not argue, and we joined the procession.

Nash, whom everyone at school called Mr Magic for his interests in extrasensory perception and astrology, was always bubbly. He told strange stories that he had read from occult and astrology magazines which sounded interesting but were in reality, preposterous. One time he told me that the ancient Rosicrucian knew the principle of gravity long before Isaac Newton discovered it. 'Nash, I think you are drunk,' I told him. He retorted. 'You call yourself a scientist but are ignorant. It is not so absurd. The Rosicrucian learnt this secret from the Egyptians.' I remembered what Azul had told me about the ancient Egyptian king-making rituals and the use of narcotics, so I said, 'Nash, the only secret the Egyptians knew was how to get high on drugs. Then it is possible to believe not only in gravity but levitation as well. Did you know that the Egyptians believed they were gods from outer space?' We argued for hours on these subjects.

As the military procession wound its way along Churchill Way, Nash, in his exuberance, walked with a gait and waved our national flag to the good citizens of Jerusha who, not having anything better to do on this forced public holiday, lined Churchill Way all the way to the Garrison Gate. Along the way, I saw Azul with other businessmen, enjoying savouries from Sukh Sagar and Chino from Moidin. He spotted me and waved at me. I waved back. Little did I know that this innocent, loving father–son bond was about to shatter.

Past the sweeping bend on Churchill Way, the procession came to an abrupt stop as the Churchill Crossing barricade came down for the 11:10 am freight train pulled by the purple locomotive from England, dubbed the Queen. This unplanned interruption confused the military band. Having run out of valorous military tunes, it began to play Bollywood tunes. These mixed with the clanking and groaning of the freight train as it entered the Crossing sounded as if this was a wedding procession. It was this military that the Israelis had come to beat into shape.

The train's rear caboose finally cleared the Churchill Crossing, the barricade lifted and the procession progressed to the gates of the Garrison Hill where the Israelis waved to the crowd and marched in neat rows into the Garrison. Nash tugged at my arm. We stepped unobtrusively on to the railway line running parallel to Churchill Way, behind a thick section of Suwakaki. Its rails were still simmering with the rumble of the Queen which had just passed. At Clipper Point we left the railway line and ran across a grass track to Jerusha Secondary. Our scramble had its genesis in a student meeting the previous evening.

My stupidity during my first year at Jerusha Secondary was to blame for the events that followed. A few months before the arrival of the Israelis, Mr Rama, the headmaster exploded a bombshell during school assembly, announcing that Jerusha Secondary would no longer be co-educational. A week after his announcement, a fence went up around one of the school wings. All the girls were marched into this Girls' Wing and a gate shut them in. In the afternoon, it opened ten minutes before the boys' classes ended. This became the daily routine at Jerusha Secondary. Loitering around the fence became an offence. A hilarious drama, *"Magic of Love"*, staged by the boys and girls, mocking the school's attitude to free mingling of sexes had precipitated the imposition of the apartheid of sexes and its architect was Mr Ben, a hypocritical lawyer, who was a member of Jerusha School Council, who argued that free mingling of boys and girls would irreparably damage school morality.

Soon after the imposition of sex apartheid, Mr Asplin, a veteran of British Malaya Campaign, joined Jerusha Secondary as a physical education instructor. Within weeks, he imposed severe military discipline and turned the school into a boot camp. He was instrumental in influencing the headmaster to ban the Academy, a boys and girls discussion group that met once a week under the *mavule* tree. Inter-house song contests were cancelled, as were co-ed dance classes. Things got to a boiling point when a student, Titus, was canned in front of the school assembly for venturing close to the Girls' Wing and passing a letter to a girl. It transpired that he was simply passing a textbook to his sister. Titus's canning galvanised the students. That evening after a football game agitated students gathered at the football ground to vent their frustration about the bad situation at school. Having just joined secondary school, a student agitation meeting was a novel idea for Nash and me. We attended it out of curiosity. In the gathering dusk, a gesticulating student was making a speech to arouse passion. Suddenly, Mr Roy, our history master, showed up next to him. This caused a stir. Mr Roy was a cult figure at school. He was rumoured to have been a soldier in Mr Bose's army for armed struggle for Indian Independence before joining Mr Gandhi's non-violent Quit India Movement.

When the gesticulating boy ended his speech, Mr Roy said, 'Boys, history teaches that it is everyone's duty to fight tyranny. Freedom and dignity are a man's right. Apartheid in any form does not belong in our school or our town.' His cryptic and short message had an electrifying effect. After he walked away, Gul, a smooth-talker, who was a year ahead of us, broke the silence and proposed that we fight the bad situation at school. Everyone except Nash and I knew of Gul's slippery character. He was aspiring to become Student Council President. A voice from the rank of the students asked. 'What mischief are you planning, Gul?' He was quick to answer, 'Honest, no mischief. I say we defy and frustrate the authorities.' Then pointing to Nash and me, he asked, 'Aren't you leading the term-end inter-house debate?'

'Yes,' Nash replied.

'Good, I will talk to you two after the meeting,' he said. After everyone had dispersed, Gul and his friends came to us. Gul put his hand on my shoulder in a gesture of solidarity and said, 'You two get the honour of planting firecrackers at the school to go off during the assembly. You look the nerdy types. No one will suspect you.' Then his friends gave us an outline of their plan and said that Ash, the Castro of Gandhi Road, will contact us later. Before they disappeared in the darkness, Gul boosted our ego by saying, 'Remember, you are soldiers in our struggle.' Our chests expanded with pride at the honour of leading Jerusha Secondary's freedom struggle.

After welcoming the Israelis, the speed of our dash along the railway line to meet Ash was proportional to our stupidity in accepting this invitation to lead the school revolution.

There was no shortage of revolutionaries in the times in which we lived. Everyone in the school had his favourite revolutionary. Nash could not stop praising Mao Tse-tung of China and his red revolution. Nelson Mandela and his *Umkhonto we sizwe*, the banned anthem of the African National Congress, was favoured by those who looked forward to the end of Apartheid in South Africa and the rainbow of Pan African Union. But the most popular of all these revolutionaries was the charismatic, bearded revolutionary of Cuba, Fidel Castro. Our school authorities feared such idealisations and kept a strict watch on student activities to ensure they were not tainted by such communist ideas.

Every Friday during the morning school assembly, the school allowed a student to make a presentation on "New Idea of the Week". One Friday, inspired by his idol Fidel Castro, Ash delivered a fiery speech on the merits of communism. 'Down with capitalism', he roared. Teachers rushed to gag him. His bravado inspired us and earned him the nickname of Castro of Gandhi Road. He became an instant hero. His soft and chubby appearance was in sharp contrast to the macho appearance of Fidel Castro. But that hardly mattered.

After the student meeting at the football ground we met Ash at Paan Café. A cigarette dangled from his lips. He was from our class but was too much of a rebel and so we avoided contact with him. Pointing to me he said. 'I hear you are good with science.'

'If you have heard, then it must be true,' I replied.

'Don't be cheeky. You prepare the cracker fuses.' He thrust a bag of wicks and sulphur powder in my hand. Turning to Nash, he said, 'I will meet you two at noon tomorrow at the Co-op Farm and give you the crackers.'

For lovers in Jerusha, the avenues of romantic escapades were limited to only three. Lovers with motorised transport had the luxury of whisking their beloveds away from the ever-watchful eyes of the elders to the height of Murima which towered behind the Railway Station. The Lover's Point gave them a few stolen moments of togetherness. Even in this rarefied realm, there was always the danger of being torn apart by self-appointed watchdogs of morality that constantly patrolled the Lover's Point for illicit love adventurers. No, love in Jerusha was not a private affair between two emotionally charged lovers. It was a communal affair. This surveillance was at its peak on full moon nights when lunar magic and shimmering Lake Vista added more allure to romance and attracted more lovers to this adventure. Given this situation, it was unlikely that anyone with a bicycle would ever think of riding his beloved up to the Lover's Point. For all such lovers and for teenagers, the next best location for love adventure was the

School Co-op Farm behind the school cricket ground. Repressive school rules and imposed sex apartheid encouraged young lovers to seek privacy in its boughs for a quick cuddle, passionate embrace, or a kiss and for exposing the murmurings of the heart. Although it was known that often more than just emotions were exposed in its leafy boughs.

For a third class of lovers who were beset more by timidity than passion, there was Mr Riyaz's Urdu class (when girls were still allowed to attend it), where love was expressed by an exchange of glances between lovers and reading of love poetry. It was where love became a literary adventure and where it was taught that it was noble to burn like a moth for love and that union was an eternal dream.

If not in this life than perhaps in next, I shall attain union.

Nash and I ran towards Co-op Farm, well aware that it was under constant surveillance to prevent love adventurers and plundering of the farm. Closer to the Co-op farm, Nash asked if I had the fuses. 'Worry not I have them.' We entered the Co-op Farm from a small hole in the thorny hedge and quickly crossed a patch of ripening pineapple shrubs. The banana patch ahead of us was crowded with banana trees lush with lathery, green leaves swaying in the hot breeze. Each tree was heavy with a loom of bananas. We looked around for Ash. 'Where the hell is he?' Nash murmured.

'We can't be here for too long,' I said. We walked hurriedly to a cluster of mango trees, when suddenly Ash jumped down from a branch like an orang-utan. 'Good grief, man you frightened us!' I hissed.

'What are you, a pair of sissies?' he asked, throwing the cigarette that dangled from his lips to the ground and stomping on it. Nash looked around and said, 'It is dangerous here. Let's do the exchange and run.' Ash pulled out two looms of German KML crackers from a bag. One look at these and I blurted out, 'Gosh, these are bombs! Are we sure we want to do this?' Ash looked at me sternly. 'Don't be a coward. Take one loom and hang it in the music corridor, while Nash and I hang this at the entrance. Give me the fuses.' I pulled out a brown bag of these from my pocket. 'These are ten minutes long,' I explained. Ash took them from me and said, 'Good, I will light the one at the entrance before the morning assembly and Nash will light the one in the music corridor. Let's go hang these and go our separate ways.'

The quadrilateral of coincidences that had opened up the seam of music in my heart and the powerful idea of God's Symphony were about to come together during my first term at Jerusha Secondary. The rocket I was riding was on its course.

Mr Bondhu, an affable Bengali maestro, was the music master at Jerusha Secondary. His kingdom was a large music studio, which stood at the end of a corridor next to the school stockroom. A *veena*, lute, dedicated to the Hindu goddess of arts, *Sarasvati*, rested on colourful pillows, at its entrance. The first time I heard echoes of tabla, strains of harmonium, and rhythmic peels of anklets of girls performing Indian classical dances, I swirled in a vortex of emotions, which brought me to tears. During the first music class, Mr Bondhu walked in with his *sarangi*, a stringed instrument very much like a cello but with heart-touching sweetness to it. I had heard that Mr Bondhu was its best player. He put the *sarangi* on the teacher's table, gently heaved himself, and sat at the edge of table, dangling his feet, surveying the class through his round, steel-framed Gandhi glasses. Then he carefully picked up the *sarangi*. Some students were seeing it for the first time and a cheeky girl screamed, 'Oh . . . is it a coconut grater, sir?' (This was the time when girls were allowed to join Mr Bondhu's music class until a lady music teacher could be found). Mr Bondhu lowered his head and looked at her from above his glasses. 'My dear girl,' he said, 'it is better you join the cookery class next door. Music will do you no good.' With this, he picked up the bow and pointed to the girl. 'Out, go!' The girl smiled and left the class. Mr Bondhu anchored the *sarangi* on his knees, adjusted his glasses, and pointed to the first row. 'Okay, now each one of you, sing "Do re me" when I play the *sarangi*.' Nash and I looked at his tobacco-stained fingers and giggled. 'I am coming to you boys in a minute, and then we will see if you are as good as your giggles,' he said as he continued to play the musical scale on the *sarangi*, which sounded sweet and mournful. As he tested the singing skills of the class, some boys refused outright to sing. To these, he said, 'You are better off in the art class.' When it came to my turn, he said, 'Yes, you, making fun of the teacher. Now, let me see how good you are. Why do you want to learn music?'

'Sir, I want to learn *ghazals*,' I blurted out.

'*Ye lo*! You fool, learn *ghazals* from cinemas, not from my class. Go to that Majnun Hall near the Picture House where all the drunkards meet and sing *ghazals*. Here, we teach music scales and tunes. I teach music of the Gods. Sing "Do re me".' I cleared my throat and started singing. Halfway through my singing, he said, 'Okay, okay,' and made an obiter dictum in Bengali, before moving on to the next student. Only later, Nash explained that he had said that my singing would frighten sleeping children. This did not dampen my zeal, and I requested Mr Bondhu that instead of vocal he teaches me how to play the harmonium. Seeing my eagerness, he relented and said that harmonium class was full and that I could join it the following term. For the present, he allowed me to attend his classes, sit behind him, and pull strings on a multi-stringed *tanpura*, whose sole function in a musical ensemble was to provide drone or continual tone during expositions of various tunes.

Mr Bondhu had a sublime voice, and his singing of difficult classical tunes thrilled me. My first term was passing in this blissful manner. One afternoon, I came early to the music room and tried my fingers at the harmonium. Mr Bondhu suddenly came from behind. 'Who taught you to play this tune?' he asked, greatly surprised.

'No one. I heard you play it on the *sarangi,* and I memorised the notes.'

'*Ye lo*. Musical ear. It's a great gift, my boy. Music is not concrete. You cannot catch it with your hands. It is only air. It is an inspiration from above. What you played was *Bhairav*, the first scale created by Lord Shiva.

After it, he created four more. Each flowed from one of his five faces. You, my boy, have grasped the essence of the first. The *tanpura* you have played for last eight weeks is the only sure thing in music. It is the eternal hum of the OM, the sacred energy of gods.' Mr Bondhu's words were like music to my ears. 'Mr Bondhu, sir, did music of OM really make galaxies dance?' Mr Bondhu lowered his head and looked at me from above his glasses. 'Why are you asking this question?'

'Because, I have heard that when God created the universe and all the spheres set in motion, it produced music and this is called God's Music. I want to hear this music.' A look of disbelief sailed through Mr Bondhu's face. He shook his head. '*Maha shay,* Esquire, you are talking above my head. God's Music! Don't run before you can walk. One step at a time. Understanding OM and God's Music will come later. But let me test you first.' He picked up his *sarangi* and asked me to listen to what he played and repeat it on the harmonium. He played a tune that I immediately recognised. 'It is *Fur Elise*, Mr Bondhu!' I exclaimed.

'Now play it.' I played it on the harmonium. 'Good,' he said. 'The scale is correct. Only one key was wrong.' Then he said something that made me happy. 'I am performing at the musical evening at Recreation Club next Saturday, and I would like you to play the *tanpura*.' I was over the moon. 'My rocket trajectory was right on course,' I thought. Destiny had well charted my course. I now had entered the gravitational pull of the elitist Circle of all the Circles of Life, the crown jewel of it all – the Classical Musical Circle – and well on course towards God's Symphony.

After the KML loom exchange, Ash and Nash left. I stood in the Co-op Farm holding the loom, apprehensive about the whole affair of planting fire cracker in the school. My hands were sweaty. During one *Diwali*, Hindu festival of light Azul had caught me and young Salim placing an empty can over a lighted KML cracker. He twisted my ear and held us at bay as the cracker went off with a loud boom. The can propelled skyward and burst open in mid-air. From that time, Azul banned these crackers from our home.

I felt reluctant to hang this loom of mini-bombs in a section of school that had become a temple of pure delight and devotion for me. I wasn't prepared to desecrate its sanctity. I tucked the loom in my shirt and wriggled out through the hole in the thorny hedge. Just then I heard ruffle of feet. Francis, the school peon, burst upon me. 'What are you doing here?'

'Oh, I am just on my way home from the Israeli procession,' I replied.

'Are you here with a girl?' he asked.

'Oh no, no girl.'

'If I find any bananas or pineapples hidden in the fence, I know where to find you. Now run,' he told me, pointing his cane at me. And, run I did. Instead of running home, I ran to the lakeshore below Old Thompson Hotel, where a fragrant lotus garden stretched as far as the eyes could see. There I flung the KML loom with all the power I could muster and watched it sink in the water. Then I went home to prepare for the debate.

Mothers are so perceptive. During dinner, I was fidgety. Rehmat surmised that I was nervous because of the debate. She said encouraging words to me. Henna was not convinced. 'Ma, he is a junior. This inter-house debate is a clash of the Titans. The girls are invited. They will all laugh at him.' Turning to me, she said. 'That Joger looks like an ape, but he is a formidable foe.' Neither of them knew the true reason of my nervousness.

Next morning, during the school assembly, pretty Wahida raised the passion barometer of boys to celestial heights by reading a Rumi love poem. Mr Rama sensed trouble and stood stiff at the podium when the assembly dispersed and the girls began a military march past the boys towards the auditorium. Suddenly coloured paper aeroplanes started flying over the girls. Taking advantage of this colourful confusion, many silent lovers threw flowers at their beloveds. This coordinated show of defiance surprised teachers who wanted to run to cool passions. Mr Rama restrained them. The girls were enjoying this aero display when a thundering barrage of bangs shook the buildings and the narrow corridors reverberated with aftershocks. Pandemonium broke through the girls' rank. Boys ran from the Assembly Square. Everyone started to move hither and thither. Soon a cry arose that the music room was on fire. This confused me. I never planted the crackers in music corridor. We rushed towards the music room. Soon, fire trucks with their bells ringing pulled up and sprayed water on the music room, flooding it. In the aftermath, I saw Mr Bondhu with tears in his eyes waiting outside. The majestic *veena,* lute, the pride and symbol of the music room, was floating in water. In the confusion that followed, students had dispersed all over the school; some took advantage and disappeared into the Co-op farm with their girlfriends. Order was restored after an hour. The debate was cancelled. A sense of tension and gloom blanketed the school.

In the class, Nash, Ash, and I were exchanging guilty glances, when the headmaster, Mr Rama and the deputy headmaster, Mr Desai brought Francis, the peon to our class. Francis studied our faces, and finally lifted his finger and pointed at me. The headmaster walked to me and said, 'To my office.'

I stood like a common bicycle thief outside by Mr Rama's office. Finally, a grave looking Mr Desai emerged from Mr Rama's office and said, 'You go in.'

Slouching in his chair and looking like the head of a thug gang of Bombay, Mr Rama thundered, 'I know how to deal with thugs like you.' His verbal assault jolted me. In the meantime, Francis, escorted Azul into the office. I was shocked to see him. He looked at me with an ashen face. Mr Rama growled contemptuously, 'Your son planted firecrackers around the school, and it caused a fire. Francis says that he saw him at the school yesterday.'

'Is that true, son?' Azul asked. I reminded Azul that I was at the military procession and had waved to him. Mr Rama was relentless, 'Then why is Francis saying he saw you?'

'Sir, I was walking back from the procession and was close to Co-op Farm when Francis saw me.' Mr Rama asked Francis, 'Is that true?'

'Yes, he was near the Co-op Farm.'

'There, sir. I was never at school and not close to the music room.'

'Then tell us who planted the crackers,' Mr Rama asked.

'Sir, I do not know. I am not involved, honestly, sir,' I pleaded. Mr Rama waved me out and talked to Azul in the office for a long time. Finally, when he emerged from the office, Azul growled, 'I will deal with you at home.' Fear chilled the roots of my being. At home, nervous and fearful, I shut myself in *Uhuru.*

Dante's Inferno

The random activations of memory projectors of my mind were propelling me forward on the rails of time, forcing me to leave the Music Room Affair behind and jump forward.

On the landscape of my life, a Singularity stood tall, like Mount Kilimanjaro. No matter what vantage point I looked from, it was there. Subconsciously, I was reluctant to approach it. Bad things happened at this Gossage Football Final Singularity. As my memory train moved on, I gently steered past it, leaving it behind. One thing was certain. This Singularity was magnetic, and it would pull me back. The picture reel in my mind would eventually run backward to that fateful Gossage Football Final. It was inevitable. But for the moment, I was moving forward . . .

. . . the constant ebb and flow of time had erased my footprints on the seashore of life. I saw that in some dry stretches the footprints were intact and faint echoes of past songs I had sung still hung in the air. As much as I desired to run back and retrace those footsteps and re-sing those songs which the heart was so familiar with, the forward motion of time did not allow me. It forced me to compose and sing new songs, which did not come easy. Like all creative processes, the creation of new songs was a heart-wrenching process.

One afternoon, after the sordid Music Room Affair, Nash and I stopped at Ylang-Ylang Grove, which was where we normally parted company.

Fragrance of yellow ylang-ylang flowers was thick in our nostrils. Suddenly, Nash made a preposterous statement. 'Do you know,' he said, 'crystal balls are able to predict future?' I seriously thought the ylang-ylang fragrance had intoxicated Nash. I mocked him, 'Are you crazy? Crystal balls can roll off and break.' My statement led to a heated debate, and instead of parting company, we walked on and continued to debate until we reached the old church at the corner of Somero Square. I told Nash that there was no need for crystal balls and that we already had equations that predicted future. He blinked his eyes and waved his hands in the air, 'Einstein, what's wrong with you? Equations that predict future?!' Undeterred by Nash's rebuff, I continued, 'Laplace, a French Scientist, said that everything that happens is predictable by theory of Determinism.' Nash stopped dead in his tracks. 'Einstein, now you are drunk. What Determinism are you talking about? Every year we have one drowning in Riyama. People say that this river demands a sacrifice every year. Science cannot predict that.'

'We have the data, except we do not know how to make predictions. In the olden days, foreknowledge of eclipses gave kings advantage in battles, throwing their enemies into disarray. They thought the king had special powers. In fact, Galileo's Equations predict . . .' Enraged, Nash ignored me and walked ahead and joined Billy who was walking towards Zanzibar Road.

Billy was one boisterous son of a bitch. He was a strong swimmer and made us weaker boys look stupid. I waved to him and shouted, 'Hey, Billy, when are you swimming the Indian Ocean?'

'Fuck off, nerd,' he shouted. I shouted back, 'I hope sharks bite your bottom off.'

When I reached home, the phone rang. It was Nash. 'Good gosh, Nash, drop it now,' I said. He whispered, 'Du Maurier Challenge is on.' I dropped my voice. 'Seriously, who told you?'

'In half an hour. Billy told me. Come quick,' he whispered.

'There is no way I can slip out. Besides, I am going to watch *To Kill a Mocking Bird* at six.'

'Pictures come and go. Du Maurier is a privilege. Come,' Nash pleaded.

Rehmat looked at me suspiciously when she saw me putting on my running shoes. 'You never go running this early. It is still hot.' I told her that I was busy later in the evening. She did not quite believe me but let me go anyway. I ran across the Allied War Memorial to Nation Park, joining a group of senior boys walking stealthily towards a rocky path leading to the thunderous Thompson Falls, the venue of Du Maurier Challenge. Suddenly, police sirens rented the air. We scattered, running hither and thither for cover. From behind a thorny bush I watched a police patrol car come to a screeching halt at the edge of the cliff. Several policemen jumped out and ran down the rocky path. Soon a cavalcade of cars of concerned parents came to a halt behind the police car. This was bad news. I crouched on all fours and made my way to Victoria Junction and took refuge in the quiet forecourt of the Hindu Temple, which had a superb wall mural of Krishna, the Hindu God, in a battle scene. I slumped on the cool marble floor and heaved a sigh of relief. My respite was short-lived. Bhatji, the head priest, naked from waist up with only a thick cotton-thread necklace around his neck signifying his higher caste and an orange shawl hanging from his shoulder, saw me and came running. In the afternoon heat, hair oil streaked down past his ears from his copious black hair. The thick red vermilion thumbprint on his forehead shone like an angry Mars. His huge belly jiggled up and down as he rushed to me. In preparation for him, I wore an appeasing smile. 'Why are you here?' he asked.

'Bhatji, I am admiring Lord Krishna's beautiful face.' My charm offensive was ineffectual. He thundered, '*Hey Prabhu,* O, God, how to keep you Muslims from defiling our temple. Boy, you are not allowed in. You are *shudra,* lower caste. Our gods don't like it.'

'But, Bhatji, your gods don't mind when you pluck frangipani for them from our garden.' Bhatji was quick to answer, 'They are Krishna's favourite. It doesn't matter if they come from Muslim or Hindu.'

'How does it not matter, Bhatji?' I tried engaging him.

'*Hey Prabhu,* this boy exasperates me. It does not matter because frangipanis are not Hindu or Muslim. They are flowers.'

. 'Bhatji, then why cannot we all be like flowers, all favourite of Krishna?'

'You are a Muslim. You are not allowed in, that's all,' he said forcefully.

'Bhatji, I am sorry,' I apologised and was about to turn and leave when he blocked my path as if he was trying to hypnotise me. 'Show me your right hand.' I lifted it to him. He grabbed it close to his eyes and studied it intently. '*Bahut kathinai he,*' he muttered.

'Bhatji, what difficulties?'

'It is all written . . .' My interest was piqued. 'Bhatji, what is written?' He contorted his face and continued to hold my hand. 'There is a lot written . . . It is too misty.' I felt frustrated. 'Bhatji,' I asked in a playful voice, 'what language is it written in?' He construed my question in a different sense. Dropping my hand, he shouted. 'You scoundrel, are you trying to make fun of me?'

'Sorry, I did not mean to,' I tried to appease him. He would have none of it. 'You rascal, you think you know too much. Now that you have asked me what language it is written in, let me tell you, only time will tell what clashing Sun and Mars in your horoscope will do.' He dropped my hand and walked away in a huff.

On my way home, I took a detour and stopped at Moidin for a Chino. Suleman stood in the slanting rays of evening sun, stirring the *deg* of boiling Chino, perspiring profusely. He wiped his face, sprinkling his sweat around him and some into the boiling Chino. Aa ha . . . this was the secret of his addictive Chino! He saw me looking at him. 'What mischief have you been up to?'

'No mischief. I just dropped by for a Chino,' I replied. He smiled and said, 'Don't have too much of it. It'll give you an erection and then you won't know what to do with it.'

'Worry not, Suleman, they teach us in school what to do with it,' I replied.

'You can't fool an old fool. I know what you do with it. I have seen many of your kind get syphilis from the Red Tower. Isn't it where you boys hang around?' This conversation was on a slippery slope, so I kept my mouth shut, had my cup of Chino, and walked home.

Henna, Rehmat, and Azul were standing by the front door. Upon seeing me, Henna rushed and hugged me. 'Dear brother, where have you been? Everyone is worried.' Her endearing voice surprised me. 'Henna, why are you singing your question?' She did not reply but took my hand and walked with me towards Rehmat and Azul. Rehmat was on the verge of tears. Azul had a stern face. Ever since the Music Room Affair, our relationship was tenuous. 'Did you go to that Challenge? Were you at Thomson Falls?' he asked.

'No Daddy, I was at the temple.' I told a half-truth.

'You are lying. Boys at police station said they saw you. Jeff, Salim, and Shamim are searching for you as we speak,' Azul screamed. Rehmat held my hand affectionately and said, 'Thank God you are safe.' Henna fussed around me. Rehmat wiped tears from her eyes and said, 'A boy has drowned. When we didn't find you, we were worried.'

'Who drowned and where?' I asked.

'Billy. In the river, during the Challenge,' Henna replied.

'Oh no! Billy, really? He was a good swimmer.' Billy's drowning sounded unreal. How uncanny that Nash and I had talked about a yearly drowning in Riyama only a few hours ago and Nash had walked to Zanzibar Road with Billy.

Jeff's BMW pulled up in the driveway. Shamim, Jeff's beautiful wife, stepped out holding little Nina, who ran to me. 'Kaku, carry me.' I picked her up and kissed her. 'Kaku, my daddy is angry with you,' she said, locking her tiny arms around my neck. 'He should not be,' I said loudly as Salim and Jeff walked past me. Jeff, as I mentioned earlier, was like a Hindu God with not three but four faces: that of a big brother, a mentor, a friend, and a foe. It was hard to tell which face he was about to show today. Salim, on the other hand, adored me and treated me like a god.

But today, it seemed, he had crossed the floor like that great English politician, Winston Churchill, and stood shoulder to shoulder with Jeff against me. Jeff assumed the face of a foe. 'Where were you? We've been looking for you.'

'Jeff, I've already gone through Act I with Daddy,' I replied. Henna kept gesturing me not to argue. Azul hissed, 'You, stop playing with Nina and listen to what we are saying. Salim is younger but is more sensible. With you, it is always new trouble. One day it is fire, the other day it is the police.' Jeff was not content to let things drop and asked, 'You know that Billy has drowned?' I was beginning to boil inside me. I put Nina down.

What happened next was a departure from our family dynamics. It was predicated on my innocent answer to Jeff's question, an answer, which had its birth in an event that had happened in Mr Valentino's geography lesson.

Stocky, with thick lips and beady eyes, Mr Valentino, the Russian, came riding into Jerusha from the desert of Sudan on a URAL Motorcycle. Until then, brainwashed by American propaganda, I always thought Russians had two horns on their heads. But Mr Valentino was a perfectly jolly human being, with an infectious laughter. He cursed Americans as ungrateful dogs. 'During the war they drank our vodka, while we killed Germans and won the war for them. And now they think they invented space. Let them eat their hamburgers and drown in their cheap California wines.'

Mr Valentino taught geography at Jerusha Secondary for two terms. He was from Leningrad and was hiking/riding his way to Cape Town. With his hitch-hiker beard, black T-shirt, and up-turned sleeves, revealing bulging muscles, he was an instant object of adoration in the school. He told stories of his travels making his geography lessons very exciting. He told us fabled stories, more exciting than *The Arabian Nights*. 'As you ride south from the windswept plains of Spain, where it is easy to hallucinate as Saint Theresa did, suddenly you come to the hills of Andalusia and there buried on a hillside is an ancient city, Al-Zahra, named after a princess, a paradise on earth.' Then breaking into his infectious laughter, he said, 'Even today, Spain has many beautiful daughters of Zahra. Oh yes, they are everywhere, copper-coloured, firmly rounded . . . ah well.' Saying this, he pulled out a wade of photographs. 'Here, look at these photos,' he said. The photos showed ruins of Al Zahra. Mixed in this bunch were pictures of bathing beauties on Spanish beaches. We were stunned and aroused.

One day, Mr Valentino brought cupcakes, a portable gramophone, and a banjo to the class. He pushed back the desks and created a centre space. Then he distributed the cupcakes and said, '*Moy droog*, my friends, you all sit, eat cupcakes, and enjoy the show.' He loaded a record in the gramophone. From it outflowed a vodka-powered Russian song, to which Mr Valentino danced the energetic stomping and knee-bending dance. As the music tempo increased, he whirled in a circle, his folded hands to his chin, squatting precariously on one bent knee, his other leg outstretched. After the dance, he sat on the table and entertained us with Russian songs accompanied by stammering of his banjo. Suddenly, one of the strings on the banjo snapped. I was sitting close to him and exclaimed, 'O . . . o, Mr Valentino, now what?' He smiled and said, 'Shit happens.' In my innocence, I picked up this expression. It became quite popular among us friends at school. My response to Jeff's question about Billy's drowning was, 'Jeff, shit happens.' On hearing it he said, 'Do you see, Daddy, the language he's picked up and the "Friend Circle" he has?' This was the fuse. The repressed anger that Azul had been harbouring since the Music Room Affair exploded like a keg. He raised his arm. His voice vibrated. 'You, rascal, is this how you talk to your elder brother, and is this what they teach you at school?' And his hand came heavy on my face. I reeled back. Nina cried out, and Shamim hid behind Jeff. The deed was done. Azul had never done this before. My pride and self-esteem crumbled like a delicate crystal. Rehmat comforted me, '*Beta*, son, go. I will bring juice to your room.'

In humiliation, I retreated to *Uhuru* like a wounded animal and sat starring at the wall. Two sand coloured geckos on the wall watched me with their bulging eyes. These normally come out at nights, zapping insects swarming around the light bulbs with their long tongues. On humid afternoons, they come out from their hot, hiding crevices and sit still on the walls to catch some air, watching the going ons around them. I ignored these and tried tuning my radio to Radio Ceylon, but reception was poor, so I gave up. I thought about Du Maurier Challenge. It was Jerusha's equivalent of Chicken Race of *Rebel without a Cause*, an annual swim across the cascades of Thompson Falls. Billy had been its reigning champion for two years. This was what made it hard for me to accept that he had drowned. A Canadian miner, who introduced fragrant Du Maurier cigarettes to the youth of Jerusha, was the first to swim across the cascades. The swim commenced from an old pumping station, at the edge of the cascades. The following year, Kharwa, a sailor challenged the Canadian, thus starting an annual tradition. In the early years, people gathered at the pumping station to cheer them. After the third year, when a lurking crocodile in the calmer waters at the edge of the thundering currents mangled a youth, the police banned the Challenge. After this it became a secret affair and was announced only a few hours before the swim. One year the police rounded up many boys at the pumping station and locked them up for a night. That time, Azul had warned me. 'Let me not find you there, ever.'

In the evening Henna came to *Uhuru* with a glass of orange. She was apologetic and asked, 'Why did you use foul language?'

'What foul language? I learnt it from Mr Valentino. What do you want me to do? I can't go out anywhere without interrogation. I can't go to pictures without being scolded.'

My afternoon encounter with Bhatji after the Du Maurier Challenge and the bad episode of "shit happens" with Azul were like the encounter with the witches in the opening act of *Macbeth*. It set up a chain of events. The first was a funny dream I had the following night. Earlier in the evening, I had a piece of cheese and bread for dinner. Truth of the matter was that Rehmat forced me to join the family at the dining table. I was still angry and felt uncomfortable sitting with Jeff and Azul. They both tried to please me with encouraging comments on trivial matters. My replies to them were in monosyllables. The silence at the table became unbearable. I picked up my plate and excused myself. This upset Rehmat. 'You will eat at the table,' she raised her voice. This upset me more. I dropped the plate on the table, picked up a slice of bread and a piece of cheese, and walked to *Uhuru. I* ate the cheese sandwich, forcing it down with a glass of water. How a strong swimmer like Billy drowned baffled me. Who could have predicted it? What if I was wrong about Determinism? May be crystal balls and psychic abilities, which Nash so strongly advocated, were the only tools to see beyond the dark mist of the future? The belief that stars and planets control our destiny was intrinsic to us. What did Bhatji mean when he said "only time will tell what clashing Sun and Mars in my horoscope will do."

I slid into a fitful sleep with these thoughts uppermost in my mind. Suddenly, I felt that I was falling into a deep void in my subconscious. I was aware of train whistles and shunting from Jerusha Station and Simba's barking. As I fell, fear gripped me. In my desperation, I was clutching at straws, and suddenly, I landed in a vast underground place. Several chandeliers, casting soft orange light hung from the ceiling. No sooner had I landed, a cuddly cat with a carat diamond twinkling in its ear jumped up from nowhere, startling me. I asked it, '*Mambo gani,* what is the matter? What are you doing in my dream, in this deep place?' The cat meowed mischievously. 'You can ask but I am not telling.' This was the same line the mysterious dancing girl had used in Suwakaki. I retorted. 'What do you mean I am not telling?' Usually cats are shy and run away from strangers. This cat was different. It replied. 'Are you dumb? I am not telling means I am not telling.'

'Listen,' I said, 'I can be dreaming about many important things rather than waste my dreamtime with you in this strange place.' The silly cat meowed and said, 'I am here to tell you about your love life.' Right then I knew this cat was up to some mischief. I immediately replied, 'It is not spring yet, a young man's fancy turns to love only in spring.'

'Never mind spring. Do you want to hear more or not?'

'If you insist,' I replied.

'Okay, here is what I tell you – Your love life is as certain as my life.'

'Are you *shanzi,* stupid? Is this what you came to tell me, you silly cat?'

'Stop trying to be smart and pay attention. It will help you,' the cat meowed back.

'You cocky cat . . .' I started to say. It did not let me finish and said, 'As you wish, silly boy. I am to inform you that I am the good part of your dreams. From here on it will go downhill.' Punch-drunk with ego, I was not listening to the silly cat; instead, I fired a question. 'Why are you telling me all this?' The cat smiled this most catty smile and meowed, 'Call yourself a scientist, and you don't know. You fool; I am a very famous cat. You are privileged that I have come in your dream to give you this personal message. I normally don't jump out of the box. The rest of the world is still struggling to solve my enigma. And, if indeed they solve it, life would be different. Now, goodbye.' The minute the cat mentioned science, my interest intensified. I humbled myself. 'You can't leave so fast, dear pussycat. When will I see you again?'

'Already want to see me again, eh? You'll see me when pigs fly,' it meowed.

'You can't be serious.' Seeing my despondent face, it took pity and said, 'You are smart. If you try, you'll find me. However, if you fail, then wait until you meet Dr Bartlemann and examine his socks. Then you will find me.' Suddenly, there was a rush of warm air, a loud whistle, and clanking of wheels. A metro train materialised from thin air and the cat jumped on to it. As the train pulled off, it shouted, 'Remember to look for Dr Bartlemann.'

What was the frisky cat's objective in telling me that my love life was as certain as its own life? Where do I find a cat with greenish blue eyes and a carat diamond in one ear to learn more about my love life? Where do I find this Dr Bartlemann? And, what do his socks have to do with a silly cat and my love life? What an enticing ploy! I was certain this was some kind of a mind game that Bhatji had started. I felt sorry I had offended him.

Early in the morning, we had news that Billy was alive. Some villagers had found him with broken leg half a mile downstream of Riyama. At breakfast Azul gave me an endearing hug. 'Do you see, son, how worrying it is for all of us when you go off and do silly things?' My anger had not subsided. I ate my breakfast in silence. I was happy that Billy was alive. However, my mind was preoccupied with Bhatji's predictions and the funny dream cat.

On a subsequent night listening to the weekly Hit Parade on Radio Ceylon I fell asleep and had a pleasant dream on the wings of a song. But, as the silly cat had said, this was the good part; in the next instance, the tone of my dream turned dark and I had a bizarre waking dream. This is how it happened. Simba started barking very close to my window. A snake or some night creature must have frightened him. I got up mechanically, and extended my hand through the window and patted Simba. It licked my hand, felt comforted, and settled down. The walls were shimmering red from the hot slag pour from the copper smelter on Murima. I lay down on the bed and began to drift back to sleep. Suddenly I felt that the simmering red on the wall became Dante's Inferno and the Nine Circles of Hell. Instead of lead, cauldrons of Chino boiled everywhere. Above me, I saw an owl, the size of an ostrich, flapping its giant wings and pursuing me. My head was screwed backwards, so I had to run forwards with my head backwards. 'What calamity?' I cried out. I asked the ugly bird circling overhead, 'You, bad bird, what is the meaning of terrorising an innocent boy?' The giant owl flapped its wings and laughed, the echoes of which reverberated through the firmament. 'Punishment in Hell is contrapasso and is divine revenge. Future belongs to God. This is your future for trying through forbidden means to look at future.' I was unimpressed, 'Ha, at least be original. You are just repeating Dante's words, and I am not in Hell. There is nothing wrong with scientific inquiry.'

The bird started to swoop down towards me like a German Messerschmitt. Words came from its mouth like missiles. 'As for Hell,' it said, 'you are not too far from it, you silly boy. Scientific inquiry must not tinker with God's domain. It leads to Hell. Determinism my foot!' From my backward screwed head, I saw the giant gates of Hell with a banner: *Abandon all hope, ye who enter here,* looming on the horizon. In my desperation, I started to run. There was no way in hell I was going to enter Hell. Like Dante, I began to fall into a "deep place" where the "sun was silent". I heard shrill train whistles, Simba's barking, and thunderous roars of motorcycles. Then suddenly I landed with a thud on a pavement, mired in blood. I heard jingles and rattles of chains and a thick voice saying . . . *Let's pull the bastard and run him over . . . kick him on the head . . .* I put my hands to my head and cried out, 'Oh, Ali, save me.' And then I woke up.

Vive l'amour

The bizarre chain of nightmares continued unabated. The increasing Apartheid terror in South Africa and deteriorating political situation in Rhodesia affected the general mood everywhere. Jerusha was not spared. There was a dramatic drop in cinema attendance which was a barometer of Jerusha's mood. Nobody talked about or went to the pictures.

On a full moon night, Refu, the roasted-groundnut hawker, who was also a petty snitch and who had bad elements of society as friends, walked up and down between the Town Hall and the Post Office, trying to hawk his roasted nuts. Not many people were out and business was dismal. Refu rested at the Post Office, whistling his favourite tune, *'Abdul is my name, I keep track of everyone'*.

At the other end of town, young Musa stood by his Vespa scooter, smoking and thinking. The full moon magic had aroused an intense amorous passion in his heart. Musa went around town with his hair styled like Elvis Presley. At one school Variety Show he had performed the best hip gyrating *"I follow that dream'"* west of Nairobi. Bulbul, a round-eyed beauty who lived in the conservative Ndebe Street, where love was a forbidden word, was wounded by Cupid's arrow. Folks on Ndebe Street loved a good romantic picture. In real life, love made them uneasy. That being so, a secret love affair still flowered between Musa and Bulbul.

Musa stopped his scooter at the Post Office and ordered two roasted nut cones from Refu. Refu asked, 'For whom is the second cone?'

'Why do you care?' Musa replied with a glow that blinked like a rainbow-coloured neon sign on his face. 'In that case,' Refu said, 'I will add extra for your special friend.' Musa paid for the nut cones and drove his scooter to Ndebe Street. He parked it in one of the alleys close to a house surrounded by a high wall with a small grilled window used for delivery of vegetables and groceries. This was the fortress where Bulbul lived. Before he turned off the scooter engine, Musa revved it up a couple of times. If he was lucky, Bulbul would come to the window when she finished her chores. Then Musa would have the vision he yearned for, and if he was lucky, he would get to hold her soft hands through the window grill. This was the only intimacy they knew. It was a dangerous game.

The passion of full moon, like the high tide at sea, was surging to a crescendo. 'Where are you Bulbul?' Musa moaned. Even before he knew, someone caressed him from behind. 'I am here Musa,' Bulbul whispered. Musa was dazed. She whispered, 'We have an hour. Everyone is at the mosque.' It was a golden opportunity. 'Let me take you up to Murima,' Musa said. With Bulbul clinging to him, he drove the scooter without switching the headlamp through the alley, past the primary school, to the hilly road to Murima. A cool wind was blowing on their faces. Musa was as if he was on a road to heaven.

At about the same time, two stalwarts from Jerusha's morality brigade, Bakor and Bandar, stuffed *paans* from Paan Cafe in their mouths and set out in their jeep for night patrol of Murima to keep away lovers who dare break Jerusha's social curfew. A full moon night was when lovers brought their beloveds to the height of Murima. This morality duo had hidden motives for such zeal. Rumour circulated among us boys that they often took advantage of the girls who came to Murima, by overpowering their lovers, well knowing that the culpability of the lovers would never allow the girl or her boyfriend to open their mouths to anyone. "Take advantage" was too soft a word. We heard rape.

Inspector Rana, an ex-soldier from the Indian Army and a full-blooded amorous Punjabi, was aware of the plight of lovers in Jerusha and the doings of the self-appointed vigilantes, and hence, on full moon nights, he patrolled Murima himself to prevent harassment of innocent lovers. He was looking for evidence to charge these goons for wrongdoings.

Musa scaled the Trinity Junction, where the road forked into three prongs. One went to Kongoro Estate. The middle went to Murima Peak and the third to Tilapia Village on the Lake. He took the road to the Murima Peak and parked his scooter in the shadow of a giant *mavule* overlooking the bay at the Lover's Point. A huge moon hung in the cloudless sky. With passion running high in his veins, Musa thought it was more silvery than usual. Peace Lake heaved gently in the raining moonlight. Musa gently lifted Bulbul and carried her to the granite rock at the edge of the cliff.

In her heart, Bulbul heard an evergreen song:

For an instant dear moon hide your face,
that I may caress and kiss him . . .

The kiss the lovers were pinning for was disturbed by the screech of a jeep, which crept up in the dark. Frightened, Bulbul ran behind the granite rock. Bakor and Bandar pounced on Musa. 'You rascal, corrupting innocent girls? Who are you here with?'

'I swear I am here with no one .' Musa pleaded. Bakor and Bandar did not give him a chance and beat him. Just about then a police patrol car pulled up. The vigilantes let Musa go. Inspector Rana accompanied by two policemen jumped out of the patrol car. Rana shone his torch on the faces of the goons. 'What's going on here?' he asked in an authoritative tone. 'Oh, nothing, Inspector,' Bakor replied, 'we are just making sure this fine young man is not in any difficulty.' Inspector Rana shone the torch on Musa's face. 'You Tyrewalla's son, are you alone here?'

'Yes, Inspector,' Musa replied.

'Ride your scooter and go home,' Inspector Rana said. Then he turned to Bandar and Bakor and barked, 'Now, you two, get into your car and drive.' He watched them get into their jeep and drive down the hill, before he and the two policemen got into their petrol car and drove up to Murima Peak. Watching the disappearing orange tail lamps of Inspector Rana's patrol car, Musa regretted not having told the truth. He realized that the fear of tarnishing Bulbul's reputation had prevented him. In the next instance, Musa realised that there was nothing to prevent the goons coming back and harassing them. He did not want to contemplate the outcome. He recovered his senses and rushed to look for Bulbul.

Next morning the joint school assembly was restless. While the new headmaster, Mr Irvine was addressing the assembly, Nash told me that some vigilantes had beaten up Musa when he was at Murima. My blood boiled. 'What the fuck is it to them if Musa takes a girl to Murima?' Nash calmed me down. It was then that Mr Irvine made a bombshell announcement that he was abolishing the apartheid of sexes from Jerusha Secondary and that girls would merge back into co-educational classes gradually over the year. The assembly broke into loud cheers. The clapping and whistling, an expression of relief and appreciation continued for several minutes. Over the last several months, a sense of defiance had developed in the school, and there was fear that any provocation could trigger a reaction from the students. Sensing the situation, Mr Irvine stopped the teachers from intervening. After the surge of the spontaneous excitement died down, the weekly "Selected Readings from Great Lives" followed. When Mr Lali, our accounting master, commenced his reading from the *Biography of Winston Churchill*, a rhythmic tick-tock arose from the assembly floor. Mr Lali stopped. The tick-tock stopped. As soon he started reading again, the tick-tock commenced. The assembly broke into laughter. Mr Asplin, the school disciplinarian, walked down from the staff-line and stood in the middle of the assembly. Whoever was doing the mischief had flouted the authority and if this challenge went unanswered, school discipline would slide into mud. Mr Asplin looked all around the assembly square. The laughing continued. His resolute expression made us all shudder. He walked slowly, looking all around, past the *mavule* tree and came and faced me. The assembly fell silent. He pulled me by the arm from the student line and barked, 'Lift your feet, boy.' I obliged. He checked my shoes. Next, he checked my pockets. He looked at my hands and between my fingers. He found nothing. A combination of the stress of the Dante nightmare and the humiliation and anger of the Music Room Affair, when I was wrongly accused of setting fire to the music room, surged in my mind. Mr Asplin was walking away when Nash, realizing that I was about to react, tried to pull me back.

'Mr Asplin, sir,' I said. He turned. I continued, 'You found nothing on me. Now, please apologise.' He looked at me with angry eyes. 'Do you want to be expelled?'

'Expelled, for what?' My challenge surprised him. 'I will deal with you after the assembly,' he said and walked away. Blinded by anger, I walked towards the podium and headed for the microphone. A murmur arose from the assembly floor. Mr Irvine stepped forward, 'Go back to your line, son?'

'Mr Irvine, sir, I would like to say something.' Before he could react, I grabbed the microphone and shouted, 'You have witnessed unprovoked search of my person. I demand an apology. I have been humiliated in front of the one I love . . .' Mr Irvine wrestled the microphone from me. I raised my fist and shouted, "vive l'amour." My action surprised the assembly and everyone clapped. Several teachers rushed and surrounded me. The assembly broke up in disarray. No apology was offered. Instead, Mr Irvine canned me.

In the class I became butt of jokes. 'Who is the lucky girl?' everyone asked. Ash and Nash reacted very differently. As soon as he saw me, Ash burst into a smile which was untypical of him. 'Bravo. Said like a man. Whom you love is your own business. I am proud that you had the courage to talk and I am doubly proud that you challenged that colonial buffoon. Vive l'amour, that is classic.' On the other hand, Nash's response was, 'Did you have to declare it to the world? One day, someone will thrash you like Musa. Society is not ready for this open love nonsense. By the way, who is she?' Nash had asked a good question. That morning in the school assembly there were two girls who thought that my "vive l'amour" outburst was meant for each one of them exclusively. Such confusions of intent and the storyline that could evolve from such utterances were exactly the plot that picture story writers loved. It was not my intention to mislead two innocent girls. I was a victim of circumstances beyond my control. A force much powerful than I had ever anticipated had put me in this unfortunate situation. At home, Henna was livid with anger. 'Do you have any shame, you idiot? Talking about love in public. You should have thought about Narika.'

How was I to tell Henna that yes, at one time, my heart had sung a song for Narika, but my uncontrolled school assembly utterance was meant for someone other than Narika and when love was driven not by emotions but by the inviolable laws of physics, then one had no defence against it. But how was I to explain this relationship between physics and love to uninitiated people? Girls were weak at physics to start with; hence, it would be impossible for Henna to comprehend me.

It was impossible to apply brakes to the vive l'amour wheel I had set in motion. I agree that Narika, the tall, gazelle-necked diva's whirling in an orbit around me was partly due to my actions. But, the truth was that she was already in a trajectory towards her Circle of Love long before then. I could not have stopped her.

I was desperate to meet my mischievous dream cat to seek explanation on its enigmatic statement regarding my love life. I wished I had paid attention to what it was trying to say. I wished it to jump back into my dream and explain things. But it did not. The other thing the dream cat had said was about meeting a Dr Bartlemann who could explain everything. This prospect seemed even dimmer than meeting the dream cat. The days of colonialist geographers like Dr Livingstone and Captain Speke coming to Africa safaris were over, so I was not hopeful that Dr Bartlemann would suddenly visit Africa looking for me. In my desperation, I had no choice but to take things into my own hands. During school recess, I went searching for this cat. Several stray cats lurked around our school gate. They lived in sewers that ran along the roads. This famous cat could be a sewer cat. When a group of girls on their way to cookery classes on the other side of the street saw me peering down sewer holes, they started to giggle and whisper to one another. I was embarrassed. In the class I started inquiring if anyone had seen any cat that wore a diamond. My sudden interest in felines surprised Nash. 'What's with this cat business?'

'I am trying to understand why cats have nine lives.'

'Well, Einstein, when you do, please enlighten me,' he said with sarcasm.

After class I rushed to our less than well-endowed public library, which stood at the corner of Sogo Square, past the Jerusha courthouse to research about famous cats and dreams. Miss Shaila, the librarian, ran the library with an iron fist. Rumour was that she was having a secret affair with a lawyer, who attended court from time to time. When I arrived at the library, she was standing at a bay window overlooking the courthouse and daydreaming. I coughed. 'Ye . . . es, what do to want?' she asked.

'Miss, I would like to sign out sections C and D of the encyclopaedia when you have time. I am in no hurry.' She reluctantly went to the reference section while I waited. After a long time, she came back and said, 'Sections C and D are missing.'

'Gone missing? Do you think a thief broke in while you were at the window, Miss?' I asked. This incensed her. 'Don't be too smart, you rascal,' she snapped.

Disappointed, I left the library and walked along Martin Road to Textile Bazaar and sauntered aimlessly through its narrow lanes lined with fabric shops with mannequins in their shop windows draped in colourful chiffons, satins and cheap nylon from Japan. At Sari Bazaar, I ordered a mug of fresh orange juice from a stall and stood sipping it. Popular Bollywood music blared from one of the shops. Frenzied women darted from shop to shop searching for outfits for the upcoming wedding season. 'What is going on?' I asked a man having tea next to me.

'Oh, it is the release of the Kanjivaram design from Japan. It has been like this all morning,' he replied.

Suddenly I had a brainwave. I gulped the orange juice and hurried to Old Gandhi Road which was well renowned for its architectural diversity spanning two centuries of Jerusha history. It comprised early immigrant dwellings of corrugated tin shacks and shoebox municipal homes standing adjacent to modern opulent bungalows. The great Jerusha flood that happened the day the mysterious girl in Suwakaki hummed the strains of God's Symphony had only damaged this section of Gandhi Road. After the flood, several of its residents were forced to live in temporary accommodations on the other side of Whispering Mahogany for a long time. Their children were forced to attend regional schools. The insurance companies dragged their feet for a long time in compensating the residents, until Jerusha town council pressured the insurers to restore the architectural heritage of Jerusha.

Nai Shop House decorated with beautiful motifs was the magnum opus of Old Gandhi Road. Nai Barber Shop occupied one section of it. One time Nash had told me that Mr Nai, the barber, had psychic abilities. I thought to myself. 'Why not ask him about dreams.'

Mr Nai was an anomaly to his profession. Barbering was far from his mind. He clipped and cropped hair like a reluctant gardener mowing a lawn on a hot tropical afternoon. He was blind in his left eye and wore a black patch over it. On some days, he was talkative and gracious and talked about weird subjects. On other occasions, he was uncommunicative. Everyone in Jerusha thought he was crazy. I found him intelligent. In the side section of his salon, he sold used English books to supplement his income.

One day, while cutting my hair, he had told me about a typhoon followed by floods in his native Sumatra that had swept away his parents and his brother's family and had marooned him with his two nephews on the roof of a barn surrounded by trees. A cobra hanging from a branch bit him between the eyes. The last thing he remembered before he became unconscious was the helpless crying of his nephews and the raging, bellowing floodwaters below him. He thought he would die from the venom, but his deep-rooted desire about the safety of his nephews, kept him alive. When he regained consciousness, the floodwaters had receded and one of his nephews was sleeping with his head on his chest and other sat holding his hand. As he clipped my hair, he said, 'When the cobra bit me between my eyes, I turned blind in my left eye. But with that I have a gift of Third Eye.'

'Third Eye!'

He pointed his finger between his eyebrows. 'There, that is where the Third Eye is.' I looked closely at his face, and sure enough, I could see the marks where the cobra had sunk its fangs.

'Incredible, Mr Nai! This Third Eye, is it like an X-ray eye or something?'

'No,' he said excitedly, 'it is better. I can tell secrets in people's hearts.'

'How did you come to Jerusha all the way from Sumatra?' I asked.

'I came to Mombasa with my nephews to work on the railway. Finally, I settled in Jerusha and built this Shop House. Floods have a connection with my life. The Jerusha flood was the second one that disrupted our lives. I sell used books to generate income. But folks here don't value books. In London and Paris, people flock to old bookshops.'

'Mr Nai, may be because in Jerusha, our Third Eyes are not open.' Mr Nai patted my back and said. 'You have a good sense of humour.'

Hoping to shed light on my dreams, I entered Mr Nai's salon. Seeing me, he exclaimed, 'You, again? You were here only a week ago.'

'Mr Nai, I need a trim.' I wore a false smile to hide my real motive. He invited me to the old rickety swivel chair and wrapped me in a white cotton sheet. Then he said, 'Let me play a tape for you. You will like it.' Lata's voice filled the salon. Mr Nai returned and pulled on my hair. 'They are dry like grass.' Saying this, he sprayed water on my hair and massaged my head and started to mow my head with his hair clipper. 'Mr Nai,' I reminded him, 'I do not want a Korean crew cut.'

'Okay, I know,' he said, grabbing my head tightly and continuing to mow it. Lata's soft voice and cool water in my hair was the magic elixir. It relaxed me, and I began to feel drowsy. Mr Nai was giving an account of the building of colonial railway in Kenya. Suddenly he said something about a prisoner of war labourer having a dream and wanting to build a church on an escarpment. I sat up alert. Mr Nai shouted, 'You, grasshopper, keep still.'

'What do you know about dreams, Mr Nai?' I asked. He stopped mowing my hair, walked around, and stood in front of me. A dream,' he said, 'it is alchemy of a lunatic mind.'

'No, Mr Nai, I've heard dreams foretell the future.' He looked at me with penetrating eyes, before he resumed cutting my hair. When he was finished, he pulled the white sheet off me and shook it in the air. At that moment, his daughter thrust her face in the doorway from the back room. 'Papa, are you ready for tea?'

'Narika, bring two cups and a bowl of black *jamuns,* fried dumplings in syrup, for our dear friend as well.' My heart trembled. I was not expecting to see Narika. Mr Nai brushed off hair from my shirt and sprinkled talcum powder behind my ears where he had trimmed with a sharp razor. I sat on the sofa while he hung a sign of "Closed for Tea" on the door. I read a newspaper cutting that Mr Nai had put under the glass top of the coffee table. 'Beautiful Miss Narika Nai gave a superb performance of classical dance at the National Theatre. One of the judges, Mr Raghuvir Kapoor, a talent scout for Bombay Art Academy, said that Miss Narika had extraordinary dancing talent . . .'

Narika came with a tray of teas and bowls of *jamuns.* My presence startled her. I cleared the pile of old newspapers from the table to make room for the tray. The accolades heaped on her by the dance judges made me think that if ever I directed a picture, I would cast her as my heroine. My impulsive outburst of vive l'amour during school assembly had given Narika an impression that she was "my love". That is what she had told Henna. I was unhappy about this confusion. There was no way to clear it. People who love are fixated in their emotional attachments.

Narika put the tray on the table. I avoided her eyes; instead, I shifted my eyes to a photo of Narika's cousins Tavi and Pal on the wall above the used book stack. Mr Nai immediately commented, 'Jewels of my eyes! Best hockey players in this part of Africa. This is when they beat West Germany at Gogo Stadium.' Tavi and Pal were jewels of only Mr Nai's eyes. Rest of Jerusha hated them. They went around on eight-speed Swift Motorcycles. We feared them. They had notoriety as bone breakers both on and off the hockey field. Unlucky was the soul that locked antlers with them. Few weeks back, they broke the hand of a boy who had whistled and teased Narika.

Narika sugared and stirred my tea. Our eyes met. She went and stood behind her father. He pushed a bowl towards me. 'Try these *jamuns*. Narika has made them.' I was sure Mr Nai was aware of the silent exchanges between Narika and me. Jerusha protocol prevented boys and girls to talk to one another in front of elders. Love or lack of it remained a silent affair. I tried a *jamun* and looked approvingly at Narika. I sensed turmoil in her soul. Mr Nai pronounced his judgment on dreams and dreamers. 'Dream is a psychosis and a dreamer belongs to the madhouse.' This shocked me. I lost interest in tea and the *jamuns*. Mr Nai said with his characteristic dry laughter, 'Stop roaming backstreets and stop fluttering about like a butterfly from flower to flower. It is better to smell the flower in front of you.' When he said this, he looked askance at his daughter. He added, 'I can catch thieves, if I want to.' I was lost for words. I had forgotten about Mr Nai's Third Eye. Until then I never truly believed Third Eye existed. I thought Mr Nai was delusional about it. His remark was accurate. He had divined my secret. To add insult to injury, he said, 'When you walked in, I knew you were like a cat that swallowed the canary.'

A scene from *The Hunchback of Notre Dame* had stayed fresh in my mind. At one point overcome by his unrequited love, Hunchback had uttered: *Would that our hearts were stones.* I never imagined I would soon utter a similar line in the presence of God, if ever there were such an entity.

I left Mr Nai's salon and walked towards the Picture House, red in the face from Mr Nai's dream analysis that had reduced me to a lunatic. It started to rain. An old sweetmeats seller was struggling to lift his pushcart on to the pavement under the roofed shop-parade on Africa Street. I was about to go help him when a hand pulled me into the alley behind Mr Nai's salon. It was Narika's. 'Why do you avoid me?' she asked. I fumbled, 'Narika, I was busy; boxing, exams. It is complicated.' Droplets of rain clung to her hair.

'When you said, "one I love" during school assembly, I felt happy. But now . . . you write love letters to a girl who does not care . . . What don't I have?'

'You are beautiful. I need time. It is not that simple . . .' I tried to explain.

'The girl you write to shows your letters around. Girls make fun of you.' She clasped my hand as I extended it to lift a lock of hair from her face that was dripping wet from the rain. 'Narika, you will catch a cold. Let's talk after the rehearsal.' She held onto my hand and said, 'Don't be cruel . . .' I did not let her finish and ran, leaving her crying in the rain. I had seen such a heartless act in one of Raj-Nargis pictures, where Nargis had sang:

> Oh, you brute, look back once,
> Abandon me not in a pit of anguish,

I ran in the face of a cold wind towards Kabir Mosque. A poster of Marilyn Monroe's *Some Like it Hot* fluttered on the Picture House wall. Dripping wet, I entered the Mosque and slumped on a straw mat. I reflected on Narika's agony. I felt wretched that I was unable to reciprocate her feelings. I raised my hands above me as if in prayers and said, *Would it be that my heart was stone, dead to pain and misery of love?* I tried to forget what Narika said about my love letters. How did she find out about them when only two other people knew?

Few days later I had a nightmare that put my monotheistic belief to test without my realizing it. Religious code of Muslims allows pleading for help only from God. But I realized that we are polytheist and in dire circumstances seek help from spirits and saints. I woke up disturbed from my dream and sat on my bed, starring at a framed picture of the Japanese Yasukuni Shrine hanging on my wall which was shimmering red from the slag pour on Muriam. Azul who had been to Japan had told me that spirit worship was common in Japanese religion. In my distress, I looked at the picture of the Shrine and pleaded to the spirit of the Shrine to stop these bad dreams. My fervent pleading worked and lo, as mysteriously as it had started, the chain of bizarre dreams abated. After my initial euphoria, I realised that I had fallen into a deadly sin of ascribing partners with God. Mullah Bashir would have boxed my ear for blasphemy if he found I had asked for spirit intervention.

Birthday Promise

My mind was like a compass needle at the North Pole, whirling in a confused circle. At this point my life, like the mid-reel of a picture, was crowded with unfinished strands of adventures of James Bond, the sleeping ghost of Watanabe and towering singularity of Gossage Football Final. As a director I have to bring these together into a meaningful sequence . . .

On the morning of geography exam, I was still half asleep when I heard Nina's footsteps. I was tired and pulled my blanket over my head. She fumbled around my bed and asked, 'Kaku, where are you?'

'Nina, please go play with Salim,' I replied.

'No, he pinches me,' she complained and continued to poke her little hands under the blanket. I threw off the blanket, picked her up, and pulled the blanket over our heads. Rays of early morning sun filtering through the blanket pores thrilled her. 'Kaku, do that again.'

'Okay, baby,' I said as I pulled off the blanket and pulled it back on. 'Kaku, I am not a baby. My mommy says I will be five soon.' Nina's statement came as jolt. I had made a promise to myself to do something special for Nina's fifth birthday which was on Thursday. There was not much time as my plan would require a visit to the USIS in Pala at the soonest.

Salim was reading the *National Geographic* when I came home from the Geography exam. He looked up and said, 'Good joy brother, finally the exams are over.'

'Yes Salim, it was gruelling,' I replied as I filled up two glasses of Coca Cola and handed him one. He took a gulp and asked. 'Are you exhibiting in the Science Fair tomorrow?'

'I have no time for it. Tomorrow is the drama premier, and in few minutes, I am meeting Vir at Moidin and then I am going to Pala to the USIS.'

'What for?'

'I am not telling you.' He did not press me and went back to reading the *National Geographic*. I was deliberately not sharing with anyone the reason for my intended visit to the USIS in Pala, which I frequented often. It had a well-stocked reference section that was my window to the wonderful world of science and technology. It also had a good section on psychology. I was intending to read up on dream interpretation.

Matatus, the shared-taxi culture that sprang up in towns and cities of East Africa owed its genesis to the French Peugeot's dull green family sedan, the 7-seater Model 403. Before the *matatus*, the cities and towns of East Africa had no urban transport service to speak of. The only mode of transport for the locals was either pedal power or walking. And that is where the shared *Matatus* became a gift of god.

After a short meeting with Vir at Moidin's, I took a *matatu* for Pala from the crowded Jerusha Taxi Stand. When I told the driver that in Pala I wanted to get off at Bolton Circle, the rascal grimaced and said, 'it will be five Ducats extra?'

'Why?' I asked. He gesticulated and replied, 'Bolton Circle is busy and I lose time in the detour.' Then he pointed and made me sit in the second row of seats. We were short of one passenger. We waited in silence. The cabin was oppressively hot, yet no one complained. This was one feature of life in East Africa. Everyone bore discomfort in silence. The loud music blaring from a speaker from a hawker stand added to our misery. Fortunately, before too long a passenger came along. A languorous *matatu* police made a mandatory inspection to ensure the vehicle did not exceed the allowed number of passengers before he allowed us to proceed.

As soon we crossed Jerusha Town limit, the driver stopped at the bustling Koroka roadside market. A bevy of young hawkers rushed to the windows with baskets of roasted cassava and groundnuts, boiled maize and all descriptions of fruits. The driver ordered me to get off and wait. A crowd waiting by the road side for a taxi to Pala also rushed and surrounded the taxi. The driver selected five more passengers, apologising profusely as he pushed two of them in the front row and the rest in the middle and the back rows. Finally, he turned to me, offered me a bottle of Pepsi that he had purchased from one of the hawkers and pointed to the front cabin. 'I will not charge extra to drop you at Bolton Circus. You are slim, so you'll be able to squeez in,' he said. I had no choice and squeezed into the front row. I was certain that Peugeot had never envisaged Model 403 to be used as a can of sardines on the roads of East Africa. Yet, loaded with twelve passengers and luggage on the roof-carrier to boot, it had enough power to negotiate the hilly road to Pala with ease. One never saw a broken-down Peugeot 403 on the road.

In Pala, as promised, the driver made a detour and dropped me off at Bolton Circle which before independence was the heart of colonial Pala. In the olden days, British banks, elegant drapers, beauty parlours, pharmacies, delicatessens and cafes had graced the Circle. The streets that radiated from the Circle had housed government offices, foreign consulates and overseas trading companies. With independence, the trading spirit of Africa burst forth. *Charuzis,* wholesalers, petty traders, hawkers and farmers from the countryside came in droves and set up pushcarts stalls around the Circle and on the streets radiating from the Circle, selling their produce and cheap Chinese goods. Everyone wanted to taste "Freedom" and trading allowed them this taste. I lingered briefly at the Circle, surveying the spirit of New Africa.

At the USIS, a sleepy guard sitting on a stool at its entrance barely moved as I approached. I entered the quiet reception lobby and signed the register. Mine was the first entry. Most visiting Americans and exchange students that normally crowded USIS had gone home for Christmas. Miss

Connie, the librarian who knew me greeted me cheerfully. I browsed through the Psychology section but found nothing interesting about dreams. I went to the desk and hesitantly asked Miss Connie about it. 'Unfortunately,' she replied, 'we don't have much on dreams.' In the next breath, she asked, 'What is your interest in dreams?'

'Dream interpretation,' I replied. She smiled and commented, 'Dreams! It is a wonderful subject. According to Freud dreams are the cognitive echoes of our efforts to work out conflicting emotions.' I did not understand all the words Miss Connie used, but her statement made eminent sense. 'How accurately put, Miss Connie!' I said. This flattered her. I realized that I had struggled with many conflicting emotions in the last few months. She asked, 'You did not come all this way just to research dreams?'

'Actually, I would like to borrow a picture.'

'We only have *Giant* with James Dean. Have you seen it?' she asked.

'Actually, no. It was never screened in Jerusha.'

'So, where exactly will you screen this picture?' she asked.

'In our garden,' I replied. This baffled her. She explained, 'I hope you know that *Giant* is in thirty-five millimetres and Cinemascope, not suitable for home screening.'

'That is fine, Miss Connie,' I assured her. At the Entertainment Section, she helped me tuck two silver cases with reels of *Giant* in my bag. I signed the register, thanked her and took out a Japanese ebony fan from my bag. 'I brought you this for Christmas.'

She opened the fan, which had flowers painted in vivid colours on a lilac silk cloth. 'My goodness! So pretty. You should not have. Thank you,' Miss Connie said. She walked me to the foyer and added, 'No need to rush the reels back. Keep them until after the holidays.' Before I left, I asked, 'Oh, Miss Connie, do you know of a famous cat that wears a carat diamond in one ear?' She looked at me quizzically. 'I know of no such cat. Why do you ask?'

I replied. 'I am trying to adopt it.' She laughed aloud. 'You are funny.'

Before returning home, I purchased a blue-and-white striped shirt from Van Heusen Shop on Market Street for a dear friend.

During dinner, I announced my plan to celebrate Nina's birthday with a picture show in our garden at seven. 'Thursday is a half day holiday,' I added. Silence greeted my idea. Henna, who was cross with me, broke the silence. 'Are you sure you will not let us down? Besides you are busy with your drama tomorrow.'

'Drama is under control. I am ready for the picture show,' I assured her. Azul asked, 'What picture show are you planning?'

'*Giant* with Elizabeth Taylor and Rock Hudson,' I replied. Henna's eyes lighted up, 'It has James Dean as well. Where did you get *Giant* for home show?' Jeff waved his hand, 'Impossible. We only have sixteen-millimetre projector. How will you show thirty-five-millimetre film?'

'You all don't worry. I have a plan,' I assured everyone. Shamim, my always-singing sister-in-law, and Henna immediately turned to one another in confused chatter and soon came up with a more elaborate party plan. I seriously thought that if UN worked with such efficiency, all our world problems would be solved. Shamim and Henna wanted to make it an affair to remember. Women were like that. They wanted to outdo others. Henna looked up and said, 'Okay, everyone, this is the plan. How if we have Nina's birthday party at four, followed by a grand buffet at six with show of *Giant* at seven?' This unleashed an animated exchange of ideas. Rehmat injected a dose of reality to their zeal. 'Girls, it's already Tuesday. Where is the time for this by Thursday?' Henna was not backing off. 'Ma, leave it to us. We will plan everything.' I left everyone talking excitedly and returned to *Uhuru* which was full of clues regarding the destination of the second rocket I was riding. This rocket had entered the gravitational pull of that special Circle, which was never mentioned by name but was in everyone's consciousness: the Grand Circle of Love. The universe enclosed by this Circle had no lighted landing strip or a control tower that guided one in. Like a bewildered astronaut, I was not even sure if I had landed or was still suspended in my descent trajectory. There was no solid ground to walk on. That was what love was all about. It was a universe of strange murmurings of the heart, a state in which a poison corroded the heart, yet it felt soothing.

Relics of such loves littered *Uhuru*. Among these were several necklaces, a rucksack full of girl's clothes, a get-well card with a heart on it, and a stack of love letters. In this letter collection, there was one, which I had no heart to read. I picked it up and put it aside. The remaining collection of torn notebook pages told a story of the flowering of my unique love whose birth was from the theories of physics and works of people such as Einstein. Secretly, in my heart, I was proud that I had stumbled upon a science based secret of love for which I should be awarded a PhD. Lonely hearts would find much comfort and happiness in love if they knew the secret of my discovery. The heart-broken *ghazal* lovers from Majnun Hall would worship me in their songs if they tasted the elixir of my Physics-Love Formula. Before my eyes, on the horizon, I was beginning to see a rainbow, and I was walking on a yellow brick road towards it. The blue mist was lifting. In the background, Mendelssohn's "Wedding March" was playing. With every step, the colours of the rainbow were getting sharper, and I was feeling their vibrancy in my heart. "Wedding March" was peaking to a crescendo. At my pace, I would reach that rainbow tomorrow afternoon, the fated Wednesday, the afternoon of the school Drama. For me, this would change the tempo of Nina's birthday on Thursday.

But the sole unread letter on the night table was a dark chapter in my life. It was a letter from someone whose tears, in my unholy haste, I had not stopped to wipe. No, love was not simply a high – far from it. The letter represented a deep nadir. Mendelssohn's "Wedding March" was fading and in its place, I was hearing echoes of a heart-piercing *ghazal*:

Walking path of new found love,
O, you unfaithful brute, forget not,
Ashes of my smouldering heart
Are scattered in your path.

I put my hands to my ears to blot out the lyrics, but they arose in the depth of my soul and continued playing like a broken record, stretching the delicate veins of my heart to breaking point.

Atom Bomb Blast?

In the misty grey of dawn, I woke up with a cry and a violent shaking and my forehead sweating like a refrigerator condenser. I was fully clothed and uncomfortably cramped on a chair. My neck was burning as if someone had gone around it with a can opener. Frightened, I jumped up and banged against a table in the dark. I steadied myself and recited the prayer Rehmat had taught me. 'When in trouble, call on Imam Ali'. At that time in my scientific pride, I had ridiculed her. 'Ma, what can Imam Ali do?' And her answer was, 'Son, I don't know, but call on Ali. He will help.' With no other avenue open I called on Imam Ali. This seemed to calm me. I realised I was in *Uhuru*. I fumbled about and switched on the light. In its ochre glow, I examined my neck in the mirror. It was red and puffed up like a pastry fresh from the oven. I pulled up my shirt and examined my throbbing back. It was lacerated blue and black. I felt an intense burning on my head. I parted my hair. A deep gash, an inch long, ran across my head. I was broken head to toe, and I had no recollection of how I had sustained these injuries. I slumped back in my chair and dozed off. Rehmat's sonorous voice woke me up. She was singing the morning *Choghadia*, devotional hymns, which she sang on Thursday mornings before she made breakfast and before Jeff started fiddling with his radio. I sat up with alacrity; if it was Thursday, what happened to Wednesday? I had no recollection of it at all. A complete day was erased from my memory. The last thing I remember was reading the love letters in *Uhuru* on Tuesday night. If it was Thursday, then it was Nina's birthday, and I remembered that I had to project *Giant* in our garden later in the evening. I also had a strong urge to read the newspaper. An inner compass told me to read the crime section of the daily paper. I hurriedly washed my face, put on a polo-necked sweater to hide the red marks around my neck, and rode out on my bicycle. I purchased a paper from the newsagent next to Moidin and was about to ride away when Suleman, who stood stirring the boiling *deg* of Chino, shouted, 'What, no Chino today?'

'I am in a rush, Suleman. Some other time.'

'No, son, you cannot run away. Come back, I have something for you.' Saying this he lowered the stirring pole on to the rim of the Chino *deg* and from his pocket brought out a small ebony box. 'Son, take this. I have carried it for days. Your daddy brought it from Japan and then forgot about it. Have it with you when we meet at JCB. Then we will ask your daddy about the skeletons in the cupboard. He will have nowhere to hide. But, promise me not to open it before then.'

'Suleman, I cross my heart.'

As soon as I arrived home I hid the ebony box in my desk drawer and then read the newspaper headline: 'Israel – Friend or Foe?' Lately the relationship between our military and Israel have soured. I skimmed through the Israeli story, which hinted that Israeli advisors may be forced to leave our country soon. I turned to the middle page for crime stories. There were none which made me happy and I was not sure why.

The rest of the house was in commotion in preparations for Nina's birthday Jeremy, our butler, was arguing with Rehmat about technicalities of cake decorations. Azul was on the phone ordering chairs and crockery. Jeff and Salim were in the dining room inflating balloons and hanging decorations. No one had time for any chitchat. This suited me fine. I went to the garden and made sure that the net canopy over the pond, protecting the falcated duck family from India, which had grown to a family of twelve, was secure. To accommodate this growing duck family, Rehmat had the henhouse moved to the east and had Azul expand the pond to twice its size.

Satisfied that the ducks would not roam free in the garden during the sundowner, I returned to the house, picked up a couple of scones and a cup of tea, and hid in the shed behind *Uhuru*, tinkering with an old thirty-five-millimetre Cinemascope projector and its speakers that had come with a consignment of junk Azul had bought from an auction house in Nairobi several years ago and had forgotten about. I had fixed most of its problems. However, I was unable to find a replacement for a broken gear. I had tried ordering it from London without success. Just before the exams, I had asked Hendrix, a trainee engineer at Lake Textiles, if he would fabricate a new gear for me in his workshop. He had agreed, but had not yet fulfilled his promise. Late in the afternoon, when the guests with their children started arriving for the party, in desperation I phoned Hendrix. 'Hendrix, do you have the gear you promised me?' Fortunately, he remembered me. 'Not yet governor. I am in the middle of an emergency. I promise to have your part by five.' I sensed tenseness in his voice, so I asked, 'Hendrix, what kind of emergency? I can't project the picture if I don't have the gear. You do remember you and your girlfriend are invited? Over fifty people will attend.'

Hendrix went quiet. 'Hello, hello,' I kept saying. Suddenly he said, 'I told you, you will have your gear. Now I must go.' He cut the phone. Frustrated, I had no option but to wait. What kind of emergency was he referring to? I went to the shed, checked the wiring on the speakers, adjusted the levers on the projector, and threaded the first reel of *Giant.* Then I ventured out into the garden. Jeff was waiting for me with angry eyes. 'Where have you been? How will you project the picture?'

'Gees. Back off. I will project the picture even if I have to pull a frame at a time,' I assured him.

'Funny,' Jeff snapped, 'I don't want a debacle like your school drama last night. I am not sure why I trusted you without seeing the projector.' Jeff was the second person to talk about a drama and associated debacle. What was he talking about? I wanted to snap at him, but controlled myself. 'Jeff, there won't be any debacle. You go enjoy the party.'

Hendrix and his girlfriend Nathalie walked in just when guests began pouring out into the garden after Nina's birthday cake cutting ceremony. Hendrix had the crucial gear for the projector. He apologized for the delay which he said was due to all none essential personnel from the textile mill being asked to return to the UK. 'They are expecting some army trouble.' He added that the army had set up a check-point at Churchill Highway. I was too engrossed with gear fitting into the projector to pay attention to what Hendrix was saying. The gear snapped into place nicely. It was only then that I noticed that the garden had a lot more than fifty people milling around. Gate crashers! A free film show was too good an opportunity to miss. Suddenly there was an unexpected stampede and many gate crashers rushed and swarmed around the buffet tables fighting for food. Henna and Shamim were shocked and dismayed. The buffet tables began to look like the aftermath of a tornado. Jeff, having foreseen this had ordered lamb chops, kofta and mashed plantains from JCB. While helpers were ferrying the food from JCB's white van to the tables, there was a stampede for chairs. Jeff threw up his hands in the air and asked me to start *Giant*. Simba, confused by the crowd came and sat close to me. Joger who sat next to me whispered in my ear, 'Junior, I never knew you had a thirty-five-millimetre projector. It is fantastic.'

An event that happened a year ago had precipitated a crisis in Joger's life and he had quit school. It sapped his zeal and reduced him to a shadow of his former exuberant self. His praise thrilled me. He added, 'Pari has returned. She is staying at the Kit Kat. She wants to reconcile.'

'Joger, will you forgive her?' I asked. He fell silent. A fiery debater and a lover of pictures, drama, and music, Joger was not academically inclined. He was not promoted after failing his exams two years in a row. This is how he joined our class or rather we joined him. In the class, I sat on a desk next to him. During one history class, he circulated a Japanese *Manga* to the boys in the back row. It made a rapid circuit, with grunts and wows from the boys, and came back to him. I stretched my neck to take a peek. Seeing nudes of beautiful Japanese girls in the *Manga*, my eyes became rounder. Joger brought the *Manga* closer and remarked, 'Sexy, aren't they? Now, don't get an erection. Girls will notice it.' I lowered my eyes. He added. 'Oh, you poor virgin. Grow up.' From then on, from time to time, he showed me a new *Manga*. One time, he told me, 'Wait until I show you the *Playboy* centrefold.' I could not wait. 'When will you bring it?' He laughed. 'Patience my boy.'

One time we decided to present a skit in the school annual variety show. When Joger read my skit, he suggested minor changes to it and said that Nash should make a cameo appearance. I told him that Nash would not agree to the role he was being assigned. 'Leave it to me,' he said. He talked to Nash in private, and to my surprise, Nash agreed. On the day of the show, Joger asked Estella, our school's Cha Cha dance expert, to dress up Nash and do his make-up. He gave her lengthy instructions. Before she led Nash away to the cookery class to dress him, Joger handed her a skin-toned pair of tights. Estella smiled and winked at Joger. I asked Joger, 'What are the tights for?'

'Never you mind,' he replied.

Our skit was the last item on the show. The mercury of the audience was already high with the whiff of a cameo appearance. Many boys had given up their seats and were crowding close to the stage. Per the script we commenced our tap dance routine. Nash and Estella were nowhere to be seen. I had fears that Nash may back out. The audience began chanting for the cameo appearance. We were concluding our tap dance, when an entourage of boys rushed on to the stage holding a white curtain. The audience went wild when they dropped it. On the stage stood a dancing diva draped in a red tent skirt with shoulder-length golden hair, spouting red lips and a pair of busts like ripe melons. Estella's handiwork was stunning. To the beat of Brazilian samba, the diva did a superb whirl. Her tent skirt ballooned up, exposing her legs to the delight of the audience. The Brazilian samba gathered pace and the diva performed a grand finale with a prolonged whirl. Midway through the whirl, her skirt flew off like a flying saucer, leaving her with nothing but skin-toned tights and her hands on her crotch. The audience went wild. Excited boys rushed on to the stage. The flying skirt landed on the top of a group of girls, who shrieked and threw it off as if it were an evil cloud. Joger, Ash, and I rushed to surround our dancing diva. Shouts of *encore, encore,* filled the auditorium. Teachers rushed to bring the curtain down. Only later we found out that Joger had deliberately asked Estella to have the skirt hook on a flimsy tether, except that he had not expected its effect to be so dramatic.

In the class with his bulging eyes shining like stars, he had said to me, 'Junior, your understanding of plots, acting, and music is superb. Let us write a story and picturize it. India is thrusting for stories from Africa. We will find money. It will be so much fun.' In the same breath, he told me, 'Give up your madness for science.'

'Joger, without science, we would be living in caves.'

'Ha . . . that's what you think,' he replied.

When I invited him to attend Nina's birthday and the screening of *Giant*, he hesitated but finally agreed. I was glad he had come.

Towards the very end of *Giant*, I asked Joger to mind the projector while I ran to *Uhuru* to fetch a relic of Joger's love for Pari which I was holding in trust for him. It was time to return it to him. When I turned the corner around the garage port on my way to *Uhuru*, I heard Mr Ben, a crooked lawyer and member of our School Board, threatening Azul. Mr Ben was not our family friend, and I was sure Azul had not invited him. I stopped in the shadow of a hibiscus shrub. I heard Mr Ben threaten Azul. 'You better sign the papers else the Sisia Affair will be in the papers.'

'Ben, you be careful, throwing stones at me. If you dare me, I will rake you over a coal fire.' I liked Azul's rebuff. I had heard that Mr Ben was a bad man and that he had thugs and goons in his payroll. He hissed at Azul, 'I have the army in my pocket . . .' It made my blood boil. They stopped talking when they spotted me. Mr Ben wore a false smile on his face. I tiptoed to *Uhuru*, retrieved a small gift box and returned to the projector.

'What took you?' Joger asked. I handed him the box. It confused him.

I explained, 'It has the necklace that was to be your gift to Pari. Give it to her when you see her.'

Early on Friday morning I was in a light sleep. Jeff's radio was playing a bewitching violin prelude and suddenly its vibrating strains induced in me a strange dream; a Pandora's Box opened up in my mind, fizzy bubbles of joy oozed out, followed by a vortex of gloom. A white mist began to swirl in my mind, and floating in it I saw blurry faces. I counted six. I expected the mist to clear at any moment to reveal their identity. But as mysteriously as it had surfaced, the dream faded and the faces disappeared with it. I had barely grappled with my frustration of not knowing the identity of the faces, when deep in the womb of my mind I heard crying of a young girl. Was it Nina? Some mornings she woke up crying. Jeff took her in his arms, sat by the rickety chair close to Phillips radio, and rocked her to sleep. I was familiar with Nina's crying. No, this crying I heard was not Nina's. It was a cry of anguish, a cry of separation. I felt as if someone was tugging at my heart with hooks, pulverizing it to bits. The echoes of the crying died down leaving me with a profound sense of sadness.

I had barely recovered from the disturbing dream, when I heard what I thought was an atom bomb explosion followed by crinkling of glass. It jolted me up. I jumped from my bed. I thought Joger had detonated the bomb. I made this preposterous association due to a discussion we had in our history class about atom bomb explosions over Hiroshima. Mr Roy, our history master had shown us graphic pictures of how people had evaporated after the atom bomb explosion, leaving their shadows on walls and floors. It had made a deep impression on me. 'This event,' Mr Roy had remarked, 'was the birth of the Atomic Age.'

Frightened by the loud bang, I ran out of *Uhuru* and met Jeff and Henna who were rushing towards *Uhuru*. Rehmat and Nina were following them. Rehmat clutched my arm and asked, 'Are you okay?' I assured her that I was fine. We all walked to *Uhuru*. Nina who was standing behind Henna looked at the floor and shouted, 'Look glass.' It became clear to us what had happened. The framed picture of Yasukuni Shrine hanging on my wall had fallen to the floor probably from a gust of wind. Rehmat grimaced. I knew what she was thinking. We were pagans at heart. Breaking of glass early in the morning was a bad omen. Rehmat had many such omens in her "Omen" dictionary. She immediately reached out and pulled Nina, Henna, and me close to her, fearful that some calamity would befall us. Azul who had joined us, guided Rehmat to the breakfast room. The gravity of this event weighed on all of us. Unable to bear the silence at the breakfast table, Jeff stood up and fiddled with his radio. Salim came to the table scratching his eyes. 'What is wrong? I heard a bomb blast.' Azul grabbed him and drew him closer. Henna stretched her hand and pulled his cheek. 'You sleepy rat, everything is fine.' Then she pointed to me and said, 'A picture fell in his *Uhuru* and that was the noise you heard.' Salim asked me, 'What mischief were you up to?' Azul defended me. 'Leave him alone. He didn't do anything.'

The broken glass had visibly affected Rehmat. Henna made her sit down. When everyone was at the table, Rehmat said that broken glass was an omen and that we ought to have a *Majalis*, a congregational prayer at the mosque next Friday. Azul countered her and said, 'But, we are booked to go to the Hot Spring Resort and we don't come back until the following Thursday. Friday would be too soon for a *Majalis*.'

'Then let's cancel the holiday,' Rehmat replied. Azul protested, 'That's impossible. It is the grand opening of the Sun Rise Resort. We also have business to conduct.'

'Well, we'll have to manage the *Majalis* somehow,' Rehmat answered. Azul, was outvoted and looked disappointed. He had a way of getting even. 'In that case,' he said, 'I shall not join the holiday.' This incensed Rehmat. 'What excuse do you have this year?' It was common knowledge in our home that Azul made an excuse every year to opt out of family holidays under one pretext or other. We also knew that he and Mr Tiano, his manager at JCB, went on a fishing trip or to some out of town business meetings. This was a thorny issue between Rehmat and Azul. Afraid that an argument would follow, Shamim interjected, 'Fresh coffee, anyone?' Judging the situation, Azul turned to Rehmat and said, 'Listen to me, dear. I am trying to support your plan. Someone has to stay back and arrange the service at the mosque. I am not even sure that we will be allowed a *Majalis* at such a short notice. Besides, invitations have to be sent out. When you return on Thursday, I will have arranged caterers and crockery and set up the marquee.' Rehmat was unhappy but kept quiet. Azul said to Jeff, 'The Resort is close to Cristobel Estate. Swing by there to pick our draft payments from Paul. They are overdue.'

'But, Daddy, Cristobel Estate is out of the way,' Jeff protested.

'Son, business is business. Paul is promising to give us sacks of his first crop of fast-growing mangoes from his agri-project. They will make excellent offerings for the *Majalis*. Besides, he loves dining. I will phone him to take you all across the border to Rwanda to a French bistro on Wednesday evening. I suggest you all take your passports with you.'

The mood at the breakfast table became less tense after this. Jeff and Shamim thanked me and said that despite the gate crashers, the Sundowner and the *Giant* picture show were a success. When everyone left, Rehmat asked me, 'Son, what happened to this girl Narika last weekend?' A dark curtain hung in my mind. I had no idea what Rehmat was talking about. Narika, why, what was wrong with her? Just then Jeremy tiptoed into the breakfast room with a crying face and said, '*Mama*, mother I show you something.' He led Rehmat through the garden which was dotted with overturned chairs and trampled flowerbeds. I followed them. Simba was having a feast on food-litter on the lawn. Suddenly, Rehmat cried out hysterically. I rushed to her side. She burst into tears, pointing to the red Singapore frangipani tree, which was her joy. One of its limbs was kissing the ground. Some fool must have climbed on the weak branch to get a better view of the *Giant* screen. I was angered. The bad omen of broken glass early in the morning had weakened Rehmat. The sight of broken frangipani added to her agony. The frangipani trees of different coloured flowers in our garden represented the bloom in our home. Their fragrance was sweetness of our home. The colours and richness of blooms in tight clusters typified our family bonding. The broken branches violated the sanctity of our home. I consoled Rehmat, 'Ma, I will graft it and it will grow again.' I knew as well as Rehmat that broken branches, unlike fractures, did not mend. Jeremy who was disturbed, stood behind us, shaking his head.

I dressed up and was sitting with Rehmat to comfort her when the doorbell rang. I rushed and opened the door. Mr Perry, the director of YMCA stood at the door. 'Good morning,' he said, 'is your daddy home?'

'No, he just left,' I replied. Seeing my worried look, he reassured me, 'It is okay, son. I am here with good news. Could I speak with your mother?'

'Yes, sir,' I replied and called out for Rehmat who came to the door wearing a pink scarf around her face. Mr Perry bowed and said, 'Meme, I am here to ask permission for your son to join our boxing training camp. We have important trials for international matches. He will join us for the whole day today and return home tomorrow.' Rehmat hesitated. In such matters, she relied on Azul. 'Ma!' I prompted her. She looked at me and nodded. I was relieved. Mr Perry smiled approvingly and said, 'Thank you, meme. I will send the details to your husband during the day.'

Stroll to the Past – Strangers in the Night

I was sitting on a corner stool in an open-air boxing ring. Spectators on the crowded stands were shouting, 'Knock-out, knock-out.' I felt tired after two gruelling rounds of non-stop exchanges of jabs and punches with an ugly slugger. A man dipped a sponge in a blue bucket, wiped my face and lifted it to the blinding sunlight. 'Remember, he has a lazy left, try the upper cut,' he said as he thrust a water bottle to my mouth. 'Rinse,' he said. I spat a mixture of blood and saliva in the blue bucket. The clean-shaven, youngish looking man then took out a towel from his back pocket and wiped my face. He was dressed in white with a black bow tie. His curly, middle-parted hair made him look like Clark Gable from *Gone with the Wind*. 'Who are you?' I asked with a grin.

'Silly boy, stop being funny. I am Zafur. How many fingers?'

'Three.'

'Where are we?'

'At Vubo Stadium in Pala,' I replied.

'Good,' Zafur said. 'And remember, if you win this round, you will be in the final.' I heard a bell. He shoved gum shields into my mouth and pushed me into the ring. 'Keep your lips tight and try uppercut. He has lazy hands,' he shouted last minute instructions behind me.

The previous year when I met Zafur at Vubo Stadium in Pala, I had progressed to the semi-finals of the Novice Boxing Championship with his encouragement. When Mr Edward, the Boxing Association Chairman, learned that I had no coach or officials accompanying me, he had asked Zafur to be my mentor. Zafur had asked me incisive questions about Jerusha Boxing Club, and when I told him that it was in the Oasis Tower, his interest perked up. 'Isn't it kind of seedy there? Some Charles has a shop there, right?'

'Yes,' I replied and asked him, 'have you been there?' He hummed as if he was lost in thoughts. 'No, no . . . I have not been there. I will visit you soon. You have guts coming here alone. Train well for next year.'

Mr Edward had told me that Zafur was an ex-middleweight champion and a Commonwealth bronze medallist and had to give up boxing after a car accident. His credentials had impressed me enormously.

Back at Vubo Stadium, from the very first bell of the third-round I went on an offensive and had an unrelenting exchange of jabs and hooks with my opponent. Spectators began to shout and chant for blood. I kept hearing Zafur's voice like a broken record, 'He has a lazy left, . . . Jab, uppercut . . . jab, uppercut.' I was tiring by the second. It was now or never. I synchronised my right foot with my left hand and dashed forward, throwing jabs. And then I saw the opportunity Zafur had been shouting for last half minute. The slugger dropped his left hand from his face and I swung an uppercut which connected with his chin. He flew in the air and hit the canvass. It was over. An elated Zafur ran into the ring and lifted me up.

In the late afternoon when I entered the ring to fight the final against a well-trained boxer from King's College, I knew I did not stand a chance. My only defensive plan was not to concede a knock-out and for the first two rounds I kept him at bay with my arms locked around my belly and face. In the final round, I did try an offensive onslaught of jabs and hooks but it was not enough. I lost on points. My loss disappointed me, but Zafur was encouraging. 'It is fantastic, what you have achieved without a coach.'

Later that night, after Participants' Dinner at the Grand Hotel, Zafur and I attended the midnight release of *Barsaat Ki Raat* at the Palladium.

This was a new experience for me. Pala had started a new Saturday night trend of releasing blockbuster Bollywood pictures at midnight. In Jerusha, me and my friends had often talked about attending one of these. This opportunity to attend the release of one of the most talked about picture of the year thrilled me. *Barsaat Ki Raat* became a memorable affair for a wrong reason.

During the interval, when Zafur went to get refreshments for us, two men followed him. I did not pay much attention to them, until I heard one of them yell, *Takh de* and was terrified to see Zafur jostled by an unruly group that included the two men who had followed him. *Takh de* had sinister connotations, the worst meaning being: deliver the blow, usually implying a knife attack. I saw one of the men drawing a *Rampuri,* the dreaded gravity dagger, favourite of Bombay thugs. I ran to Zafur's rescue. The ruffian swung his *Rampuri* in my face. I threw my hands up in the air. I had just come from nearly winning the boxing championship and had delivered a knockout to one of the most talented boxer of the competition. Seeing a thug haphazardly swing a dangerous weapon in my face caused an adrenalin rush to my brain. Jab . . . uppercut . . . the routine that Zafur had drilled into me, flashed in my mind. I saw the face of the thug like a punching bag. In swift sequences, I clenched my fist and threw jabs at him. It shook him up, and he swung his *Rampuri* like a wild orang-utan, grazing my left arm. Little did he expect the uppercut. It caught him square on the chin like a solid hammer blow, and as per the script he flew in the air and hit the floor like a stone. His *Rampuri* scuttled under the seats. The other assailants, shocked and surprised, ran, abandoning their floored comrade. Zafur and I ran in the opposite direction. In the safety of his car, Zafur explained to me that Bisney gang thugs had been harassing him for months. Someone was paying them to break up his friendship with his girlfriend. After my first meeting with Zafur, I had done some asking and had found that Zafur was no saint. In London, he had lived and boxed in a tough immigrant area called Brick Lane in East London which was notorious for the exploits of the nineteenth century serial killer Jack the Ripper. In Brick Lane Zafur was known as the Jungle Slugger. I asked him, 'What sort of a girlfriend do you have that warrants a *Rampuri* attack?'

'Listen young man, what do you know about love? It just doesn't happen in pictures. People fall in love in real life and the one I love is worth dying for. I met her in London. We were both strangers. Then I found she was from Pala, and I followed her.' Zafur saw me clutching my left arm. 'Good lord, you are bleeding.'

'It's nothing, just a surface wound,' I replied. He drove me to his flat, cleaned my wound, and put an antiseptic band aid over it. Late at night, he drove me to Jerusha.

At breakfast, seeing my puffed-up face, Shamim started crying. Rehmat brought out her medicine chest and started preparing a paste of turmeric and other strange ingredients to apply to my face. I laughed and ran away to *Uhuru* to escape her remedy that would leave my face as if I had jaundice. Later when the commotion died down, I told Salim that I had been to the midnight show of *Barsaat ki Raat*. Instead of being thrilled, he laughed. 'You're nuts, losing sleep over third rate Bollywood pictures.'

'Salim you are wrong. In fact Frank Sinatra released his popular "*Strangers in the Night*" after Rafi's "*Never shall I forget this Rainy Night*" from *Barsaat ki Raat*?'

'Are you saying Sinatra copied Rafi?'

'You be the judge,' I replied. Salim fell over laughing. 'You, my brother are not only crazy but as Jeff says, delusional too. This boxing business has shaken the roots of your brain.' I was not sure if what Salim implied was true, but Bollywood pictures influenced me a lot. In them, every situation of life had a song associated with it. I thought of life as a picture. A song played in my mind at all times. I tended to judge and scale a situation by what song fitted it. This was not to say that I did not like Western music. I only pretended to irritate Salim and make him defensive. In fact, my unhappiness was that I had not watched any of the greatest Hollywood musicals such as *Dancing in the Rain* and *Funny Face*. Of course, Salim did not know this and always fell for my ploy. While Salim and I were arguing about the merits of Bollywood pictures and their music, Jeff came and said, 'Listen, your success calls for a celebration. Let me treat you all to a dinner tonight at *La Trottoria*.'

It was the first time we went out together for dinner after Jeff got married. After his marriage he had drifted away from us. Before then we were always tight together. Jeff took us on forest hikes and picnics. After his marriage, his attention shifted to his beautiful bride. We felt neglected. We felt that even Jeff secretly missed our company. When we heard that he was planning to move to a new house, it depressed us. Salim punished Shamim for this. One Saturday evening, he told Shamim that he had an early tennis game the next morning and would like breakfast at six. Shamim, wanting to feel part of us, got up early, laid out a hot breakfast for Salim and waited. Salim was fast asleep, for he had no tennis game to go to. Poor Shamim kept waiting and fell asleep on the sofa. When Henna woke at eight, black, fat ants were swarming on the table and devouring Salim's breakfast. On seeing this Henna shrieked. Shamim woke up dazed, and started to cry. I rushed out and realized what had happened. I woke up Salim and cautioned him that Jeff's attack was imminent. We both ran away to Moidin for breakfast.

After our dinner at *La Trattoria*, the starry sky from our roof terrace seemed to hug us. 'Salim, let's have a sing along,' Henna suggested. It was our wont to sit on the roof terrace, sometimes by ourselves and sometimes with friends and have jamming sessions. Jeff and Shamim excused themselves. I fetched Salim's harmonium and we sat around him as he sang. A few minutes later Shamim and Jeff joined us. This surprised us. We insisted that Shamim sing a song. She was reluctant at first, but when Jeff asked her, she sang a Lata song, which left me gasping. She had a beautiful voice. Anyone who rendered Lata with such panache was instantly my favourite.

'Shamim, you are amazing.' I complimented her. A beautiful smile spread on her face. I think from that time Shamim became part of us. A week later Jeff told us that, he had postponed the idea of moving to a new house. This made us all happy.

The Meeting with 007

Mr Perry drove me to the Lake Textile Boxing Club across the newly opened Riyama Dam which was basking in brilliant sunshine. He complimented me for my boxing talents and we talked about school and such subjects. Churchill Highway had no army check-points or evidence of any army troubles that Hendrix had experienced the previous evening. At the Lake Textile Boxing Club Mr Edwards, the organiser of the Boxing Training Camp, greeted us all cheerfully and said that the first camp was only for meet and greet and more intense camps would be held during the year and added that later in the evening we would be attending a gala dinner in Jerusha. I did not see Zafur, and when I asked Mr Edward, he replied that we might meet him later. The rest of the day was filled with lessons on boxing techniques by several well-known boxing coaches and in the afternoon, we watched clips of great heavyweight boxing fights. Towards the evening we showered and freshened up and waited for a charter bus to Jerusha for the gala dinner.

A purple coloured bus decorated with posters of Sportsman cigarettes, Kimbo butter and Ambi skin lightening cream rolled in, blaring Elvis songs. A *Luo* driver was at the helm and when we were all seated he chuckled, 'Dear boys, I am Odhiambo. I know you all are very good boxers so I must be civil to you. I have selected some very...very good songs for our journey.' There upon he increased the volume on the tape player and we set off towards Jerusha with Elvis crooning us. On our approach to Riyama Dam I realized that for the last half mile there was no traffic in both the directions to the Dam. A pall of darkness was spreading over the forested hills surrounding the Dam. At the arch leading to the Dam, Mr Odhiambo, who was hanging on to the steering wheel and rocking to Elvis's *"She's a Devil in Disguise"*, failed to notice two soldiers waving at him to stop. He drove on to the Dam straight past them. Rifle shots from behind! We panicked and ducked below the seats. Mr Odhiambo slammed the brakes, hurling us forward. Elvis tape kept playing. The soldiers came running and climbed on to the bus and screamed at Mr Odhiambo. *'Wewe shenzi. Shuka chini,* you moron, get down.' Confused and frightened, Mr Odhiambo kept hanging on to the steering wheel. One of the soldiers rammed his rifle butt on to this shoulder. Mr Odhiambo shrieked and ran out of the bus. The other soldiers ran after him, caught him, and continued to beat him. The soldier, who remained on the bus, kicked the tape player with his boot. The Elvis tape stopped playing. He then pointed his rifle at us and shouted, *'All of you,* get off, *haraka,* hurry.' Afraid for our lives, we filed out. The soldier, who was beating Mr Odhiambo, left him grovelling on the road and joined his partner. The two pointed their rifles at us and asked us to march to the Dam railing, below which were the sluices from where Riyama thundered out, pounding the riverbed. Wilbur, a fellow boxer from Bira College crept close to me and clutched my arm. *'Funga macho.* Shut your eyes and kneel down,' one of the soldiers shouted. We obeyed. I heard a dull thud of a rifle butt on one of the boxer's shoulder. *'Wewe shenzi, funga macho.* Moron, keep your eyes shut.' We kept squatting on the narrow pavement with our hands on our eyes. The sun disappeared behind the hills, and Riyama Valley plunged into darkness. The amber lights on the Dam that made it look like a necklace did not come on. After a while we heard the roar of a motorcycle followed by rumble of trucks from behind us. They drove past us. The soldiers guarding us took their eyes off us. We lowered hands from our eyes and in the eerie light, I saw a scene that drove the terror of hell in my heart. The trucks reversed against the Dam railing, the bright red of the reverse light shining like the boiling cauldrons of hell. More soldiers jumped from the truck cabin, opened the back hatches, and we witnessed a gruesome spectacle, which until that moment was a rumour. Bodies were being pushed from the trucks into the river. The news about army trouble and tribal purge was true after all. '*Funga macho*. Keep your eyes closed,' the soldiers guarding us hissed. We covered our eyes. My heart was palpitating uncontrollably. I continued to recite prayers to Imam Ali. The dirty task of dumping the bodies took only a few minutes. The truck hatches were pulled up. The motorcycle roared again, and the trucks drove past us led by the motorcycle. Soon their rumble died down. I thought of the Japanese saying: 'See no Evil, Hear no Evil, Say no Evil.' The soldiers ordered us back on the bus and let us proceed.

Mr Odhiambo, jolted by the rough treatment at the hands of the soldier and frightened by what he had seen, drove hastily towards Jerusha. Was what we saw real or imagination? The amnesia that accompanied my head injury was acute now. We crossed Zanzibar Road rail crossing. Ahead of us loomed the dark wall of Suwakaki. I suddenly became confused. I stood up, opened the bus door, and was about to jump, when Wilbur ran after me and restrained me. 'It is okay,' he comforted me. I sat down and took deep breaths. I felt as if I was losing grasp of my sanity. I was sliding into a waking dream and had the most shocking realisation of my life that there was a dead man hidden in Suwakaki. I broke into a cold sweat, shut my eyes tight, and put my hands to my head. I had no idea why I had such a frightening thought. I had no idea who the dead man was or how I knew him. I now understood why I was so eager to read the paper for crime stories in the morning. I opened my eyes only when we were past Suwakaki. The bus was travelling on palm-lined Lake Drive. Wilbur turned to me and asked if I was okay. 'Yes, I am fine,' I replied. We passed the familiar Krishna Temple, European Cricket Club, and Japanese Shinto Shrine. Mr Watanabe, a dam engineer, was instrumental in construction of the Shinto shrine. There were bizarre stories about him. In our home, Watanabe's story was a taboo. We knew that when Rehmat was informed that Azul had purchased JCB, the cafe and bar in the Business District close to Jerusha's Market Square, she was unhappy and had challenged Azul about it. She had asked, 'What about Watanabe story and about some problems with JCB freehold land title?'

Azul's reply was very simple, 'Like many foreigners, Watanabe drank at JCB and that's all. As for freehold title, there is nothing that a good lawyer cannot fix.' There was no telling where and when Watanabe's ghost may rise again.

I was lost in my thoughts when the bus stopped. I looked out of my window and realized that we were on a hill overlooking Jerusha Pier. Mr Odhiambo turned off the bus engine and kept sitting, clutching the steering wheel. Gone were his gleeful outbursts. We stepped off of the bus. Everyone was quiet, jolted by the *Funga macho ordeal*. In front of us Pier Park eased off gently towards Jersusha Pier. The horizon still had some streaks of pink. In the gathering darkness, the Pier lights twinkled like distant stars. The lights on the masts of boats along the jetty bobbed up and down. Behind us the flames from torches surrounding the majestic Old Thompson Hotel's garden fence danced about in the gentle breeze, casting warm glow on Old Thompson's Tudor façade. The charming fairy-tale setting lifted our gloom of *Funga macho ordeal*. My fellow boxers found their wit.

During the olden days, Old Thompson Hotel was the domain of the colonialists. Its remaining boorish attitude was kept alive by an old-time door attendant, Peter, who allowed only those folks into the hotel whom he deemed worthy. From what I had heard, his method had no rhyme or rhythm to it. For this reason, I had never set foot in Old Thompson.

A man with a French beret studded with medals and decorations came to attention at the entrance as we stepped down from the bus. One look at the man and I concluded that he was Peter. Aware of his notoriety, Mr Edward stood beside him to avoid any incidents. Contrary to the stories, Peter was most gracious and greeted us with courtesy.

Mrs McGuire, a debonair woman, greeted us at the reception. I was surprised to see her. I had met her first at JCB when she had come to drop her husband for drinks. Being new in town, at that time Mrs McGuire had asked me to accompany her to a grocery store. After shopping, when she saw the poster of *Splendor in the Grass* at the Picture House, she had asked me to accompany her to the picture. I was hesitant. 'It's not something that's done in Jerusha,' I told her.

'It is okay. Terry will not mind.' During the picture I was moved by Natalie Wood's portrayal of anguish of love. After the show, Mrs McGuire and I went to Rose Cafe where she told me interesting stories about her life in her native Canada. She asked my opinion of *Splendor in the Grass*. I cobbled an answer. 'It is a tragic picture. It's unnatural for a father to suggest that his son find a girl . . . I mean sleep with a girl, other than his girlfriend before marrying. That's what destroyed Natalie.' Mrs McGuire was candid. 'Sex before marriage is not unusual. Girls face this dilemma every day or lose the boyfriend.'

'It's an unusual situation for us,' I replied. Mrs McGuire smiled and said, 'I had fallen in love with Terry when I was seventeen, and we made love six months after we met. When you are in love, it just happens.' I sipped my hot chocolate, hot under the collar by the nature of our conversation. Then she asked me. 'How do you meet girls, here?' I held the hot chocolate cup in my hand for a long time before answering her, 'Mrs McGuire, we don't.'

'What do you mean, you don't?'

'That is what I mean. We don't meet girls. Our school has separate streams. I mean girls attend a different wing. Boys are not allowed anywhere near the girl's wing. Meeting girls is seen to be a sin or something like that. We watch Bollywood pictures and see middle-aged heroes, old enough to be our fathers, chase eighteen-year-old heroines around gardens, and we dream and drool. And when Helen is on the screen, it is a riot.'

'What do you mean a riot?' Mrs McGuire asked. I explained, 'Helen is the dance queen of Bollywood. Pictures that have her dances are box office hits. Boys fight to get the closest seat to the screen in the third class in the hope that when Helen does her dance whirls and her umbrella skirt fans out, we would be able to see her legs. And the closer you are to the screen, the better the view. One time, Nash did a gig like that in school and we almost got expelled. In Bollywood pictures, Indian heroines wear baggy pantaloons underneath, unlike Marilyn Monroe in *Some like it Hot.*' Mrs McGuire burst out laughing. 'Oh . . . you make me laugh, you do.' When she recovered, she asked, 'Do you mean to say that you can't ask girls out on dates?'

'Oh no, Mrs McGuire, that is out of the question. Our Indian pictures teach us that love is only a desire and not a fulfilment.'

'This is so brutal, you poor boys!'

Mrs McGuire finished her round of meeting and greeting the guests and came to me. 'Why, young man, fancy seeing you here? Are you with the Boxing Team?'

'Yes, Mrs McGuire. I am surprised to see you too,' I commented as she led us to Emerald, which was the heart of Old Thomson. On the way, she explained, 'I help part-time to pass the time. There is nothing else to do in Jerusha.'

In the Emerald, Zafur who was with Mr Edwards immediately came over to greet me. I noticed lines on his face, which were not evident when I saw him a year earlier. I fired him a barrage of questions. 'Why didn't you get in touch with me? I was curious how things went with you and your girlfriend after that *Rampuri* attack.'

'Simmer down,' he said with a smile, 'I meant to contact you, but I manage this place and things were busy. As for the girlfriend, you'll soon find out.' Just at that moment, a group of guests entered the Emerald, causing a stir in the dining hall. 'James Bond and his crew,' Zafur whispered. This astonished me. '007, seriously?' I looked at the group but was unable to spot Sean Connery. Instead I spotted Savi from Jerusha accompanying a blonde girl. Zafur walked away to attend to the Bond

VIPs. The Bond group sat down at the dining table under the ornate chandelier in the middle of Emerald. We sat two tables away. Savi, whose photo hung in our school's Hall of Fame, sat next to the blonde girl. She captivated my attention. She lifted her face and ran her hand through her tumbling hair. I blushed as I realised that I was staring at her. This was the first time I was seeing her in person. I had seen her on TV when she was hosting School "Mastermind" series from Pala.

After dinner, I asked Zufur about the real James Bond. He patted my back and said, 'Good gosh, you won't see him in this lot. These are all doubles. They are all here on location search for a new James Bond picture.'

The hotel band started playing lilting tunes, and couples swayed gracefully on the dance floor. My fellow boxers drifted towards the bar to chat with the serving girls. Zafur talked to Savi at the bar. Cigarette smoke was wafting up to the ceiling. I lifted my two hands, made a frame with my fingers and thumb, enclosing Savi and Zafur in it, pretending that it was a scene for my next picture. Zufur and Savi walked towards me holding hands. I lowered my eyes and tried not to stare. 'Young man,' Zafur said as he approached me, 'meet Savi. Keep her company until I come back.' I stood up and shook her hand. 'I am . . .' I started to say. 'It is okay, Zafur has given me your introduction.' Savi looked adorable in a light blue frock with a dark blue medallion of aquamarine choker around her neck. I became tongue-tied. 'Are you going to ask me to sit, young man?'

'Oh, I am sorry.' I offered her a seat next to me. She sat down. Fragrance of a fruity perfume engulfed me. She asked, 'Are you not related to Jeff from JCB?'

'Yes, he is my elder brother.'

'Were you not involved in a school drama on Wednesday and this girl had to withdraw?' I fumbled for words. My mind was still confused about events. I had a vague recollection of a drama and a chase in the Suwakaki. 'How did you find out?' I asked.

'Ishrat told me on the phone that a girl from Gandhi Road had a dance routine.'

'Narika,' I mechanically answered. I was surprised by my answer. Did Narika really have a dance routine in a drama? It was as if Savi heard my question. She answered, 'Yes. What a shame things went sour. Such a sweet girl. A champion dancer.'

'Do you know her?' I asked.

'My dear, we have a secret sisterhood in Jerusha. We feel pain when there is violence against women, mental or physical.' What violence was Savi referring to? What happened to Narika? I felt frustrated that the fog in my mind that shrouded Narika, the drama, and a lot more remained as thick as before. Suddenly, Savi drew closer and asked, 'How long have you known Zafur?'

'Actually, I met him at Vubo Stadium during boxing tournament. He looked like Clark Gable. He made me win two rounds,' I replied. Savi was listening to me, but her eyes were roving Emerald looking for Zafur. In an effort to push out the thoughts of Narika, drama, and violence out of my mind, I asked Savi an intrusive question and waded into forbidden territory. I regretted it immediately. 'You must be in love with him?' It was as if a lightning bolt had struck Savi. Her fingers gripped mine, and she blushed. Her eyes changed many shades until they assumed radiance and lustre that were easy to recognise but not easy to describe. 'You have asked me a very personal question, young man.' She lowered her head and looked down. The play of emotions on her face reminded me of a song:

Ask not about love . . .
Gaze not on my face . . .
Isn't lowering my eyes
my confession?

She held my hand and said, 'I like you. You are honest.' Then she asked me an innocent question that displayed the sense of pride and exclusivity of people who belonged to the most secretive of the Circle of Life, the Circle of Love. I had seen this same attitude in other people who had asked me the same question in the recent past. Savi pulled my cheek. 'What would you know about love?' The directness of her question touched a nerve in my heart. In fact, I could ask her questions of my own: What was love? Can a heart fall in love a second time, a third time, and possibly a fourth time or was it all a make-believe deception? I trembled. I steadied myself. We sat in silence for a while and then we talked about a mural facing us. It was a paradisiacal scene of two women in colourful *khangas,* calico flowery prints, facing a lake and forested hills beyond. The mural was painted by Mr O'Leary when he first came to Jerusha. When I told Savi that I had watched him paint a mural at the Hindu Temple, during his second visit to Jerusha, she immediately became interested. She commented that there were stories about him. 'What stories?' I asked. A bearded man from the Bond entourage interrupted Savi. I found this interruption untimely. While Savi talked to the bearded man, I studied the wall mural. What did Savi mean by 'There are stories about him?' Artists always had skeletons in their cupboards. When the bearded man left, Savi turned to me. 'Sorry, it was the director. He wants to shoot before daybreak. Where were we?'

'We were talking about Mr O'Leary and you said that he had a past.'

'Yes, not many know about it. In fact your JCB is at the centre of his story.' This surprised me. 'Tell me, tell me, about it please,' I pleaded. My boyish zeal amused Savi. A waiting staff brought us fresh coffees in gold-rimmed cups. Savi sugared her cup and looked at me. I gestured her two spoons. 'Sweet tooth!' she remarked. She sugared my coffee, stirred it and gently tapped the spoon against the rim, producing a sonorous peal. She put the spoon in her saucer, took a sip of her coffee, and said, 'Watanabe came to Jerusha many years ago to work on the dam and stayed at the Kit Kat Lodge opposite JCB. In the evenings, he used to dine and drink at JCB. Is there a Blue Room in JCB?'

'Yes, many foreigners drink there,' I replied.

'That explains it. People say that Riya Hill looks like Mount Fuji from a window in the Blue room. It reminded Watanabe of his home in Hakone, in Japan,' Savi said.

'Yes, that is true. On sunny days Riya looks beautiful,' I added.

Savi continued, 'People say that over the years, Blue Room has developed a reputation as a "literates" haunt. I have never visited it so I don't know. This Watanabe was a regular at Blue Room. As luck would have it, a Japanese nurse, Miki, came to Jerusha Hospital with the VSO (Volunteer Service Overseas). She used to visit Blue Room and Watanabe and Miki developed a close bond. Miki was expressive and bold. She had studied in San Francisco. She was not shy, which is unusual for a Japanese girl.' I wanted to differ with Savi, but I restrained myself. My mind reflected on Japanese *Manga* that Joger circulated in our class. In them I saw Japanese girls in all positions of nudity, and they did not appear shy to me. I was sure all these *Manga* girls must have been high on hot *Sake* before they posed for the nude pictures.

I wanted to find out how O'Leary and Miki fitted in with the story of Watanabe, whose ghost always appeared in Jerusha folk lore. Stories always become interesting with the introduction of a female character. Miki had never surfaced in Watanabe stories before. Savi took a sip of her coffee and continued, 'After the dam project was postponed, Watanabe was not busy, so he made a proposal to the old proprietor of JCB to make several paintings for Blue Room.' "What kind of paintings?" the old proprietor asked. "Japanese landscapes," he replied. The old proprietor was honest and said, "Sure, but I have no money to pay you."

"Money, no problem," Watanabe replied. Watanabe started his painting project in earnest. It was during this time that wild Mr O'Leary came to Jerusha from Sorbonne. With shoulder-length hair and a green bandanna around his head, people came to call him crazy Hindi. Mr O'Leary also gravitated to Blue Room and was mesmerised by Watanabe's mastery with water colours. His distinctive Japanese thick *shodo* brush strokes captivated O'Leary's imagination. Soon Watanabe's Blue Room project and O'Leary's colour in motion paintings from Jerusha gained fame among the foreign community. Blue Room became a hive of literary types attracting people from as far as the Sugar City. Late afternoons and evenings became most busy. There were lively debates about art, literature, philosophy, and everything in between. Talkative Miki became a darling of Blue Room. "You foreigners," she said one evening, "you are here with hidden motives. Some of you are Christian zealots, some of you are here with political agendas, and some are simply economic thieves." Everyone listened to Miki with amusement. "But Japan," she continued, "has no such ambitions overseas. We provide true aid, without any hope for benefit." This polarised the "literate". Mr O'Leary sided with Miki. Strangely, Watanabe opposed Miki.

'After this debate, Miki Kawai acquired not one but two serious admirers, Watanabe and O'Leary. Both fought for her attention. While Watanabe was busy painting Japanese landscapes, Miki started spending more time with O'Leary. This made Watanabe unhappy. After his third painting, he lost his concentration.'

Savi's next statement added a new dimension to the story. 'It is rumoured that in his paintings, Watanabe has weaved a secret. And there was a third person in the Miki story.'

'What secret? And third person? Who?' I asked.

'No one knows,' Savi replied.

'Savi, you said three paintings, but Blue Room has five paintings of Japanese landscapes. I am not sure if they are Watanabe's.' My statement surprised Savi. 'Five? Watanabe only painted three. Are these landscapes still at JCB? When can I see these?' I thought for a while and said, 'If you come to JCB next Saturday, I will show them to you.' Savi took up my offer. I told her, 'If you come early we will have dinner in the cafe. Later, it gets very crowded. JCB has the best mashed plantain and kofta in Jerusha.'

'Oh, are you inviting me on a dinner date? This is so exciting,' Savi said, patting my hand. The dimples on her cheeks deepened with her spreading smile. The band started to play Dean Martin's "Say Si bon". Savi became playful and said, 'Are you going to ask me for a dance?' I was more eager to hear the rest of Watanabe's Story and find out who the third person was, so I said, 'Please finish the Third Man Story.' She was astonished. *'Arre,* you are like an old woman, gossip hungry. We can finish the story next week. At this very moment, there are men dying to spend time with me and you don't want to dance with me?' She pulled me to the dance floor. We danced in silence. She dropped her head on my shoulder, and I felt a sort of resonance with her. Actually, I felt a raging storm in her heart. She lifted her head for a brief instant, and I looked into her eyes, which told a story. The mind can understand such stories of the heart. We continued dancing. She dropped her head again on my shoulder. I felt drops of warm tears on my shoulder. I heard a soft sob. It surprised me. The lilting "Love is a Many Splendour Thing" tune was stirring up emotions in her heart. I did not stare at her. I let things flow. I was not sure what made her cry. People in love behave irrationally. That I know. I pulled out a handkerchief from my pocket and gave it to her. We continued to dance as she wiped her tears and gripped my fingers. 'I am sorry. You must be wondering. I will explain it all one day,' she apologized. We bonded in an unfathomable manner. I felt a pat on my shoulder and heard Zafur's voice, 'Thanks, young man, you have been a great help.' He winked at me and whispered, 'What do you think?'

'Zafur, superlative,' I replied. He smiled and said, 'Join us for breakfast tomorrow and then I will drive you home.' As I handed Savi's hand to Zafur, she whispered in my ear, 'Did you know Watanabe was murdered here in Old Thomson?'

Tired but too tense to go to sleep, I took a short walk across the road to Pier Park for fresh air. A man followed me with long strides, startling me. 'It is okay,' he said as he caught up with me. 'It is me, Refu.'

'You frightened me,' I said.

'Sorry. I thought you may want some nuts.' Saying this, he offered me a cone and continued walking with me. 'Say, were you in for dinner in the restaurant?'

'Yes,' I replied.

'I hear that beautiful Savi is with the foreign party. Is she still in there?' His question made me uncomfortable and I was not sure what he would use this information for. I crafted my reply. 'I can't remember.'

'Oh, then she must be still in there.' Saying this, he turned and left.

I looked back. Old Thomson stood silent like a Tudor Castle. Flickering candles in Emerald appeared like twinkling stars. I walked a little further and sat on a park bench, listening to the wind singing in the trees and gentle waves lapping the lakeshore. I looked at the star-studded sky. My mind dwelt on the events of the evening. Why would Savi cry when at this very moment she was in the arms of her lover? The tears she shed were certainly not of joy. Our Bollywood pictures have many twists on love stories. I felt that Savi was harbouring a big sadness in her heart. If half the stories I had heard about her were true, then she had many ups and downs and anyone can shed a tear or two because of it.

And Watanabe murdered in Old Thomson! I had never heard that before. This was a new angle to an intriguing old story, and it had an immediate relevance to me because I grew up looking at the five paintings in Blue Room. What secret had Watanabe weaved in his paintings? I also personally knew Watanabe's contemporary Mr O'Leary from the time when he was painting the Krishna mural in the Hindu Temple. Who could be the third men in Miki's love story?

This Mr O'Leary was an interesting character. When I sat with him watching him paint the mural at the Krishna Temple, he told me an interesting bit about his youth, which raised my sexual mercury to its zenith. When he was at Sorbonne, he fell in love with a Romany gypsy called Lola who lived in one of the flats above a quaint art studio along the Seine. Mr O'Leary was open and told me all about his afternoon love marathons with her and his desire he said was to be granted eternal youth like Endymion, the son of Zeus, adored by the moon goddess, Selena, who came every night and mounted him.

'Would you not tire?' I asked. Mr O'Leary replied with a boyish grin, 'That is why you require eternal youth, silly boy.' I found Mr O'Leary's love philosophy interesting. This was before my Sex Lessons 1, 2, and 3

On my way back to Old Thompson, I heard a high-pitched altercation between Refu and Peter. By the time I reached the gate it was over and I saw a car pulling away. I crossed over to a dimly lighted parking lot, skirting a parked Jaguar. Two lovers, undisturbed by the shouting and commotion at the gate, were locked in a passionate embrace. A fruity fragrance hung around the car. I was certain it was Savi's scent.

A fragrance-laden breeze was blowing in from the open window when I went to Kaiser Suite. I fell asleep as soon as I hit the bed. A heavy banging on the door woke me up. I opened the door. Zafur stood at the door. 'Sorry to disturb you, old chap,' he apologised. 'They will start filming soon, if you are interested. Come to the Emerald for coffee and hot buns. It'll wake you up.' I freshened up and joined a group of people gathered around the coffee table. Savi, who was talking to the bearded director, came over to me. 'Did you get any sleep?' she asked.

'May be an hour or so. How about you?'

'Zafur and I sat and talked,' she replied. A coy smile played on her face. The director came over and requested Savi to have the fence torches lighted again. Savi disappeared with Zafur. The director and his team gathered in the garden around the camera trolley flanked on either side by two powerful camera lights. I followed them. A bright moon hung in the sky. Old Thompson looked surreal. The Jaguar, in which I had seen Savi and Zafur making love, was now parked at the front gate. The director signalled to the cameraman and the shooting began. One of the crew gave a bump to the rear wing of Jaguar as if it had just stopped. Mr Bond stepped out of the Jaguar and opened the door for the blonde girl. One of the peacocks from the Old Thompson garden was startled and shrieked. The director made rolling motion with his finger. The camera kept rolling. Suddenly, an assailant jumped out of the darkness and knocked the blonde girl down. Mr Bond jumped on the assailant. The director did not like some technical detail. There were several re-takes of the scene. Close to the fence, Savi and Zafur stood snuggling. Moonlight was waning. I was getting tired and sleepy. I returned to my room, drew my curtains, and went to sleep.

Green Ford: Love of Cinema

Take-offs and landings are the most critical phases of aeroplane flights. It is the same with sleep. Dreams, visions, and psychological events happen during falling asleep and waking up stages of light sleep. It was déjà vu. There was a banging on my room door like soft mallet blows. I bubbled up from sleep and opened my eyes with difficulty. Outside, in the garden, there was an orchestra of bird songs. Sunlight blinded me as I opened the door. The time on my watch was 8 am. 'Good lord,' I cursed. A hotel bellboy held a calling card to my face, 'You have to come urgently. Madam is waiting in the car.'

'Madam who?' I glanced at the calling card: Dr V. Bajaj. In degrees, I connected the card to the German-trained double-degreed women's medicine specialist. How did she know I was at Old Thompson? I prayed everything was well at home. I washed my face, picked up my sports bag, and joined the bellboy who led the way. I asked him if Zafur was awake. 'No, sir, Mr Zafur left the hotel very early and has not returned,' he replied.

'Well, please tell him that I will not join him for breakfast.' The bellboy handed me Madam's card and answered, 'I will. Madam's car is at the side entrance.'

Madam Doctor was waiting in an old green Ford. She leaned over and opened the door for me. 'Sorry, I had to wake you up so early.'

'Madam, is everything all right?' I asked as I sat in the car. 'All is fine. We are taking a short drive.' A tape was playing Brahms Symphony #5.

Madam Doctor lowered the volume. 'I know you don't like classical,' she apologised.

I replied, 'In the morning, it is soothing.' Then I asked, 'Madam, what happened to your MG? Why this old car?' She smiled, 'The MG would have been too loud early in the morning.' Saying this she drove off on Lake Drive and then turned north on Zanzibar Road without stating our destination. The heaviness of Brahms Symphony #5 and lack of sleep fatigued me. I dozed off. A black and white spiral rotated anti-clockwise on my dream screen, and I slid into the depth of my subconscious.

My riding in Madam Doctor's green Ford had its genesis in the past . . .

Like a woman, Jerusha's beauty was in the magical congruence of facial lines and curves in correct proportion and a hip to waist ratio of 0.7. The hills of Riya, Murima and Garrison which surrounded Jerusha, were in the right proportion. Peace Lake, which reflected the colours of morning and the grey of misty evenings, and Riyama, which gushed forth from Thomson Falls, which was the venue for the notorious Du Maurier Challenge, were cosmetics that accentuated its beauty. In the early days, Riyama Dam, which partially drowned Thomson Falls, was only on the drawing board. Murima Hill which stood behind the railway station was the most charming of the three hills. On its eastern slope, a path zigzagged up until green forest consumed it in its upper reaches. Halfway up the western slope, at Trinity Point, the mud road forked to Kongoro Estates on the left, Tilapia Village on the right, and the middle led to the summit where shady mavule trees swayed gracefully overlooking Peace Lake. Lover's Point was about twenty yards below the summit.

One morning during breakfast I suggested that we ought to climb Murima to welcome the sun. This was before Jeff was married. As soon as I suggested it, I realised that Jeff would pulverize me for saying it. In any event once I had put my foot in my mouth, I had to continue to shove it further. I avoided looking at Jeff and said, 'Daddy, I have heard that Peace Lake turns into a sheet of gold. We can enjoy a picnic breakfast up there.' Jeff put aside the *Filmfare* he was reading. I braced for his assault. 'Are you crazy, climbing Murima at dawn just to see the sunrise? What did you dream about?' Azul jumped to my defence, 'In Japan, every year, thousands climb Mount Fuji at night to greet the sun as it rises. It is considered very sacred.'

'There, you see,' I said triumphantly, looking at Jeff.

Not too long after this, at the crack of dawn, one Sunday, only Azul and I packed a picnic breakfast in my rucksack and crossed railway tracks at the station to climb Murima. Mist covered the forested path. We climbed in silence. Suddenly, a buck ran across our path frightening me. Azul put his hands around me. 'It is okay. It won't hurt you.' Further up the path a troupe of colobus monkeys shrieked in mad frenzy, jumping from tree to tree at our approach. We stopped to watch them. We reached the summit when the eastern sky was turning blood red. We sat on a granite rock in anticipation of the sunrise. Mavule and eucalyptus trees swayed in the morning breeze around us. To the south stood Riya Hill with its peak rising above the morning mist. Beyond it stretched malaria ravaged McKenzie Forest looking benign and inviting. The roofs of army barracks on Garrison Hill were beginning to take shine from gradually brightening eastern sky. 'Beautiful,' Azul commented.

'Daddy, did you climb Mount Fuji in Japan?'

'Yes, I did. Our party reached the summit just before sunrise. I must admit son that I never reached the summit. One member of our team was oxygen starved and I had to turn back.' While we were talking, I thought I heard peals of laughter. Sure enough, smiling Jeff, happy Henna, and mischievous Salim burst upon us singing "Happy birthday to you", from behind a thick trunk of a mavule. Henna was holding a birthday cake with sparklers throwing out stars. This surprised me, 'Daddy, I never knew . . . You all, you are impossible!'

'We wanted to surprise you,' Jeff said with a smile bigger than usual. Azul explained the reason for Jeff's big smile. 'He will be married soon.' Azul's announcement was a surprise. 'Hooray,' Henna clapped and hugged

Jeff. 'Who is the lucky bride?' she asked. A beaming Azul replied. 'A beautiful girl from Kenya. Her name is Shamim.'

When the sun climbed the sky, Peace Lake turned into a sheet of gold as I had said. Even Jeff was impressed. Henna laid out a scrumptious picnic breakfast. Handing me a piece of imported cheddar, Henna said, 'Jeff drove all the way to Pala yesterday for this.' I thanked Jeff. He simply waved his hand and said, 'Whatever.'

'Why didn't Ma come?' I asked.

'She is cooking a birthday lunch for you, you fool,' Jeff answered. 'Leave him alone on his birthday,' Henna defended me.

After breakfast, we played hide-and-seek among the granite rocks and lost track of time. Azul looked at his watch and exclaimed, 'O, I have to be at the "Dam Planning" meeting.' We gathered together the breakfast spread and rushed him to the old town hall. Until that day, I had not noticed the construction boom that had gripped Jerusha. Cranes and dirty dust-laden trucks crowded Sogo Square where a new town hall was under construction. A prison complex was coming up on the slopes of Riya Hills. Just below it, an industrialist had built a sand-dredging station on the lakeshore, destroying its fragrant lotus garden. Not too long after we had witnessed the magic of Peace Lake turning into a sheet of gold from the summit of Murima, its tranquil beauty became a memory. A Canadian Company began construction of a copper smelter at the summit, cutting a deep channel along the steep path along which Azul and I had climbed to the summit. A funicular rail was installed along it to shuttle ore and copper ingots back and forth to Jerusha Station below. The tall smoke-billowing chimney of the smelter and nightly slag pours that turned the sky cherry red became icons of Jerusha. Many nights I sat in *Uhuru*, watching rivulets of slag running down the hill, the trees in their paths bursting up in flames like ghosts. Over time, slag and fumes reduced the rain forest into a smouldering, gloomy clump. Only tropical rain from above shed tears for this devastation. Nonetheless, the rain by itself was not able to reverse the destruction or regenerate the forest to its former glory. I often wondered what happened to the bucks that called the forest their home. As if forest devastation was not enough, a far more disturbing event happened at Murima, which changed, forever, Murima's standing in Jerusha.

As much as I wished it not to, my mind played the memory segment of that event which obliterated the good standing of Murima and shattered the cloak of secrecy that surrounded Jerusha's Circle of Love. That day the bluish tinge of the Circle of Love turned crimson red at the Lover's Point on Murima.

Jerusha had begun to take notice of Musa and Bulbul's secret love affair. When one fateful, full moon night they came up to Lover's Point to share a few intimate moments, the taboo and Victorian norms of Jerusha confronted them in the face.

My clenched-fist declaration of "vive l'amour" the day after Musa and Bulbul's escapade to Lover's Point caused a great stir in the school. That day a rumour began to circulate that Musa and Bulbul had eloped. Neither had returned home from their outing the previous night. With my clenched-fist declaration, everyone thought that I had some knowledge of this. Mr Irvine summoned me to his office where he and Mr Desai grilled me about Musa and Bulbul affair. 'Sir, I do not know anything about them. I am not even friends with Musa.'

In a surprise move, Mr Irvine asked Mr Desai to leave. Then he closed the office door and asked me, 'Son, are you in love? What prompted you to say "vive l'amour"? Is there anything bothering you?' Mr Irvine had put me on the spot. If I was not careful, I may have to utter untruths. 'Sir,' I replied, 'I regret my assembly outburst. Mr Asplin had no right to search me in front of the whole school.'

'I am fully aware of the situation, and we are trying to change things. If you have any problems, do not hesitate to talk to me. If you have any information about Musa and Bulbul, let me know. Their families are very upset. You may leave now.' This was the first time any teacher had spoken to me with respect.

At the police station, Inspector Rana was not convinced about Musa and Bulbul's elopement story. He was conducting his own private investigation. Only later we were to learn that he had taken Bakor and Bandar into custody for questioning. As days wore on, many different spicy bits were added to the Musa and Bulbul story. People reported seeing them in Pala; others said they were in Nairobi. Bulbul's family was in shame. In the conservative Ndebe Street, such events were seen as a blot on the whole community. Everyone felt that the root of the evil was the free mingling of boys and girls at school.

It was not until Friday when the Musa Bulbul Story took a turn. A villager cutting wood in the valley below the Lover's Point found the broken body of Bulbul. Barely thirty yards from her was Musa's body pinned under his scooter. These discoveries sent shock waves through Jerusha. Their bodies were sent to Jerusha Hospital for post-mortems. Mullah Bashir and other mullahs from Jerusha's different mosques got involved in the case on behalf of the distraught families. Not wishing any ugly truth to mar and destroy the honour of the families, they wanted Musa and Bulbul buried at the soonest. Post-mortems were concluded post-haste, and deaths from multiple injuries due to falls from height were registered. Inspector Rana was persuaded to declare no foul play in the case. He had no option but to release Bakor and Bandar for lack of evidence. His personal view was that Bakor and Bandar had complicity in the case and had probably returned to Lover's Point after a while and had overpowered Musa and molested Bulbul. Forensic experts from London would have probably proven the case. But that would have taken time and the families did not want to face such an ugly truth.

Musa and Bulbul were buried on the following Monday. On Tuesday, during school assembly, school bugler, Kelvin, and drummer Vinod, played "Last Post" while the school flag was put to half-mast. Mr Irvine declared a holiday in memory of Musa and Bulbul.

In an out poring of grief, students marched up to the Lover's Point with flowers and heart-touching messages. In time a group of students built a wall at Lovers Point in memory of Musa and Bulbul and Mr Sara, the art master painted a scene of lovers reclining under a tree with a cask of wine and grapes. He titled it "Adonis and Venus" and wrote: Farewell beloved Musa and Bulbul. Underneath the painting, he wrote, "Vive l'amour." That was how the bluish Circle of Love turned crimson red.

But these sordid events were still in the future. After my birthday celebration at the summit of Murima, where I had seen Peace Lake turn into a sheet of gold, we rushed down the hill to drop Azul at the old town hall for the Dam Planning meeting. On our way, home we saw a large crowd gathered on a vacant lot opposite Sukh Sagar. Jeff told us that it was the ground-breaking ceremony for a new cinema. I was delighted. 'When will it be ready?' I asked.

'May be in a year or two,' he replied. Further along Boja Road a huge banner hanging outside Picture House greeted us.

NAGIN

In Geva colour. Grand Release – Next week

'Salim, it is in Geva colour. It will be fantastic,' I exclaimed. Until then, all Bollywood pictures were in black and white.

Nagin celebrated silver jubilee in Jerusha due to its sole and exclusive engagement and Mr Lorne, the proprietor of Picture House hosted a grand fete on Boja Road to commemorate this occasion with free shows of *Nagin*. I fought the crowds to catch a free show of *Nagin* when I spotted Gul, who had a lot to do with the dreaded Music Room Affair. He was with a muscular boy whom I had not seen before, harassing Narika and her friend near the Maxi Car's show room. I should have minded my own business. Narika had two nephews, Pal and Tavi, who were capable of looking after her. Against my better judgment, I dashed across the road and stood face to face with the muscular punk blocking Narika's path and asked him to let Narika pass. Gul whispered in his ear. I was sure he informed him that

I was a boxer. In street situations, boxers got two types of reactions. Either people backed off or looked for a fight. I think the punk chose the latter option and pushed me with his strong arms. Narika and her companion ran. Gul lunged at my arms, locked them, and shouted, 'No fight please.' In that instant, I saw the punk's fist loaded with a silvery object fly past Gul's arms. A knuckleduster blow to my right ribs took the wind out of my sail. I gasped. Gul and his companion merged in the crowd. I slumped on the pavement on my knees with an excruciating chest pain, struggling for a breath. After resting for a while on the steps of Maxi Car, I trudged to Picture House, slumped into an empty seat, and passed out in pain. When I regained consciousness, my head was resting on the shoulder of a girl. She was gently rubbing my neck and shoulder. I was in too much pain to resist or react to her affection. While Vyjayanthimala, looking beautiful in Geva colour, was singing a love song on the silver screen, the girl drew closer and kissed me. It was Narika. Then she left. When I walked out of Picture House, it had turned dark and the crowded Boja Road was all aglow with colourful Chinese lantern lamps cris-crossing Boja Road. The razzmatazz of Silver Jubilee fete was at its peak. Popular *Nagin* songs blared from Navin Paan Shop next to the Picture House. Down the road, a Tombola (Bingo) stall was busy calling out numbers. When Vir, a class fellow saw me, he commented, 'Gosh, what's wrong with you? You look as if you are coming out from *Dracula* and not *Nagin.*'

'Vir, there's nothing to laugh about. I am not feeling well.' I replied. Vir, unlike many other village boys who came to Jerusha Secondary during school term, was more sociable. He was sitting behind me in the music class when Mr Bondhu had asked me to sing Do Re Me. When Mr Bondhu had arrested my singing halfway through, Vir had chuckled. 'What is so funny?' I had asked. He had replied, 'It's not funny. I like your spirit. You cannot sing, but with your persistence you'll make it on the Radio Ceylon Hit Parade.'

I discovered that like Jeff, Vir was a right-wing conservative, with only a minor difference. He did not read old copies of *The Telegraph* and hence was not as deeply coloured in Tory ideology as Jeff. But nonetheless, he was a conservative and did not like my "Friend Circle".

Outside Picture House when he saw me clutching the rails, he said, 'You cannot walk home in this state. Let me ride you home.' In *Uhuru*, I took two Aspros, the new magic pill; a cure for all ills as touted by VOK's morning commercial programme, and crept into bed.

In the morning, the knuckleduster blow to my chest had turned blue. Before breakfast, I took two Aspros to ease my pain. At breakfast, Henna was fluttering around Rehmat with two blouses asking, 'Ma, which one will look better?' I asked her what the fuss was all about. 'Oh, I am going to the Fete with Rosie, Narika, and a bunch of other girls,' Henna replied.

'Why Narika, she is not part of your circle?'

'She phoned this morning and said she wants to be with us.'

'Be sure you don't go anywhere by yourself.'

'Yes, big brother,' Henna replied in jest.

East African immigrant life revolved around four axes: commerce, cinema, religion and social clubs. For the Asians, their entire week was spent in commerce and anticipation of upcoming Bollywood picture releases and then a scramble for the advance tickets to the cinema. With "cinema-worship" on weekends, "god-worship" occurred at mosques and temples during the week.

Before independence ruling White folks, stayed close to their "white only" communes. They were mostly administrators and civil servants. They were graced with Hollywood and English picture shows at the Indian owned cinemas on Friday and Saturday nights. Rest of their leisure time was spent at their exclusive social clubs and church services. In some towns and cities there were small English theatres where they staged some good English plays.

The Whites and the Asians immersed in their self-centred stupor hardly took interest in African life. The social life of urban Africans, who worked in factories or as domestic help, revolved around bars in towns and local beer dens and dance halls in their shantytowns. But there were exceptions to this. When I started playing music at JCB, an immigrant Luo from Western Kenya asked me to play a song from a Bollywood, black and white picture called *Albela*. This surprised me and I asked him, 'Sambuka, how do you know this picture? It is a very old movie.' He beamed with inner joy and replied, 'When I was young, my mother used to put me to sleep with this song.'

'Naturally, it is a fantastic lullaby,' I replied. From that point on Sambuka used to make me special requests to play him Bollywood songs. 'I like Bollywood pictures very much,' he used to say, 'there is so much family drama, and song and dance.' He was not shy to admit that he sometimes cried during the pictures, when a touching scene reminded him of his family in Kisumu. I found out that Sambuka and a gang of his compatriots used to frequent Bollywood movies every week. When word spread that there were free shows of *Nagin* during the Fete these became an instant hit with the Luo. I was lucky to get a free seat during the afternoon show. Like the Luo I watched pictures with wide eyes. Cinema was my foible and worship. Projections through celluloid film strips which brought actors alive on silver screens fascinated me. My favourite pastime was collecting cut film strips from Picture House and projecting them on *Uhuru* wall with a homemade projector. That was how I recognised the genius of Vyjayanthimala who exploded like a bombshell in tragic *Devdas,* with her vibrant dances and portrayal of unrequited courtesan love. Her Geva colour dance sequences in *Nagin* established her as the dance queen of Bollywood. My amour with these cinema heroes was in no small measure due to the small Picture House where characters on silver screen assumed magical aura. I felt an intimacy with Natalie Wood when Mrs McGuire and I watched *Splendor in the Grass*. We were saddened by young Miss Wood's love life. Mrs McGuire captured my feelings when she said, 'Watching a film in this little cinema is as if we are there and feel the pain of the actors. Oh, and I love that cinema smell, what is it?'

'It is roasted nuts, samosas, and cigarettes.'

I remembered Mrs McGuire's mellow expression when Miss Natalie Wood, spurned by her lover, tried to explain the famous lines from William Wordsworth's poem '*Ode on Intimations of Immortality*':

> What though the radiance which was once so bright
> Be now forever taken from my sight,
> Though nothing can bring back the hour
> Of splendor in the grass, of glory in the flower

Miss Natalie Wood became my favourite Hollywood actress.

Famished, I left *Nagin* to look for food and bumped in to glum-looking Joger who had volunteered to run the Lions Club's Lucky Dip Stall. Business was dismal. I told him that a Lucky Dip Stall was not a crowd-puller. 'Do you have any other ideas?' he asked in a dejected tone. I told him to set up blackjack tables. His eyes dilated, 'What do we need?' I told him to get four decks of cards. Without a word, he left and returned several minutes later with several decks of cards. We rearranged two tables inside the stall and put a board outside: 'Blackjack – Come Break the Bank'. I told Joger to invite people using the same words that were on this board. Like a true showman, Joger stood outside the stall and sang the message at the top of his voice. Luck was in our favour. A giggling troupe of women led by Rani Raman, the wife of an industrialist, came in. I signalled Joger to join me. We shuffled two decks each and stood behind the tables with smiles on our faces, ready to milk beautiful ladies off their money. They milled around, laughing and chatting, dipping into their purses for money. 'Welcome, ladies. Minimum bet is 100 ducats,' I told them. Joger's bulging, round eyes got rounder when he heard the exorbitant sum. Rani, who was wearing a diaphanous silk blouse with a choker around her neck, threw several notes on the table and said, 'For all my friends.' During rounds, I gave them hints on winning strategies. But these rich wives did not care for money. They giggled and kept increasing their bets on lousy cards. Word got around, and gamblers attracted by the presence of rich wives showering money on the tables, packed the stall. Seeing influential players at the tables, Mr Nirmal, the chair of Lions Club, came with several officials and took charge of the stall and booted us out. Rani and her friend tipped us generously.

East African towns had a unique method of advertisement. Companies painted entire façades of shop houses on commercial streets and market squares with bright, colourful signs and pictures of their products, be it cigarettes, face and hair creams or butters and margarines. The decorations, flags and colourful lamps for the Fete were simply cosmetics to a Boja Road already resplendent with rainbow colours of such advertisements. Walking along crowded Boja Road we bumped into Arvind, the Casanova of Jerusha. Joger started to talk to him. I spotted Henna across the road. I rushed to her and handed her the tip money. This surprised her. 'What do I do with it?'

'Spend it. Have fun with your friends.' Henna's friends giggled. Refu came by, shouting, *'Njugu,* groundnuts.' Narika bought a cone and executed the classic Jerusha "silent love" gesture in which a lover presented a trivial gift to one she loved in front of her friends. Narika offered me the cone. I was in a dilemma. If I declined, she would be humiliated. If I accepted, it would signal a bond between us. I accepted it. Henna smiled. I realised that I had committed an error. When *Nagin* was in its twelfth week, I had stood outside Picture House and whispered sweet nothings to a coffee-tanned girl with arched eyebrows to whom I had lost my heart.

I hurried and joined Joger and Arvind at the food stall table. I heard Joger asking Arvind, 'Well, how is your progress with Rosy?' Arvind was in good form. 'No, not Rosy. Talk about the other one. I was at the netball grounds, last Tuesday...what thighs, marble white! Boobs firm and ripe like pomegranate, pink and red.' Curiosity had the better of me, so I asked, 'Arvind did the boobs just jump out! How did you see the colours?'

'You jerk,' Arvind reacted, 'how will you see anything? You are too busy watching picture clips that you scour from trash bins of Picture House.' I bit my tongue. Joger came to my aid. 'Arvind, don't take your frustration out on him. This Palita is pretty, but she'll use you like a doormat.'

'Never mind all that,' said Arvind and pointed to the balcony above Lake Sport Shop, 'Joger, look there is your heart-throb. You have to kneel and recite, "What light breaks through that yonder balcony, it is the east and Pari is the sun . . ." ' The sight of enchantress Pari on the balcony, her hair flying about her face in the evening breeze awed Joger. He whispered, 'Arvind stop it. It is no joke.' I had heard rumours about Joger and Pari. To take my mind off of the grave error I had committed accepting Narika's cone, I asked Joger, 'Are you in love?' His bulging eyes fixated on me like spot lights. 'Junior what would you know about love?' Without meaning it, Joger had displayed exclusivity of love, as if it was a monopoly of a chosen few.

Later that evening, Nash dropped by *Uhuru* to inform me that Mr Bondhu had a serious car accident and had suffered a fractured leg. I was sorry for Mr Bondhu. Ever since the Music Room Affair, my relationship with him had suffered a serious setback. In the days that followed everyone flocked to Jerusha Hospital to visit Mr Bondhu. One evening Nash asked me to join him. I shook my head. My hurt ego stood in the way.

Yet another Circle of Life?

I realized that life was like a mountain range. No sooner did I scale one peak, another peak loomed behind it, challenging me. I had thought that I had discovered all the Circles of Life. Little did I know that there was yet another circle pulsing like an X-ray ring from a faraway galaxy which intersected with every other Circle of Life and created turbulence. The discovery of this Circle came as a result of events taking place far away.

Soon after his election, Mr Kennedy crystallised USA's resolve to put a man on the moon. Not to be outdone, the Russians fired a rocket and put an unmanned spacecraft on the moon ahead of the Americans. And so was born the Space Age. These events elated me and I thought that the Atomic Age was dead. I hated what atom bombs had done to the people of Hiroshima and Nagasaki. But alas, Atomic Age was not dead yet. On the horizon, deafening drumbeats of Third World War began to sound. This was the new Circle of Life that I discovered, the Circle of War and Conflict. Its centre was far away, in corridors of political power. Ordinary people had no influence or control over its orbit.

The crisis began when USA discovered that the Russians were secretly planting missiles loaded with atomic bombs in Cuba, aimed at American cities. Russia denied this accusation. But things got to a boiling point when USA discovered that a fleet of Russian ships was on its way to Cuba, loaded with these missiles. USA did not waste any time and pointed its missiles loaded with atomic bombs towards Russia and imposed a Naval Blockade around Cuba. Russia in turn aimed its land missiles at USA. The world thus teetered on the brink of an atomic war. One would think that such global events would not affect small people in a tiny country of Africa. How would the speeches of President Kennedy and debates at the UN in New York bring about the confessions of love(s) in Jerusha? Or for that matter, drag Rehmat into the vortex of war. But then the turbulence of intersecting ripples could do anything.

I was following these exciting developments on the radio when Rehmat interrupted me and gave me a message that Joger had called twice and wanted me to meet him at Caltex Station urgently. I reluctantly left home to meet Joger.

At Caltex Station, a white van mounted with loudspeakers was playing Elvis's and Modammad Rafi's latest songs and showering free Clipper cigarettes on a crowd. This was the latest cigarette marketing ploy in Africa. Joger with his spiked hair and bright orange shirt stood out from the crowd. He rushed to me. 'Junior, what took you?' he asked, his perspiring face was flush with excitement. Without waiting for my answer, he said, 'Let's go. We are late.' He walked briskly ahead of me on Africa Street and stopped at the door of his uncle's Vision Film Distributors office at Rizvi Chambers. He tidied my hair and arranged my shirt collars before he ushered me into his uncle's office. Joger's uncle, with his glasses at the tip of his nose, was surprised to see us. Joger reminded him, 'Uncle, you had said to come in the afternoon.'

'Yes, I do remember,' he said. Next to Joger's uncle stood a man wearing light brown trousers, a clashing flowery yellow shirt, and Al Capon white shoes with golden buckles. His dark hair moulded in the shape of a torpedo protruded beyond his forehead. He was chewing a *Paan* and wiping red saliva drooling from the side of his lips with a red handkerchief. Joger saw my expression and quickly interjected, 'Uncle, this is my friend.' Joger's uncle turned to the clown and said, 'Mr Raghuvir, my nephew and his friend.' Turning to us, Joger's uncle said, 'This is Mr Raghuvir, talent manager for film studios of Bombay.' Mr

Raghuvir put his handkerchief to his lips and wiped his saliva. 'Boys, I heard good things about you.'

Joger's eyes lit up. 'Mr Raghuvir, my friend is good with music, film scripts and dance. He has won a first prize for short story in The Daily Standard Competition.' Mr Raghuvir replied, 'That is very much *phantastic*. Do you have summary, some example of a story?' Joger did not waste time. He said, 'Yes, *In the Shadow of Kilimanjaro*. An Indian heroine while climbing Kilimanjaro gets trapped in a time warp, falls in love with a magical prince and the story goes like that.' Joger's half-truths about my talents and the storyline of *In the Shadow of Kilimanjaro* flabbergasted me. Joger and I had talked about making a picture, but *In the Shadow of Kilimanjaro* was certainly not flowing from my brain.

'Truly *phantastic* storyline,' Raghuvir said. Turning to Joger's uncle, he said, 'There is very much demand for young talent in Bombay. Much interest for Indian stories from Africa. You boys send me your story when it is *phinished*. Your uncle has my address.'

Outside of Rizvi Chambers, Joger had a broad smile on his face. I did not mince my words, 'Joger, you rascal, you told lies. I am not working on any Kilimanjaro story.'

'Then start working on it.'

Rehmat was no fool and on my return home asked me about the high-pitched commentaries on the radio. I explained to her that the world was sliding towards a Third World War. This jolted her. She had very bad memories of the Second World War. 'Ma, this time it is going to be very different. Russia and America will explode atom bombs over each other and then it will be all over. Everything will be destroyed in an instant and all our food will be radioactive, and those who survive will die of cancer and disease.' She became very alarmed and put her hands around me. 'When will it happen?' she asked. 'Ma the D-day is upon us. Russian ships are already sailing towards America.' I felt guilty for painting such a frightening picture. She shook her head and said, 'I will pray to Imam Ali.

He is all powerful.' In that delicate moment of fear, Rehmat displayed one of her most adorable characteristic, her simple faith. She sang a stanza of a *Ginan,* poem of wisdom:

> Gardens bloom with His compassionate grace,
> Even arid deserts bloom with His single glance…

'My dear boy,' she concluded, 'I will start a midnight vigil until this war is avoided.' Her faith and resolve left me speechless.

Rehmat started her vigil in earnest. At midnight, surrounded by several *ghee* lamps, she sat in the lotus position in the nook behind the breakfast room. I took a break from the radio debates and sat watching her while she sang heart stirring stanzas of the supplications of Pir Kabir's epic '*Unending Spiritual Poem*' beseeching mercy and compassion from the Almighty. Everyone woke up, surprised and gathered around her. After completing her upstanding supplication, she briefly explained her vow.

In the days that followed, there were no diplomatic breakthroughs in the Missile Crisis. Rehmat continued her midnight vigil. We all joined her. On the fourth night, during her upstanding supplications, she slumped on the floor and fainted. Henna shrieked; I was alarmed. 'Ma,' I cried out. Jeff immediately phoned Dr Scott, who arrived within ten minutes. By this time, Henna had sprinkled water over Rehmat's face and she had regained consciousness. Dr Scott checked her and declared that a chest infection had caused her fainting. He prescribed medications and ordered her bed rest. Rehmat's sudden sickness frightened me. To cap it, Jeff and Henna cornered me and reprimanded me, 'Now, look what you have done, frightening her with bad war stories.' I defended myself by saying that I had told her what the pundits were saying on the radio. 'You fool,' Henna said, 'you must use some judgement.'

From that point, the glamour of war lost its lustre. I felt that this particular Circle, the Circle of War and Conflict, was evil. For the first time, I prayed with utmost sincerity to Imam Ali to end this Crisis and to restore Rehmat's health. That night, despite everyone's protest, Rehmat continued her vigil. The breakthrough in diplomacy that I was hoping for did not happen. The Crisis deepened.

During this time Mr Irvine, our headmaster, was attending a three-day conference at Jerusha Town Hall. Mr Desai, the deputy headmaster, had the school helm. He sat in his office and followed the Missile Crisis on the radio. Teachers were relaxed and during lesson changes, gathered in the corridor around Mr Roy, the world history expert, who gave them analysis of the Crisis. During geography class, Mr Silvio came to our class, assigned some work, and joined Mr Roy's discussion group. With no teacher in the class, boys were busy trading stamps and picture cards, and girls were busy writing notes to each other.

At times Joger, like Aristotle, had good insights into nature of things and characteristic of people. Once he told me, 'Junior, teachers are different than normal people.'

'How?' I asked him. He explained, 'When teachers see sexy pictures, they do not get an erection. They get angry.' This confused me even more. I asked, 'Why?' He replied, 'Junior, trust me. I just know.' As the world teetered on the brink of Third World War, Joger's observation was to come into full play. Mr Silvio assigned us work and joined Mr Roy's discussion group in the corridor. Joger circulated a *Playboy* which made a leisurely round of the class with wows from the boys. I anxiously waited for it. Joger calmed me down, 'Junior, it is coming.' Finally, when he got his hands on it, he turned pages and stopped at the centrefold. My eyes became rounder. Suddenly Mr Silvio burst upon us from behind, grabbed the *Playboy* and flipped through the pages. Just as Joger had said, his face beamed red. Everyone fell silent. 'You, two, out,' he said and marched us to Mr Desai's office, where he handed him the *Playboy*. Mr Desai opened the centrefold, and like the comic Mr Magoo, brought it close to his nose and studied it. When the image finally registered in his myopic eyes, his face glowed red like a burning charcoal. 'You, rascals,' he yelled. If his yell was even half an octave higher, I would have pissed in my pants. He adjusted his glasses and shouted, 'Is this why your parents send you to school?' He put the *Playboy* on the table and took out a well-oiled cane from his cupboard and gave me ten smacks. He turned to Joger and said, 'You are a rotten apple. I suspend you. Come back to school next term.' Mr Desai kept the *Playboy* with him. He had the ammunition he needed. And he would bid his time.

Joger was waiting for me at the school gate when school ended to tell me to meet him at Tembo na Membe, (Elephant and Mango), at six to follow the crucial UN speech on Missile Crisis.

'Joger, I cannot. I have a curfew at nine. Mother is not well, and I don't know what will happen if Henna announces that I was canned.' Joger did not pay attention to what I said and walked away saying, 'I will see you at six.'

When I told Henna that I planned to go to Tembo na Membe at six she was livid. 'Brother, you will distress mother. We all worry when you are out. Don't get into any trouble.'

Tembo na Membe at the junction of Zanzibar and Gandhi Roads was pulsing with excitement and free flow of Tusker beer. Here, there was no vigil for world peace except a desire to consume as much before the world ended. People huddled around several clusters of radios tuned to BBC or VOA. Joger introduced me to Gina, a youngish Israeli girl. 'Junior,' he said, 'just before you came, Gina was asking about a special blend of coffee. I told her that you know everything about coffees. She wants to send some to her family in Israel; that is if we are not all dead.' Before I replied, all eyes turned to a side corridor. It was Tuesday, and Miss Suku, Tembo na Membe's burlesque queen, who lived in red-tiled "geisha" house around the corner, made a grand entrance. There were rumours that she had only one breast. One time when Joger and I participated in a Dart Tournament at Tembo na Membe, she planted kisses on our cheeks. 'For good luck,' she said. From that time we were Miss Suku's fans.

Dressed in red with matching high-heeled shoes, and holding a gold cigarette holder in her hand, Miss Suku made her entrance with a sashay.

Those foreigners who had heard about her but had never seen her gasped at her figure. Close to the stage, she put her hand below her breast(s) and lifted them up. This risqué but elegantly executed stroke caused giggles all around. Gina blushed. Miss Suku took a puff of her cigarette. The blue smoke swirled up in small vortexes and cast an aura of romance. She handed the cigarette holder to her aide and waved her hands in the air. Aretha Franklin's enchanting voice wafted from the speakers to which she performed a sexy dance.

Joger and Gina had drifted off. I stood sipping orange juice and listening to BBC commentary when Gina re-joined me and asked if I was able to get the Red Berry Mountain coffee for her. I told her that this coffee came from our own plantation. This surprised her and she asked if I could get couple of Kilos of it before the weekend. 'Where shall I send it to?' I asked.

'You can deliver it to the Garrison Hill gate with my name,' she replied. Then she reached into her sling bag and pulled out a small box which she presented to me and asked me to open it. Inside it I found neatly arranged insignia of Israeli Military, Air Force and the Navy. 'These are fantastic. Are these for me to keep?' I asked. 'Yes, for sure,' she replied.

Confessions

During the seven pm BBC news, Ash made a sudden cameo appearance in Tembo na Membe. I always knew he had a flair for dramatics. Lately, he was sporting a beard to maintain his image as the Castro of Gandhi Road. He stood facing me like an Oracle, his face pregnant with some vision of the future. He sucked on his cigarette and puffed out ringlets of smoke before he spoke. 'You phoney Einstein, if you love someone, now is the time to confess, before we go up in smoke.' I replied, 'Ash, seriously, I can't think of anyone.' In my heart I knew that I had lied. When I asked him if he had anyone that he wanted to confess to, he shook his head. 'Well,' he said, 'now I must rush. I have to attend to other business. Please give the same message to Joger.'

From the news summary, it was clear that there was no new twist to the Missile Crisis so I told Joger that I was leaving for home. He said, 'Let's go outside, it is too stifling in here.' A bearded man standing outside Tembo na Membe jumped into my path and waved a placard in my face. 'Confess, my son. Redeem your sins with the Saviour. The world will end soon.' The suddenness of his "John the Baptist" action unnerved me. I told him, 'I have not sinned, Sir, honest.' He clutched my arm, 'That's your good heart speaking. You are too young to fall into sin. Come away from these sinners. Accept Jesus.' Joger freed me from his clutch and shouted, 'Leave him alone. Go redeem sins elsewhere.' I was shaken and asked Joger, 'What did he mean by confess?'

'Pay no heed to him,' Joger comforted me. As we walked to his Mini he made a statement that was totally out of character. 'It is only during crisis or wars that people confess their loves or write love letters.' Saying this he pulled out a necklace from his pocket and added, 'this is for Pari, and I am about to confess my love to her. You should do the same.'

'Joger, this is a beautiful gift. Has she reciprocated your love?' I asked.

'I have enough for the two of us,' he replied. When I asked him when he intended to present it to Pari, his face beamed. 'Junior, this Saturday my uncle is releasing *CID* and *Solva Saal*. *CID* has that hot Shakila and *Solva Saal* has Waheeda. Both pictures will run at Picture House and City Light simultaneously. I plan to give it to her then.' Joger's statement baffled me. 'How is it possible for two pictures to run at two cinemas with one set of reels?' I asked.

'We will alternate the reels between the cinemas. And wait. My uncle has made me in-charge of bookings at the City Light. I have booked you all for the Saturday matinee. That Arvind is over the moon. His beloved Palita is attending the matinee. He is begging me to give him a seat near her.' This was the second time Joger had mentioned Palita. I asked Joger, 'What is special about Palita? Every time I hear you and Arvind talk about her, he starts drooling and you salivate?'

'Junior, haven't you seen her? Finest of Hindu blood! Real top-class, rose petal skin, and tulip face. We can talk about her some other time. Now we have to go to Flamingo. After that I will drop you home.' "Redeem your Sins" incident had frightened me. I did not want to be late coming home and distress Rehmat. I had serious reservations about going to Flamingo Bar, so I told Joger to drop me home first. Joger was insistent that I go with him. 'Junior it will only take five minutes. I enjoy your company.'

He drove his Mini a short distance on Gandhi Road, a right turn on Boja Road, and stopped at Flamingo Bar. The newly constructed City Light Cinema, opposite Flamingo was ablaze with rainbow-coloured neon lights with its walls plastered with wall-size posters of *CID* and *Solva Saal*.

'What business do you have in Flamingo?' I asked. Joger replied that he needed to contact Harry who was to transfer the picture reels between City Light and Picture House. I stopped dead in my track and expressed serious reservations about drunkard Harry. This amused Joger, 'There is nothing wrong with Harry. He transfers papers for the banks.'

'Joger I don't like him. Anyone who goes around with Gul is a rotten scoundrel,' I replied.

Flamingo was like a lion's den with no guarantee of life. Its raw energy hit us in the face. Here, "World Coming to an End" excuse was not needed to get drunk. It was the norm. Fights and stabbings were routine. Several girls were dancing to the thunderous beat of Congolese Jazz. Under congenial, safe conditions, Flamingo Jazz was not bad music to listen to. Two prostitutes slithered to our sides. 'Hello darlings. Come, let us make you happy.' Joger moved to my side and warded off the one who was beginning to rub her protruding breasts against me. 'Leave him alone mother.'

'Fuck you, I am no mother,' she lashed at Joger. We looked for Harry and found him sitting at a table surrounded by several girls. A man with his back towards us sat opposite Harry. Upon seeing Joger, Harry shouted, 'Dear Joger, the world is ending tomorrow. One last drink with you is all I desire.'

'Harry, we will have opportunity to drink later. Please see me at ten tomorrow.'

'I will come, but you have one drink with me. Bring your friend here. He can taste any one of these girls. They are all free.' The man with his back to us turned. He was no other than my nemesis Gul. He stretched to shake Joger's hand. Upon seeing me, he shouted, 'Ah, it's you? Harry, leave this nerd alone. He cannot get an erection. He shags that Barber's daughter. What's her name, Nerd?' A black curtain descended over my eyes. In flashbacks, I saw his shenanigans, and my blood boiled. 'You f**king rascal,' I screamed, 'this is for insulting Narika, for the blow to my ribs, and for fire in the music room.' He was within easy reach, and I lashed out at him with a jab. It caught him square in the face. Blood sprouted from his nose. Joger had not seen this coming and was dazed.

'Junior no, not in here,' he shouted. In a flash, Gul pulled out a *Rampuri*. A bouncer swooped on me and locked his arms around me. I was defenceless. Gul threw the chair that was blocking his path to the side and rushed towards me. I struggled to come away from the arms of the bouncer. In this confusion, an athletic man with one golden tooth and remaining teeth red from chewing *Paan* jumped into the melee in my defence. 'Leave him alone,' he shouted and barred Gul's path. The bouncer let go of me. The man screamed at Joger. 'You leave, now.' Refu lurked behind him. I recognised the man. He was the one who had donated money to our Free Bird Charity when we won the Dart Trophy at Tembo na Membe. His office was in the same parade of shops as Jerusha Boxing Club. A crooked, rusty sign with his name "Charles Atlas – Export/Import" hung on his office door. His name was associated with stories of extortion and even murder. I waved at him for saving my life as we left.

In his Mini, Joger calmed me down. 'Junior I should have seen it coming. That Gul has something against you. This is the second time you have fought with Gul for Narika. Junior, confess to her like how I am about to confess to Pari. Love is a wonderful thing. Narika is a superb girl.'

'Joger, there is nothing between us. It is all a mistake,' I replied.

'Anyway Junior, it is your decision.'

It was only eight, so I asked Joger to drop me at the JCB. Before he drove away Joger cautioned me, 'Gul is nasty. Stay out of his way. He will try to get even with you. If you suspect anything, let me know.'

I sat in JCB courtyard and had a cold Pepsi. I opened the box of Israeli Military insignia and examined them. They were superbly crafted metal pieces from Israeli Navy and Air Force. Someday they would be valuable for a trade with one of the boys. I walked to the JCB cash register and hid them in a secret compartment at the back and then walked home just in time for dinner.

Stroll to the Past – Narika's Dance

Rehmat had not noticed my absence. Despite her delicate health, she had taken charge of the kitchen because she said that Jeremy did not know how to cook Italian dishes. She asked Henna to fill up my plate with a generous portion of saffron risotto. 'Ma, I can't eat so much.'

'Sure you can. It is your favourite. You are a growing boy.' We were all pleased that she was her old self again. The mood at the table was pensive. There was no breakthrough in the Missile Crisis. The Russian Ships with atomic missiles continued sailing towards Cuba. Knowing Rehmat, we were all certain that she would not relent from her midnight vigil. For her sake, we were secretly hoping for the Crisis to end. After dinner I changed and crept into bed listening to VOA, with the intention of joining Rehmat for her vigil. Late at night, drifting in and out of sleep, I heard Andre Gromyko, the USA Secretary of Defence, giving the Russians an ultimatum. 'Call back your ships to avert an all-out Atomic War.'

As I drifted back to sleep, a spiral rotated anticlockwise in my mind . . . What I had told Joger was only half the truth. Narika had come to *Uhuru* once after Gul's friend had punched me with a knuckleduster outside the Picture House. In coming to *Uhuru*, Narika had crossed a formidable wall of Jerusha custom. The afternoon she came, the sky was blue, and the sun was shining, yet we had gloom over Gawa Crescent due to what was happening to our neighbour, Commander Leman, the joint commander of the armed forces of our country.

He was a nice family man, and everyone on Gawa Crescent liked him except Rehmat and Mrs Inderjeet. His estate next to our home extended deep in to Suwakaki where he had a barricaded enclosure where he practiced shooting. Rehmat hated the loud afternoon bangs when Leman and his associates practised with guns. 'So dangerous discharging live bullets close to home,' she used to say. Mrs Inderjeet agreed with Rehmat. Leman, aware of this silent dislike of him, made extra effort to woo everyone. Some weekends he went around Gawa Crescent distributing meat of the game he had hunted on his patrol of the border areas.

Suwakaki behind our home was a dense equatorial forest; a twisted web of tall elephant grass, bush, and tall trees intertwined with vine and liana. The entire forest grew and propagated at prolific speed, throwing its dark green tentacles in every direction. I knew names of maybe five trees, bushes and liana in the forest. The rest were unknown. Rehmat, who maintained our garden with a yard boy, constantly struggled to contain the forest from consuming our garden.

I considered Suwakaki my personal forest. Before Salim had a nasty fall from a tree, we used to play "Tarzan" swinging on the liana immediately behind the granite rocks that marked our garden boundary. When Salim fell and sprained his ankle, Rehmat pulled my ear and forbade me from going into Suwakaki. She planted Bougainvillea around the granite rocks and in time, these blanketed the rocks. Some afternoons, despite Rehmat's warning, I ventured into Suwakaki as far as the lovely cluster of palms, almonds, and a fig tree past the brook where I had the encounter with the girl who had hummed God's Symphony. Beyond the fig tree, Suwakaki was uncharted territory with incredible stories of goblins that lived on a huge Suwa mango tree deep in the forest. On some rainy nights, as the stories went, the Suwa tree lighted up in a strange bluish mist and some practitioners of *Tantra* Yoga gathered there, smeared with ashes of newly-cremated dead on their bodies, and danced in circles in terrifying rituals.

One day while bird watching under the fig tree, I heard ruffle of dead leaves. I hid behind the tree and was surprised to see Azul and Leman, carrying hoes, shovels, and other tools, pass by. I followed them, keeping out of their sight. They stopped at a spot between tall mavule trees, about a hundred yards from an electric pylon, and started to dig a hole in the ground as if to bury someone. They worked with military precision. As Azul dug, Leman filled up the dirt in small gunny bags and went in different directions dispersing it. They alternated doing this. When it got dark, they hid the tools, covered the hole with leaves, and left. This routine continued for many days. When the hole was large enough, they brought in camouflaged panels and started to assemble these in the hole. I had read in the newspaper that many people in the USA were building bomb shelters in their backyards as protection against atomic war. I was certain this was what Leman and Azul were building – an atom bomb shelter. Upon completion of the shelter, Commander Leman and Azul covered it with dead leaves. In time, climbers, shrubs, and grass grew around and over the bunker. I made a mental map of the location of the bunker using the overhead electric cables and the pylon as my reference markers.

One afternoon Leman and his soldiers were target-shooting in an enclosure behind his estate when a small snake climbed up his boot and bit him in his leg. By the time the soldiers brought him to the hospital his leg was swollen as if he had elephantiasis. He was not responding to the anti-venom medication and his condition deteriorated. He turned blue and lingered in this condition for a day and a night as life began to ebb from his body.

Two weeks before this event, an outbreak of coffee disease in South America had caused a dramatic jump in coffee price in London. Sensing a financial opportunity Azul rushed me to our Nirambeya Plantation to grade and ship tons of coffee we had in stock. He was unable to attend to this himself due to work commitment at JCB. When I returned home from the coffee estate after two weeks Rehmat told me about Commander Leman's condition and added that he was clinging to life with the skin of his teeth at the hospital and that if he didn't pull through during the night, death was certain. This upset me.

Early next morning, the doctors at the hospital gave up hope and moved Leman home to die. Things became tense around Gawa Crescent. Neighbours gathered at Leman's house, talking in hushed tones, waiting. Many important army and political people came in expensive cars to pay respect to him. Soldiers loitered around Gawa Crescent aimlessly. To escape the gloom, Jeff, Shamim, and the girls went shopping to Pala. Salim went to play tennis. I went to Suwakaki and sat under the fig tree for a long time. When I was tired, I came and hid in *Uhuru*, projecting clips of Vyjayanthimala and Natalie Wood on the wall. Rehmat came to *Uhuru* shortly before lunch and asked me to accompany her to the herb garden, where I helped her pick delicate roots and leaves. Back in the kitchen, she asked me to pound these into a fine paste. While I did this, she continued adding strange ointments and a black powder from her medicine chest to it. There was no drama of "bubble bubble toil and trouble" of Macbeth proportions in her effort, but I knew Rehmat was practicing an ancient art of herbal medicine she had learnt from Granddaddy. Satisfied with the consistency of the paste I had pounded, Rehmat put it to boil in a copper walled vessel normally used by alchemists for their cooking. She added chunks of lamb fat to it. In another pot, she made a thick lamb fat soup. When the poultice had cooled, Rehmat, accompanied by Azul, took the soup and poultice to the commander's house. I followed them. Commander's wife, who was resigned to his fate, was desperate to try any remedy. Her eyes lit up when Rehmat talked to her. She immediately cleared everyone from the house. Seeing this exodus, people surmised that either the end was near or the commander was dead. A woman started to sob. Leman's daughter came and told the crying woman to hush up. Rehmat and Leman's wife disappeared into his room where they applied the poultice to his festering wound.

With nothing else to do in the afternoon, I hid in *Uhuru* tinkering with an electric gramophone I had picked up from a trash pile when there was a knock on the door. I looked up. A smiling Narika stood at the open door. 'Henna is not home,' I said. My casual answer masked an error of judgement.

I could count two pictures from Bollywood and Hollywood Cinema that had the best sequences that captured the essence of these pictures. These pivotal sequences were superb in their build-up to deliver the essence of the stories. The first of these was the sequence from *Splendor in the Grass,* in which Natalie Wood tried to explain the meaning of a Wordsworth's poem and broke down, overcome by grief of love.

The second was from the tragic *Devdas,* in which shy and beautiful Paroo, with shackles of village custom around her ankles was pining to meet her lover who had just returned to the village from Calcutta. A meeting was impossible. The day turned into night. Paroo was restless. Superb cinematography was at work. In a long shot, the camera showed darkness descending on the village Square. A street cleaner was sweeping an edge of the Square and a dog was muzzling through the trash he was collecting. The camera showed the clock on the tower. It was approaching midnight. Next the camera focused on the long portico leading to the entrance of the palatial home of Devdas, where a night watchman extinguished the portico lamps, stretched on the floor, and pulled a sheet over his head. In this grey emptiness a figure with a shawl wrapped around its head entered the Square. In slow steps it walked towards the palatial home, past the sleeping watchman. The camera zoomed on the face of the figure. It was Paroo. She entered her lover's chamber. The build-up of the entire scene portrayed the gravity of her action. She had flouted the village norm and scaled the tall, forbidding wall of social custom to meet her lover, alone, at night; an action which if discovered would cast her into deep nadir of social death. If her lover spurned her, her afterlife would be brothels of Bombay or Calcutta.

Narika entered *Uhuru.* She said she wanted to learn electromagnetism. Without waiting for my answer she kicked off her shoes and jumped onto my bed. When I tried to show her an example of electromagnetism in the record player's power supply, she ignored me and instead picked up a deck of cards from my table. 'Come, lets play rummy,' she invited me. She sat in a graceful lotus position as we played. She won most of the games. 'It is just Lady Luck,' I said to save my face.

'Einstein, grapes are sour,' she pulled my cheek. She deflated my ego and booted me to size. I dropped my cards and said I was tired. She came closer. I tensed up. 'Henna was right,' she said, 'you are shy.' Then she asked if the gramophone worked? I nodded.

'Then play me something romantic.' I loaded a 78-RPM vinyl. 'Come sit with me,' she grabbed my hand as she said this. A *Nagin* song vibrated in the air. She drew closer and put her head on my shoulder. Before I knew, she was kissing me. 'Narika,' I tried stopping her. She gave me a long kiss. 'Narika, what if someone comes in?'

'You could be a good kisser if you try.' I pulled away from her. She commented, 'You fool, listen to the song.' Lata was singing:

Forsaking this world
Scaling its tall wall
Beloved, I have come . . .

Then in a cat-like motion, she jumped from the bed and started to dance Lord Shiva's gentle dance *Lashya*. I watched her, mesmerised. As she whirled, her hair flew about her face. Her grace surpassed my screen idol, Vyjayanthimala. The song ended. The record continued to turn with a rhythmic hum. She came and sat at my feet, with her head in my lap, her face like a beautiful moon in dark clouds, her hair hanging down to her hips, and her hands around my waist. 'This is how I feel about you,' she whispered. I cupped her face. She spoke softly and said the magic words, which a girl uttered only when the dam of emotion in her heart brimmed, 'I love you.' Her eyes were moist and unfathomable. The echoes of her words reverberated in my heart. She sat in my lap, wrapping her hands around my neck.

'Say you love me,' she said as she kissed me. I sensed the tenderness in her heart. My heart was in a quandary. I had already lost my heart to a coffee-tanned beauty at the Picture House when *Nagin* was in its twelfth week. My encounter with her had put me in an orbit away from Narika. I sat at an important juncture, and as much as I would have liked to, I could not reciprocate Narika's love. I felt as if my heart was in a vice.

At night, I fell asleep after a long struggle. A banging woke me up. I jumped out of bed, certain that Leman was dead. Azul and Rehmat were standing at the front, door talking to Leman's daughter. 'Mama,' she was saying, 'you must come urgently.' Rehmat wrapped her pink shawl and left with her. The whole family was awake. We sat at the dining table. Shamim percolated a pot of coffee and brought a tray of scones, butter and jam. Jeff poured coffee for all of us and asked, 'Daddy, if Leman dies, what will happen?' Azul looked tired. After a long pause, he said, 'Son, that Kikuna is an animal. He is ruthless.'

The night wore on. Everyone went back to sleep. Azul and I sat at the table lost in our thoughts, waiting for Rehmat. Sad notes of First Post from Garrison Hill announced the approaching dawn. A cockerel crowed from the garden. Rehmat finally returned when the eastern horizon turned pink and orange. I wrapped my hands around her. 'Ma, what took you?' She kissed me and came and sat next to Azul and said, 'There is a glimmer of hope. Leman has coughed and there is sign of life. It is up to Ali now.'

At eight when we were at breakfast, Leman's daughter rushed in and hugged Rehmat. 'Mama, it is good news. He has opened his eyes. The doctors are back, and they want to move him to the hospital.'

More Trials of Love Await You

Commotion from the breakfast room woke me up. I snapped out of my journey to the past when Narika had danced in *Uhuru*, and Leman had come back miraculously from the dead and the Arrow of Time was in mid-flight towards that Singularity which dominated the landscape of my life, the fated Gossage Football Final.

My radio was crackling. I remembered falling asleep, listening to the USA Foreign Secretary's ultimatum to the Russians. I did not remember hearing Rehmat's midnight vigil or the First Post from the Garrison Hill. I rushed to the breakfast room. Jeff's radio was pulsing with excited chatter. My goodness, was the atomic war on? Rehmat stood with a spatula in the doorway. Azul was sitting at the breakfast table with hands around Salim who was scratching his eyes. 'Jeff, did America fire an atom bomb?' I asked. He smiled and said, 'I thought you were following the news on your radio.'

'I fell asleep. What happened? Is it the start of the Third World War?' Jeff grabbed my shoulder and said, 'No, the Russians have blinked. Their ships have made a U-turn in the Atlantic. It is over. For thirteen days, we were on the brink of an all-out atomic war.' Overjoyed, Rehmat hugged Salim and Henna. She put her hands around me and said, 'Thank God, it is all over and you all are safe. I told you, Ali has all the power. You have to beseech and beg him.'

Henna was happy, 'Ma, I was worried about your own health.'

'My dear child,' Rehmat replied, 'it is all worth it. Now we have peace.'
She looked beautiful like her prized garden flower, the pink frangipani.

After the BBC news summary, Jeff tuned his radio to the VOK's *Bhor Ki Bela*. I was not sure what it was, but like the dream projectors of my mind, which at times just projected the same dream over and over again, fate conjured up signs and signals that reminded me of the same subject: Narika. The radio played the *Nagin* song to which Narika had danced in *Uhuru*. I had a vivid recollection of her confession of love in *Uhuru*. But with it came the jarring memories of the events that happened when the Arrow of Time hit its target: the Gossage Football Final. I consciously arrested my mind from projecting this footage. My heart was not ready to experience the disturbing events of that day. However, in the aftermath of those events, my inner universe had suffered an atomic winter. My heart was frozen. It had just begun to thaw. At some point, I would have to let the Gossage Football Final footage play to heal my heart but now was not the time for it. Now was the time to celebrate spring and to welcome the start of another round of events that would re-usher me in to the Circle of Love and teach me the true meaning of lyrics I had heard at the *Majnun Hall*.

Beyond stars innumerable universes
Await you,
More trials of love
Await you.

For the present, I was relieved that the Missile Crisis was over and that the world would continue to exist. The fact that the box office hit *CID* was releasing in Jerusha, after a two-year delay, excited me. Two of the hottest heroines of Bollywood cinema had their debuts in *CID* and both had meteoric rise in their screen fortunes. I started to float on silvery clouds of sweet anticipation. At the bottom of it, my joy was not *CID* but the fact that during the night, as I listened to the gloomy speeches of atomic war, I had taken to heart my friends' advice about confessing love. The object of my love was no other than Narika who had waited patiently for me. The fragrance of her love had begun to intoxicate me. Hearing the *Nagin* song on VOK, I had a sudden flash of inspiration during which I realised that the sweet murmur of love in the heart was somehow associated with God's Symphony. The *Nagin* song floating in the airwaves aroused exquisite emotions. I felt that time was ripe to take Narika in my arms and confess my love to her.

After feasting on Rehmat's special "Peace Breakfast", I paddled to Nur Gift Store, whistling a tune, and purchased an exquisite pearl necklace for Narika. I had no idea how or where to present it to her. But, I was full of brainwaves. On my way home, I decided to invite her to the sensational, death defying "Well of Death" show close to the Central Taxi Stand at one o'clock. This show had been playing to packed audiences for last several days. I knew that Narika was interested in science and the magic of daredevil motorcyclists riding around the wall of a wooden well at high speed, defying gravity, would thrill her. After the show, we would walk to JCB, get two packets of kofta, and have a picnic lunch at the primary school's Rose Garden. And then in that lush and beautiful setting, I would declare my love to her. I had goose pimples thinking about it and arrived home intoxicated by my inspiration. Azul caught me in the breakfast room. 'Son, I need a favour. JCB needs cooking oil. Take Jeremy with you and get some cans from NTC warehouse in the Market Square.'

'Daddy, can it wait until tomorrow?'

'Son, JCB has only a drum left. These NTC black marketers are out to kill business, and during this Missile Crisis, they have been ruthless.' In my euphoric mood, I did not argue. I showered, put on a blue New Yorker striped shirt, smeared by hair with Yardley hair cream and set out with Jeremy to NTC for oil. I checked my pocket to make sure I had Narika's necklace.

We waited in a long queue with other irate NTC customers for oil, starring at *CID* and *Solva Saal* posters plastered all around the Market

Square. Loud speakers from the Well of Death Show were playing a song from Dev Anand's picture *Black Market* over and over again. The roars of motorcycles from the Well of Death and the *Black Market* song were barrowing into my mind like miners drills. The sun reached the zenith And the pavement of Market Square sizzled in intense heat. Baggers who normally loitered up and down the Square, withdrew in the shadow of Market walls. We covered our heads with newspapers. Street boys did a roaring business selling cold Pepsis and Fanta to angry NTC customers. My striped shirt was drenched in sweat which made me mad. I looked at my watch. It was approaching one o'clock. I became frustrated when yet another Well of Death show got underway with roars of motor cycles. Suddenly, the rhythmic roars of the motorcycles sputtered, followed by a loud bang. Cries arose from behind the Market Square. Everyone became frenzied and a crowd ran towards Well of Death. Jeremy joined them. Something terrible seemed to have happened. I waited for a while, watching the pandemonium. My heart was with Narika. Despite my sweaty shirt, if I hurried, I still had time to meet her. I walked against the crowd when a man started to walk with me. He told me that one of the stunt motorcyclists had fallen and that his motorcycle had punched a hole in the wooden wall. I asked him if anyone was hurt. He said contemptuously, 'I don't know. Foolish! How can a man ride a motor cycle round a vertical wall?' Science was my weakness. I stopped for a brief second to explain to him the science behind the Well of Death. A second! Less than a heartbeat. Little did I know that second contained infinity within it. I started to explain to the stranger, 'By centrifugal force, it is possible . . .' The man became agitated, 'Even you look foolish.' With these words, he turned and left.

MG and the Lady with Marble-White Thighs

That delayed second changed everything. Someone behind me cried out, 'Hello, could you please help me?' I turned around. A woman in a lilac skirt and a white coat with her Sophia Loren cut hair flying about her face was struggling to hold her shopping bags. I took the bags from her hands. She tied her hair in a bun. The diamond studs in her ears sparkled in the sunlight. She asked. 'What is wrong? Why is everyone running?' I explained that an accident had happened at the Well of Death. I added, 'Madam, you should not come here alone. Anything can happen. Besides, this heat will burn your beautiful skin.' She narrowed her eyes. Her spouting lips tightened and an apologetic smile played on her beautiful face. She mumbled and excuse and said, 'You are right. I should have been careful.'

'It is all right, meme. I'll help you to your car,' I comforted her and walked with her around the Market Square to Pele Road where she pointed to a sports MG and said, 'That's my car.' I immediately recognised my companion. She was the wife of Mr SB John, son of an industrialist, who often came to Tembo na Membe and bought rounds of drinks for everyone. She was a doctor trained in Germany, specialising in children and women's medicine. She had a busy practice on Gandhi Road. I exclaimed, 'I now know who you are.'

'What? Didn't you know until now?' she asked, with a sense of thrill. I apologised and said, 'I didn't recognise you in your work clothes.' I dropped her shopping bags in the back seat of the MG and prepared to leave. She threw her handbag on the seat and said, 'No. *Arre*, where are you going? You have to help me all the way home.' I reluctantly sat in the MG. She tied a scarf around her hair before we drove off on to Boja Road. At Anglican Church, she turned into a lane and parked the MG in the shaded porch of a huge mansion. I picked the shopping bags from the back seat. She exclaimed, 'No need, no need, the servants will do that.'

'But you wanted me to help you.'

'That was just so you will come home with me.' Her remark made me nervous. She led me through an arched entrance into a huge living room. Soft strains of classical music greeted us. 'Do you like classical?'

'It is not my favourite. I am a music manger and I like jazz, and African and Indian music.' She laughed. 'You brainwashed boy, all the Indian tunes you hear are adaptations of Beethoven and Chopin.'

'Madam, only in your imagination! Even Beatles came to Indian for inspiration,' I argued.

'Witty, I see. You said you are a music manager. Where?'

'At our cafe, JCB. On Saturdays, when we don't have a band, I play records for the evening. In the saloon, I play local music. Blue Room has an international crowd. They love Indian music. Mr Suleman is waiting for me to play *CID* songs,' I explained.

'*CID*! I saw all those posters in Market Square. The women in the clinic simply would not stop talking about it for last two days. I must see this *CID*.'

'Madam, I doubt if you will get tickets. We have tickets for the City Light tomorrow.'

'You, talkative boy, let me fetch you some refreshments,' she said as she kicked off her shoes, unbuttoned her white coat, and threw it on the chair. She was wearing a matching lighter shade pink blouse underneath. She left the room and returned with a plate full of strawberries and whipped cream. This surprised me. Jerusha weather was harsh for strawberries. She lurched forward to hand me the plate, revealing her cleavage from behind open top buttons of her blouse. I lowered my eyes. 'These are fresh . . .

from Germany,' she added as she sat on the sofa and unfurled her legs, with her skirt halfway up her marble-white thighs. 'At your age, you should be rocking with Elvis,' she commented.

'I like Elvis. But I don't get a feel for his beat. I like the sixteen-beat Indian music.'

'Well, then play Indian for me from SB's collection,' she said pointing to the music cabinet. I put the strawberry plate on the side table and walked to the cabinet, flipped through the LPs and said. 'I will play Ghalib poetry.'

'Oh, you like poetry, do you? You don't look the type.'

'Our literature mistress says that looks can be deceiving,' I replied as I loaded the turntable and waited until it played. Lata's soulful voice filled the room. Madam Doctor beckoned me to come and sit on the sofa. I looked at my watch. If I hurried, I still had time to ask Narika out and tell her what was in my heart. 'Please, I must go,' I said.

'But you haven't finished telling me what else your literature mistress says.'

'She says that poetry is the language of love.'

'Oh,' she exclaimed. I reached for my strawberry plate and stood holding it.

'It's okay. I won't bite you. Sit.' I sat at the other end of the sofa. She stretched her legs. Her toes touched my thigh. 'And do you understand this language of the heart and love?'

'Well, Madam, if you hear the lyrics of this Lata song, it tells a lot.'

A loving heart is distilled
From the fury of a million storms,
Only a loving heart has the strength to
Bear the storm of rejection.

'Bravo,' Madam Doctor clapped, 'I didn't realise that they teach such poetry in school. Didn't I hear that they stopped teaching poetry after an infamous symposium?'

'Actually they don't teach it. I learn it by listening to good songs. And yes, there was ban on Urdu poetry.' Madam Doctor dug her toes in to my thigh. I looked at my watch.

'Where do you have to go?' she asked.

'To the boxing club. I can walk.'

'I'll drop you. We must talk more some other day,' she replied.

We were approaching City Light decorated with blinking, colourful lights. People were pouring out from Kabir Mosque after the mid-afternoon prayers and most of them were heading towards City Light for *CID* tickets or for afternoon tea at Sukh Sager. Two giant boom box speakers which stood on either side of Sukh Sager entrance were blasting *CID* songs at full volume. Several vans, picking up *CID* advertisement posters and pamphlets from Lake Printers to distribute them to surrounding towns and villages, crowded Flamingo Square. I asked Madam Doctor to stop and let me off. She insisted on dropping me right to the door of the Boxing Club. It was never my intent to go to the Boxing Club. All East African cinemas had large photo boards on their exterior walls where they pinned photos of the scenes from the current and upcoming pictures. I was most eager to see the photos of Shakila and Waheeda, the two debut actresses of *CID*, before I met Narika. Close to City Light, a large crowd was milling around for tickets. 'The booking office has opened today,' I commented. Madam Doctor surveyed the scene and said, 'Good gosh, it is like *Diwali* celebration already. My interest is aroused. I will ask SB to get tickets.' At Moon Bakery, I signalled her to stop. 'I will get off here.' She stopped and asked if she could look at the inside of the Club. I agreed reluctantly, relieved that it was early for other boxers to be at the Club. Madam Doctor looked up at the "Red Tower" and commented, 'I hope you don't get into any mischief here without condoms.' I shook my head without understanding exactly what she meant. I knew it had something to do with sex. If she had said Durex, I would have understood because it was the most popular brand of sex protection. Madam Doctor continued,

'Filthy men who come here don't use any protection. I see the results every day. Infecting their wives with dangerous diseases.'

'What is a tampon?' I asked. Immediately, I felt ashamed of my ignorance. Madam Doctor was unruffled, 'It's a good question. Men don't understand it at all.' Once inside the clubroom. Madam Doctor looked around and was about to sit on a ledge. I stopped her, 'Please don't. It'll soil your skirt.' She spread a handkerchief on the ledge, pulled up her skirt, and sat on the handkerchief. Then she explained to me the female monthly menstrual cycle. When I lowered my eyes, she said, 'No, don't be shy. You need to know.'

Before she left, she told me, 'Keep up with the poetry. Take my card to the Lake Sports Shop and buy new boxing gloves. I will pay them later. You can't box with these torn gloves. What if you cut your handsome face with these?'

After she left I sat and reflected on the strange encounter. Madam Doctor's explanation of female biology made a lot of sense. The dry biology lessons had never sunk in. I mean sex and anything to do with sex were taboo in our school. It was not even appropriate to talk about it with friends. Immediately, I thought of Savi and her bold but futile efforts to change all that at our school. Sex education was often conjectures and untruths. The subject that Madam Doctor so eloquently taught me was often a subject of ribald jokes among boys. 'Oo . . . she is having her period. She'll need a tampon.'

I realized that Madam Doctor's biology discourse was lesson number three in my sex education. Lesson number one was Joger's saucy Japanese *Manga* of nudes. From these, I learnt that females have swollen breasts and vaginas have hair around them. I also learnt that looked at from many different angles, the female form was always attractive. Lesson number two would come during a cricket match at the PWD grounds.

Joan of Arc

Savi was a goddess of Jerusha women's field hockey team. Under her captaincy Jerusha had thrashed Holland in an international match, with Savi scoring two goals. But her fame or notoriety stemmed from her tireless effort in the field of education reform and specifically sex education in Jerusha Secondary. The humiliation and stigma she suffered as a result made her Jerusha's Joan of Arc.

When Jeff was at school, girls attended primary school and dropped out, usually getting married before they were sixteen. The question of admitting girls to secondary school divided the school board for many years. Finally the board relented and a first batch of brave girls joined Jerusha Secondary. Savi joined three years after the first batch. Jerusha Secondary and the school board had no idea what dynamite they had introduced in the male-dominated keg of Jerusha Secondary. In her first year, Savi formed a girls' field hockey team. Within two years, she shook the roots of the old Jerusha School establishment by declaring her candidacy for the presidency of the most powerful school establishment, the Student Council. There were old guards who wanted to bar her from the election. There were moderates as well who welcomed this revolution. Savi's candidacy became a subject of a hot debate at the monthly school board meeting. One of the old guard, Mr Ben, a prominent lawyer, in a private conversation, warned the headmaster. 'Under no circumstances should girls be allowed the presidency of the Student Council. It's a slippery slope and will lead to moral degradation.'

An editorial in our daily newspaper said that Savi's candidacy was a crucial barometer of the direction of equality of sexes. Despite running a hard campaign, Savi lost the election. Nevertheless, her candidacy punched a wide hole in the very heart of the old guard's thinking. In a defensive move, the old guard headed by Mr Ben introduced a draconian measure of separate streams for boys and girls. Society, they argued, cannot and should not be allowed to slide into a morass. Free mingling of the sexes in the classes and in the school was a recipe for disaster. It had to be stopped.

Progressive people of Jerusha, including Jeff felt that Jerusha Secondary's policy of separate streams for boys and girls was more akin to the South African apartheid model rather than the one man one vote of Abraham Lincoln. They argued that when progressive white Americans in the USA were marching hand in hand with black Americans for civil liberties, it was morally wrong to take a backward step and put a fence between boys and girls in Jerusha Secondary. But the school board was adamant. Thereafter the only common platform boys and girls of Jerusha shared was a monthly morning school assembly where the headmaster asked teachers to read from texts extolling the virtues of celibacy and pure living. He had them read the story of Original Sin. They read from the novel *Saraswatichandra*– which preached the virtue of abstinence and sacrifice.

Savi went to London and earned a degree in Political Science. Meanwhile Jerusha Secondary's development progressed more or less along the Apartheid model. This was the state of union at Jerusha Secondary until the arrival of Mr Irvine as the new headmaster. He turned the tide of the board's demented slide to Victorian morass by merging the separate streams and dismantling the fence that separated boys and girls. The likes of Savi who had returned from London helped his efforts.

I was to learn from Henna that Savi's arrival in London was at the beginning of Women's Liberation Movement. On the campus of London School of Political Science and Economics (LSC), besides learning all about political revolutions, Savi had lessons in sex revolution. It was rumoured that Savi had been to Scandinavia, which was known as Tundra of Hot Sex made famous by Anita Ekberg in *La Dolce Vita*. I knew about the French and the Marxist Revolutions, but these sex revolutions were new to me. Mr Roy, our history master who was a world authority on revolutions, never mentioned anything about these. Henna told me that in fact there was not one but two sex revolutions. I asked her, 'What does sex revolution mean? Does a man become a woman or the other way around?'

'It is very simple,' she explained. 'Men have turned women in to slaves. Sex revolution is women fighting to regain their freedom from men's abuse.'

'Seriously? I did not know it was so bad for women.'

'It can be bad,' Henna said with a sad face. She only made such a face when she was dead serious. 'Henna,' I observed, 'in our home, women are not slaves. You have all the freedom. I think Daddy is afraid of Ma, and Shamim, why Ma says that Jeff will not even drink a glass of water without asking her? How can that be abuse or slavery?'

'The slavery I am talking about is totally different,' Henna replied. Not satisfied with Henna's explanation, I asked, 'What has sex revolution to do with women throwing their bra and underwear on the streets in protest? It is so rude.' Henna replied that I would not understand this complicated subject. 'All men are like you. They cannot grasp the essence of this matter.'

Savi paid a heavy price for her efforts to bring about a revolution in attitude. The coup de grâce of Savi did not happen in a day. It had a lot to do with Mirza Ghalib, the poet laureate of Urdu, whose anniversary Jerusha Secondary celebrated with pomp every year. It was said that the stress of Victorian taboos of love and sex in Jerusha School found its deserved relief in Urdu classes under Mr Riyaz. Urdu was imminently suitable for this task. It had no less than nine words that conveyed the emotional richness called Love. Of these *ishq*, love desire and *wasl*, union could be used in profane sense or in spiritual sense as in love or union with the divine. In the hands of poets, this richness and wordplay became potent weapons to shatter the taboos of love and sex. Mirza Ghalib and his contemporaries often used these words that could be construed as profane.

The momentum of Savi's Sex Revolution built a tremendous sense of anticipation in Jerusha. When asked in a newspaper interview after her return from London as to how far she would take it, she replied, 'Wait and watch.'

Jerusha Secondary's internationally famed Urdu poetry symposium called *mushaira* to celebrate Mirza Ghalib's birthday was still under male dominance. Lovers of Urdu poetry flocked to it from all over the world. The symbolic use of *Ishq*, love desire and *wasl*, union found their incisive power during such poetry recitals where poets sought to portray hopelessness of unrequited love in delicate language. Despite its sad theme, the Symposium was always a jovial and humorous affair, as it allowed audience, with their individual love grief, to find relief in lyrics.

When Mr Riyaz announced the twenty-fifth Symposium, demand for tickets exceeded expectations. The school auditorium, where the Symposium was normally held, was too small. To add to this predicament, Savi, who had freshly returned from London and Jerusha Secondary's nightingale, Ishrat announced their joint intention to participate. This attack on the only remaining bastion of male domain threw Jerusha Secondary's management into confusion. However, there was nothing in school rules to stop Savi and Ishrat from participating. This novel development electrified Jerusha. People, who ordinarily did not have interest in the Symposium, demanded tickets. This forced Jerusha Secondary to erect a huge marquee on the football pitch.

The stage was set for the Symposium of the century. Mr Riyaz and the members of the Mirza Ghalib Society, sensing the international interest in the Symposium, spared no effort in decorating and furnishing the marquee to mimic the historic opulence of the ancient Mogul Court of Lahore, where such Symposia first took place.

Savi and Ishrat, clad in pink and lilac *kameez shalwar,* long top coats with matching baggy pantaloons, made a grand entrance, when all guests were seated. Mr Riyaz, a man of drama, came to the microphone and said,

'My dear sisters and brothers, this year we bring down the net curtain dividing the male and the female sections so that our sisters can enjoy the Symposium to the fullest.' The audience greeted this with clapping. Mr Riyaz continued, 'We are also making history on another front. Two of our own lovely girls are again the torch bearers and will participate for the first time as contestants. We are eagerly waiting to witness how they lock antlers with their formidable foes.' The audience stood up in a standing ovation for Savi and Ishrat. When the clapping died down, the Honourable Mayor cut the symbolic tape and declared the Symposium in session. Mr Riyaz came to the podium again. 'My sisters and brothers, it is time to introduce you to the grand master of the Symposium.' Thereupon he raised his hands in a grand gesture and sitar music blasted from the loud speaker. From the wing, a white man in a tie and suit walked towards the stage. This confused the audience. A murmur arose from the audience. Mr Riyaz continued, 'My sisters and brothers, I introduce to you Mr Arnold Hales from the United States as the grand master of the twenty-fifth Symposium. I will let him make his own introduction.'

Mr Arnold greeted everyone in Urdu. 'Sisters and brothers, just as you all are surprised; I was surprised when I was invited to this grand occasion. I had never heard about Jerusha, but later, I found that it has been host to one of the world's most respected Symposium. Yes, you are thinking what does a white man know about Urdu Poetry? I am a professor in languages and have spent time at Allahabad University in India. My specialisation is poetry of Amir Khusro, and Mirza Ghalib. And now without much ado, I set the mood with a recitation of Amir Khusro's famous poem:

What tavern was I in last night
All around me were bleeding lovers,
burning in agony
There was full bosomed beloved with a rose-like face
Ruthlessly pulverizing hearts of lovers

Mr Arnold's Urdu prowess impressed the audience and everyone burst out with appreciative *vah vah*. When the commotion died down, Mr Arnold continued, 'On this twenty-fifth anniversary of Jerusha Secondary's Symposium, we will celebrate the concept of "love" with the theme of Flame and Moth. Flame of love, which is a divine impulse in the heart, attracts a moth, the lover, which scarifies its life trying to attain union with the flame.' The audience clapped in ecstasy. Mr Arnold continued, 'The winner of last year's Symposium, a bright star in the firmament of Urdu poetry, Ahmed Khan will open today's Symposium, per its tradition and rules.'

Mr Arnold took his seat behind the podium and nodded, indicating the commencement of the Symposium. Mustaq, a handsome boy, lifted a golden candleholder and put it in front of Ahmed Khan. *Irshad,* commence, the Grand Master said, raising his hand. Ahmed Khan recited the first poem of the Symposium in the form of a challenge:

Think not it is Love,
That impels the moth
To self-immolation in the flame.
Nay, it strikes the flame, crying
Destroy the light,
'*Wasl* (union) can only be in darkness.'

Vah vah the audience clapped. Mustaq carried the golden candle to the next participant who continued the theme impromptu. For the next two hours, succession of participants, reclining on colourful cushions, jotting down their answers to the challenges posed by preceding poets, recited exciting poems. Finally, Mustaq put the golden candleholder in front of Savi and Ishrat. A sense of anticipation gripped everyone. Savi and Ishrat requested permission from the grand master through Mushtaq to sing their composition instead of reciting it. Mr Arnold conferred with Mr Riyaz. The audience got restless. Mr Riyaz came to the microphone.

'Sisters and brothers, we have a situation. Our lovely ladies, Savi and Ishrat, have requested to sing their composition. I have conferred with the grand master and this permission is granted.'

Mr Arnold raised his hand and Savi and Ishrat sang four stanzas of their composition that held the audience spellbound. The moth was saying to the flame:

If I attain not your love,
Let me then suffer eternally
In your *Ishq* (love-desire)
If I attain not your *wasl* (union),
Let me then burn eternally
In your *wasl*-desire.

The audience erupted in a *vah vah*. Just when the commotion was dying down, a catcall arose from the rear of the marquee. 'Honey, why burn eternally in *wasl*-desire? I am ready for a full "*wasl*" now!' A wave of consternation and derision sailed through the entire marquee. Female audience was appalled. People rushed to gag the catcaller.

Sunday's newspaper carried an editorial praising Jerusha Secondary and Mr Riyaz for the history-making firsts and praised Savi and Ishrat for their courage. 'The divas of Jerusha Secondary,' it wrote, 'have lighted the torch of Women's Liberation and their foray in the male-dominated Symposium is welcome.'

However, close to home, the tinder of that single catcall only needed an evil wind to burst in to a conflagration that would destroy everything. Critics of liberalism, headed by Mr Ben, seized on this event and branded the whole experiment a failure. School board reprimanded the headmaster for an error of judgement, who in turn took the unusual step of transferring Mr Riyaz to a regional primary school. Censorship was imposed on Urdu classes, and for a time, Mirza Ghalib was taken off from the syllabus.

Cults are born when basic freedoms are denied, that is what Mr Roy said when he heard about the censorship of Urdu classes. A secret concept that had coinage in Mr Riyaz's class even before the imposition of censorship devolved into a cult. Like Freemasonry, there were only rumours about it. Elder boys whispered it in riddles. When I joined Jerusha Secondary, I heard sketchy accounts of it. The word that came up in these conversations was '*Udhric*'. Wild tales of "naked dancing and sex orgies" of *Udhric* circulated among boys. I had no idea what the girls thought about it. Parents shunned it; establishment hated it. I tried to break its secret many times. Our poorly stocked school and public libraries did not allow much opportunity in this respect. As time went on, I learnt that this *Udhric* concept was the centre of the Circle of Love and coloured all of us who loved and was the backbone of all our tragic Indian pictures.

Mr Ben's reappointment to the school board re-initiated the game of divide and rule. Boys and girls were again put in separate streams. Savi renewed her battle cry, now not as a student but as a concerned citizen to overhaul girls' education. Mr Ben and his supporters thumped the table and said, 'We told you so. Empower a woman and this is what you get.' Other more progressive members agreed that the education system needed modernisation. But Savi had saved her salvo for an appropriate occasion. At the Town Hall meeting, she lighted the fuse and called not only for abolition of sex-apartheid, but introduction of sex education, 'Descriptions of sex organs in biology class is not sex education.' The sonic boom of this demand reverberated across our country and the neighbouring countries. Newspapers were aflame, 'About time we debunked the old Victorian sex taboos. Miss Savi has fired the first salvo in this battle.'

Conservative religious groups denounced this as immoral and painted Savi as a sex crazy bitch. Someone pasted a poster-size photo of Savi alongside Anita Ekberg of *La Dolce Vita* at the Town Hall with a caption – Tropic of Hot Sex – Right here in Jerusha.

At Parents' meetings Mr Ben and his clan drove fears of breakdown of morals if Savi and her immoral ideas were allowed to take root. 'Do you want our girls to do what they are doing in London and Stockholm? Do you want teenage pregnancies?' they asked.

In an underhanded move the School Board setup a committee of head priest from the temple, head mullah from the mosque and a Catholic priest to safeguard Jerusha's morality and convince Savi's father to rein in his daughter. They pressured Savi's father to sign a letter denouncing her which appeared in the Friday Edition of the paper. Savi's father regretted signing the letter. But it was too late. Savi had no idea about all this when she came home on Friday afternoon. Her father was out visiting customers. Savi's stepmother spared no mercy, 'Welcome, you shameless girl.'

'Mother, what are you talking about?'

'Don't pretend you don't know, you prostitute. Look at this letter. Pack up and get out.' The stepmother thrust the newspaper to Savi's face. Savi read the letter and grimaced. 'Where is Papa?' she asked, fighting tears.

'He has nothing to do with you,' the stepmother replied. Savi felt as if someone had thrust a dagger in her back. She realised she was naked without a family. All along, she did what she did in the knowledge that the one person in her life whose esteem she enjoyed was her father. Without him, she was like a twig trampled on by elephants. Holding back her tears, she left.

Later, she resurfaced as TV host for popular school quiz program Master Mind in Pala.

Build Up to *CID* Release

I snapped back to reality from my memory stroll. Madam Doctor had forgotten her handkerchief on the ledge in the Boxing Club. I folded it and put it in my pocket with her card. Then I remembered. Narika, good lord! I was planning to meet her before I was waylaid by Madam Doctor. I looked at my watch and realised that the Primary School's grounds would be crowded for the evening sports practices. Delicate declaration of love would be impossible under such conditions. That magical moment to hold Narika in my arms and declare my love to her had passed. Fate had conspired to fail my intention. In that instance, Shakespeare's quote came to my mind:

There is a tide in the affairs of men.
Which, taken at the flood, leads on to fortune;
Omitted, all the voyage of their life
Is bound in shallows and in miseries . . .

A lecture by Professor Pinto, our physic master had a lot to do with what happened next.

There is no correlation between physics and love, to speak of. Yet during *CID*, this was what I derived in my mind. My mental aberration arose from a lecture Professor Pinto had delivered in our class some months earlier. He commenced his lecture by telling us about a famous 1927 conference in Brussels attended by giants of physics such as Albert Einstein and others. At this conference, they discussed the mysteries of microscopic Quantum Universe where laws of Relativity broke down and matter began to behave in strange ways. The class became very attentive. Professor Pinto stood rolling a piece of chalk in his hand for a while. His idiosyncrasies were responsible in no small measure to my accepting the things he told us that day as Gospel. Young and athletic, Professor Pinto taught physics with an infectious zeal. Few brave girls that attended his physic classes swooned when he wore bright shirts and flowery ties. They giggled and wrote secret notes to one another.

During the Quantum Universe lecture, Professor Pinto said that at microscopic level a single particle could be at two different places at the same time or could tunnel through matter and re-appear at different location defying time. Joger who never took interest in physics waved his hands and exclaimed. 'Professor, how is that possible? It would mean that the particles are in two different universes.'

'There,' Professor Pinto said, 'we scientists do come up with some interesting ideas.' Continuing Professor Pinto said that an additional quark of the Quantum Universe was that some particles which were separated over vast distances could influence the behaviour of other particles without any communication between them. When he saw that the class was confused, he gave an example by saying that twins sometimes exhibited similar behaviour. 'If one of the twins living in Australia had an accident, the other living in America would feel the pain. In Quantum Universe, this property of the particle is called Entanglement.' Professor Pinto added that Einstein did not like all this mumbo jumbo of Quantum Universe and said it was not science but Voodoo. Niels Bohr, another scientist calmed him down and explained that at Quantum level particles were behaving normally and were happy to be Entangled and conjoined with each other and be at two places at the same time. The strangeness in their behaviour was only noticed when we tried to observe the subatomic universe with our everyday large instruments. This intrusion disturbed the equilibrium of the Quantum Universe and a Wave Collapse happened which forced the particles to behave irrationally. Concluding his lecture, Professor Pinto said, 'So, boys and girls at this very moment, you may be Entangled with your double on Mars who is in resonance with you and thinks like you.'

I could not sleep that night and thought about professor Pinto's Quantum lecture. At dawn when the bugler played First Post on the Garrison Hill and Hukum Singh sang devotional songs, I had flashes of inspiration and realised that in Quantum Universe, we exist as ideas of pure light and each one of us has a soul mate. There is no chance or uncertainty in this Universe. God is resting knowing that we are all united and there is peace and harmony. Then mysteriously we splinter into a multitude of individual souls in our Space and Time Universe. What happens when this splinter occurs?

Your guess is correct. A big Waveform Collapse happens. Time is born. Where there was light, now there is darkness; where there was harmony now there is chaos; where there was love, now here is hate. Life becomes unpredictable and we become separated from our soul mates. However, deep in our heart remains a memory of the love and a longing for our soul mate. If during our normal life we meet a soul that awakens a dormant love song in our heart, bang, we construe it as love at first sight. However, it is not so. This chance meeting of the souls is the seed that revives forgotten love. This is when a stranger says to another, I have the same dreams as yours.

One of Jerusha's paranoia was an uprising or a tribal war in the army. This was due to the fact that there was an intense rivalry between Commander Leman who controlled Garrison Hill and General Kikuna who controlled Gama Garrison, which was only fifteen kilometres away.

The morning radio news bulletin reported the Jerusha Well of Death accident. A motorcycle jockey was in hospital with a broken leg. I was relieved that there were no fatalities. I lazed in my bed. Garrison Hill was basking in brilliant sunshine. I thought about my meeting with Madam Doctor. My Quantum Love Thesis and my failed attempt to meet Narika flashed in my mind. Why not meet Narika and invite her to *CID*?

I decided to put my idea into action and meet Narika as soon as possible. After breakfast, I showered and was ironing my shirt, humming a song, when a breathless Jeremy came back from the wet market and shouted, *Na Anza* which literally meant "it has commenced". This was the dreaded Jerusha code word for a tribal war. We had a well-rehearsed procedure for this eventuality. I dropped everything and ran out to shut the front gate. Azul and Jeremy closed all the windows and doors to the house. Rehmat led Nina, Salim and Henna into the cellar. Jeremy fetched a machete and a spear and stood like a Zulu warrior behind the front door. He cut a comic figure. Azul tried calling out on the phone but all lines were jammed. Salim, Henna, and Nina kept giggling in the cellar. Rehmat kept scolding them. We waited. Finally, at one o'clock Jeff and Shamim who were out playing badminton phoned to inform that *Na Anza* was a false alarm. Jeff said that the police and Commander Leman's men had arrested Andrew, the director of NTC for black marketing. Azul aired his misgivings. 'Andrew is Kikuna's clan brother and will seek revenge. Our troubles are not over yet.'

With less than half an hour before premiere of *CID*, I had to abandon my plan to meet Narika. I informed Azul that after *CID* I would sleep over at Ash's, as we would be attending a dance at the Lake Textiles Club. Rehmat was upset that I was running away without eating lunch. 'But Ma, you have not even started cooking and *CID* starts like now.'

'It will be ready soon,' she shouted behind me.

Spring of Love

Flamingo Square was thronged with people due to the congruence of the premier of *CID*, non-stop Jazz Festival at Flamingo Bar and the lunch time crowd at Sukh Sager from the Tri-country Cricket Tournament. I fought my way up the crowded steps to the foyer of City Light looking for Joger. An angry crowd surrounded him, jostling for tickets. 'Brothers, it is Full House. I have no more tickets,' Joger was yelling. Upon seeing me, he tried to break away from the crowd and said, 'Junior, late as usual. Take this ticket.' The crowd reacted angrily with shouts of "favouritism" and started to get unruly. I got worried for Joger's safety. He apologised profusely to the mob, 'Brothers, I am holding a ticket for him for a week now.'

'Where are Nash and the rest?' I asked, raising my voice above the din. Joger did not answer and simply waved to an usher who came over, and flashed a torch in my face. I followed him into the dark cinema hall. 'What is my seat number?' I asked.

'There is no number. Just take one of the extra chairs,' he whispered and shone the torch to an empty chair next to the wall. I squeezed in. A Disney cartoon was playing on the screen. At its conclusion, *CID*, in an action-packed opening murder sequence, blazed on the screen with *cinema noir* seriousness. A superb, tense opener, I thought. Relief came when the camera zoomed on the face of a sweet girl of eighteen filling her car at a petrol pump: Shakila! This was her debut. The pit crowd burst into claps and whistles. A group of boys jumped up and danced near the stage. Cinema staff came and calmed them down. I turned and looked to my side. A smiling Madam Doctor was holding my hand. 'You were so engrossed, I did not want to disturb,' she whispered. She put her hand on my thigh and turned her face back to the screen. At that moment a pair of girls came and occupied the empty chairs in front of us. The first of the girls occupied the empty chair in front of me and as she did, she threw her head back and her long, thick braided plait fell into my lap. She was unaware of this. Her hip rested against my knee which was wedged between her chair and the wall. Fragrance of Pantene hair lotion engulfed me. Professor Pinto's Quantum Universe lecture and my earth-shattering thesis of Quantum Love were fresh in my mind. I held the long, thick pigtail of the girl in my hands. In the flashing silvery light, I saw a ribbon and a bow clipped to the end of it. The dual acts of my contact with hip of the girl sitting in the chair in front of me and her pigtail falling into my hand were the essential tentacles of a Quantum Trap into which I fell. Every nerve in my body tingled. A forgotten song from Quantum Universe sprang in my heart. The dream that I had dreamt when time was born, flashed in my mind. I knew right away that a Waveform Collapse had happened. I knew that the girl whose pigtail I was holding in my hand was none other than Palita, the girl that Joger and Arvind had kept talking about all the time; the girl with marble-white thighs, rose petal face, and long hair that hung to her hips. I also realised that the dream that flashed in my mind was her dream as well. With the Waveform Collapse, I realised that our souls which were ideas of pure light, were joined together from the time the universe was created. By Quantum Entanglement, Palita and I were entangled from long ago. I had a realization that I was in love with her. I shivered uncontrollably. I sat holding her pigtail like a jewel. Its Pantene fragrance intoxicated me. Madam Doctor's tight grip of my thigh kept me grounded in the reality of my surroundings. I could not tell if she was stroking my erection. On the screen *CID*'s smash hit song

The spring of first love...
. . . a charmer from magic land
with bouquet of love has arrived.

was playing with charming fury. The uniqueness of my feelings of love for a girl whose face I had never seen absorbed me utterly. Its surge, like a tidal wave, swept away my previous emotional attachments.

Absence of Janitors

S omeone shone a torch in my face and I heard Joger calling my name. I came back to reality with a jolt. On the screen, Dev, the detective hero, had been implicated in the murder of a prominent newspaper editor. Joger was saying, 'Come Junior we need you.' He guided me in the dark narrow alley between rows of extra chairs. Just when my heart was throbbing with a new rhythm in anticipation of coming face to face with Palita during the picture interval, I was torn away from her. In the next instance fear gripped me. What if Chaucer's adage of time and tide wait for no one came into play? What if I never saw Palita again? This thought unnerved me. Joger left me in the foyer with a cryptic message, 'Junior, wait for Nash to explain to you what has happened.' My heart was with Palita in the cinema. Nash came running up the stairs and without much ceremony asked me to follow him. We fought our way through a crowd jostling for tickets for the next show and boarded a waiting taxi. It sped along Boja Road, coming to screeching halt at the junction of Tembo na Membe to allow a convoy of army trucks to pass. As we waited, Nash said that Ash was in love with Tara. I lost my balance. 'You idiot, did you pull me out of *CID* to celebrate Ash and Tara's love. What the fuck do I care?' I shouted. Nash tried to calm me down. I was beyond rage. 'How can I calm down? Only two days ago that idiot went around telling everyone to confess love. Did he confess?' Nash was apologetic and explained that Tara's family was forcing her to be engaged to an industrialist's son from Pala on Monday.

'Do they not know about Ash?' I asked.

'You fool since when do girls tell their families about their love affairs? They will skin her alive if they find out,' Nash replied.

'So now what?' I asked. Nash explained that Ash was already in Pala trying to work something out. However, he added that the only sure way to avert Tara's engagement was for Ash's family to send a telegram before Monday to Tara's family with a counter proposal. And if Tara agrees then Ash stands a chance.

'Why can't Ash's family talk directly to Tara's family?' I asked.

'According to custom, only a telegram will do. Here is the text of the telegram we have to send. No post offices are open at this hour. So, our only chance is the telegram machine at Kira Estate guardhouse. You worked there two years ago. We can try using that machine. Ash will wait for us at ten tomorrow.' I became alarmed. 'Nash, Kira is past Gama Garrison. You do know what has happened this morning to Andrew, Kikuna's brother? It is dangerous to be around Gama,' I said shaking my head. Nash assured me that we would be in and out of Kira guardhouse in no time. I had cold shivers as our taxi sped past an orderly and calm Gama Garrison towards Kira. The Garrison's barracks' roofs simmered orange red in slanted rays of sun filtering through tall trees of Wiri Hill.

Kira guardhouse was hidden in the lengthening shadow of the towering hills surrounding it when we arrived. The taxi dropped us at its entrance and waited. A young boy, Taban, with a ponytail, minding the desk greeted us. I introduced myself and told him that I knew his father when I worked for him. When I told him that I wanted to use the telegram machine, he directed me to the back office without hesitation.

The back office was exactly as I had left it two years ago. I switched on the telegram machine which made strange whirling noises. I waited anxiously. As soon as a small green light came on, I keyed in Ash's text message and waited while the machine quietly digested it. Suddenly, it came alive again and spewed out a ticker tape. I was relived. I spliced the tape, pasted it to an official telegram paper, and inserted it into a brown envelope. Then I sealed it with red wax and stamped it with an official stamp and tucked the sealed envelope in my secret trouser pocket below the belt.

In the office, Taban informed me that his father was in the bungalow behind the guardhouse and would be pleased to see me. I felt obliged to at least say hello to him. Taban opened the back door leading to the bungalow for us. Nash and I walked out and skirted several empty oil drums towards a wooded path. Suddenly, from the darkness that had descended rapidly, two trucks came to a screeching halt in front of the guardhouse. No sooner had the noise of the truck engines died down we heard a barrage of gunshots. Nash gripped my arm. We saw our taxi speed away. 'Nash, our taxi is running away,' I shouted. A violent explosion drowned my words. The guardhouse shook violently. I saw Taban escape from the back door. Nash and I dived behind the empty oil drums, puzzled by the suddenness of the gunfire and an explosion. The aftershocks of the violent blast reverberated in the surrounding hills.

The memory projectors of my mind rolled to the time when we were foolish and immature. Many afternoons we went to the swath of Suwakaki surrounding Garrison Hill and watched military exercises, hiding in trenches that crisscrossed Suwakaki. We were familiar with sounds of gunfire and blasts of hand grenades. On one occasion after the military exercise, Joger and I strayed from the exercise area and found a tunnel behind a rock. We crawled halfway through it when Ash and Nash, startled by our absence, shouted for us. We turned back. Joger went and joined Ash and Nash. Before leaving the area I searched for unexploded bullets and found several different types. Some were short, others were medium length. One bullet that I found which surprised me the most was fat and the size of my long finger. I had never seen it before. I pocketed all these. Later that evening sitting at Paan Cafe, I showed my friends my bullet treasure.

'What are you doing with these?' Joger asked.

'Add them to my collection and cut them open to see how they work,' I replied. Joger became alarmed and said, 'You crazy scientist, you want to understand everything. I think you should throw these away. And this long one looks like it can kill an elephant.' I ignored Joger's advice and put the bullets back in my pocket. Instead of taking them home, I went to JCB and hid them in my secret box behind JCB's cash register.

Kira Guardhouse burned in the aftermath of a grenade explosion. Several shadowy figures ran into the woods from the other side of the guardhouse. Three soldiers ran in our direction from the waiting trucks and were soon upon us, pointing guns at us. 'Arrest these foreign spies, and bring them to MIC,' one of the soldiers barked. The mention of Military Interrogation Centre (MIC) under the control of General Kikuna drove the terror of hell in us. MIC was never mentioned openly. Foreign newspapers occasionally carried reports of torture and brutal killings of prisoners with hammer blows to their heads at this dreaded centre.

We were herded on to one of the trucks and led to MIC in the shadow of Riya Hill. The truck came to a stop in a dimly lit compound. Behind us stood the ghostly summit of Riya Hill and to our right stretched the vast Peace Lake. A guard threw open the back hatch and shouted '*Shuka chini*, get down and marched us into a cell infested with smell of urine and faeces. We sat on the bare floor, traumatised. 'What will they do to us?' Nash asked.

'We have not done anything wrong. They'll let us go,' I comforted Nash. Internally I was terrified. Nash kept blabbering that we had overstayed our welcome in the country and the minute the immigration law in Britain was passed, he would leave. In this state he fell asleep on my shoulder. I eased him on the floor, stretched besides him, and drifted into a disturbed sleep.

I felt a powerful kick to my side. A soldier pulled Nash and me by the shoulders and marched us into a brightly lit room occupied by a uniformed man who sat behind a desk and a civilian who walked up and down the room. I would have never imagined that the thin, fragile strand that we call life was so crucially dependent on the absence of janitors that day. We were to soon discover this.

The civilian came and stood behind us and barked, 'You spies!' The officer shouted, 'What do you know about the deserters from Gama Garrison?'

'Sir, we are students,' I replied. The civilian whacked me with his cane, 'Liar. What were you doing at Kira?'

'We were there to see Mr Diambo,' I replied. The officer became animated. 'Diambo is a dog, a traitor. He killed our people in the north. Did you know that?' I looked down. The civilian put his cane under my face, 'Look up and answer the officer.'

'No, sir, I did not know,' I replied. The officer was unrelenting, 'Are you planning a rebellion? Today fourteen soldiers ran away from the barracks to meet with you and Diambo.' Suddenly, he reclined on his chair and stretched his foot on the desk. Frightened, Nash and I came closer together. The officer pulled out a fat cigar, lighted it and sat smoking it, rocking his foot. The room kept filling up with smoke. A few minutes later, a girl in a crumpled uniform brought a tray of coffees and *mandazi* and put it on the table close to the officer's foot. We waited in silence. The officer continued to smoke and rock his foot, his shoe grazing the *mandazi* in the tray. The room was thick with cigar smoke and appetizing aroma of coffee and *mandazi*. Suddenly, Nash started to cough. The civilian came and punched him in the face. 'Quiet,' he barked. Nash reeled back in agony and in a violent spasm, spat blood on the floor. The civilian gave out a blood-chilling growl, 'You dog, how dare you spit in front of me?' Seething with rage he raised his cane to strike Nash. I raised my hand to protect Nash and pleaded, 'Please, sir.' My move electrified the interrogation room. The civilian threw his cane in the air, pulled a revolver from his pocket, and shoved its muzzle into my mouth, 'You bastard, attacking an officer? I kill you. I kill you . . .' The officer jumped up. His boot knocked the coffee and *mandazi* tray to the floor. On impact one of the cups exploded like a KML cracker. The officer ran towards us screaming. 'Sembe, no . . . no, don't do it.' He came and pulled his partner away from me. 'Sembe it will be a big mess. We'll have to do it to both. We have no janitors to clean up until Monday. No transport to dispose. Leave them.'

Sembe barked, 'Look what you had the commander do?' He caught my neck, forced me down, and rubbed my face in the spilled coffee. 'Now clean it up.' I crawled on the floor, picked up broken pieces of the cup and the soiled *mandazi* and put them in the tray.

After several hours of interrogation and canning, when no substantial information came from Nash or me, the officer left us. Sembe checked my pockets, found some money and Madam Doctor's card together with her handkerchief which she had forgotten in the boxing club. He kept the money and the card and gave me the handkerchief before he left us.

Alone in the interrogation room we realised that no one would be looking for us. Joger was busy with *CID* tickets. Ash was in Pala, and both Nash and I had told our families that we would be sleeping at Ash's. This thought frightened us. Overcome by fatigue Nash curled up on the floor and fell asleep. I started to think about pleasant things. I thought about *CID* and Palita. I thought about Narika. Despite my best efforts to keep awake, I fell asleep. A prodding to my side woke me up. Sembe was standing above me. 'You are free to go,' he said. Then he showed me Madam Doctor's card. 'Who is this?'

'Sir, my family doctor,' I replied.

'Before you go we need a guarantor. Call this doctor to come. Use the phone.' I made a phone call to Madam Doctor and explained to her the situation. She listened to me patiently and then asked, 'Where exactly are you?' When I told her my location she fell silent. After a while she said, 'I will be there soon.'

We waited outside Sembe's office and watched the ripples over the lake taking on a pinkish orange shine from the brightening sky. Madam Doctor came at sunrise. Sembe escorted her to his office. The door was ajar, and I saw him talk to her with emphatic hand gestures. I saw her give him money. I felt rotten for having exposed her to this humiliation. She came out looking ashen. 'What have you been up to? Do you have any idea what this place is like?' she hissed. Both Nash and I felt ashamed. Outside, I thanked her. She came close to me and said, 'Remember to help me when I need you. Don't forget.'

'I will not forget,' I replied. I handed her the handkerchief that she had forgotten in the boxing club. She smiled as she took it from me. She drove us to Zanzibar Road and dropped us near Moidin.

Bonfire of Love

Simisu took our order and asked if we had come straight from *CID* midnight show. 'There was no midnight show,' Nash replied. 'Yes there was due to confusion in the afternoon show,' he said, with a foxy smile. During breakfast Nash declared that he was taking the first plane to the UK once the immigration law had passed. I told him that our MIC ordeal was an isolated incident and that he ought not to make a rash decision based on it.

At ten we walked to Tara's house and delivered the telegram as required. Then we phoned Ash. He was delighted. 'I will wait at home to hear their decision,' he said. I went home and slept. In the evening I played Ludo with Henna and Salim. Tired from my ordeal at the MIC, I had an early dinner and was in bed listening to Radio Ceylon when Vir knocked on my door. He was out of breath. 'You must come urgently. It is about Joger,' he said. I slipped out and we rode out on his bicycle towards Naran Road where he led me to a figure sitting by a log fire in a secluded passage behind Moon Bakery. At close quarters I realized it was Joger. He sat staring at the dancing flames. On seeing me he said, 'Junior, it is all over. What was wrong with my . . . ?' he stammered. He was drunk and incoherent. I had never seen him like this before. Vir explained that during Saturday's evening show Harry was on his way to the Picture House with *CID's* second reel when Pari stood like a temptress on the balcony above Lake Sports Shop. There was a coy exchange between the two. She invited him up. Her folks were at the City Light. One thing led to another. At the cinemas there was no sign of Harry or the picture reel. Angry patrons besieged Joger and Mr Jeg. Shows at both cinemas were abandoned. Pari's folks returned home from unfinished picture show to find Harry on top of Pari. I was confused so I asked Vir, 'What do you mean on top of Pari.'

'Well on top means on top, like how to make babies. You are the one who watches all those *Manga*. In any event, Pari's folks caught Harry and thrashed him, dislocating his shoulder. Like a true showman, Joger said that the show must go on. Mr Jeg the manager at City Light and Joger retrieved the *CID* reel and calmed the angry crowd with a special free midnight show at the City Light. After the midnight show, Joger drank at Flamingo until dawn and left with bottles of Scotch. He lighted this bonfire and this is where he has been sitting all this time.' I sat down and held Joger's hand. He kept moaning. 'Junior, I loved her.'

'Joger I know. Did you give her the necklace you showed me?' He shook his head. 'What use now? I burnt it,' he replied pointing to the fire. I took a stick and retrieved a charred box from the ashes. I asked Vir to wrap it in a piece of paper. We tidied Joger, washed his face at Maru Temple and walked him home. On seeing me his father showered me with profanities, 'You rascal I will talk to Azul tomorrow. You are a rotten apple. What manner is this coming home drunk? We have been searching for him for two days.'

We attended Ash's engagement to Tara a week later. Joger did not attend. That evening, I confronted Joger at the City Light. He hid in the booking office.

'Joger, listen . . .' I tried reasoning with him through the ticket window. He would have none of it. I recalled the glint of excitement in Joger's eyes at Tembo na Membe, when he had shown me the necklace he wanted to gift Pari and declare his love. Looking at him through the ticket window I felt as if I was looking at a ghost.

In the days and months that followed, Joger withdrew into a shell. He dropped out of school. His behaviour confused his family. His father apologised to me for his tirade the night I had brought him home. 'What is wrong with my son?' he kept asking me.

'Uncle, I don't know,' I replied.

'Take him out. Take my car and go see a picture in Pala,' he pleaded.

'Uncle I will try,' I assured him. I tried reminding Joger about our picture project and Kilimanjaro story. My words fell on deaf ears.

We all knew that Pari was a flirt but pragmatist Nash asked me incisive questions. 'Who saw Pari in that position? What if Harry tried raping Pari?' Nash's questions and comment set me thinking about Pari's innocence.

Mr Irvine's absence from the school during the Cuban Missile Crisis and the infamous incident when we were caught ogling at a *Playboy,* cost Mr Irvine dearly. Seizing on this incident, Mr Desai executed a dirty stroke. When Mr Irvine's policy of abolition of Apartheid of sexes was in progress, Mr Desai connived with the cliquish conservative core of the school board and forced an extraordinary meeting at which he tabled the *Playboy* as a smoking gun to prove that Mr Irvine's liberal policy of free mingling of sexes had gone terribly wrong and that school morality was on the slide. When Mr Desai's underhanded shenanigans to oust Mr Irvine became known, the Student Council staged a populist two-day strike. Ignoring it, the board unceremoniously demoted Mr Irvine and posted him to the regional Regwa Secondary School and appointed Mr Desai as the headmaster.

Back to Green Ford: Kofta for Lunch

Every event has its genesis in a preceding action. My riding in Madam Doctor's green Ford towards an undisclosed destination was likely a repayment for favour she had done me when she had rescued Nash and me from the MIC.

We were driving steadily on a dirt road through a thick forest. Brahm's Symphony was rising to a crescendo. Madam Doctor made a sudden sharp turn on a grassy track to the edge of a lake and stopped between trees intertwined with dark green-leaved climbers. A man waiting in a small boat ferried us a short distance across the water to the tip of a densely-wooded island. Chirping of birds greeted us. I followed a cheerful Madam Doctor on a red-mud path bordered by towering mavule towards a fence overgrown with colourful bougainvillea behind which stood a bungalow. My imagination ran wild. Is she turning me in to a sex slave or something? A bungalow in the middle of a jungle island, a pretty, middle-aged woman and a teenage boy: it was a perfect script for a sex picture. In reality, my mind was far from picture scripts. I made a comment. 'Beautiful. Is this yours?' Instead of answering me Madam Doctor continued walking. We entered the bungalow through a side door. A girl came out of one of the rooms when she heard us enter. Madam Doctor stood between us. 'I was expecting you sooner madam,' the girl said in a voice that sounded familiar. 'Breakfast is ready,' she added.

'Good. I'm sure our friend is hungry,' Madam Doctor replied and stepped aside. A tornado hit me when I saw the girl's face. I controlled myself. 'This is Amina,' Madam Doctor said. A spectrum of emotions sailed through the girl's face. I stood speechless. I was not sure if Madam Doctor noticed our reactions. I stepped forward and extended my hand to her. 'Amina' is all I managed. She blushed and shook my hand. She turned and went to the kitchen. We sat down at a small breakfast table. Madam Doctor asked Amina through the kitchen door, 'Where is the little brat?'

'Madam, the ayah has taken her out for a walk. Last few days she has no temperature,' Amina replied from the kitchen. I assumed that Madam Doctor was making a patient visit. Many thoughts went through my mind. Did Amina have a baby? Soon Amina came with a tray with a tea pot, toasts and jams and butter. She poured tea for me. Her hand shook. We noticed it. She stretched to pour tea for Madam Doctor. Her hand grazed my neck. Her closeness gave me goose pimples. She put two toasts in my plate and turned to go to the kitchen, saying, 'I will be back with fried eggs.' Soon there was appetizing aroma of frying eggs. Madam Doctor saw the quizzical expression on my face. 'I will explain everything after breakfast,' she assured me. Amina came and served eggs to Madam Doctor. She moved over to me. I looked up. Our eyes met. She served me two eggs, cooked American style just the way I liked. Madam Doctor invited Amina to join us. She came and sat to my right. Her face was sad. In the past I had cupped her beautiful face like a delicate flower in my hands and had known its former radiance. It pained me to see her like this. We ate in silence, exchanging glances.

After breakfast Madam Doctor invited me to the garden. 'I want to explain a few things,' she began to say when a young voice shouted 'Mama,' from behind us. I turned and saw Amina holding the hand of a young girl of five with golden hair and a fair complexion. The girl ran to Madam Doctor. 'My sweetie pie,' Madam Doctor said as she lifted her. Upon seeing me the young girl buried her face in Madam Doctor's shoulder. 'He is a friend sweetie,' she said. 'And this is Jill.'

'Hello Jill,' I tried to cajole her, but she continued to hide her face. We walked back to the bungalow where Amina took Jill for a bath. Madam Doctor handed me a copy of a thick annual edition of *Filmfare* and followed Amina to the bathroom. I sat miffed, trying to recover from the shock of this chance meeting with Amina. I leafed through *Filmfare* and got absorbed in reading an article on upcoming *Mughal-e-Azam,* starring the stunning Madhubala, one of the most iconic and beautiful heroine of Bollywood cinema when Madam Doctor came out of the bathroom, carrying a giggling Jill. A fragrance of Eau de Cologne surrounded them. Amina came and announced that she will prepare kofta for lunch. I caught a fleeting glimpse of the former radiance in her face. 'Kofta,' I repeated mechanically after her. The dream projectors in my subconscious came alive as if "kofta" was a switch. I saw a black and white spiral rotate anticlockwise and my mind went back in time.

Stroll to the Past – You are A Devil

Shamim delivered Nina two weeks early at home. It happened a day before the Grand Women's Association Gala in Pala. Jeff was still away on business in London. In fact, Rehmat, Shamim and Henna were busy making last minute preparations for the Gala when Shamim's waters broke. She delivered Nina that night. This put Rehmat in a quandary. The Gala in Pala was an annual marriage bazaar where families scouted for prospective brides and grooms for their sons and daughters. Rehmat was to be installed as the vice chairperson of the Association. To add to this excitement Azul had tickets for *Cinderella on Ice* at Vubo Stadium on the evening of the Gala. Shamim's early confinement disrupted our family plan. Rather than cancel the entire trip, Azul arranged a staff girl from JCB to come and stay with Shamim and Rehmat arranged for Nurse Lily to come and spend time with Shamim so that the planned trip to Pala could happen. Azul asked me to stay behind to manage the house. I was looking forward to *Cinderella on Ice,* but had no choice in the matter.

After the family left for Pala, I sat in *Uhuru,* switched off the ceiling lights and watched my collection of cut-frames from pictures on my home projector. There was a knock. 'Come in,' I said. A girl walked in and stood in the full glare of the projection. I saw a round, tulip face adorned with big arched eyebrows. The girl seemed same age as Henna. She shielded her eyes from the glare and asked, 'Where are you?' I switched on the ceiling light. 'Ah, now I see you. I am Amina, I am here to help Shamim. What are you doing, hiding in here?'

'I am watching a slide show,' I replied. She turned and looked at the projection and asked, 'Pretty; who is she?' I explained, 'She is Vyjayanthimala from film *Yasmeen*. This sequence was three minutes long without the camera moving away from her face.' She laughed. 'Good. You can tell me all about it later. Now come and eat.'

Shamim was already at the dining table. We hardly started lunch, when Nina started to whimper. Shamim and Amina left in a hurry to attend to her. I finished my lunch alone.

In the afternoon, Nurse Lily dropped by to spend time with Shamim and Nina. I was slugging away at my punching bag when Amina came looking for me. On seeing me she ran into the house and came back with a towel. I stopped to see what she was up to. She rushed to me and began to dry me. I put up my hands and laughed, 'Stop! I am not allowed to use regular towels. Mother says they smell.' Amina continued to dry me and said, 'It is okay. I will wash it. You go for a shower now.'

When I came back after the shower, Amina was hanging the washed towel on the drying line. Pointing to a machine next to the hen house, she asked, 'What is that thing?'

'It is a sugar cane juicer. Would you like some?'

'Yes, do you have sugar canes?' I showed her the plump, purple skinned '*dongosi*' sugar canes in the garden. 'My goodness!' she exclaimed, 'I have never seen such fat canes.' I cut a couple of these, picked up fresh limes from a lime tree, and made a frothy jug of juice while Amina checked on Shamim. She returned and said that Nurse Lily was busy teaching Shamim how to breastfeed and that she would be a while. I gave Amina a glass of the juice. She sat on our garden swing slurping the juice and surveying the garden. In the afternoon heat her satin soft skin was drenched in perspiration. I took out my handkerchief and wiped her forehead. She smiled and continued enjoying the juice. When she finished, I said to her, 'Come, let me take you to the stars.' With a twinkle in her eyes she asked,

'How?' I gave a big push to the swing, jumped on it, and continued to push. Amina giggled and screamed. I pushed harder and the swing climbed higher, rising above the mango trees. 'Hold tight,' I shouted. Suddenly, she let go of the chains and held on to my legs. The swing swayed side to side. Afraid of an accident, I sat down, locked my legs around her, and held her tight. As the swing slowed, she clutched me and rested her head on my shoulder. When she recovered, she said. 'You are a devil.'

Next morning at breakfast, Amina asked me what I wanted for breakfast. I told her to make me two American-style eggs. She went away to the kitchen. When she did not come back for a long time, I followed her and saw her standing with raw eggs in her hand, looking puzzled. 'What, haven't you made the eggs yet?' I asked.

'Prince, I don't know how to. What are these American-style eggs?' she asked. I took the eggs from her hand, cracked them in the hot pan, and when one side had cooked, flipped them by a move of the pan. This surprised her. 'Who taught you that?'

'Oh, from Ma.' Then on an impulse, I told her, 'I like you. Stay with us.'

'You are sweet. I will consider it.' After breakfast, she helped Shamim with the baby chores. Later, she came to *Uhuru,* and I played songs for her. These fascinated her. 'What are they saying, these songs? They are nice.'

'Indian songs are all about love and hurt of love,' I replied.

The Aftermath of the Music Room Affair

Fate extinguished all the engines on my special rocket that I was flying towards Grand Circle of Music, the Classical Circle. The fountain of my happiness thus far was that I had the magical key to King Solomon's Treasure, which would lead me to God's Symphony. With the sudden loss of power my rocket plummeted to the ground. The key to King Solomon's Treasure was lost, and my happiness vanished with it. This had everything to do with the dreaded Music Room Affair.

Azul's bark of "I will deal with you at home" when he came out from the headmaster's office after the school music room fire, was worse than his bite. At home, he ordered me to *Uhuru* in solitary confinement. I sat lonely and frightened, staring at the wall. I was sad that I had fallen low in Azul's esteem. Towards the evening, I sneaked out of *Uhuru* and ran to Mr Bondhu's quarters on Teacher's Lane. I knocked on his door and waited. He had asked me to play *Tanpura* with him the following Saturday at a recital he was performing at the Recreation Club. I already had a practice session with him. I wanted to explain to him that I had nothing to do with the music room fire. His wife opened the door. 'Yes?' she asked.

'Meme, I would like to speak to Mr Bondhu, please.'

'*Aji,* (dear), there is a boy wanting to talk with you,' Mrs Bondhu shouted. I heard ruffle of flip-flops, and Mr Bondhu came to the door, scratching his face. Upon seeing me, a flash of anger sailed through his face. '*Aae . . . lo,* after burning down my music room, why are you here?'

'Mr Bondhu, really, I did not do it. Honestly, sir.'

'Out, I don't want you to come near the music room.' With these words, he shut the door on me. Losing Mr Bondhu's trust and respect compounded my hurt and humiliation. Much later I was to learn that Gul had planted the crackers which led to music room fire. He had a score to settle with Mr Bondhu who had him nearly expelled for fondling a girl during a dance class. He had set fire to the music room to get his revenge.' This made Gul my public enemy number one

The humiliation of Mr Bondhu slamming his door in my face left me devastated. My special rocket on a trajectory to God's Symphony plummeted to the ground and with it my happiness vanished in a puff of smoke. I drifted like a rudderless ship on high seas and gradually began to adopt physics as my pet subject. The idea of scientific determinism had already taken root in my mind. I took up boxing to Rehmat's dismay. 'Play tennis, like Salim. It is more respectable,' she pleaded.

It was in the sphere of music that I made the greatest adjustment. My path to God's Symphony now became the soundtracks from cinema and especially Bollywood. Lata Mangeskar was the playback queen of Bollywood. There was no picture that did not have her playback. Every heroine had lip-synced to Lata's voice. Every song of hers was on the chart of Radio Ceylon's Hit Parade. She became my music goddess. Her velvety voice took me to heights of ecstasy. And so began my zig-zag path to God's Symphony.

During this time, despite my belief in scientific determination, I consulted the Tarot Card to see what future had in store for me. Its message was very encouraging: *The mist will lift and a path shall appear.* And so began to flower in my heart a hope that the promise of the Tarot was about to be delivered and that the Universe was conniving to fulfil this promise and a cosmic locksmith was at work shaping a key to a treasure.

My tension with Azul due to the Music Room Affair continued to simmer unabated. At dinnertimes heaviness hung around the table. Rehmat was uneasy. Jeff was more polite than usual. One evening during dinner, a beaming Azul said that he had engaged La Bohemia, the Belgian Jazz band to play at JCB next evening. 'Son,' he said to me, 'you like Jazz. Come and listen to them.' I mumbled an answer, nibbled at a few morsels, and excused myself from the table. After dinner, Henna and Salim came to *Uhuru*. 'Listen, brother,' Salim said, 'don't be so glum. We have brought you ice cream.' Henna hugged me and said, 'We know you are angry. But, let things simmer down. Daddy is trying to please you. Please, go to JCB and listen to La Bohemia. It'll make Daddy happy. But be careful. Only stay in the cafe. Don't go to the Blue Room. Jeff does not like that. I heard him argue with Daddy.'

'I would have come,' Salim said, 'but I have booked the tennis court at the YMCA.'

Internationally acclaimed La Bohemia playing in Jerusha was a feat if not a miracle. The following evening, I fought my way through a jazz-crazy crowd to get into JCB pulsing with excitement. I met Azul and asked him how he managed to engage La Bohemia. He beamed. 'Son, I thought of you when I heard that the band was stopping over for a night in Jerusha on their way to Nairobi. I made them a handsome offer, and they agreed.'

Mr Tiano, the manager, dapper in his signature tweed jacket and bowler hat, was delighted to see me. 'Welcome, son, it's going to be a fantastic evening. You just hang around by the stage and don't go into the crowd. I'll ask someone to look after you.'

At seven, La Bohemia made an entrance to a rapturous applause from the crowd and performed for almost an hour before taking a break. Enraptured in La Bohemia's solid gold performance, I had not noticed that every corner of JCB was packed, with spill over crowd sitting on the walls and others hanging like orang-utan on trees surrounding JCB. Suddenly, I heard a voice call out my name. I turned around and saw standing before me a coffee-tanned diva with arched eyebrows. A red hibiscus adorned her hair. 'Do you remember me?' she asked in a sweet voice. With the phantom strains of saxophone and trombone ringing in my ears, these words conjured up a world of romance. My mind reeled to the time when this beauty had come to our home to keep company with Shamim and I had tried to take her to the stars. Only a few days back, when I was trying to hear God's Symphony from our roof terrace, watching the night sky, her face had emerged mysteriously in the stars. I came to myself and said, 'Yes, you are Amina.' She handed me a tray of refreshments, 'This is for you. Don't stray from here.' Then she turned and left. Mesmerized, I watched her swaying hips as she walked and merged in to the milling crowd.

During the second half, I was absorbed in La Bohemia's Congolese and African Jazz renditions when I felt someone's hand on mine. I turned around and saw a smiling Amina sitting close to me. 'I came as soon as I finished my chores,' she whispered, pressing her shoulder against mine, her warmth radiating through my body.

The days that followed my short but sweet encounter with Amina at JCB became dream-like. My desire was to meet her again and again. My inner excitement was matched by the wave of excitement gripping Jerusha. At the Picture House, *Nagin*, the musical melodrama was breaking box office records. It was in its eighth week. Folks from surrounding towns and villages were flocking to Jerusha for it. To add to the excitement, our mayor performed the ground-breaking ceremony for a new town hall at Sogo Square in the presence of the newly arrived Israeli military advisers, amid much pageantry and fanfare. Businesses were booming, and Azul and Jeff were inordinately busy at JCB. One night during dinner, Azul and Jeff, with broad smiles on their faces, announced the construction of a wine garden at JCB. Explaining the details, Jeff said, 'The new dam construction is good for business. Many foreigners are coming to town. The Israelis will be here for several years. The cafes and bars along Boja are too rowdy for families. Our Blue Room already has a good reputation. When completed the wine garden will look like a miniature Crystal Palace.' Looking at me and Salim, Azul added, 'Our mayor will perform the ground-breaking tomorrow. Why don't you boys come at three for the ceremony?'

As usual, Salim was busy with something else and I went alone to a transformed JCB for the ground-breaking ceremony. Bunting and colourful paper decorations covered the front of JCB. Reclining couches and chairs lined the front saloon and cafe for the invited guests. Amina, in a green frock with hair sliding to the left, was busy directing a bevy of girls serving finger foods and libations to the invitees. The ease with which she mingled with people surprised me. When I had met her at our home, I had imagined her to be shy. She saw me and waved at me. Soon after, the City Brass Band played a Mendelssohn Symphony, and our honourable mayor performed the symbolic ground-breaking ceremony for the Wine Garden. 'Splendid design,' the mayor complemented Azul as he sipped a glass of wine after the ceremony. He added, 'Old chap, this is a superb wine. Best I have tasted since I came from the old country.'

I loitered around, hoping to talk to Amina. When it appeared this was not possible, I sighed and said aloud, 'I wish I could meet her alone'. Then I joined a gang of workers knocking down a shed behind the Wine Garden site. The key to the treasure that the cosmic locksmith was fabricating was about to be thrust into my hand. Many of my secret wishes were about to come true.

The shed behind JCB had always intrigued me. No one seemed to have a key to its locked door. When a worker jammed a crowbar and cracked open the door to the shed, the mist of future lifted. Eureka! The treasure that I had hoped for lay before me. Under a tarp were hundreds of 33-⅓-, 45-, and 78-RPM vinyl records and reels of audiotapes. This discovery flabbergasted me. Until that time, the only access to music I had were a few records in my collection and my Grundig shortwave radio that gave me fuzzy and crackling access to Radio Ceylon, VOK, and BBC. The Music Shop in Pala probably did not have as much music as what lay before me. Excited, I ran out to Azul. 'Daddy, I have found Ali Baba's treasure.'

'Son, what are you talking about?'

'Daddy, come,' I pulled him to the shed. Mr Tiano followed. The heaps of records and tapes surprised Azul, 'Good lord, this is incredible. I didn't know the old proprietor was music crazy.'

Mr Tiano pulled one record from its cover. 'Look at this one,' he exclaimed. It was Luis Armstrong's "Mack the Knife."

'This is good jazz gold,' he said. For the rest of the afternoon, Mr Tiano and I helped the workers move the record collection to the safety of Pumzika, which was a seldom-used staff room next to the kitchen. Pedro, JCB's head chef, argued with Mr Tiano not to use Pumzika as Amina used it as a prayer room. 'It's okay,' Mr Tiano replied, 'this won't prevent her.'

A thought has the potency to unleash conspiring events that seek to fulfil it. Discovery of Ali Baba's treasure was first such event towards fulfilment of my wish to meet Amina again and again. The next day, I came early to Pumzika and started to go through the priceless collection. It was world music at its best. Around noon, the door to Pumzika creaked. I looked up and saw Amina tying a scarf to her head. 'Sorry,' I apologised, 'I did not hear the prayer call.' As I prepared to leave, she bid me to sit. Soon she was engrossed in her prayers. I sat, pretending to work on the records, but her presence increased my heartbeat. She finished her prayers, untied her scarf and caught me looking at her. I quickly shifted my gaze to the records on the table. She smiled and asked, 'I have never seen so many records. What are they?'

'They are rock, jazz, country, Indian, everything. And I haven't yet touched the tapes.' Puzzled, she asked, 'What will you do with them?' I shrugged my shoulder. 'I don't know; listen to them, make a music library.'

'Okay, you play with your records. I will come back soon,' she said and left Pumzika and returned after a few minutes with a tray. 'Hold this,' she handed me the tray as she made room on the table. 'Please be careful,' I cautioned her as she moved the records.

'Relax, I won't damage them. Now leave the records and eat,' she commanded.

'What am I eating?'

'JCB special kofta.'

'Amina, you looked beautiful yesterday. I mean you are beautiful now,' I ventured.

'I knew there is something with you, you flirt.'

'I mean it,' I said. She extended her hand and felt my face. 'Good gracious. Are you shaving?' I felt embarrassed. 'That's good. Grow up fast so I can marry you,' she said. Her comment whipped up a storm in my heart.

I spent the next two weeks of school holiday cataloguing, and listening to a wonderful collection of world music. Mr Tiano asked a carpenter to build lockable cabinets in Pumzika to house the collection. Amina came every lunch hour and we ate lunch together after her mid-day prayers. One afternoon, I played her a record. 'What song is this?' she asked.

'It is from *Nagin*, picturized on Vyjayanthimala,' I explained.

'Who is she?'

'Don't you remember? Her projection was on my wall when you came looking for me.'

'Yes, I remember and you were shy,' Amina teased me, rubbing my leg with hers.

'I am surprised you don't know Vyjayanthimala,' I replied and extended my arm under the table and caught her leg. 'There, now you can't tickle me.' She giggled and asked, 'What music do you like the best?'

'Bollywood songs. Have you seen any Bollywood pictures?' I asked. She shook her head. 'No, never.' This surprised me. Amina's charm was beginning to entice me and lead me into a beguiling world. I resolved to take her to one picture show. But several hurdles stood in my way. We were prisoners of our prejudices and customs. One of the most powerful of these was the corner stone of the Circle of Love. It dictated whom one could mingle with and love. This irrefutable truth dawned on me when I toyed with the idea of taking Amina to *Nagin*. Ordinarily, it should be simple. However, in reality, it was not so. Despite Jerusha's easy-going social milieu, we were tribal. During the day people mingled with each other amicably. But, there were strata of class, caste, religion, and colour, which ruled our lives. In the evenings, we all went back to our homes, cast off our masks, and became tribal. There was no simple way for me to take Amina to a Bollywood picture or to any picture for that matter. I could not simply walk out hand in hand with her. First was our age difference. That was our first unwritten law. She was probably sixteen, and I was some years younger. Ruling social custom would never allow that. Next was her vocation. She was an uneducated bar hostess. It did not matter to me. However, in Jerusha, it would have significant social impact for my family. Then there was the question of tribe. This was one of the most formidable unwritten rules of all. Even tribes were stratified. Within Christians was the great divide between the Catholics and the Protestants. Muslims had the most vehement divisions between the Sunnis and the Shia. Hindus had their caste system. Amina was a Creole and in a different category altogether. My family, with all its outward liberalism, would raise an eyebrow at my association with her. And if I was able to somehow escape the watchful eyes of my family, there were the self-appointed morality police from society that would stop us. Our mingling within the confines of JCB, so long as it was innocent and not seen as leading to anything, was tolerable. Even in JCB, I had to be careful especially from the watchful eyes of Jeff. He did not like me walking into the Blue Room or the saloon. If I were bold enough to walk out with Amina, I would need to declare an intention of why I was with her. When I first told Amina about my intention to take her to a picture she asked in disbelief. 'Are you crazy? How?'

'I will think of a way. You will love *Nagin*. Some of the dances are in Geva Colour,' I replied.

'My crazy prince,' she commented, shaking her head.

Due to the heavy demand for *Nagin* tickets, I only managed to get advance tickets for an evening show two weeks away. The homely Picture House was too small for a popular picture like *Nagin*. The management overcame this disadvantage by putting extra chairs in every free corner of the cinema, adding to much confusion. This would give us an opportunity to sit together without too much attention. I gave her a ticket. 'It's a two-week advance ticket for Saturday's six o'clock show. Please make sure you arrive in time and go direct to your seat. Any seats not occupied after the lights are out will be taken.'

'Are you sure it will work?' she asked.

'Don't worry, I will follow you.'

'I will try,' she replied. Her lukewarm answer made me unsure if she would come.

A secret affair brings an emotional rush of a special kind. I arrived at a crowded Picture House clutching two Cadbury bars, anxious, excited and happy at the same time and waited for Amina. I was afraid that a large crowd would deter her so I stood on my toes looking out for her. As soon as I saw her, I rushed and made an eye contact and followed her into the cinema, which as expected was packed to capacity with extra chairs lining the aisles. I took my seat next to her as the lights dimmed and curtains lifted. I nudged her and handed her a Cadbury bar. On the screen, *Nagin* began to roll. We came to one song sequence with Vyjayanthimala in the frame on a moon-lit night. A gentle breeze played with her hair. In a close-up, Vyjayanthimala, love brimming from her eyes, was in the arms of her lover. The camera zoomed closer and then shifted and focused instead on the moon. The eroticism of a Bollywood picture was in what it omitted to show. The Indian Censor Board made sure no kissing was ever shown. The camera re-zoomed on flushed face of Vyjayanthimala. Then she lip-synced to the voice of Lata and danced:

O, my magician beloved
It is high time
My home is far
Release me from your love spell . . .

This scene transformed the homely Picture House into a magical far away dreamland. Amina and I were huddled together in the aura of enchanting magic of celluloid romance. She was clutching my arm, and her legs were entwined with mine.

Hyperbola of Life

Madam Doctor's voice reeled me back to the reality of her jungle bungalow. 'We'll leave as soon as I finish my notes.' I picked up the *Filmfare* that had dropped to my side. Jill, who was wearing an orange dress, wriggled down from her hands and ran to me. 'Tam, let's play horsey,' she said. It surprised me that she decided to call me Tam. She was holding Mickey in her hand. With injuries on my back, there was no way I could play horsey with her. 'How, if we paint in your book?' I replied and picked up pencils and a colouring book from the floor. 'Okay,' she said. I leaned against the sofa. She curled up in my lap. I sketched a flower in her colouring book and told her, 'Now colour this flower.'

'Tam, what colour do you like?' she asked.

'Pink,' I replied, pulling her cheek.

'Okay,' she said and started to colour the flower in black, looking up to me from time to time and giving me a coy smile. When she was bored, she pointed to the back garden.

'She'll enjoy a walk to the lake,' Madam Doctor, who was sitting at the table, said.

Jill walked holding my hand for the first few yards of the wooded path leading to the lake. Then I picked her up. As we came closer to the lake, only the increasing murmur of the waves lashing the rocks disturbed the soul satisfying stillness of the forest around us We stood at the edge of a cliff. Sunny glare from the lake dazzled us. Jill buried her face on my shoulder with her hands around my neck. I put my hand around her and cocooned her close to me. We stood in silence. Suddenly, she lifted her head and said, "Mickey". She had left him on the sofa. We walked back to the bungalow. She wriggled down, picked "Mickey" from the sofa, and ran to Amina. 'She is tired,' Amina said. I looked at my watch. Madam Doctor noticed this and said that we would be on our way soon. Amina put Jill to bed. Madam Doctor asked me to follow her to Jill's room. Jill was sucking her thumb, half-asleep. Madam Doctor lifted up her blanket and pointed to Jill's chest which was heaving up and down like a bellow. 'Hole in the heart,' Madam Doctor whispered. We walked out of the room. Amina and Madam Doctor stood talking in the corridor. Jill's heart condition distressed me. I thought of Nina. Why was Madam Doctor sharing all this information with me? Amina stood with her back towards me. I wished she would turn so I could gaze on her face, a face that I had grown used to. 'Grow up, so I can marry you' was what she had told me at JCB. It had thrilled me then; I mean who would not be thrilled with an invitation like that. Then the tide turned and our lives went off in different directions like the ends of a hyperbola on the day of the Gossage Football Final.

During one Algebra class, Mr Husna weaved the magic of mathematics. He wrote an equation on the blackboard and said, 'This equation represents a hyperbola. It is like an Australian boomerang, with its two ends going off to infinity. They never meet.' For the rest of his lesson, I played with the hyperbola equation, trying to grasp the idea of infinity. At the end of the lesson, I approached Mr Husna, 'Sir, when the two ends of hyperbola go off to infinity, how far do they go?' Mr Husna looked at me, perplexed and said. 'What do you mean, how far do they go? They go off to infinity.' The projected ends of a hyperbola disappearing in space confused me. I told Mr Husna my idea of how to bring the two ends of the hyperbola together. He laughed and said, 'Good try, but it is impossible.'

My first impression of Madam Doctor at the Market Square was of a mathematician who could bring back together the two diverging lines of a hyperbola. I had no idea why such a thought came to my mind. On reflection, I did not think Madam Doctor was as helpless as she had pretended to be at the Market Square. I think she had carefully play-acted the whole episode of being helpless. Seeing Amina talking to Madam Doctor, I now saw the reason why I had thought of Madam Doctor as a mathematician who could bring together diverging lines of a hyperbola. She had indeed succeeded in that impossible task. How else could have Amina emerged from the womb of time, when I had made an understanding with fate, against my belief in determinism, that she was gone forever?

However, I also realised that life was not how it used to be. The Waveform Collapse that happened in the City Light during *CID* in the intervening years had rewritten the script of my life. In Palita I had found my soul mate from before the creation of time. My heart resonated with her. I was in Quantum Entanglement with her. With acute pain I grasped the essence of the philosophical statement: a river is never the same, twice.

Back in Green Ford: Cold Kofta and Pepsi

We are simply product of our antecedence. My current state was a result of past events; all linked tightly together like a chain. The precision with which everything had happened amazed me. Nina's Birthday which we had celebrated only on Thursday, seemed so long ago. Following it, yesterday, Friday at dawn I had a dream in which I saw six faces. This was an important link in this chain of events. I did not know whose faces they were and what they meant. Soon after this dream, Yasukuni Shrine picture fell from the wall in *Uhuru* which in my sleepy state I thought was an atomic bomb blast. Rehmat thought that the breaking of glass early in the morning was an omen and that ancestor spirits were unhappy. I secretly thought this not to be plausible, but Henna prevented me from saying anything to the contrary as it may offend Rehmat who had decided to hold a *Majalis* and following it a feast next week to appease the spirits of the dead. Soon after, Mr Perry from the YMCA came home and invited me to join the boxing training camp at Lake Textiles. This was no small honour for me. I was not even that good a boxer. In the evening, meeting Zafur my boxing coach, at Old Thompson Hotel came as a complete surprise. I had not met him since the night the ruffians had tried to attack him with a *Rampuri* at the midnight show of *Barsaat Ki Raat* at the Palladium in Pala. At the Old Thomson, Zafur introduced me to Savi, the legend of Jerusha Secondary School who was with James Bond Film Crew. However, when dancing with her in the elegant Emerald at Old

Thompson yesterday I sensed a great sadness and turmoil in her heart. She cried on my shoulder. It disturbed me, but I did not probe Savi about it. I was to have breakfast with Zafur and Savi in the morning, but when I left the hotel, the concierge told me that Zafur had left the hotel at dusk and had not returned. I surmised that may be Zafur had gone to the Saturday dawn Fish Market. I also wondered if Savi and Zafur had spent the night together. If that was the case tongues would wag all over town. Savi was already maligned enough. I liked Savi. I would do anything to protect her. I was looking forward to our "date" at JCB a week on Saturday to view Watanabe's Hiroshige paintings. Madam Doctor interrupted my chain of thoughts, 'Now, we leave.' On hearing this Amina's eyes became clouded and she asked, 'Madam, would you not stay for lunch?'

'Sorry I have another appointment in the afternoon, and this young man must go home before he is missed,' she replied.

We drove in Madam Doctor's green Ford in silence towards Jerusha. Madam Doctor was pensive. I was not sure why she had brought me in a hurry to the jungle bungalow. Things remained unexplained. I waited. I put my head on the headrest. The drone of the Ford relaxed me. The black and white spiral rotated anticlockwise in my mind . . .

Amina was the magnet that pulled me to JCB. While I catalogued and organised JCB's music library she kept me company. Handling JCB's music collection, I understood that God's Symphony, if ever there was one, must encompass not only Indian Classical Music which Mr Bondhu said flowed out of Lord Shiva's five faces, but also world music. I realized that music had infinite forms. The soul-shaking vibrancy of African American gospel in the thundering voice of Mahalia Jackson, the ecstatic vibrations of the Spanish guitar and Flamenco dance music, the playful simplicity of Congolese Jazz or the hip-shaking, emergent phenomenon of Elvis and Bill Haley's Rock music and Beatles pop songs were all part of God's symphony. I had to simply synthesize these into one mighty orchestra to hear God's Symphony. I had the dictionary in my hand. All I had to do was to weave a story.

With Azul's permission, during school holidays and weekends, I started to play selective music from the collection for the Blue Room. Mr Tiano built me a booth just to the right of the saloon, on the cafe side, but in reality, it was more within the saloon. He set up two different stations within the booth, one that channelled the music to Blue Room and the other to the saloon. The "literate" loved what I played. De facto I became the music manager for JCB. Many folks brought their own music for me to play. A new trend began. The "literate" began to bring their wives and Blue Room became civil and elegant. For JCB's more pedestrian front saloon, I selected local music. Azul paid me a compliment. 'Son, your music is leading very nicely to the opening of the Wine Garden.'

One evening when Jeff was not around, I ventured into the Blue Room. Amina was with a group of Canadian wives, topping their glasses with bubbly champagne. She looked irresistible in her turquoise dress. She ignored me, which made me restless. I hid in the music booth. After a while, to my surprise, she brought me a glass of orange juice and hung around without saying much. I pretended to be angry. Suddenly, she bent down and kissed me smack on my lips. I felt her moist lips on mine. Before she left she said, 'Prince, I want to be with you.'

'Amina, we can go to *Chori Chori* releasing next week,' I suggested.

'No, no picture, I want to be alone with you,' she replied. It was a daunting task to find a place where we could be alone. I had an idea so I said, 'Meet me next Saturday at seven near Naran Road at Sikh Temple.'

Sex education in Jerusha came packaged in curious modules. Despite efforts by crusaders like Savi, it remained self-taught. Sex became a topic of hot discussion in our class around the time of my first escapade to *Nagin* with Amina. We slurped up anything that satisfied our curiosity. Japanese *Manga* and Taiwanese girly magazines showing beautiful nudes in inviting poses became a huge success in our class. Three weeks after *Nagin* Silver

Jubilee, Arvind caught up with me in town and asked me, 'Einstein, would you like to play cricket? We are a player short in our Ragota Eleven.' I still had pain in my chest, thanks to the knuckleduster blow from Gul's companion during *Nagin* Fete. Seeing my hesitation, he said, 'I will give you cut-frames from *Lolita*.' I agreed. This friendly match against the English was memorable for two reasons. Despite my rib injury, I took two wickets and forced the English to declare. The second reason was Sex Education Lesson 2 which I learned during the game. While the Ragota opening batsmen battled the English, the rest of us sat in the pavilion, sipping orange juice and munching samosas. As was the routine at such gatherings, the subject of love, and sex came up. Taking a gulp of orange juice, Arvind declared, 'Do you know, if you have sex with a girl whom you don't love, your erection will never go away.' Everyone laughed. Arvind was serious. Anu, the wicket keeper retorted, 'Arvind, you talk rubbish. It is the other way around. If you don't love the girl, she can lock you in.'

'How do you mean, lock you in?' Arvind asked.

'That's what I mean, lock you in. During sex, she asks you, "Do you love me?" If you lie, she would not release your key until you say you love her.' There was lot of hand waving and laughter. I was in the company of boys, three or four years my senior. I just listened. Everyone had a good laugh debating these interesting perspectives on sex. However, for me, these issues raised a very important point about love and sex. What Arvind and Anu said stuck in my mind like a mantra: No love, no sex. This was my sex lesson 2. The idea of a permanent erection or being locked in the keyhole of a girl due to loveless sex was so humiliating. I discussed this in private with Joger. He asked if I had heard it from Arvind or Anu. When I confirmed, he laughed, shaking his head. 'Permanent erection? Where is your scientific brain, you gullible virgin? These boys are taking you for a ride. Do you know some people have difficulty even getting it up let alone permanent erection?'

I bought two takeaways from Sukh Sagar and waited at the corner of a quiet Naran Road for Amina. I saw her silhouette against the bright lights of the Sikh Temple, walking towards me. Eager to be with her, I crossed the road and joined her and together we walked towards Moon Bakery. 'Where are you taking me?' she asked.

'Some where safe.'

'I hope it is not like how you wanted to take me to the stars,' she teased me.

'Trust me Amina. I have the keys to our Club. We could dry off and eat there,' I comforted her. At the Club, I locked the door behind us and lighted a candle that we always kept due to frequent power cuts. The walls turned amber. 'I am sorry about the sweaty smell,' I apologised. Amina smiled. 'It is all right. I am used to it. You should smell some of the people in the saloon when they come after work.' Her eyes followed me in the wavering candlelight as I spread sit-up mats on the floor. I told her, 'Amina we should have gone to *Chori Chori* at the Picture House. These Raj and Nargis pictures are very popular. I hear one song setting is very sexy. I have the record. When I come to JCB, I will play it for you.'

'And what is the story?'

'These pictures are romance at first, bit of crying and problems in the middle, and a happy ending. We can go see it. I personally don't like Raj. In one picture, he dragged Nargis by her hair. What lover would treat his beloved like that?'

'Prince you are too nice . . . that's why I love you.' As soon as she said this, Amina blushed. It was hot in the room. I undid my shirt buttons and took out a towel from my sports bag that hung on the wall and fanned it to get some air. Amina rummaged through the food bags and asked, 'What have you brought?'

'Kofta from Sukh Sagar. I am not sure how it compares with JCB?'

'JCB's is the best in town' Amina replied as she gathered the takeaway bags and sat close to me. In the dancing candle-light her skin glistened like gold. Her wet clothes clung to her form. 'Amina your hair is totally wet. Shall I dry it?' I asked. She tilted her head in my direction. I dried and massaged it. 'It feels nice' she said, running her hand over my bare chest. I drew her closer. She looked up. Our lips met. I fumbled and undid her blouse. There was hesitancy in our ardour but our desire overcame the clumsiness of clothing. I felt the silkiness of her skin. Our bodies met and we became one. We stayed together for a long time. Late at night we shared the cold kofta and a Pepsi which I always hid behind an air vent.

The Ghost of Somero Square

The enchanting morning reflected my inner state. I woke up happy, savouring the sweetness of my intimacy with Amina. Without even knowing it, I had walked over the threshold into manhood. With this realisation, my mood changed. The mantra of my sex lesson 2 exploded in my mind like a bomb: No love, no sex. I checked and was comforted that I did not have a permanent erection. Gosh it would be so scandalous if I had one! But that was not the point. I had broken my own rule. In Amina's company and in the heat of the moment, my mantra had not surfaced into my consciousness. The romance and the heart thumping reality of being alone with Amina had kept out all other thoughts. In the muggy reality of morning I asked a fundamental question: Did I love Amina, or was it loveless sex? I examined my feelings for her. I enjoyed every minute of every day I spent with her. I fantasised about her and yearned to be with her. My heart trembled when I thought of her. Was this love? The bluish mistiness of the Love Circle confused me. I felt that after our intimacy I needed to open my heart to Amina and express my feelings at the soonest. This thought and sex lesson 2 kept playing in my mind over and over again.

Then my mind took a turn and I thought of Narika's dance in *Uhuru* and her confession of love. There was no way I could have responded to her love. I knew from *Splendour in the Grass* what unrequited love did to a heart. Natalie Wood portrayed it well. I felt sorry for Narika. I was on an emotional seesaw. My urge to confess my love to Amina and at the same time, my feelings of tenderness towards Narika were causing me deep anxiety. Despite free-love mania sweeping Europe and its light-hearted and often frivolous portrayal in Hollywood blockbusters, in our nick of woods, love was a serious business. Unlike Oscar Wilde's portrayal of faithfulness in love as a confession of failure, faithfulness in love was everything in our part of the world. Oscar Wilde lived and loved in London and geography in love did matter. Jerusha was not London and did not have exposure to or freedom of mingling with the fairer sex in schools, social clubs, theatres, and lovely parks which encouraged the resonances and de-resonances of hearts at the drop of a hat. Under these conditions faithfulness in love could be a confession of failure. In Jerusha the germination of romantic feelings between young people could only happen in two settings: school assembly or Pier Park on Sundays. The choice was limited. A single smile or a false murmuring of heart for the fairer sex was amplified a million times in the mind and a beautiful poetry or a *ghazal* was written in commemoration of such an event.

How can I rest,
When she has cast her eyes on me
With such love

Faithlessness under such circumstances would be unthinkable and if it did happen, then the affected party would seek to drown his sorrows in neat Scotch at the *Ghazal* Circle or contemplate Hara-kiri. The weaker sex would burn in fire of inner hell as portrayed in so many Bollywood pictures. Most of the popular Lata songs were laments of faithlessness of the lover.

You, who have spurned me
Let your faithlessness burn you
And make you shed tears of blood

My morning passed in such musings. In the afternoon, I was walking across Somero Square on my way to Tembo na Membe to play darts with my friends when a ghostly shadow grabbed my arm. It startled me. In bright sunshine Somero Square, which in reality was a quadrangular, was a lovely place. Several old mavule trees graced the square. Old Somero Church stood at the Zanzibar Road end of the Square. We played cricket in the Square on weekends. An overgrown patch of shrubs, and spiky acacia interlaced with red bougainvillea occupied the space between the church and the cricket pitch. In the middle of this patch were several old graves. In the distant past as the story went, a woman was raped and murdered here. Since then all sorts of ghost stories circulated. As years went by more stories were added to it.

I regretted having walked across Somero Square in the rainy gloom of Sunday afternoon. The hand that grabbed me was that of a boy. 'Gosh, Luke,' I cried out aloud, 'you frightened me.' He pulled me to the shelter of Old Somero Church. 'Luke, what is the matter?' I asked. I could not fathom his expression in the darkness.

I first met Luke under excruciating circumstances at Recluse Lane behind Nur Gift Shop which was a hangout for petrol-sniffers and grog addicts. Over time people who had withdrawal tendencies began to live here in corrugated sheet shacks. An old custom of Recluse Lane encouraged many people to become day recluses on Thursday when a man parked a trolley at the entrance to the Recluse Lane and sold refined grog concocted from methylated spirit and rum. And it was cheap. It was a day of great rejoicing. To enhance the joy of revelry, an eccentric recluse carried an HMV record player, a collection of 78-RPM vinyl records, and played requests for a Ducat. Some of the recluses, petrol-sniffers and grog addicts formed a circle and danced around the HMV player.

One afternoon Rehmat had sent me on an errand to Market Square with Jeremy. A trip to Market Square was always an adventure. Mid-afternoons were particularly energetic when promoters showered free cigarettes on eager crowds or gave away key chains. Fortunately, on the afternoon I arrived at the Market Square, no such promotions were in progress. I made the necessary purchases for Rehmat and handed the bag to Jeremy. 'You please go home. Mother is waiting. Don't loiter,' I told him.

'Give me two Ducats for a drink. It is too hot,' Jeremy demanded. I threw him a couple of Ducats. He was happy and was on his way home. I crossed the Market Square to the crowded bazaar and was near Nur Gift Shop on my way to Moidin for a cup of Chino, when I saw a jeering crowd at the entrance to Recluse Lane. Against my better judgment I walked closer to Nur Gift Shop to see what was happening. Mr Nur, the proprietor of Nur Gift Shop was standing on an elevated ledge of his shop looking into the crowd. On seeing me, he shouted, 'Quick, save that boy. They will beat him to death.'

'What has he done?' I asked.

'May be stolen something…be quick, before they kill him.' This thieving business in Jerusha as in the rest of East Africa was a serious offence because every person survived on bare minimum; everyone was poor and respected the dignity of labour. The pittance that people earned went to purchases of a small scoop of cooking oil, few ounces of salt or sugar or a loaf of bread or flour to feed the family. A thief who stole from the poor was at once seen as a blot to society and if caught would be beaten mercilessly unless the police intervened and saved him. So, that afternoon when Mr Nur asked me to intervene to save a thief, I hesitated and said, Mr Nur if I interfere people would turn on me.'

'*Arre,* don't be a coward,' Mr Nur hissed, 'here, take this.' He gave me a green pass and a wade of one-Ducats notes. 'Show them this poll tax pass. Throw this money to the crowd. Say you will hand him over to the police; hurry.' I could not ignore Mr Nur's challenge. Without much of a thought I grabbed the green pass and the money and plunged into the crowd. At the epicentre of the disturbance the mob was savagely beating a young boy. He was about my age. I held the green pass in the air and shouted. 'Stop, please. I have his poll tax pass. He works for Azul.

Chukwa pesa, take this money. I will hand him over to the police. Please.'
The colour of money worked wonders. The beating stopped. A man said,
'He stole from me.' I handed him several Ducats. The rest I threw in the
air. People ran for the money. I grabbed the bleeding boy and rushed out
of the crowd. Mr Nur signalled me to bring him to the back of his shop
where we cleaned his wounds with swabs of Dettol and applied tincture of
iodine to his wounds. Between his sobs the boy told us that his name was
Luke. He had come from the dreaded McKenzie corridor south of Jerusha
which had been ravaged by a second malaria epidemic. He was an orphan.
'Why are you at Recluse Lane?' Mr Nur asked. 'I was hungry. I wanted to
forget my shame with spirit.' Mr Nur gave me money to bring food from
the market for Luke.

Mr Nur sheltered Luke in the storeroom behind his shop for the night. At
home, I told Azul about Luke and begged him to help Luke. 'Bring him
to the warehouse tomorrow. We need a yard boy,' he replied. The next day
Azul employed Luke in one of our coffee warehouses on Spice Road. 'He
can live in the quarters behind the warehouse,' Azul said.

Luke and I became friends. I found him angry and with a knot in his
heart. One Sunday afternoon, while fishing in shallow waters of Peace Lake
at the edge of the lotus garden near Old Thompson Hotel, I watched him
stand in knee-deep water with a bamboo spear in his hand, in meditation
like a heron. He stood still, his deep sunken eyes trained on the gentle
waves, looking beneath the water. He fitted the Christian description of
a fisher of man. He taught me the art of Zen. 'Just look at the water. Do
not strain. Let your mind focus on the image of a fish and it will come to
you. You will be able to look beneath the water.'

I mimicked him. I began to see beneath the waves. I was delighted
when I speared one fish. He complimented me. 'You are fast. It took me a
week of frustration before I could spear one,' he added.

When we had speared two fish, we walked ashore. Luke gathered
some kindle and started to light a fire to barbeque the fish. I sat beside

him and asked, 'Luke, what is burning in your heart?' The abruptness of my question surprised him. He continued lighting the fire. I waited and watched kingfishers dive in the simmering waves. When the fire was lit, Luke handed me a leather-bound book from his bag. 'What is it?' I asked, watching his face, which reminded me of Moses in *The Ten Commandments*. His lips tightened. He looked up and the lines on his forehead came together like folds of an accordion. He spoke, 'When my family died of malaria, the missionaries came and took us to Sia on the shore of Lake Salisbury for three years.' The pit fire flamed out. Luke knelt and blew on it to rekindle it. Then he continued, 'A priest befriended me. This father did bad things, painful things. I stole this book from him. After doing those bad things, he read aloud from this book.'

I leafed through the book with faded handwritten notes in the margins. 'Luke this is a Bible. What did this father read?' Luke grimaced, clasped his hands together in pain of recollection. 'One afternoon this father held me back in a farm shed. I wanted to leave with the other boys, but he said he wanted my help. In the shed, he did me. I felt dirty and angry.' Tears streamed down Luke's cheeks. He continued, 'Afterwards this father held the book and knelt down and prayed, "Lord, I am of the people of Lot. Have mercy on me".' I was speechless. I held the Bible tightly in my hand. Luke put his hand on mine. 'You are my good friend. Please find from this book where he read and explain to me about Lot, and why this father did what he did to me.'

I cleared my throat. 'Luke it is difficult to find exactly where in the Bible he read from. I have not read the Bible that well.' Luke heard me yet he did not. His voice became intense, 'You read me . . . read me, read me.'

I cast back my mind. I had done one year of Bible studies with Mr Githinji. I remembered him talking about sin and hope in the Bible. I remembered that he had quoted some verses from Genesis that mentioned Lot. I eagerly opened the Bible to Genesis and leafed through it. At verse 19, I found what I was looking for. I looked at Luke. 'Tell me,' he said eagerly.

I said to him, 'I will tell you a story from Genesis. Tell me if you heard something like it.' He invited me to speak by his hand gesture.

'God saw that Sodom was a place of sin and wickedness. He sent two angels in the form of men to Sodom to find out how wicked the men were. When the men of Sodom saw the two strangers they followed them. Lot, who was a pious man, saw the evil desire of the wicked men and gave the two angels shelter in his house. The people of Sodom demanded that Lot give up the two angels. He refused and offered his virgin daughters to them instead. The men declined this, and the angels struck them blind. Even in their blindness they wanted to break Lot's door.'

'Yes,' Luke grabbed my arm, excited and shaking and said, 'this is what he read.'

'What else did this father say?' I asked. Luke thought for a while. He remembered, 'What does Lamb of God mean?' he asked.

'Luke I am not sure, but Jesus is known as Lamb of God. When he came to John the Baptist, John said "Behold, the Lamb of God who takes away the sins of the world".'

'That is what this father said to me after he did his dirty thing. He put his hand on my shoulder and said, "Be happy my lad. For it is in sin that we experience the mercy of the Lord. The Lamb of God shall take away my sin. And . . . and he will bless you for being the vessel through which I experience his mercy".'

When I heard Luke, I burst out, 'That is wicked what this father did and said.' Luke buried his face between his knees put his hands to his head, and wept violently. After a while he lifted his head. His eyes were burning like red charcoals, 'What did God do to Sodom?' he asked.

'He destroyed Sodom.'

'Destroy mean kill?' he asked angrily.

'Yes destroyed Sodom with a fire of sulphur,' I replied. Luke shook his head and started to cry again. I put my hand around him to comfort him. Finally, he said in a low voice, 'I destroyed him. I destroyed this father. That afternoon in that farm shed he did something he had never done before. He knelt and prayed holding me. Then he unzipped his trousers and offered me his . . . in my mouth. I turned away. He scolded me . . . made me kneel and forced me. My mouth was full. I was frightened and ashamed. He continued to thrust and then . . .'

'And then what?'

'I closed my mouth with all the strength. My teeth bit into him. He cried beating on my head. He was like the fish that we speared today flapping about and helpless. My mouth was full of blood. I left him bleeding. He groaned and twisted on the floor. I ran away.'

'Oh, my goodness! . . . My goodness! What happened after?' I asked.

'I went back to my dorm and washed my face. I lay in my bed, praying. In the morning, there was a loud cry in the mission. Priests found this father hanging in his room. They were too ashamed to talk about it. After a week, I ran away from the mission.'

Luke worked in our coffee warehouse for a few months. During weekends, we played cricket. He jumped with joy every time he stumped me. Then he ran away. I never saw or heard from him until the ghostly encounter with him in Somero Square when I was on my way to meet my friends at Tembo na Membe.

'Where have you been all this time, Luke?' I repeated my question.

'I joined the army,' he replied. 'We were killing children and women. I hated it. I ran away. My wife is ill. I need money. The doctor says she'll need medicine for months.' He groped for my hand in the dark as he said this. I pulled out a wad of Ducat notes. 'Is this enough?' Luke lighted a match and held it up between our faces. From close-up, his face looked older and rugged. I put the money in his free hand. He said in a choking voice 'Junior I owe a lot to you and your daddy. I will repay you.' The matchstick flamed out. He melted away in the darkness.

Don't Stand and Stare

I made my way to Tembo na Membe and had hardly played a round of darts with my friends when Azul came to fetch me home. This surprised me. On our way, he informed me that due to a breakout of coffee disease in Brazil, the coffee price in London had jumped. We had tons of coffee in our warehouse in Nirambeya which needed to be graded and shipped out. 'It is a good opportunity for profit,' Azul said. He wanted me to stay in Nirambeya to help grade the coffee. 'It will take only a few days' he pleaded. 'But Daddy, I have plans for my school holidays. Why can't Jeff go?'

'Jeff and I are busy with the Wine Garden construction. And besides there are people who want to steal JCB from our hands. The Canadian Mining Company has plans to build their head office and a warehouse around Market Square and JCB is gold dust. That Ben is grabbing as much land as he can. I can't leave JCB for a minute.' Azul left me no choice. At home, I packed my bag and Azul drove me to Nirambeya. All my plans were ruined. I was yearning to meet Amina and declare my love to her. I was angry.

Nirambeya had its own charm and rewards. The last time I visited it I had become aware of God's Symphony. There was something interesting in store for me during my second visit. The coffee grading which Azul said would take a few days took good two weeks. On the last day before my return to Jerusha I went to a local jungle market with Masrubu, our foreman, to look for custard apples. While Masrubu was busy scouting the market for these, a trader enticed me. 'Young man, come look at my wares. They are magic cures for everything. This will make you a stud and women will fall at your feet asking for more. But for you, I have something special. You wait.' Something about this trader captivated me. He returned and dangled a green agate necklace with mesmerising quality in front of me. His deep guttural voice rang in my ears, 'This is a stone of love. Behold the two hearts on it. You have a friend who loves you and wants you to buy this stone. She has an angelic face. She is calling for you . . .' I began to drift into a trance and a smiling Amina stood right in front of me. The vividness of the impression gave me goose pimples. I reached out and grabbed the agate in my hand, and threw money at the foxy trader like confetti. Sla . . . p, I felt a violent smack to my face. 'Junior,' Masrubu's voice thundered in my ears, 'what are you doing? This man is a magician. He is casting a spell.' Masrubu grabbed all the money that he could from the trader and rebuked him. 'You rascal, *na danganya,* cheating a young boy.' The foxy trader pocketed some of the money he already had and wrapped up his stall.

What was I thinking? Having seen Rudyard Kipling's *Kim,* I should have known better not to stare at a dangling stone and be mesmerised. When I counted my remaining money, I had paid handsomely for the necklace. On scrutiny, the agate appeared to be more valuable than what I had paid for. Green agates were rare, and this one had within it crystallised inclusions known as drusy which had formed two shadowy heart shapes on its face.

When I returned from Nirambeya, Jerusha was pulsing with a different rhythm. At the heart of it all was football, the passion of Africa. A venue dispute between cities had forced the Football Federation to stage upcoming important matches of Gossage Tournament in neutral Jerusha. This was nothing less than the announcement of a Papal visit. When I returned to Jerusha, cigarette, soda and beer companies, Kimbo margarine and Ambi and Moono Snow skin lightening cream companies had plastered every conceivable free space on Africa Street and Boja Road with their bright, colourful advertisement posters. Nearer home Captain Leman, who had almost died due to a snake bite, had revived after Rehmat had applied a poultice of home remedy to his wound.

The first match kick-off was at five. Just before noon I rushed to JCB to meet Amina. In my hurry and anxiety, I had forgotten to take with me the precious agate necklace for which I had paid good money to the foxy trader at Nirambeya market. I did not have enough time before midday prayer to go home and get it. Not wanting to meet Amina empty-handed, I purchased a white silk scarf with a rosette of pink Sakura flowers from Nur Gift Shop. The recluses from Recluse Lane were milling around the refined grog vendor for their weekly spirit fix, just behind Nur Gift Shop. Many recluses high on spirit were dancing around the one-Ducat gramophone jukebox. I stopped briefly to watch their merriment. A bearded recluse with beady, playful eyes stood patiently in the queue for his spirit. I recognised him. He was a good artist. One of his paintings hung at the Grand Hotel reception in Pala. He saw me looking at him and growled. 'What are you starring at?'

'I am sorry I didn't mean to. Actually, I wanted to ask you if you have any paintings I can buy?' He scratched his unkempt beard. 'Ha . . . how you know I paint?' he asked.

'I have seen you deal with the art dealer,' I replied.

'That rascal he is robbing me blind,' the recluse lamented.

'How much does he pay you?' I asked. The recluse shook his head and replied. 'He only pays for the spirit. I asked him to get me some white and grey pastels and I am still waiting. He has reduced me to making my own colours by rubbing bricks and mixing it with this spirit. I must admit the effect is stunning.'

'Why did you become a recluse?' I asked. He blinked his eyes and made a dismissive hand gesture. I asked the same question again. 'You are an obstinate fellow,' he commented and then told me that he had imported

Rayon Technology from Japan and had set up Smart Axle. His girlfriend and his lawyer betrayed him and wrestled the company away from him. I asked, 'Are you Mr Axle?'

'Yes' he replied. When I asked him how he learnt the Japanese painting techniques, he explained that he had attended a painting school in Japan where he learned Hiroshige paintings techniques. I felt sorry that "fate" had turned a talented man to paint with brick powder. I told him to wait. I rushed to Nur Gift Store and purchased a 128-piece painting set, making sure it had white and grey pastels, and gave it to him. He thanked me with tearful eyes. 'I can't repay you. That rascal Nur does not allow us in his shop. He says we make his shop smell.' Before I left, Axle said to me, 'Come back next week. I will have painted you a nice Sakura, scene with cherry blossoms in full bloom in Tokyo. Families picnicking . . . children chasing floating cherry blossoms in the park. I will paint that magic for you.' I promised him that I would come back for the painting and went on my way to JCB

The Arrow of Time

An unusual sight greeted my arrival at JCB. People were milling about on the pavement, sipping beers. The front double doors of JCB which never closed, were drawn in. This was unusual. I asked a man what had happened. He gulped beer from a bottle he had in his hand, wiped his face and replied, 'Electrical problem. Everyone had to evacuate.' Mr Tiano saw me and came rushing. 'Son, take our driver and get a new fuse box from Jack's Electrical before the health inspectors show up. There is a fire in the back. All food will be ruined. We are starting the backup generator.'

I rushed off to get the fuse box. When I returned, the rag fire was tamed. The electrician installed the new fuse box and JCB was humming again. I immediately rushed to Pumzika to look for Amina. It was locked. I ran to Blue Room. Amina was not there either. A jazz band started playing "Take Five" in the Wine Garden. I heard the midday call to prayers from the mosque. Hoping that Amina would have made her way to Pumzika, I walked towards it and stopped at the door of a cubicle called Sofa Room opposite Pumzika. In the olden days, Sofa Room was where customers spent their "happy hour" in the company of females. During planning of Wine Garden Mr Tiano reprieved it from demolition to convert it into a wine storage room.

Over the hum of the standby generator and hammering of the piano and the puffing of trombone in the Wine Garden, I could hear moaning from the inside of the Sofa Room. I put my ear to its cracked door. Some

215

sort of struggle was in progress. I took a step back and kicked the door open. Two semi-naked men had sandwiched Amina between them. Her crumpled skirt was above her waist. One man was gagging her. A volcano erupted in my mind. My muscles tensed and in black rage I grabbed a piece of wood lying by the door and rushed in and whacked the man nearest to me. The piece of wood broke into pieces. The man slumped to the floor with a grunt as his chest deflated like a burst balloon. I punched the man who was gagging Amina. Blood sprouted from his face. Amina slumped to the floor. I cried out and knelt down to support her. I pulled down her skirt. My cry must have alarmed people outside the Sofa Room. Pedro, JCB's head chef, rushed in and grabbed me by the shoulder. 'What happened?' he asked. More men appeared at the door. It turned dark. Pedro whisked me out. Mr Tiano calmed me and asked Osmani, our driver, to take me home.

I sat on my bed trembling, taking deep breaths. Osmani informed me that I was not to leave home and that he would stay and watch me. 'It is Mr Tiano's order,' he replied. He went and stood at the gate like a sentry. Rehmat and girls were at a women's party which would go on until late. During sport events and political rallies when men were busy, women organised such parties.

I sat in *Uhuru*, numb, not knowing what to do. The gory event at JCB corroded my heart. I tried to read a book, but nothing made sense. I switched on the radio but did not have the motive to tune it. It sat making hissing noise. It began to turn dark. Birds made their homecoming calls, circled above the trees, and settled down in their nests. Osmani stood guard at the gate, smoking. The house was quiet. Why was no one coming home? I was frightened. I wanted to be with Amina. Where was she? Finally, I put on my canvass shoes and ran on to Forest Drive through the back gate. I jogged along the railway tracks. My feet led to Amina's rooming house where she shared a room with another girl. It was in darkness. I knew that the landlady did not allow male visitors so I walked stealthily to the back, skirting a garden overgrown with grass and shrubs and started to climb up a drainpipe to the balcony. A yellow light shone from Amina's room next to the balcony. I was half way up when a clamp broke with a loud metallic bang and the drainpipe swung out. I hung on to the drainpipe like an orang-utan. In the meantime a girl shouted, 'Thief . . .' I lost my balance and fell. My left leg buckled under me at the knee as I hit the ground. I cried out in agony as something sharp punctured my sole. I felt I was drowning in the murky waters of hell. A curtain of darkness blanketed me. When I regained consciousness, the girl was still shouting, "*muisi, muisi,*" thief, thief. Someone blew a panic whistle. A light came on in the balcony. The electric shout of "*muisi*" and succession of short bursts of the panic whistles mobilised many people. A mob ran towards me. It would beat me to death unless I hid. I straightened my knee, pulled my leg away from whatever was poking through it, and crawled into the safety of a bush enmeshed with climbers. A few men reached the spot where I had fallen. They looked at the dangling drainpipe and surmised that the thief must have run into the back alley. I held my breath. The men ran into the back alley.

The pain and burning in my sole became excruciating. I extended my hand and felt a piece of glass poking through my blood-soaked tennis shoe. I pulled off the piece of glass, took my shoe off and pressed over a deep, oozing wound. Fear of *muisi* phobic mob on the prowl out in the alley forced me to stay where I was. I chewed on grass blades, made a fibrous pad and tied it over my wound with the scarf I had purchased for Amina. My left knee felt like a rock. I lifted my leg, wedged it against a tree trunk with great difficulty, and pressed it with my right leg. Then I levered my body. The knee bone snapped into place with an explosion that shook every fibre in my body. I shivered and began to feel faint. 'Keep awake,' I kept repeating. I lost track of time. I ran my hand over the blood-soaked scarf. It was tight and snug. I put the shoe back on and stood up with a numbing pain. I trudged home at a snail's pace through dark alleys avoiding all lighted areas.

Simba greeted me with a wagging tail. He sensed something was terribly wrong. He put his head to my bleeding foot and started to whine. 'It is okay, Simba,' I patted him. The house was in darkness. I sat by the *Uhuru* door, took my shoes off, wrapped them in newspapers, and threw them in the trash can. I stepped in *Uhuru* and wrapped a boxing bandage over my ballooned knee. I soaked more bandages in Dettol and tied them over the bleeding wound. I took two Aspros, pulled a blanket over me and went to sleep.

I slept in fits. Thoughts in my mind turned 'porridgy' and I became delirious. When I woke up, the sunlight filtering in through the window was unbearable. 'Someone draw the curtains,' I shrieked. I closed my eyes. I heard a great commotion around me. When I opened my eyes, Henna sat holding my hand, sobbing, with panic written all over her face. 'Ma, what is wrong with him?' Azul was standing by the bed nearer to my head. Rehmat was hysterical and was saying, 'Answer me someone, how did he get hurt?'

Azul was defensive. 'Osmani was with him . . . was not hurt in JCB.' Rehmat was having none of it. 'Did anyone care to check on him?' she yelled.

'Dr Scott is here .' Salim ran in and announced. Everyone moved aside.

'Right, everyone out now,' Dr Scott barked. 'Azul you stay.' He checked my temperature and listened to my chest. He pulled the blanket off my blood-soaked bed. 'Good lord!' he muttered. When he tried moving my leg, I cried out. 'Azul he is burning, knee injury and has lost lot of blood. What happened here?'

'We don't know,' Azul replied.

'We move him to the hospital,' Dr Scott said.

I lay in Jerusha General for several days with a swollen right knee, infected left foot and high fever that refused to abate. Dr Scott was afraid that I might develop blood poisoning. He arranged me to be airlifted on a mercy flight on the Canadian Mining Company's Cessna to the United Nation's military hospital on the boarder of Rwanda and Congo. Azul accompanied me.

Our arrival at the UN Hospital was at the height of the Congo insurgency. After several examinations and X-rays, a French surgeon, in a delicate operation extracted a long piece of clear glass from my heel. He said that the glass was wedged in such a way that if not extracted correctly it could have cut vital nerves.

After my return from UN Hospital, I became uncommunicative. No one talked about Amina's rape or my injuries for fear that it would trigger my pain centre and invoke bad memories. The swelling in my knee had subsided somewhat, but it pained when I walked. Azul and Jeff barred me from JCB. This added to my frustration. I felt like a caged animal. I stopped listening to the radio and sulked in *Uhuru*. Many times, Henna came to play Snakes and Ladders and left halfway because I was glum.

While I was in UN Hospital, Narika had knitted me a blue Nordic wool sweater. It sat on my night table with a "Get Well Soon" card. She had drawn a red rose and a heart on the inside flap. I understood the emotion behind it. But my heart was possessed by Amina. I wanted to run to JCB and meet her. How was she? Whom could I ask?

One afternoon, I limped to an alley behind JCB and waited for Pedro to finish his afternoon shift. He was pleased to see me and asked me to meet him at Moidin where he told me things that plunged me into a depression. He shed different light on the events of the Gossage Football afternoon. The two animals that raped Amina were footballers. They took advantage of the confusion during the electrical fire and cornered Amina into the Sofa Room. One of them almost died due to a punctured lung from a nail in the wooden piece I had hit him with and had to be airlifted to Pala. The other had a fractured jaw. Police arrested Azul and Mr Tiano. Jeff had to work with the mayor and Dr Scott to get them released. 'What happened to Amina?' I asked Pedro.

'There was something between you two, wasn't there?' Pedro asked. I nodded.

'I knew from the way she brought you lunches. She was a good girl.'

'What happened to her?' I repeated my question. Pedro told me that she was taken to Jerusha Hospital and then she disappeared. 'What do you mean disappeared?' I asked.

'That's what I mean. A curtain fell on her story.'

'Even when she was raped?' I asked.'

'It happens in our business. What do you know about her?' Pedro asked.

'Not much,' I replied. I had never asked Amina about her past. The limited time we enjoyed together did not allow such conversations. Pedro gave me an account of Amina's life which changed my perception of her. She was from an important Creole family in Seychelles. She grew up in Congo. Her father held an important bank post in Leopoldville. Before the war he was planning to send her to a school in Europe. When the rebels stormed Leopoldville, they massacred many people including Amina's family. She escaped and took refuge in a hotel where the rebels captured her and a Western Journalist and retreated to the jungles from where they were waging their insurgency. She was in captivity for eight months. Pedro stopped his narration, took a sip of Chino, and passed me a wade of photographs. 'Junior I found these in her belongings. They were taken by The journalist who was with her.' I saw shocking and gruesome pictures of Amina with cropped hair, wearing army uniform with gun-toting soldiers in fields littered with dead villagers. Pedro took a swig of his Chino and continued, 'Amina had told me that the only way to survive with the rebels was to become one of the concubines of the crazy rebel leader. If not she would be at the whim of the soldiers and gang rape. When an opportunity came, she escaped with the Western journalist.' I became sick to my stomach looking at the photos. Pedro saw my reaction and pushed the cup of Chino closer to me. 'Pedro I don't feel like drinking,' I told him.

'Junior, she is not the girl you think she is. She has probably gone back to Congo.' I was convinced that she had not gone back to Congo. Before Pedro left I asked him one last time, 'About Amina, can I ask Mr Tiano?'

'Junior let her go. Mr Tiano has taken a long leave. He is in Kenya,' Pedro replied.

There after I made rounds of every bar and club in Jerusha and Pala looking for Amina without success. One day returning from Pala in a taxi, a woman named Mala sat next to me. She was a nurse at Jerusha General. I inquired about Amina. She asked, 'Can you describe the girl?' Not wanting to sound too familiar with the case, I said, 'She must be eighteen or something like that. Copper tan.' Mala thought for a second. Then she replied, 'There was a case like that at Jerusha General. I will have to look at the records.' At the end of our journey she invited me to come and see her at the hospital and she would look up the records. The following afternoon I plucked some flowers from the garden, wrapped them in a newspaper and presented them to Mala at the hospital. She thanked me and said, 'Ah, you want to find someone.'

'Yes, a girl . . . something happened on Friday of the Gossage Football.'

'I remember,' Mala said. Her reply kindled a hope in my heart. She dropped her voice. 'It is a very unusual request. I think it was a police case. Are you a relative?'

'No just an acquaintance. I never found out what actually happened.'

'You wait here dear.' She put the flowers in a vase on the desk and left the ward. I waited in anticipation. When she returned, she looked concerned. 'I am sorry it took so long, but the record clerk says he can't remember such a case. He says that the records are all in the vault and their release requires departmental head's permission. That needs a bit of, you know what. A little something.'

'Do you mean money?' I asked. She nodded. I was hooked on solving Amina's case, so I brought out a few Ducat notes from my pocket. 'I only have this much.'

'Not so openly! That should be plenty.' Mala whisked the notes and tucked them in her bra. 'Tomorrow I will keep the records ready.' I left, a little puzzled but hopeful.

At night after many months, I listened to Radio Ceylon. I was hopeful that I was close to solving Amina's mystery. Jerusha Station was alive with shunting steam locomotives. Past midnight the goods train left the station with two whistles on its night journey to the copper mines. Simba, as was its wont, started to bark immediately after. I got up from my bed and stood at the window watching the slag pour on Murima. I went to the kitchen and had a glass of milk. I tossed and turned and fell asleep only after the playing of the First Post on Garrison Hill. I did not sleep too long. A morning thunderstorm woke me up. When I came to the breakfast table, Jeff sat eating a bowl of cereal. Upon seeing me he complained. 'What's wrong with you? You kept walking about all night.' I sat in silence ignoring Jeff. Rehmat came and asked, 'Why aren't you eating?'

'Ma I am not hungry,' I replied. She went away to the kitchen. Jeff looked up and scolded me, 'Enough is enough. You worry everyone. You are going from bad to worse.' I wanted to explode. I banged my plate on the table and went back to *Uhuru* and sulked in bed until mid-morning. Then I sneaked out and met Mala at the hospital. She had the same look of helplessness. 'Listen,' she said, 'I made some inquiries. The police say it was not a rape case. The girl was a known prostitute.'

'A prostitute . . .'

'Yes, and the police want to question you,' Mala said, patting my hand.

'But I can't get involved,' I said defensively. 'Exactly, I told the record clerk the same thing. The police are insisting. It will need more . . . to keep them off your back.' I had sweaty palms. With a shaking voice, I said, 'But, I don't have that kind of money.'

'You come from a good family and you can't be involved with a prostitute.'

I came home disturbed. I thought of talking to Jeff. However, with his acidic comments in the morning he would not be of much help. Although no one at home was saying anything I sensed that I was a cause of anxiety in the house. Hint of blackmail might topple the proverbial apple cart. It would raise all sorts of questions for which I had no answers.

End of the Dark Night of Despair

My night of despair finally ended when Nina started to walk. As her limbs grew stronger, she began to run around the house and wanted to continually run to the garden and chase Simba. I was afraid for her. This equatorial garden was no place for a child. Many creepy crawlies and snakes slithered around. I continually ran after her and brought her in. Some mornings she ran to my room and tugged at my blanket, wanting to be carried and cuddled. She was such a bundle of joy. It was amazing how she filled me up with love and tenderness. I started to build my stamina and started boxing again. My friends noticed the change. Nash asked me if I was in love or something. 'No,' I replied, 'why do you ask?'

'You seem very happy lately,' Nash replied.

'Well maybe I am ready for love,' I made a joke. This is when the idea of fate began to confuse me. Was coming together of random events to a recognisable outcome fate? It was uncanny that the quantum Waveform Collapse that brought Palita into my life during *CID* happened exactly at a time when I was beginning to accept Amina's disappearance and was ready to declare my love for Narika? Was this fate? After falling in to a Quantum Trap of love during *CID*, I realized that Palita was my long-lost soul mate. Narika became just another girl. The City Light became temple of my love.

Jogger's and Arvind's conversations about Palita had formed a lovely image of her in my mind. The fact that I had never seen her did not matter. I was in no hurry to have a face-to-face encounter with her. Subconsciously

I avoided it. I was content to hold it as a mystery. This bestowed perfection to my love and made it ageless. I could fly on wings of imagination, not constrained by name or form or time or space. Palita was whatever I imagined her to be. Sometimes she was Venus, the Roman Goddess or Hera, the Greek Goddess. I gave wings to my blind love in the best way I knew how. I wrote love letters to Palita on perfumed rice papers from Nur Gift Shop. Actually, these papers were part of one of those Japanese kits that came with beautiful pens with small pots of coloured ink and an assortment of fancy envelopes. For my first letter, I agonised for days about what to write. To simply say "Palita, I am in love with you" would be like dead curriculum vitae. She would throw it in the trash bin without a second thought. I had to be innovative. I knew that girls liked mushy poetry. I selected a dark turquoise ink for my first letter. After a lot of thinking, I glued a dried hibiscus to a pink, scented paper. Dark red on pink with dark turquoise letterings: the effect was dramatic. I penned the following.

Dear Palita,
I held your silky smooth hair in my lap through CID
I wish to hold it for eternity.
This hibiscus is my pulsing heart,
Whisper, in return, whisper . . .
if it has a place in your HEART

I sealed my letter in a matching envelope and tied it with a golden ribbon. My romantic handy work impressed me. I had no idea that I was such a genius! What girl would not be thrilled to receive such a love letter? I gave my letter to soft-spoken friend Vir, whom I took in my confidence and who was related to Palita. He took my letter reluctantly and commented, 'She is very snobbish. You are wasting your time. Look at your reputation; mingling with overage boys and boxing in the seedy part of town.'

'Vir please, let her be the judge.'

I waited eagerly for her reply. Days turned into weeks. No answer. I was beginning to doubt if my letter ever reached her so I asked Vir about it. He was brutally honest, 'Maybe she does not like you.' Palita not liking me had never crossed my mind. Why would she not like me when my love was born out of Quantum Entanglement? Then I rationalised that it was not necessary that entangled souls should both have the same realisation. This point was not clearly explained by Quantum rules. I meant to ask Professor Pinto about it but never did. A few days later, Vir came to me. 'Smile, you have a letter.'

'Seriously?'

'Yes,' he said, handing me an envelope. This was a very momentous occasion. With a fluttering heart, I went to the school library and selected a quiet spot behind science section. If Palita was not interested she could have simply ignored my letter. The fact that she responded meant something. I opened the letter, a page torn out of a notebook; it had no perfume or decoration of any kind.

Dear Lovesick,

Should you not be studying for exams instead of writing love letters? I knew someone was playing with my hair during CID. If I had raised an alarm, they would have broken your bones. You write well. As for your flower, it is too big for my heart. Why start a story whose end we don't know?

After an exchange of letters in which I made pledges of love and Palita wrote single sentences of ambivalent nothings I began to doubt the validity of my Quantum Love. What if after exams Palita was forced in to a marriage like many girls without realizing the beauty of my Quantum Love. With this thought I became desperate and started to search for ways to write an epic letter that would colour Palita with my love. The inspiration I was waiting for came one afternoon. I immediately walked to our public library to research Napoleon's love letters. His love letters were famous, that was what Mr Roy, our history master had said. Maybe I could use some of Napoleon's amorous ideas to spice my letter. I was dreading to see the moody librarian Miss Shaila. Fortunately, she was in a good mood. 'Everyone is busy with exams. Why are you here?' she asked.

'Miss, I want to research the volume N of the Encyclopaedia.' Before she gave it to me she asked me to run to Rose Café and get her coffee. She proceeded to give me money for it. 'Miss, no need I will buy it for you,' I said.

When I saw the girl at Rose Cafe make coffee, I was appalled. There was no pride in her coffee making, not like how Suleman did it at Moidin's. She dumped a spoonful of instant coffee in a cup, topped it with hot water, and gave it a dash of milk. 'Does she dish out such tripe to the lawyers every day?' I thought to myself. Back at the library I exchanged the coffee for the Encyclopaedia. I sat in the library veranda reading about Napoleon's love life.

Napoleon's love life disturbed me. He was in love with Josephine, an ex-mistress of an older general. She pretended to love Napoleon but secretly thought that he was a bore. Soon they were married. During his Italian Campaign Josephine stayed behind in Paris and carried on with many lovers, while Napoleon wrote her love letters, begging her to come to Italy. She made excuses and even wrote that she was pregnant, when in reality she was barren.

For some reason, my mind went off at a tangent. I thought that Napoleon's love story would make an excellent school drama with plump Ash as Napoleon and tall Narika as Josephine, singing a romantic duet by Kishore and Geeta. The minute I thought of Kishore, I remembered a serious incident that happened to Salim.

Our part of the world had many dangerous tropical diseases that afflicted perfectly healthy children. One day, Salim came down with fever and became bedridden. Rehmat and Shamim attended to him day and night. Salim's condition was such that Rehmat's home remedies were ineffectual. Dr Scott eventually made a correct diagnosis and special medicines had to be flown from London to treat his condition. A few weeks later, Salim was getting better, but still confined to bed. He was hankering to go out, so one evening I made sure that his temperature was normal, tucked him in Narika's Nordic sweater, and we slipped out through the back gate. 'Where are we going?' he asked.

'Just follow me,' I replied. At the Picture House, we bought third-class tickets for *Be Gunah,* starring Kishore and Shakila, purchased a cola and a bag of tapioca chips and took our seats, just as the curtain was rising. The cinema hall was practically empty. It baffled me why Mr Lorne had decided to release such a star-studded picture on a weekday and when the schedule clashed with Christmas Light Ceremony at the Town Hall. *Be Gunah* was a sizzling political drama with memorable songs. Kishore was superb in the role of a political double agent on the run. The song "*I am a beautiful fairy*" provided Shakila an excellent platform to reveal her dancing talent and charms. Salim's eyes were glued to the screen. 'Brother this is fantastic,' he kept saying as he scoffed the chips and gulped cola. I extended my hand to grab the cola from him and found him burning like a furnace fire. I became alarmed. I jumped up, pulled Salim behind me and we left the cinema. We walked briskly. Salim started falling behind. "Salim, are you OK?' I kept asking and walked close to him holding his hand. He nodded his head and continued walking, but I could see that he was getting tired and weak. I heaved a sigh of relief when we sighted Gawa Crescent. We tried to slip in through the rear gate, but Azul, Rehmat and Henna were waiting for us. Azul was pacing up and down the drive way. Rehmat, with pink scarf over her head, was holding Henna's hand and standing at the porch. When he saw us, Azul growled, 'Where did you take him?'

'We went to a picture, Kishore's *Be Gunah,'* I replied.

'Why didn't you ask permission?'

'I am sorry Daddy,' I apologised. Rehmat rushed and felt Salim's forehead and shrieked. 'He is burning hot. Please call the doctor.' She rushed into the house with Salim. We followed them. Henna fetched a bucket of water and dumped a bottle of Eau de Cologne into it. Rehmat put Salim to bed. Henna applied cold compress to his head. Rehmat unbuttoned his shirt and gave him a towel bath. 'You,' Azul pointed at me, 'go to your room and stay there.' Jeff came to *Uhuru* and rebuked me. 'How could you? There is no limit to your stupidity. You almost killed him.' Later Henna brought me food. 'How is he doing?' I asked.

'His temperature is down and Dr Scott has given medication.'

In the days that followed Salim's condition improved. He thanked me for *Be Gunah* and said that we should go see it again. 'Dream on brother' I replied and explained to him that *Be Gunah* had been banned and all its prints were burned, the show we attended was one in five in the whole of East Africa. Salim was disappointed. Only later did I learn that in the annals of black and white Bollywood Cinema, *Be Gunah* became a cult picture.

At the Jerusha public library, my desire to emulate Napoleon's love letters evaporated due to tragic connotation and infidelities involved in his love life. Miss Shaila looked at me and commented that I did not look happy. 'Yes' I replied, 'Emperor of France, Napoleon, was not a happy lover.' She looked at me quizzically. 'Is that what you came to research when everyone else is busy preparing for exams?'

I had noticed that lately Jeff was hiding old copies of English newspapers in the cabinet under the Phillips Radio. When I came back from the library, I took advantage of his absence to find out why he was doing so. In the cabinet I found copies of *The News of the World* with front page semi-nude pictures of Miss Christine Keeler in very sexy positions. I quickly read some of the stories and found out that Mr. Perfumo who was a British Cabinet Minister was caught having a secret affair with Miss Keeler who was a prostitute and who was also sleeping around with a Russian General. It was a big scandal in London. Now I understood why every Friday there was a big line up of customers that included some very prominent citizens of Jerusha at Heptulla Book Store. It was a very hush hush affair. No one made eye contact with anyone. The manager at

Heptulla Bookstore discreetly gave out brown begs for the customers to take away. The hypocrisy of it all amused me. It was the same reason why it was impossible for any student to purchase Lady Chatterley's Lover from Heptulla Book Store.

In the evening, while helping Shamim make *rotis* for dinner, I asked her what I thought was a very innocent question. 'Shamim, how many girls can one love?' She stopped rolling the *rotis* and put the rolling pin on my wrist. 'What do you mean how many girls? How many are you playing around with?' Her reaction surprised me. I fumbled, 'I mean, can one love more than one girl?' Just then Henna came to the kitchen and our conversation stopped.

After dinner, I was fiddling with my radio when Shamim came to *Uhuru*, handed me a cup of hot milk and said, 'You did not eat well so I thought I would bring you milk.' I was embarrassed by my question to her in the evening. She said, 'I am sorry we did not get to finish our chat. Love is exclusive. It is a special feeling one has for another person. The heart does not have the capacity to love more than one. There cannot be many beloveds.'

'Shamim it is nothing like that. I was just curious,' I mumbled.

'Henna tells me that you have something going on with Narika who comes here from time to time. She is beautiful. Don't fool around with other girls,' Shamim advised. She lingered for a bit, wanting to talk more but then she turned and left. I sat drinking the warm milk that Shamim had brought when Vir knocked on my door. He had a smile on his face. 'What is it Vir?'

'This is too important. I had to come right away,' saying this he thrust a box and a blue envelope in my hand and left. I examined the box which was wrapped in an expensive, stars-embossed blue gift paper tied with a matching silk ribbon. Only the Brompton Gift Shop in Pala carried such expensive paper and ribbons. I put the box on my bed and opened the blue envelope and pulled out a perfumed letter.

Dearest Lovesick,
I can't write as well as you do.
I dream the dreams that you dream
Even my heart cries for you
I play in Badminton Tournament next Saturday at the European Club.
Please come. At the club door say you are my guest. And, please wear my
gift. Bring me flowers. Yours . . .

I could not believe what I read and saw. At the bottom, instead of a signature there was an imprint of a kiss in deep red. I was elated and kissed the letter. I opened the gift box. Inside was a black hat with a knotted rope and a buckle. It reminded me of Al Capon. Palita's gift choice surprised me. I put the hat in the box. I sat at my desk and wrote a reply.

Beloved,
A lover is like clay on a potter's wheel. I will come as you have desired
Yours Lovesick

I sealed the letter in my traditional style and in the morning, gave it to Vir.

Guilt is a heavy burden. Just when Ash's love affair had culminated in his engagement to Tara and just when I was floating on cloud nine, smug in the knowledge of the flowering of my Quantum love for Palita, Joger's love life was in a ditch. The Pari Affair after *CID* broke his heart and he dropped out of school. After the stern rebuke I received from his father the night I brought him home from his bonfire of love behind Moon Bakery, I had stopped visiting him. When I next visited him, he looked like a prisoner of war from *Bridge on River Kwai*. I felt that Joger's pathetic condition was brought about by the curse of the secretive *Udhric* around which a cult had formed after the imposition of censorship on Urdu classes. There were wild stories of orgies and strange rites associated with *Udhric*. Anyone cursed by the rituals of *Udhric* was doomed. Names of poets like Ghalib, Rumi, Hafiz, and others were also linked with *Udhric*. From the limited familiarity, I had with the *ghazals* and poetry of these famous poets, I was convinced that however mischievous their ideas, vulgarity was not part of their character and neither curses and charms their trade. In fact, *ghazals* introduced me to all that was sublime in the heart. I felt that Joger was imitating the behaviour of heroes of tragic pictures and was on a path of self-destruction. If I were ever to make a picture, I had to understand this destructive impulse and know how the cannons of *Udhric* fitted in with the Circle of Love. Week after week, we saw this self-sacrificing behaviour in pictures like *Devdas* and read about it in tragedies of Romeo and Juliet. The turbulent love tragedy of Musa and Bulbul who leaped to their deaths from the Lookout Point on Murima attested to this dark and grim reality of *Udhric*.

The answer to *Udhric* Enigma finally came at Ahmed Mosque, which was in the poorer part of Jerusha, on the other side of Gembe Stadium. Just before the fasting month of Ramadan, I was delivering supplies to the Mosque for the upcoming month-long evening festivities, where I met Jamal, a young *Imam* in-training who had recently come from Yemen. He spoke good English. With his curly hair and dark tan, he looked like a playboy rather than an *Imam*. I told him so. Contrary to getting angry, he looked at me with respect. 'Well you have a good observation. *Imam* does not mean I have given up pleasures of life. I can enjoy all the pleasures allowed in the Koran.'

'Including sex?'

'Yes, that too, if you must know,' he replied with a smile.

'Then you are having the best of both worlds,' I told him.

'Nothing to stop you from following my example,' he replied. We talked about many subjects until our conversation led to a point where we talked about poetry. I seized the opportunity. 'Tell me what do you know about *Udhric?*' I asked him. Before answering me, he gave instructions to one of his helpers. Then he said to me, 'Let's sit. I will explain it to you.'

We sat in the forecourt of the Mosque. It was stifling hot. Jamal wiped his face with a white towel. His helper returned with a tray loaded with a shiny brass coffee pot, dates, a plate of pink *halwa,* and two small porcelain cups. Jamal offered me a cup of black coffee and said, 'This heat you can only fight with hot and spicy coffee.' One sip and I fell in love with the coffee. 'Oh, it is so tangy,' I commented. Jamal said, 'Try it with the sweets.' As I savoured the coffee, dates, and sweet *halwa,* Jamal said, '*Udhric* is associated with Arabic love-poetry. In all societies where there are too many restrictions, love-poetry thrives. What else are people supposed to do when they cannot meet with their sweethearts? Imagination takes over and people gather on street corners and Chai Houses and talk about love and things like that. There are two love-poetries specific to the geography of Arabia. The first is the poetry of Kufi. It is very different. It does not beat around the bush. It is explicit and erotic.' Jamal's statement surprised me. 'Jamal, I thought Islam did not allow such language.'

'So you would think. However, humans are humans and sex excites everyone and Islam does not deny that. So, these Kufi poets make full use of religious openness to express naughty things and use old style of *majun* (shocking and mocking) as a tool,' Jamal stopped.

'Can you give me an example?' I asked. He looked at me with a naughty smile and said, 'It goes like this: If length of penis is a mark of manhood, then mule would be the king.' I wanted to burst out laughing but controlled myself. Jamal poured me more spicy coffee. 'And what about *Udhric?'* I asked.

'Ah, *Udhric!* It is the Cadillac. The desert tribe of *Udhra* of Arabia are well known for their love unto death. When one of its tribesmen was asked who he was, his reply was: I am from the tribe where we die when we love. In *Udhric* if there is an obstacle in path of the lovers, and union is unattainable, such a love is transformed to a love of high devotion of the beloved. The lover dies as a martyr to love. It is the poetry of union beyond death.'

I came home with a glow of knowledge in my heart. I now understood the basis of cinema tragedies and the impulse of sacrifice in love. Hopeless love transformed into something lofty: die for love – eternal love. I understood the reasons behind the "Flame and Moth" theme in Urdu poetry and the popularity of an Urdu couplet that went like this:

Sitting in your forecourt, I will cry
And burn in the flames of immolation,
Yet will not divulge to you my love pain.

The reports of secret *Udhric* meetings attended by the likes of Savi and others at which poetries of Ghalib, Rumi, and other love-mad Sufis, dripping with the ecstasy of love, were read and where virtues of love unto death were extolled, began to make sense. It raised love to a spiritual height and removed profanity from it.

When I next met Joger, he had taken up smoking and lighted a Sportsman. He puffed out rings of smoke. His bulging eyes stared at me lifelessly. Armed with knowledge of *Udhric,* I confronted him, 'Joger, do you remember we wanted to make a film of love with blood-stirring emotions?' He took a drag of his Sportsman and said, 'Cut the crap. What do you want from me?' I spared him no mercy and lashed out, 'I am tired of your brutish behaviour.' He screamed back at me, 'Then stop coming to see me?'

'You f**king swine that is not an option. I do not expect this from you. You want to be my partner and make a picture with me; then stop living this life of *Devdas.* I know the secret of *Udhric* and this die for beloved nonsense. You can make a good picture with that kind of crap. You don't have to live that experience. And why the f**k are you smoking?' My outburst shocked him. When I evoked *Devdas*, he knew exactly what I meant. 'Junior . . .' he searched for words.

'Say it. Get it off your chest.'

'What do you know about love?' he asked. This was the second time he had asked me the same question as if love was a monopoly of a few chosen people. I put his question aside and asked, 'Tell me about love?'

'Pari is constantly in my mind. I cannot get her out. It is not love. It is a disease.'

Mumtaj Mahal

My outburst was an electric jolt that shook up Joger. A day after that he confessed that he had behaved badly. From that point on he changed. Knowing his weakness for drama and theatre we trapped him to act in our school play *Mumtaj Mahal – Story of Eternal Love*. At first he argued and said there was nothing like love and it was all a mirage. Nash told him that there was no one more suited than him to play the role of the Emperor Shah Jahan, who build the Taj Mahal for his beloved Mumtaj. Joger replied, 'You are asking me to play a role that I don't believe in.' Nash was ready with an answer. 'Joger that is exactly what a good actor does. He becomes the character.' Joger succumbed to our gentle pressure. 'If you all insist I will try,' he finally agreed. I sealed his consent with a concrete plan. 'Exams are seven weeks away. If we try we can be ready by the term end. Miss Sue is ready to help us, and she has the headmaster's permission.'

Miss Sue, a blonde with degrees in drama from York and mathematics from Imperial in London was in Jerusha for the African experience. She hugged our Mumtaj Mahal Project how a mother hugs her baby. It took her some time to understand the subtlety of the plot which was full of emotional and tearful dialogues. 'Does the Emperor have to say these dialogues?' she asked when she read the script.

'Oh, yes Miss Sue definitely. Our audiences love these tearful emotions. Without these, they would feel they have not eaten rice in their meal,' I explained. The project got underway and rehearsals were progressing

well. As yet I had no one to play the ghost of Queen Mumtaj so I asked
Henna to ask Narika if she would play the role. The smile on Henna's face
evaporated. She burst out. 'You mistreat her. Why mess around with her?'

'Henna, nothing happened between us. I never encouraged her.'

'You fool,' Henna hissed, 'there are no secrets in Jerusha. Your name is
stuck to her like glue. We know she came to you in *Uhuru*. Do you know
what it means to a girl's reputation? If you were not interested why did you
accept that nut cone from her? We all saw it.'

'Henna, please just ask her. Let her decide.' Two days later Henna told
me. 'She has agreed. I think she is a fool.'

The badminton tournament at the European Club was on. It was the
day to wear Palita's gift of Al Capon hat and go meet her. At breakfast Jeff
asked me, 'What is the smile for? What did you dream about?' I ignored
him. After lunch I showered and groomed my hair with Yardley cream. I
smeared a dab of Nivea Cream on my face to give it a shine. I wore pleated
trousers, a lilac dress shirt of the type George Chakris wore in *The West
Side Story,* and a matching pink tie. I picked up Palita's gift box and on
my way out I cut roses and wrapped them in an origami paper. I walked
across the open field from Forest Drive to European Club, skirting several
marabou vultures that stood still as statues. At the club, I walked past
a queue of cars waiting to drop off dapper couples to this annual "By
invitation Badminton Tournament" which was a "who is who" affair of
Jerusha. Close to the entrance I put on the Al Capon hat, held the origami-
wrapped bouquet in my hand, and walked to the front entrance. The
doorkeeper looked at me quizzically, 'Good afternoon; your card please?'

'Er . . . I am Miss Palita's guest,' I replied.

'That's nice. You must still have a card,' he said.

'Could you please check with Miss Palita?' I asked. The man turned to
an official who was chatting with other guests. The official walked to me.
'What seems to be the problem?' I lifted my hat from my head and replied,
'Oh, there is no problem. I am Miss Palita's guest. Could you please check

with her?' The official glanced at the long queue of guests behind me and said, 'I am sorry. That is not how it works governor. It's impossible to look for this Miss . . .'

'Miss Palita.'

'Yes, Miss Palita. It is not possible to look for her. You must have an invitation card. Now if you will please let others in.' I stepped aside. People in the queue looked at me with curiosity and talked to each other in hushed tones. I knew I looked like a clown with the Al Capon hat and a bunch of flowers in my hand. To save further embarrassment I turned and walked out, feeling humiliated. Just as I stepped out a photographer jumped out from a waiting Mercedes and took my picture. 'Thank you,' he said as he retreated. I heard laughter and giggles from inside the car. I tossed the bouquet and the hat over the hedge and left the venue, unobtrusively. At home, I sat in *Uhuru*, angry and embarrassed. Had I lost all dignity in love? I remembered the Sufi saint, Rumi, alluding to that very same subject. He had said that lovers lose sense of pride and dignity in divine love. A Sufi in love for God will suffer and bear insults and privations. Unfortunately, I had reached that Sufi state in profane love. In my simmering anger I tore a page from my notebook and wrote:

Palita,
I donned a clown's hat for your love,
I suffered insults for your pleasure. My love has not diminished.
Rather my resolve now is to pluck you from your own castle

I was serious about storming her house and carrying her away. Quantum love was wearing me down. I knew my love life was taking a new direction. How would it work? If I carried her away, would it be kidnapping? If she consented, then it would be an elopement. She could live with me in *Uhuru*. She had hinted at that in her letter. Azul and Rehmat would have to get used to the idea of a new member in the family. Jeff would go berserk. But would I care? I could marry Palita once I finished my school in three months.

On my way to Vir to give him the letter I stopped at Somero Square. It was that time of day when Somero transformed itself from a mavule graced quadrangular to a haunted junction. The dark ghost-like edifice of Anglican Church at the Zanzibar Road-end was the heart of African Christian worship in Jerusha. Its history was closely linked to colonial history of Jerusha. Built a century ago it was an enormous, open-walled hall with corrugated sheeted cathedral roof. In the early days, the white colonialist congregated here, but as time progressed and African Christianity took root, the elitist whites felt it necessary to assert their superior position and built an exclusive white-only church on the road that lead to Madam Doctor's palatial home. Once white patronage was lost, the Church fell into disrepair. Asian businesses from time to time contributed to carryout necessary repairs to the roof. Electricity was never connected to the Church and important service was conducted only on Sunday morning when hundreds of Africans flocked to the Church. These simple folks believed in the hopeful message that the weak and the poor shall inherit the Kingdom of God.

I sat on the Church nave and grappled with my dilemma. With the gathering darkness, the clamour of birds on the mango trees gradually died down. The loneliness of Somero helped me concretise my plan. It was very simple. I would ask Vir to find out what size clothes Palita wore. Then in the morning I would ride to Socram, which opened at ten and purchase necessary toiletries, dresses, and other necessities for her. I would stock my refrigerator with food. Then I would tell Vir to bring Palita to *Uhuru*. I felt that there was enough sparkle in my Quantum Love to convince her to stay back in *Uhuru*. I knew that if a thing was planned properly, it was easy to execute it. Laughter from bougainvillea-covered grave patch woke me up from my meditation. I felt frightened. I bicycled to Vir's with double urgency. 'Good lord,' he commented when he saw me, 'do you ever rest?'

'Vir it is urgent,' I said as I handed him my letter. 'I need an answer by tomorrow.'

'You are impossible. You have no regard for time or occasion. Tomorrow is Sunday,' he pointed out.

'Vir, please be an angel, go to her now.'

'Do you know I have never met a persistent lovesick fellow like you?'

'Vir do me one more favour. Ask her to come to *Uhuru* in the afternoon. I have this great slide show. It is fantastic. She will love it. Oh, by the way, could you ask her dress size?'

'What?' Vir shook his head in utter disbelief and left me pondering my grand scheme.

In the morning when Jeremy saw me take a full plate of samosas and a jug of orange juice to *Uhuru*, he protested. 'Junior, if you hog a full plate I have nothing left for others.' I snapped, 'Jeremy nevermind. Prepare more.' He wanted to answer me back but held his tongue. At ten I cycled to Socram, quickly collected the things I had on my list and selected a medium-size flowery dress, a green skirt and colourful blouses for Palita. At the cash counter, I waited for Kala, the cashier to put her newspaper down and attend to me. A man with well-oiled dark hair that stumbled down to his neck stood close behind me. I had never seen him before. My imagination went into an overdrive. With his drooping lips and a scar on his left cheek, I thought that he could be a perfect cast for a villain in our picture. Many times I had seen a group of such men gather at the Gymkhana in the evenings and practice wrestling. Vir had told me that these men were nasty nationalist radical types who had assassinated Mr Gandhi in India. 'Vir what are they doing in Jerusha?'

'Maybe they do dirty work for the mill owners and disappear,' Vir had replied.

The man stood too close to me. Kala looked at the dress and the blouses I had selected and asked, 'Are these for your sister?' The gymnast stepped closer and stretched his neck to listen to my reply. It made me uncomfortable. 'Sort of,' I told Kala. Then I turned around and said to the gymnast, 'My brother, there is enough room behind you, why so close to me?'

'No there isn't,' he replied. His arrogance incensed me. Not wanting an argument, I kept quiet. Kala said to me, 'These may be too loud and flowery. On some girls, they would look like paintings. Why don't you ask your sister's choice?' I felt embarrassed.

'Okay I will change them if she doesn't like them.' I replied.

'Exchange within three days okay? So sweet you think of your sister,' Kala said as she put my purchases in a bag. On my way, home I picked up groceries from Lobo Stores. Back in *Uhuru* I stuffed all the groceries in my refrigerator and hid the rucksack with the clothing and toiletries under my bed. I waited. Late in the afternoon I heard chimes of Vir's bicycle bell. I rushed out. 'Vir, where is Palita?'

'Well she is not at your command. She was at the temple. I had to wait. She gave this.' As I took the envelope from Vir he said, 'She was asking questions about you and Narika. What are you up to, you two-timer?'

'Honest nothing's between me and Narika.'

'Well isn't she acting in your play?' Vir asked.

'Vir, it is strictly business.'

'I don't care. Please don't bother me tonight. I am busy,' he said as he left. I opened Palita's letter with trembling hands.

Dear Lovesick.

I am sorry for the Badminton joke. I wanted to test you. I am a wingless caged bird. Do come and pluck me from my golden cage. I am sorry I could not come in the afternoon. I am eagerly waiting to be with you on Janmastmi.

My beloved Krishna,

I am your eternal Radha

I was stunned. Was Palita playing another joke? The insult of Al Capon melted away. I clutched her letter, sat in the patio and reread the ending of Palita's letter. 'I am waiting to be with you on *Janmastmi*. My Beloved Krishna I am your eternal Radha.' Could there be a clearer proof of her feelings for me?

In Hinduism, "Radha Krishna" is a sublime love story. Krishna, an incarnation of the powerful Vishnu of the Hindu trinity, is a symbol, par excellence of love between a god and his devotee. From a very young age, Krishna was a charming flute player. In the garden of *Brindaban*, whenever Krishna played his magical flute, all his female devotees abandoned their chores and ran to *Brindaban* for love play with this coy and erotic Krishna. From all his devotees Radha was his beloved. For over 2,000 years, Krishna's love play with Radha is a rich fodder of inspiration for ancient poets and Indian picture song lyricists.

Krishna devotees celebrate his *Janmastmi,* birthday, with much pomp. At Jerusha temple, celebrations always commenced with giggling devotees pampering a toddler Krishna. This was followed by enactment of Krishna's childhood pranks. Towards late evening the celebration reached its climax. Dark-complexioned Krishna now an adorable youth of extraordinary charm, wearing his orange robe with a peacock-feathered crown on his head, his flute to his lips, stood like a divine axis, in the middle of a circle formed by love-desirous devotees. Exhilarating divine tunes flowed from Krishna's flute, intoxicating the devotees who would lose all sense of time and would swirl in a circle around him. This was the much celebrated *Raas Leela,* love-play of Krishna. He would spread a net of divine magic to quench love thirst of his swirling devotees. This enactment symbolised the eternal hope and desire of every Krishna devotee to, once in his or her lifetime attain this spiritual ecstasy of playing *Raas* with Krishna and experiencing a union of mind and body with him.

While I was floating on cloud nine after Palita's Radha-Krishan letter, Rehmat was watching me carefully. 'You are again not eating well. Look at those bags under your eyes. Why have you taken on so much?'

I comforted her, 'Ma, I can handle it.' But there was a secret that I had not shared with her or for that matter with anyone else. Night after night I was having a nightmare. I was lying on a dark road in a puddle of blood, and a thick sinister voice was saying . . . *Let's move the bastard to the middle of the road and run him over.* In the dream, I was desperately trying to get up and run but my limbs were limp. I was crying for help but no sound came from my throat. I was convinced that after *Janmastmi* when Palita came and lived with me this nightmare would stop.

When Miss Sue and I looked at the calendar we found that *Janmastmi* coincided with the staging of Mumtaj Mahal. It was a Wednesday. We consulted with the headmaster who ruled that Mumtaj Mahal should be a matinee rather than an evening show to allow students to attend *Janmastmi* finale later in the evening. I argued that this would cut out several hours from drama preparation time. The headmaster was firm in his decision. This added to my anxiety.

There was no one more committed to a cause than Joger when he put his heart into it. His talent began to shine during the drama practice. He took Narika under his tutelage. One Friday he gathered us all to show us the progress on Narika's dance sequence. While we were waiting, Narika came and stood by me. We stood tongue-tied for a minute. She untied her ponytail letting her hair down and re-tied it. She broke the ice, 'I like the way you direct. I want to do my best for you.'

'That's because you are a good actor. You love what you do,' I told her.

'Walk me home tonight. I have something important to tell you.'

'Narika, I would love to but today we have special Friday service at the mosque, and I have promised mother that I would attend. Why don't we do it tomorrow?' She looked disappointed. She went and joined Miss Sue. In the meantime, Nash played the selected *Yasmeen* song and Joger asked Narika to demonstrate her dance repertoire. After the dance, I complimented Narika for her dance and made a gaffe that would change lives. I was not sure what impelled me to say what I said. 'Do you know Narika, you and Joger make a good pair? I mean you share the same passion . . .' Narika winced and stiffened up. 'You of all people saying this?'

'Narika,' I fumbled and tried to undo the stab I had inflicted without realising that serious bleeding only started when the dagger was withdrawn, 'I don't mean it in that sense . . .'

'I don't care what you mean; you heartless brute.' Her outburst shook my heart. What was I thinking? Her eyes welled up. 'I love you. I would give my life for you and all you can say is that I make a good pair with Joger.'

'Narika, I am sorry.' I was lost for words. I felt stupid.

After Narika's dance to the tape music, Joger and I felt that it had no vibrancy. The following evening, when we gathered at the school Narika avoided me and kept close to Miss Sue. Joger surprised us by arriving with Ishrat of *Wasl Queen* notoriety, together with Chandu and Rahim who were the best tabla and flute players in our country. In the intervening years since Ishrat participated in the *Wasl Queen* Symposium, she had grown in proportion and could be described as plump. Two gold earrings adorned her ears. Joger told us that Ishrat had agreed to sing for us. I was delighted and thanked her. She asked if I was the director. I nodded. She threw a curve ball, 'Well, the song you have selected requires harmonium and *sarangi*. Without these it will not flow. We need them now.' I told her that I could get Salim to play the harmonium. But to find someone to play *sarangi* was impossible. Joger interjected, 'Not so impossible, Mr Bondhu is the best *sarangi* player.' I began to shake my head and said, 'Joger, he won't agree. Remember the fire in the music room?'

'Junior, if you beg he will. Now stop wasting time and go with Ishrat and convince Mr Bondhu to play. I will go fetch Salim.' Joger left me no choice. Ishrat and I walked a short distance on Teacher's Lane to Mr

Bondhu's house. I was convinced that on seeing me he would slam the door. I rang the doorbell. His servant opened the door. 'We would like to see Mr Bondhu,' Ishrat said. The servant invited us in and led us to the living room. Mr Bondhu sat on a sofa with his left leg resting on a stool. I was seeing him after two years. His face had withered. I knew that his fractured leg never healed properly, and he limped. He was also unable to sit on the floor for long periods during music recitals. Seeing Ishrat he beamed. 'What an honour to have one of my best students visit me! An accomplished singer, you make me proud.' Ishrat made a graceful bow at his feet. He blessed her. Then he looked at me with an expression of puzzlement. '*Ye lo*, and what about you, *maha shay,* esquire, where have you been all these years?'

'Mr Bondhu, sir, I heard about your accident and . . .'

'And, what? Never once did you inquire. Or ever came to the music room.'

'I came, sir, to explain but you closed the door on me.'

'*Maha shay,* I am your *guru.* I was angry. You are my student. You must beg. You played *Tanpura* for me. The eternal AUM of Shiva is heard when the universe is created and when universe is destroyed. The *Tanpura* you played awakens that hum in the heart. That is what I wanted to teach you. But you were too drunk in your pride. But days are gone when students respect their *guru.* Now I hear you have earned a name in science.' I hung my head in shame. Ishrat looked puzzled. I realised that during the term when I had attended Mr Bondhu's music classes, I had established a special relationship with him. 'Mr Bondhu, sir, forgive me. I should have come sooner. I apologise.'

'Nevermind, to what I owe this honour?' he asked.

Ishrat answered, 'Well, Mr Bondhu, a school play has a dance and a song. It's a picture song. We need you to direct the song, and play the *sarangi.*'

'When do we start?' he asked. Ishrat was quick to answer, 'Mr Bondhu now, today! Everyone is assembled at the school.'

Immediately on reaching the school, Mr Bondhu set to work and had the song synchronised within an hour. Narika's dance became vibrant with live orchestra and Ishrat's velvety voice. 'It is a wonderful scene,' Mr Bondhu said after the dance and added, 'Narika dances well, and of course, Ishrat is without a parallel,'

Narika missed drama rehearsal for two days. This was unusual for her. I was getting concerned and had made up my mind to visit her home if she did not show up. Fortunately, she showed up. I was relieved. After the rehearsal I was rushing to talk to her when Sudama interrupted me to show me the pulley and tackle for Narika's grand stage entrance from the ceiling. I signalled Narika to wait. I inspected Sudama's contraption and it appeared weak, so I showed him where I wanted extra clamps. Just then Joger walked in with a man. 'Junior, you do remember Mr Raghuvir?'

'Yes' I replied, 'we met at your uncle's office.' Mr Raghuvir, his mouth full of *paan*, shook my hand. He continued to apply a handkerchief to his lips to arrest the free flow of red *paan* juice. I found it repulsive. He patronised me and told me that Joger talked very highly about the drama. He added, 'You boys are doing so *phantastic*. Superb. You must *phinish* Kilimanjaro story soon.' When he spotted Narika, he rushed to her, putting his hands on hers and making wild gestures like an Italian gigolo. This made me jealous and angry. I pulled Joger aside and asked, 'Joger, why is this man here, and why is he talking to Narika?'

'He was one of the judges at the National Dance Competition. He knows her. Junior, he is well connected in Bombay.' Privately I did not like Raghuvir's antics with Narika. I wanted to rescue her from him when the headmaster's peon came and asked me to go to his office. I left reluctantly. Once again an opportunity to talk to Narika was lost. When I came back, everyone had left. My faith in my Quantum love wavered. What if Palita's Krishna–Radha letter was a joke? The strange emotion that possessed me at that point was in favour of Narika. I had to tell her something. I rushed out looking for her. On the way I met Sudama and asked him if he had seen Narika. 'Yes, she and Miss Sue left in that Bombay clown's car,' he replied. I felt rotten. I walked to Somero Square and sat on the church steps, thinking about Narika, Palita, and Quantum love.

On Saturday evening Rehmat insisted that I attend a wedding to which our family was invited. I declined. When the family left, I busied myself with exam reviews. The phone started to ring. It was Rehmat. 'We have forgotten the wedding gift and a car is blocking ours. Could you cycle it to the Town Hall?' she asked. I resisted, 'Ma, I am busy and not dressed.' Rehmat insisted, 'Son, please help, Shamim will wait for you in the foyer.'

At the Town Hall, there was no sign of Shamim. Tired of waiting, I walked into the chaos of the wedding hall through a heavy door. A wedding song blared from speakers. I walked towards a gaily decorated *mandap,* a wedding stage, and halted behind a pink net curtain to escape glares of guests. I looked around for my family. Suddenly I became aware of a pair of girls with their backs towards me. The curvaceous one with a waist to hip ratio of 0.7 was Narika, the object of my affection. To her right stood the object of my desire, my Quantum love, Palita. I guessed this from her long black ponytail, which cascaded down to her hip. She was closest to me, only about half a meter away. I swooned. This was my first close encounter with her since *CID.* She was shorter compared to Narika, and was clad in a pink sari. Diamond studs adorned her ears. Narika was wearing a loose turquoise dress with a matching ribbon in her hair. I stood as if in a trance. When the wedding song ended, I heard the echoes of the priest's deep voice, '*Kanya padhrao,* commence the bride walk'. I felt that any second Palita and Narika would turn on their heels as their eyes followed the bridal walk, and reveal their faces. Every fibre in my body tingled. A hand tagged me from behind. 'What are you doing in here, dressed like a tramp?' Henna hissed in my ear. I whispered, 'I could not find Shamim. I had to come in.' Henna took the gift box from me and said, 'What if Narika saw you like this? Go home.'

I took a parting glance at the *mandap*. The bride and the groom had commenced their seven circuits of the sacred fire while the priest chanted from the scriptures. At the end of it, the groom would put a dab of vermilion in the bride's hair and that would make them man and wife. No power in the universe would be able to separate them after that. This thought froze in my mind. This wedding ritual conducted in the witness of the god of fire was all that was needed to solemnise a bond of love.

I realized that vermillion, the important ingredient in the wedding ritual, was missing from the supplies I had purchased for Palita. On my way home I stopped at Socram and purchased a small bottle of it. I stopped at the temple and waved at Bhatji who was conducting the evening prayers. I waited. He came out after the prayers. I asked him, 'Bhatji, are you allowed to perform weddings on *Janmastmi*?'

'*Hey Prabhu,* O, Lord, what wedding? Who's wedding?' he asked in exasperation.

'You have to perform a wedding. I will tell you later. There will be a good reward for you. You will remember, *na?*' He shook his head in disbelief.

The End of an Affair

At home Simba had run away somewhere. He did that from time to time, making his escape from a hole in the fence. I rushed to *Uhuru* and pulled out the rucksack with clothes for Palita from under my bed. I put the vermilion bottle in it. After seeing Palita's elegance, I acutely felt the inadequacy and rusticity of the dress and blouses I had purchased. There was no going back now. I justified my selection in the knowledge that everything was fair in love and that she would wear the selected dress as robes of pure love. After Bhatji performed our marriage on the evening of *Janmastmi*, I would smear vermilion on Palita's forehead, and then there would be no need for her to hide in *Uhuru* any more. I would be able to shower her with dresses befitting her beauty and dignity. While I was pushing the rucksack under the bed there was a knock on the door. I opened it. Gul stood facing me. I blurted out, 'You bastard you nearly killed me last Thursday. What do you want?'

'I am sorry. Please help me. I want to talk to you. Please let's go to my BSA.' I locked *Uhuru* door and followed him to his BSA under the street lamp. He stood with his back to the lamp, which hid his face. 'It is about Narika,' he said.

'What about Narika?' I became tense. He hesitated and cleared his throat, 'She is . . . I mean . . . she is pregnant. I am sorry.'

'How could she be pregnant? I just saw her at the wedding,' I shouted and began to feel faint. How could a beautiful and intelligent girl like

Narika get involved with Gul? How? Things just did not add up. I was sure Gul was lying. The tender feelings for her in my heart began to surge. She had uttered beautiful magic words, "I love you" to me in *Uhuru*. My inability to reciprocate her feeling had caused me deep anguish, and when I heard sleazy scum like Gul say that she was pregnant, it infuriated me. I was seething with black rage. I said the prayers Rehmat had taught me to control my anger. I heard Gul say, 'I would like you to take her to Kongoro to "drop the baby".'

'Drop the baby?' I shouted. I could not believe what I heard. 'What do you mean by drop the baby?' I asked, shaking with rage. My sex lesson 2 surfaced in my mind. Without waiting for Gul's answer, I yelled, 'You bastard if you did not love her, why did you get her into this mess? Marry her.'

'I can't. Her nephews will kill me and her,' Gul replied.

'Where is she, you lying bastard?' I asked.

'She escaped from the wedding. We have two hours before she'll be missed. She is at Somero Square.' The idea of Narlika alone at Somero Square drove me insane. The veins in my brain began to pulsate. 'Take me to her right now,' I demanded. Gul was blabbering desperately. He was tugging at my arm. 'Please help me. We have not been the best of friends . . .We have an hour.'

'Gul, why aren't you taking her to Kongoro yourself?' I gained control of myself.

'She is crying for you. She will only go with you,' Gul replied. I wished Rehmat was home. She would be able to find a solution to Narika's predicament. I told Gul to wait. My hands were sweaty. I was desperately trying to come up with a solution other than "drop the baby". I remembered Madam Doctor. She was specialist in Women's medicine. I rushed into the house and phoned her. There was no answer. The thought of Narika alone at Somero Square overwhelmed me so I told Gul to bring me to her. On the way, I told him, 'You bastard, if anything happens to me, my family will kill you. If anything happens to Narika, I will kill you.'

'Please, don't worry,' he assured me.

At Somero Square, Gul switched off the BSA engine and freewheeled to the Church in darkness. I saw Narika's shadowy figure sitting on the Church steps. She stood up as she saw us. We got off the motorcycle. Gul went and talked to her. He returned after a while and said, 'I told her that you would take care of her.' I sat on the BSA. Narika sat at the back. Gul thrust a bag to me. 'What is it?' I asked. 'Towels,' he whispered. The bastard had come well prepared. He stuffed my shirt pocket with a stash of money. 'Kongoro Estate, Look for Street C, house number 44,' he said.

We made the painful journey on Murima Road towards Kongoro Estate on Gul's BSA. Narika held on to me tightly. My heart was in a knot. After what seemed like an eternity, we reached the Trinity Junction. I stopped and switched off the engine. A concrete thick silence descended upon us. To our right was the Lookout Point, where in the shadow of the old mavule stood the *vive l'amour* monument dedicated to the memory of Musa and Bulbul who had plunged to their deaths from the overhanging cliff. In the darkness, Peace Lake was a glassy, grey sheet, stretching far into the horizon. At the summit, the silhouette of smelter chimney spewed vaporous fumes into the atmosphere. An amber glow of cooling slag made everything look surreal. I remembered the time when we celebrated my birthday at the summit, when it was still a green meadow. When the Smelter was first built, people came up to the Lookout Point to watch the nightly red hot slag pours. It was a novelty until noxious fumes made people sick. In the distance, just below the overhanging mounds of frozen slag, stretched sickly haze of Kongoro Estate. I looked back and asked Narika, 'Do you still want to do this?' I heard her sniffle. I said, 'Please change your mind and talk to your mother or someone.' She did not answer. 'If we wait until tomorrow I could bring you to the seminary. I know Sisters Beth and Carol. I could talk to Dr VB on Gandhi Road. I insist we wait until tomorrow.' There was no answer. I asked, 'Will Gul not marry you?' Her sniffles continued. I gave her time to recover. I waited, not knowing how to comfort her or lessen the enormity of the situation. After a long pause, I asked the dreaded question, 'Narika, why?' Her body heaved violently. I heard a sob of deep anguish. I dismounted, parked the BSA and gently lifted her off. She let go her dammed-up emotions, and clung to me and cried. It pulverised me. I held her tight in my arms. 'I am with you Narika. Dr VB will help. I swear, I will not let any harm come to you.' We stood for a long time before I loosened my arms around her. Between sobs, she asked, 'You ask me why? For many days, I am trying to talk to you. If you had read my letter and seen the photographs, you would know.'

'But, I never got your letter,' I replied.

'I put it in your physics book. I told you to walk me home. But, it's too late now,' she said.

'It's not too late. Please, tell me what happened? Why, Gul?' I asked. She shook with violent sobs. I took her in my arms again and comforted her. When she calmed down, she looked me in the face. 'He was going to hurt you. He showed me photographs of you touching me, kissing me. It was a picture of when we talked behind my house.'

'But how could I have touched you, kissed you. It's a lie ." I said holding her hand.

'He said he will return the photographs if I met him. He fooled me. When I met him, he threatened that he will show them to Tavi and Pal and get them to beat you up. I was afraid for you. Then he forced me . . . He infected me.' She broke down.

'The bastard, I will kill him . . . You did all this for me?' I said, trying to put my hands around her. Her crying overwhelmed me. For the first time, I felt the depth and purity of her love and that realisation transformed my heart with a Midas touch. I trembled. I hung between feelings of love and guilt. Why hadn't I paid more attention to her? Narika sniffled and pulled out something from her side pocket and handed it to me. 'What is it?' I asked.

'Look and you'll know it,' she replied. In the glow of the cooling slag, I saw that I was holding a gold pendant. My mind reeled to the past. My goodness! The pendant that I had given to the girl in Suwakaki in exchange for telling me the words to the tune she was humming; the tune that I had thought was God's Symphony, the girl that I had thought was a divine Nymph. My jaws dropped. 'Narika, how did you get this?'

'How do you think? You gave it to me,' she replied.

'Oh, Narika, was it you that danced in the forest and hummed that tune?' In the pink glow of the cooling slag, her face looked like an angel. In an instant, I saw the resemblance. Why did I not see it right away? For all these years, God's Symphony was at hand. If only once she had given me a hint or said something, the gyrations of love that I had performed would have not been necessary. The thought of the pain I had inflicted on her pained me. Narika broke the silence. 'I followed you ever since you were in junior school. Then Jerusha flood destroyed Daddy's business and we had to move to Jujuka and I lost touch.'

'Narika if only once you had mentioned after you came back to Jerusha, things would have been different. We were young. I did not recognise you. God is my witness.' I stepped closer to her and whispered to her, 'I will marry you, Narika, no matter what. And I will take care of you. I will not let any harm come to you.'

'It is no use. I want your love, not your charity. You have no feelings for me. You said that I make a good pair with Joger, that is what you said.'

'Narika, I love you . . .You don't know how much . . . I meant to say it . . . Narika . . .' I heard what I said, and I meant every word. Her selflessness overwhelmed me. Somewhere deep in my heart, there was a voice asking, 'What about Palita your Quantum Love?' I realised there and then that life was a forked road. It was all about choices. I had made a choice. I tried to put my arms around Narika. She held me at bay with her elbow. 'It's all over. Please let's go,' she said, pushing me away with her hand.

I rode with Narika down the mud road to Kongoro Estate with my heart in a quandary, crying silently for the way things had turned out. Until two hours ago, when I saw Palita and Narika together, I felt strong and entirely enamoured by Palita – my quantum love. But by stiff arming me, Narika had turned the table on me. I now became the tragic hero, spurned by the beloved. I felt weak and became acutely aware of the numerous slights I had heaped on Narika. As always, my mind searched for a cinematic situation that paralleled by wretched state. A powerful Talat song played in my mind:

I am a dishonoured lover of a doomed love,
　　And burning in the fire that I have lighted myself
What good now to save my skin from
　　its leaping flames

Below us, Jerusha with its teeming lights simmered like a mythical city. Jerusha Station was alive with shunting locomotives puffing out clouds of exhaust steam. The BSA was groaning. We rode into Kongoro Estate from its north entrance. Smog hugged the ground as in "Dante's Hell." A few functioning street lamps cast sickly yellow pall over the matchbox-size houses rising above the smog. I drove around trying to find Street C, hoping never to find it. I mean what was so difficult to find Street C, when streets were in alphabetical order. I hoped that an earthquake would strike and destroy Kongoro. I wished the slag running downhill would consume it like lava consumed Pompeii. Street C stared me in the face. I turned into it and stopped midway where it was darkest. The smog made breathing difficult. We dismounted the BSA. Narika held on to me. We heard heavy footsteps behind us. Alarmed by their suddenness, I turned. Shadowy figures snatched Narika's hand from mine. A heavy blow to my head knocked me down. I felt a kick on my back. I curled up putting my hands around my head. I felt shearing lashes of clanking chains on my back. In the distance I heard Narika crying, 'Leave him . . . don't hurt him. He is innocent.' I wanted to get up and protect her. Then I heard a thick sinister voice in the darkness say, *Let's pull the bastard and run him over.* My blood curdled up. For past several months, I had heard these sinister words in my dreams. I shivered. Fear of dying gripped me. I tried desperately to get up and help Narika, but my limbs turned into jelly. My head was hurting. I tried shouting for help but no sound came from my throat. I heard the sound of a car. I heard hurried footsteps. I kept saying, 'Narika, Narika.' A heavy kick to my head . . . a curtain of darkness descended over my mind.

When I regained consciousness, I was in a brightly lit room with a strong smell of antiseptic and Dettol. Someone was shining a torch in my eyes. 'Where am I?' I asked. I heard Joger's voice. 'Junior, you are hurt in the head. Tavi and Pal beat you up at Kongoro. You are in good hands at Dr Samuel's Clinic.'

People came to Dr Samuel's Clinic in Gembe for discreet medical treatment. I was pleased that Joger had the good sense. Dr Samuel kept me under observation for a long time, frequently checking my eyes, nose and ears for internal bleeding and urging Joger and Nash to keep me awake and talk to me. Finally, around midnight he applied tincture of iodine to the gash in my head inflicted by Narika's nephews, checked me one more time and released me. He advised Joger that the serious blows to my head may cause amnesia and that if I showed signs of confusion or had bleeding from nose or ears I should be rushed to Emergency at Jerusha General. 'In any event,' Dr Samuel said, 'bring him back for a check-up in two days' time.'

In *Uhuru,* I examined my back. The chain lashes had turned blue. The inch-long gash in my head which Dr Samuel had irrigated with tincture of Iodine was burning like a seam of lava. I changed into my nightclothes and dumped my blood-stained clothes in the trash heap by the hen house where no one would find them. Then I crept into my bed. I was in a surreal stupor. In this distressful state, I speculated if metaphysics had anything to do with the events of the evening. That my recurring dream about someone trying to run me over would turn to reality on a dark street of Kongoro Estate and involve innocent Narika unnerved me. Her cries still rang in my ears. Nash had always told me. 'You phoney Einstein, there is a lot more beyond science.' Frightening reality of my ordeal at Kongoro Estate made me think seriously about fate and predestation. Was mine and Narika's fate predestined? A scientific part of me rejected it, but another part of me accepted that predestation had a role to play in the drama of life. This admission was like a lightning bolt. It brought flooding back to my mind Bhatji's prediction of Sun and Mars clashing in my horoscope.

Early next morning I searched pages of my physics textbook for Narika's letter. To my dismay I found an envelope stuck in the flap pocket. In it I found a letter and black and white photographs which showed me kissing Narika. I was certain Gul and his accomplices had doctored these. A rage built up in me. I was about to open the letter when Joger dropped by to check on me. He told me that after dropping me, he and Nash hunted for Gul and Harry. 'I thrashed them good. That Gul has run away to Congo. He is never coming back. As for Harry, he will never find a job in Jerusha. He is history too.' I had never seen Joger so animated. I asked him about Narika. 'Shusss, it is best not to talk,' he said, 'that Gul destroyed her.' Joger fell silent. I sat fiddling my fingers. My guilt was killing me. I felt responsible for Narika. The grief I felt caged me. I made up my mind to correct the situation. 'Joger, I will take blame for everything and I will marry Narika. My family knows her.'

'You are too late,' he told me. He added that during the night she ran away to Bombay with Raghuvir on Ethiopian Airlines. 'I don't know what promises Raghuvir made to her. He was like a vulture circling above. Bombay is not for innocent Narika.' Joger's stark statement dismayed me.

The secret motto of *Udhric* came to my mind. Narika had lived by it. She had put her life on line for me. I must do something for her. I told Joger, 'Maybe if I go to Bombay I can bring her back.' Joger stared at me, 'Have you gone crazy? My innocent friend this is not Jerusha Secondary

School drama. This is bad business. Concentrate on our drama.' When I argued, Joger read the riot act and said, 'Junior, the show must go on. Cut out Narika's dance.'

Late in the evening I phoned Joger with my suggestion. Joger liked it. He came over and we drove to Hendrix's, where we convinced Nathalie, Hendirx's girlfriend to play the part of the empress Mumtaj. She said she was honoured that we thought she was capable of playing such a character. Turning to Hendrix she said, 'Can you imagine I will be an empress?' He laughed. 'Remember, darling you are only a ghost. You have no substance.' I liked their chemistry.

At home Henna cornered me. 'What do you know about this Narika business?' I pleaded ignorance. 'You better not have anything to do with it. I told you not to get her involved. Now see what has happened.'

'Henna. can we talk about this after the exam?' I asked.

Congruence of Events

Vir had the only piece of good news for me since Saturday when Narika's nephews had beaten me savagely and Narika had run away to Bombay. When I came back from Pala with the reels of *Giant,* he was waiting for me and invited me to Moidin's. At Moidin's he was playful and asked me, 'Where do you get all this energy from?'

'What do you mean?' I asked him. He said, 'You continued drama rehearsals during exams, upsetting your drama team. Your heroine has run away to Bombay with some pimp. I don't know what relation you had with her, but your name keeps coming up. You have the Mumtaj Mahal debut tomorrow. You are relentless in chasing Palita and want to meet her tomorrow during your drama. Now you have brought reels of a film from USIS. What for?'

I sat listening to Vir, numb from all that was going on. 'Well, Vir,' I explained, 'I made a commitment to show *Giant* in our garden for my niece's birthday on Thursday. It is just that the film, the drama, *Janmastmi* and this Narika thing have come together at the same time.'

'Don't get a nervous breakdown,' he cautioned me. Simisu brought us cups of steaming Chinos and a plate full of *mandazi.* Vir took a *mandazi,* dunked it into his Chino and sat savouring it with gusto. I was getting exasperated. 'Vir, why did you bring me here?' He replied, 'Well my friend, Palita has agreed to attend Mumtaj Mahal.' Vir dunked another piece of *mandazi* in his Chino and while waiting for it to soak, he said, 'Wait, there is more. She said that you wear a red tie, and she'll wear a red hibiscus in her hair.' My heart swooned. 'Seriously?' I asked to be sure. I was suspicious if this was another Al Capon joke.

'She is serious. I have delivered my last message. She has finally fallen for you. I have to leave now.' I made Vir Sit down and said, 'You cannot leave so fast my friend.' From my sling bag, I pulled out a wrapped gift package and handed it to him. 'What is it?' he asked. 'Vir, open it.' He tore open the wrapping and saw the white-and-blue-striped Van Heusen shirt. 'Good gosh you didn't have to!' he said in gratitude.

'Vir, it is for our friendship. Without your help, nothing would have been possible.' Vir clasped my hand and said, 'It is a wonderful gift. You have raw charm. Palita said that too.'

On Wednesday, I woke up feeling miserable. The injury to my head from the kicks from Narika's nephews was pulsing. My back was sore from the chain lashes. I lumbered out of bed and phoned Joger and forgot what I wanted to tell him. Dr Samuel was right. From time to time my mind went blank. I convinced myself that everything was fine. Then I remembered what I wanted to tell Joger. I phoned him again. 'Joger, make sure Sudama rechecks the pulley before the curtains this afternoon.'

He assured me. 'Junior, relax. We'll take care of it.' I ate two Aspros and rested. The flywheel to pluck Palita from her castle was now in full motion. I went over my plan. After Mumtaj Mahal show, Palita and I would walk the short distance through War Memorial to Krishna Temple for *Janmastmi* Celebration. There I would watch Palita perform her *Radha* dance. Then I would hold her hand and lead her to the temple fire pit and ask Bhatji to perform our marriage with the god of fire as a witness, after which I would put a dab of vermilion in her hair. That would make her mine for ever. I had goose pimple simply thinking about it.

Time was crawling ever so slowly. I rechecked the rucksack from under my bed. In the last four days, I had done this five times. I threw out the stale groceries from the refrigerator. I peddled to Lobo Stores and bought new groceries. I peddled by the temple where preparations were in progress for *Janmastmi* celebration later that evening. When I came home, I saw Bhatji plundering our garden. Rehmat did not allow him to go closer to the Frangipani patch and told him that she would personally cut these for him.

'Please, madam give me all the colours. Do you know these were Krishna's favourite?' he pleaded with Rehmat.

Rehmat cut bunches of frangipani of all the colours and put them in Bhatji's basket. Then, she went indoors. I followed Bhatji and reminded him about the wedding he had to perform in the evening. He had forgotten all about it. 'Whose wedding?' he asked, scratching his bulging belly. 'Bhatji, I will tell you in the evening, after *Janmastmi.* Remember, there will be a very big gift for you. You have to perform a wedding after *Janmastmi.*'

'Okay, come to the fire pit, opposite the temple. Whose wedding?' he asked again.

'You will find out. And here, take this advance gift,' I discreetly handed him Ducat notes which surprised him. After he left, I shaped my hair with Yardley to hide the gash on my head and dressed up for the drama. Henna saw me and immediately blurted out. 'Why the red tie? Who are you trying to trap now?' I sensed sarcasm in her voice. I offered no answer. I was happy that at least she was communicative. I skipped lunch, which made Rehmat very unhappy. 'This is a sure way of falling ill,' she complained. 'Ma I will eat a big dinner after the drama,' I told her, as I collected my drama script and notes. Just when I was leaving for school, Henna came over, hugged me, and said, 'Good luck with the drama. I'll see you later at school.'

It was curtain time. Just when the headmaster was ready to make his introductory speech, Nash rushed to me, 'Einstein can we delay the curtain? There are people without seats. In our rush, we forgot to set up the stands at the back. I need help.' I asked Miss Sue to hold back the headmaster. Joger and I organised a group of boys to help Nash. Mr

Bondhu and his orchestra played light classical melodies to entertain the audience while Nash and the helpers set up the stand at the back. When Nash gave thumbs up the headmaster made a short introductory speech. The lights dimmed, and the stage curtains lifted to soft strains of Gustav Mahler's ninth Symphony. Mahler had written it to celebrate triumph of love over death. I wanted it to portray the emperor's nostalgia and the triumph of his love for his beloved Mumtaj. In a way, I wanted it to symbolise the triumph of my Quantum love.

On the stage bathed in orange, Joger's commanding figure, in his emperor's regalia, began delivering a powerful performance. Imprisoned in the Red Fort by his son, the emperor was pacing his cell, admiring the symbol of his eternal love, the Taj Mahal, in the distance. The props were superb thanks to our art master Mr Sara. Until this point I had deliberately not looked at the auditorium for Palita. I was waiting for that delicate moment when Mumtaj made her stage debut from the sky. Mahler's ninth was reaching its grand finale. Stage lighting turned translucent blue transforming Taj Mahal into a surreal edifice. Mr Bondhu introduced *sarangi,* flute, and harmonium notes to the dying strains of the ninth. Kintu turned on the fan, and swirling mist began to spread on the stage. Everything turned surreal. The audience sat spellbound in anticipation of some momentous event. Nathalie, hanging by a harness just above the curtains was ready to descend on to the stage. She looked stunningly beautiful in silk. All at once, the music tempo changed, and Ishrat's velvety voice filled the auditorium.

From beyond the nine spheres,
Compelled by your longings,
Your love...I come...

Mumtaj alias Nathalie began to descend gently from a misty blue sky. The emperor was romanticising about the time when his love with Mumtaj was in full bloom.

Beloved, rekindle the flame of our love.
This Taj Mahal . . .generations of eager hearts,
In its shadow shall
Reaffirm their love.

The vibrancy of music and the passion of poetry built up a world of anticipation in me. We were approaching that moment when I would look at the second seat in the third row and see the face of my beloved; the other half of my soul separated from me in the violent aftermath of the Big Bang. Just when on stage, Mumtaj would quench the emperor's love thirst, I will fill my chalice with Palita's love, our eyes would meet.

Boom . . . there was a loud bang followed by a sudden crash. A pandemonium broke in the auditorium. It dragged me rudely back to reality. The temporary stand at the back of the auditorium had collapsed. Ash and I rushed to it. A plank had given way from overweight. We pulled people from top of one another. There were minor bruises and bumps. Then, someone shouted 'Lambu is trapped.' We frantically lifted the planks and pulled crossbeams to rescue trapped Lambu. A pipe brace protected him from debris above him. In the meantime, someone had called an ambulance. With it came the police who shut down the show. Lambu had a dislocated shoulder. Ash and I went to the hospital with him. When I came back, the auditorium was deserted. For me, an excellent opportunity of having a face-to-face with my Quantum love was lost. I surveyed the deserted auditorium with sadness in my heart. Vir stood quietly beside me. Miss Sue came and joined us. 'Don't feel sad,' she said, 'we had no control on how it turned out.' I remembered Professor Pinto's lectures on Quantum Physics. 'Randomness and uncertainty are hallmarks of life,' he had said. I could not share my disappointment with anyone. Vir comforted me, 'It's not your fault. She waited for you. Then she left for the temple for her *Radha* dance. Oh, and she gave this note for you.' I opened it.

Dear Lovesick,

I love you. I am sorry for the mishap. I want you to see my dance at the temple. I will dance for you, only for you . . . my Krishna. Make me your flute, so that I may rest on your lips forever . . . Radha.

I tore a piece of paper from my diary, and I wrote her a reply:

Dear Princess
My heart is heavy. My love for you knows no bounds
What is Krishna without Radha?
After your dance, wait for me by the temple fire pit.
Bhatji will perform our union.
No matter what, please wait for me.
By this eve, we shall be one.

'Vir, please, give her this,' I said apprehensively.

At home, Salim shared my disappointment. Everyone consoled me. This made me weak and tearful. Then Azul said, 'Son, why did you agree to the extra stand without the headmaster's permission? Now that Ben is making a big deal about some boy getting hurt. The police are involved. You do things without informing anyone.'

'Daddy, what you said is not true,' I protested. Azul was charged. The furrows on his forehead seemed deeper. He raised his voice, 'Son I gave you freedom in this drama and cinema business and you are already talking to people behind my back about going to Bombay – and we at home know nothing about it. This drama business has upset you. I want you to disengage from all this for a few days. Stay home tonight. Do you understand?'

The imposition of a curfew surprised me. I hung my head in silence. 'Answer me son,' Azul pressed. The anxiety and the disappointment of events had the better of me. I reacted in a fashion unlike me. I burst out, 'Listen you all, I am not going to Bombay. Why do I get the finger pointed every time? Daddy, why are you imposing a curfew? You question me if I go to the pictures. You beat me up if I go to the river. What do you all want me to do? Shrink and die!' My outburst shocked everyone. I stormed out.

Jeff came over to *Uhuru*, 'You should be ashamed to talk like that to daddy. It was about time he called spade a spade. You have been out of control. Family is tired of you.'

'Jeff, I have too much on my mind. Leave me alone.'

'Yes, I know what's on your mind. You are crazy.' I did not want to argue with him. I was more worried about how to bring my plan to marry Palita to fruition. I did not want a debacle similar to Mumtaj Mahal. My vision was clear. There was no way I could stay indoors. Not tonight, come hell or high water. I would have to disobey Azul. I had to bring Palita home.

'Don't do anything stupid,' Jeff said as he left *Uhuru*.

I dressed up in a white bush shirt and jeans and put the agate necklace for Palita and money for Bhatji in my jeans pocket. I fished out the small vermilion bottle from the rucksack and put it in a paper bag. From the garden, I collected a bunch of flowers and added them to the vermilion bag. I took a small pocket torch and tucked it in my belt to shine Palita's way at night. Then I waited. Rehmat came to my door. 'Son, don't mind your daddy's comments. We do it only for your good. Please come and have dinner.'

'Ma I am not hungry. I will eat later.'

'You are not cross, are you?' she asked. 'No Ma, everything is fine. I am just tired.' Rehmat knew my moods and gave me space. 'Okay eat when you are hungry.'

At sunset when birds settled down in the trees, I turned on the radio and deliberately increased the volume and left *Uhuru*. Simba followed me. He sensed my stealth and did not bark. At the Bougainville Rocks, he stopped and wagged his tail. I hugged him. He looked at me as if he knew my intent and was telling me, 'Go, get your prize.'

'Simba' I whispered to him, 'when Palita comes home, she will be your best friend.' He licked my face. I plunged into Suwakaki on my journey to my beloved. I had a warm glow in my heart knowing that Palita was waiting for me. A strange force was pulling me towards her. I remembered a quote by Einstein: gravity is not what makes people fall in love. In my case, not gravity but Quantum Physics had everything to do with love. I kept Einstein's idea at the back of my mind for later analysis. I walked on Jackson Crescent towards the temple. Strains of a popular *Janmastmi* folk song were wafting from the temple.

I had an eerie feeling that something was not right. I glanced back and saw a car following me with its headlamps switched off. I became alarmed and reciting *Nade Ali*, the spiritual SOS of Shia, I broke into a gallop and ran into the War Memorial. The car jumped the curb and switched on its headlamps. I ran between neat rows of memorial tablets. The car kept following me, cutting a swath of destruction in its wake. I ran towards the woods on my left. Suddenly, the car bogged down in the soft terrain of the War Memorial with an agonising whine. I glanced back and saw its drooping headlamps. 'Good,' I said. I continued running, emerging on Sycamore Drive and paused for a breath. All at once, from the shadow of the darkness, a man emerged behind me. It unnerved me. The dazzling halo of the temple was now behind me, where Ishrat had started singing, "*Amorous Krishna*", the grand finale of *Janmastmi* celebration. I was certain Palita was dancing. Her eyes must be roving, looking for me in the crowd. I said aloud, 'Dance my darling; I will be with you soon.' Without a second thought, I dived into the dark, inviting wall of Suwakaki to confuse my predator. I ran from tree to tree, pausing, trying to pick up the noises of my predator. Chirping of crickets and croaking of frogs pervaded the Forest. I followed the brook to get to the familiar twin fig trees. From there, I wanted to trace my footsteps to Commander Leman's bomb shelter and home. Suddenly a shadow jumped on me. A flock of birds flew away with great clamour. I raised my hands in defence; the sudden attack disoriented me. 'Caught you, you bastard,' a man hissed. He threw a noose around my neck and continued to tighten it. He hissed, 'You want to pluck her from the temple? You filthy shit, you want a priest to marry you. You want to pollute pure Hindu blood?' My eyes were bulging out. My lungs were bursting. The veins in my brain were ready to explode. *Nade Ali . . . Ali help me*, I whispered. I had may be fifteen seconds before I died and went to heaven. Zafur's face flashed on the dream screen room of my mind. I went back to the day when Bisney gang had attacked him at the Palladium during the *Rainy Night* midnight show and I had saved his life. When we were safe in his flat, he had showed me a trick, 'This is a sandwich clap. It is dangerous, but when you have no other line of defence, use it.'

I realised it was time to use the "sandwich clap". My pocket torch was in my left hand. I clenched my fists around it. With remaining power of mind over matter left in me, I raised my arms and brought my fists together like a clap on my assailant's temples. It was my last proverbial Dead Cat Bounce. 'Ahe . . . eeh,' he cried out and fell to the ground with a grunt. His grip on my neck loosened. Air gushed into my lungs, and blood rushed to my head. I felt dizzy and fainted.

When I regained consciousness, I was lying face down in complete darkness. I sat up and wiped my face. Frightened and confused, I fumbled for my pocket torch in the darkness. I found it near my foot. I switched it on and flicked the bright narrow beam side to side. My assailant was on his back to my right. I shone the torch on his face. I was shocked. It was the face of the arrogant man who had stood behind me at Socram and had tried to listen to my conversation with Kala, the cashier, when I had purchased clothing for Palita. I put my hand to his nostrils. Not breathing. My heart sank. Was he dead? I put my head to his chest. No heartbeat. Good grief, did I kill him? Panic and fear were drowning me. I jumped up with a suddenness that surprised me. I wanted to run. There was a dead man at my feet. I took deep breaths and counted to ten. Murder lessons from gruesome Hitchcock pictures that I had come to memorise came rushing to my mind. I needed to hide the body. I held the torch in my mouth and dragged the dead man with difficulty towards the bomb shelter twenty meters away. He was heavy, and his limp hands kept slipping from my grip. Nearer to the shelter, my torch dropped from my mouth and turned off. Suwakaki plunged into darkness. I pulled my assailant in the dark, propped him against the low wall of the bomb shelter, and covered him with climbers and leaves. Then I ran back to *Uhuru*.

I crept into my bed. Amin Sayani was concluding the Hit Parade on Radio Ceylon. My mind was far from music. I began to shiver and felt feverish. I had killed a man. It was self-defence . . . I kept repeating in my mind. I heard Rehmat calling me, 'Son, I did not hear you, all evening. You did not eat dinner or any fruit.'

'Ma, I am not hungry,' I replied. Rehmat left me alone. I sat up in bed. How did my assailant know about my motive? He must have read my last note to Palita. My goodness, did Vir betray me? Did Palita conspire? Did Bhatji reveal my intention? Who hired the killer, for that was what he was? I had heard stories of families hiring such killers to end undesirable liaisons. I broke into a cold sweat at that very thought. Up on Murima the Smelter chimney was belching noxious fumes like an angry dragon. In the distance, Jerusha Station was alive with its nightly locomotive shunting. I agonised if I should wake up Azul, tell him about the dead man, and face the consequences. Then I deluded myself that no one would find him. He was well hidden. I remembered that in Hitchcock's *Strangers on a Train*, the perpetrator thought he had gotten away with murder, but not so fast. Murderer always left a clue behind. A smart sleuth always stumbled upon it. I remembered that in my haste I had left the torch and the bag with the vermilion bottle and flowers in the vicinity. This thought immobilised me. My mind projected all kinds of story lines on dream screen of my mind. I regretted breaking Azul's curfew. Jeff's words came to my mind, 'Don't do anything stupid.' I had no choice. Palita was waiting for me. Did Mahiwal fear the raging river for love of Sohni? And then there was the *Udhric* motto – *when we love, we die!*

Back in Green Ford: Madam Doctor's Grand Plan

There was a screech. Madam Doctor had stopped the Ford inches from a pair of deer in the middle of the road. I jolted back to reality from my Time Travel with the painful knowledge that my master plan to pluck Palita from her castle had not materialised. A man lay dead in Suwakaki behind our home. To complicate matters, a new dimension had opened up. Amina had come back into my life.

The deer stood in the middle of the road, looking at us, wriggling their tails and ears. Madam Doctor exclaimed, 'Beautiful creatures! I would have knocked them down, if I was not careful.' The deer trotted off into the forest. Madam Doctor drove a short distance, turned into a small lane, and stopped the Ford on the brow off a hill overlooking the vast expanse of Peace Lake. 'I am sorry I dozed off,' I apologised. Madam Doctor put me at ease, 'It's okay. I woke you up early this morning. We should refresh.' We stepped out of the Ford. Madam Doctor had brought with her a flask from which she poured cups of tea and asked, 'Mr Perry told me about your boxing camp. How was it?' I had run out of patience. 'Madam, whose child is Jill? Why the bungalow?' She smiled, 'I was about to explain.' She gave me a brief explanation. She fell in love with Heinz, a visiting research fellow from Germany when she was teaching at Pala University. She conceived Jill at the University. Heinz was the father. And after that it was all a Bollywood Picture love story. Heinz returned to Germany and in the meantime Madam Doctor's family forced her to merry SB. She had to conceal her pregnancy and Jill's birth. Heinz, when he found out, was devastated and continued to live in Germany. Madam Doctor wiped her tears as she added, 'Jill has grown up in that Bungalow from her birth. Only four people including you know this story.'

'Madam, how does Amina come into this?'

'She came to Jerusha Hospital with a broken pelvis. She required surgery. It was a sad story of gang rape by some footballers. The police were under pressure to drop charges against them. In a fight that followed her rape, one of the footballers was knifed. He was close to death with a collapsed lung. The other had a broken jaw. We treated all three at Jerusha Hospital. Later, we moved Amina to Dr Barnard's clinic on the Island when she had a body cast on her. Marina, the ayah, was looking after Jill in the Lake Bungalow at that time. Later, I moved Amina to the bungalow while she was recovering. She was alone and needed help. She faced a vagrancy charge. Later, when Marina was unable to look after Jill, Amina started to help.'

'Madam, why are you sharing your secret with me?'

'Do you remember, young man, one time I told you I will need your help. Well, my daughter has a hole in the heart and she needs help very quickly. A team of specialists is in Nairobi next week from Cleveland. I would like you to accompany Amina and Jill to Nairobi. I have no one else I can trust. I cannot slip out. My mother-in-law has me followed.'

'Can Mr Heinz not come from Germany?' I asked.

'He will meet you in Nairobi. There isn't enough time for him to come here to fetch Jill,' Madam Doctor explained. I made excuses to wriggle out of travelling to Nairobi. Madam Doctor reminded me of my promise. She said that she would facilitate my trip by getting Mr Perry and Mr Edward to issue letters to the Kenya Boxing Association for me to study their training preparations. 'That will be a reason enough for your family to allow you to travel.' Madam Doctor left me no other options.

My agreement, to an extent, was influenced by the fact that I would be with Amina. Madam Doctor looked relieved and added, 'Amina would be with you to take care of Jill. She is very motherly. I have arranged for a driver. You have driver's license, don't you? Avenue Garage has a VW Beetle to drive to Nairobi.'

'Drive to Nairobi? Can we not just fly? It is so much easier.'

'Next week is the big Africa Summit in Pala. Our airport will be on high alert. Then our president goes to Arusha, so travel through airport is impossible with a child when you are not the natural parents. Driving will take only six hours.' I had no choice. I agreed.

Nairobi – The Star of Africa

Azul bid his time until we sat down for dinner on Sunday before he announced that I had been invited by the Kenya Boxing Association to go to Nairobi. I marvelled at the efficiency with which Madam Doctor had put into action her grand plan. Azul's announcement surprised Rehmat, 'Will he not join the holiday?'

'So it seems. He has to leave by tomorrow. A car will await him at Avenue Garage,' Azul replied. This upset Rehmat. 'Nairob! I have never let him go further than Pala. Nairobi is too far. He has to be here for the Friday *Majalis*.' Azul ignored her and sang my praises, 'The boy has to grow up and he is smart. He'll be gone only a few days and will be home by Thursday.'

After dinner Azul handed me my passport. To Jeff, he handed a bunch of passports and said, 'These are the rest of family passports, just in case you go across the Border to Rwanda with Mr Ramji for dinner. There is a nice French Bistro across the Border.'

I started packing my duffel bag for the trip to Nairobi. My radio was at full volume and I did no hear Jeff and Salim come in. Salim lowered the volume. I anticipated a verbal assault from Jeff for some flimsy reason. Instead he dropped a bombshell saying that he and Salim had a gift for me at Pumzika. A gift from Jeff was a new one for me. I wanted to immediately cycle to JCB and retrieve it but decided to wait until the following Saturday when I had a "dinner date" at JCB with Savi to look at the Watanabe Paintings.

Due to a miscalculation, Mr Safi of Avenue Garage had no driver for me. I did not get the keys to the VW until after lunch. I phoned Madam Doctor and updated her on the situation. 'Well,' she said, 'in that case, you will have to drive.' We agreed to meet on a quiet street behind the Station.

As arranged, Madam Doctor was waiting with Amina and Jill in the innocuous Green Ford. There was a quick transfer. Amina put Jill in the back seat of the VW and hopped in the front. I loaded their luggage. Madam Doctor handed me Jill's medical papers and her passport. She explained that Amina had own passport. Just before we drove off she handed me a half-torn 1000 Ducat note and said that she will explain its purpose on the phone. A short goodbye and we were off, driving east towards Kenya Border.

The responsiveness of the souped-up VW Beetle and the lush green landscape flying past us lifted my spirit. Anxiety about Palita loosened its grip on my heart. Narika's fate simmered below the surface. Jill was snug under a blanket in the back seat. Amina was beside me listening to the songs and music that we used to enjoy together in Pumzika.

A few miles past Giri, I took the road towards Ronko Check-point. Mr Safi had advised me to use the Ronko and the not the Bulaya Check-point. 'It is less used and immigration is much easier,' he had said. Bulaya Highway was the main asphalted transport artery from Kenya to our landlocked country. Ronko Road was a different story. Within a few miles the asphalted section ended and we began travelling on unpaved road. The surface of such roads comprises gravel and fine dust of red mud that is often used by the locals to plaster their huts. The VW started to float on the thin film of dust like a hovercraft. The soothing drone of the engine turned into a shrill whine and I had to increase the speed to keep control. The cabin was intensely hot so I rolled the window down for air. The whine of the engines and rushing air made it impossible to enjoy the music. As we drove, African homesteads of thatched huts and allotments of cassava shrubs and banana and mango trees appeared and disappeared like a mirage. Soon, open savannah of tall grass and shrubs gave way to thickening forest and signs of civilization faded. Ahead of us loomed the forested Ronko Mountain Range, already beginning to look like a dark wall in the evening sun. Air became cooler and we rolled up the windows. I inserted a tape in the player to keep us company.

The sun set rapidly behind the hills and it turned dark. We entered the Roko Mountain Range and the VW started to groan as we zig-zagged along the torturous Zinga Pass towards Ronko Check-Point. Africa was beautiful in brilliant sunshine, but when it turned dark, the unsigned mud roads that often became washed-out grass tracks, the tall elephant grass, the umbrella shaped trees and thick walls of dark jungle bordering the roads assumed unnerving quality. The tape ended. Amina sensed my anxiety and made conversation to keep me company, 'What will the doctors do to Jill in Nairobi?'

'Amina, these specialists may treat her in USA if required.' Amina went quiet. I asked her a question that was on my mind ever since I saw Jill, 'It must be difficult for Madam Doctor to keep everything about Jill a secret.'

'Yes, sometimes when she visits, she cries,' Amina replied.

'I've heard that her husband has a mistress in Pala.' I said.

'No, it is not a mistress. He has a he-stress. He likes man and not woman.'

'Seriously? It is very bad for Madam Doctor, if this is true,' I commented. Amina giggled and said, 'She told me that he loves a man, a musician who plays at La Quinta Club in Pala.' I began to understand Madam Doctor's temptations, and her actions in the City Light.

The Ronko Border Check-Point was a mosquito infested small hall with a light bulb that cast a dull orange glow on the walls. A generator hummed somewhere in the darkness behind the hall. A sleepy immigration officer stamped our passports and allowed us to eat our dinner in a room adjoining the main hall. But before that he sprayed it with DDT from a Fleet Pump. 'This will kill the mosquitoes,' he added. Jill was awake and playful. Amina fed her a bottle of Gerber and gave her medications. We ate cold kofta and shared a Pepsi, which reminded us of our intimacy in boxing club. Jill wanted to drink Pepsi. Amina cautioned me, 'She will get high and won't sleep.'

Just before we drove off, the immigration officer cautioned me in private, 'Be careful of these roads at night.' My fear of darkness became more concrete. I drove with caution. Jill fell asleep to the drone of the VW in Amina's lap in the back seat. I relaxed when we finally joined the asphalted Nairobi Trunk Road. Contrary to my expectation, the forested Trunk Road was as dark and lonely as the Ronko Road we had travelled. Ghostlike trees flew past us, mesmerising me as I sped up. I wanted to be at Norfolk Hotel by midnight. To lift the mood, I inserted a tape. Lata's voice filled the cabin. 'What song is this?' Amina asked.

'You have not heard this before. *Amaar* was a love story with a twist.'

'What kind of a twist?'

'On a rainy night, a circuit lawyer who was to marry the local landlord's daughter makes love to a village girl and gets her pregnant. The story is the struggle of the hero to do the right thing and marry the village girl.' Lata continued to croon. After this Amina went quiet. Suddenly, a loud thud shook up the VW and it wobbled. I slammed the brakes. Amina was alarmed, 'What is it?'

'Nothing to worry, Amina, let me look.' I left the engine running, fetched a torch from the glove compartment and stepped out. My fear was that we had hit an animal. This was leopard territory. I went around the car and found no damage. I opened the engine hatch to check the engine. It was purring smoothly. In the distance behind me, high beams of an approaching vehicle pierced the darkness. Sign of human company encouraged me. The light beams disappeared as the approaching vehicle went around a curve in the road. The VW head lamps fought hard to ward off the darkness. The approaching vehicle re-emerged from the curve and its multiple head beams dazzled me as it approached. A Tata transport truck was soon upon us. It stopped. From its high window, a Sikh driver leaned over. 'What is the matter, brother?'

'I don't know. Something hit us but no sign of damage,' I replied.

'Arre, *Pape*, brother, it is the *kondos*, highway robbers. Check your tires. They must be flat. They put nails on the road. Quick, you must abandon this car and get in the truck.'

'Abandon the car? What do you mean?'

'That is it, *Pape*, abandon the car. These *kondos* rob and kill. They only did not come yet because they saw us coming. They are hiding close by.' I checked the tyres, and found two flat tyres. Panic swelled in me. I opened the car door and took sleeping Jill from Amina's lap and asked Amina to grab Jill's food and medicine bags. Amina did not ask questions. The Sikh opened the front truck door. I helped Amina climb into the cabin and handed Jill to her. The Sikh and his two turn-boys helped me transfer all our bags to the back of the truck. I picked up the document folder with Jill's birth certificate and passport and made a last check to make sure I had everything, climbed in to the truck and slammed the door shut. I took sleeping Jill in my lap. She started to cry. Amina patted her to sleep. The Sikh drove off. Once on the road, he looked at us in disbelief. 'Are you mad, stupid or both? How the hell do you travel this road at night with a child and a wife? Very dangerous road. The *kondos* rob your car and leave you on the roadside. We carry guns. Lucky, I came just in time.' I pleaded ignorance. He shook his head and muttered. 'Stupid.' The Sikh, whose name was Perminder, drove steadily through the night and we reached Nairobi's Dagoretti Corner just when the sun was rising.

Despite the loss of VW to the *kondos*, my enthusiasm for Nairobi, the Star of Africa, came back. Only a rail junction on a windswept African Savannah at the turn of the 20th Century, Nairobi had blossomed into an exciting metropolis with broad avenues, several cinemas, International hotels, jazz clubs and a thriving centre of commerce within a span of sixty years.

Cyclists, motorcycles, buses, and Peugeots 403 *matatus,* all honking their horns or ringing their bells clogged the roads into centre of Nairobi. In the cold and crispy morning, smoke and mist hung like a pall over the shanty town that littered both sides of the road.

'Welcome to Nairobi,' a grinning Perminder said. 'Where are you staying?' When I told him to drop us at the Norfolk Hotel, he shook his head. '*Pape,* why stay at white man's hotel? Too much trouble around this hotel. Stay at Parklands, good Indian hotel.' I replied that it was too late to change the booking. At Norfolk, I thanked him. Before he left he said, 'You can report your stolen car. But it won't help. Look after your family.'

I immediately fell in love with Norfolk's colonial façade, especially Lord Delamere Terrace, about which I had heard many stories. From the room, I made a brief phone call to Madam Doctor and informed her of our arrival but made no mention of the VW incident. 'Remember,' she concluded, 'Heinz will call you. Match the half 1000 Ducate note I gave you before you trust anyone. Keep phoning me.' I also phoned home and told Jeremy to inform Azul that I had reached safely.'

Late in the afternoon, we walked a short distance to Nairobi City Centre and enjoyed the sights and sounds of the bustling metropolis. Amina was impressed with the broad avenues and sleek ladies' shops on Government Road and Delamere Avenue. I told her that once we had finished with Jill's medical examinations, we would spend a whole day shopping. Amina was excited and pointed out to me the dresses and the cosmetics she wanted. At the Ice Cream Parlour Jill went insane, wanting to try every ice cream flavour. We had to leave halfway through a sundae to control her tantrum.

Back in our room, Jill fell asleep halfway through her dinner of peas and carrots, holding Mickey in her hand. Amina made her comfortable on the bed and went for a shower. I slept on my side to ease the pain I had on my back from the chain lashings. I thought about the room arrangement. I would have thought that Madam Doctor would have booked two rooms. With these thoughts in my mind, I dozed off. When I woke up Amina was kneeling by the bed gently massaging my back. We became aware of our closeness. Before my Quantum Love for Palita, I had shared intimate moments with her. My sex lesson 2 flashed in my mind: no love, no sex. Although I was never able to verbalise my feelings for her after our intimacy in the Boxing Club, there was an implicit understanding of a shared commitment between us. With the knowledge of her pain, and suffering after her rape, what was my commitment to her?

As she massaged my back, her fingers pressed on a tender spot where Tavi and Pal had lashed me. I cried out. This startled her. 'What's wrong?' She pulled up my shirt. The blue bruises horrified her. 'It is okay, Amina. It was nothing, a small fight.' She held my head to her bosom. I put my arms around her. When she calmed down, I asked her, 'What about dinner?' She pointed to sleeping Jill. 'We have to eat in the room.'

I got out of bed and told her, 'I will take a walk and order room service.' At the restaurant, I ordered dinners for room 113 and took a brisk walk around the Norfolk. The National Theatre, VOK Radio Station and the University which surrounded the Norfolk were bathed in pink of setting sun. Crisp Nairobi air was a new experience for me compared to the steamy sunsets in Jerusha. When I came back to the room, Amina ran in to my arms with an ashen face. I became alarmed and kissed her on her cheek, 'Amina, what is it?'

'Madam wants us to hand Jill to her father who would take her to Germany,' she replied. I asked Amina if she gave any reasons. 'No,' she said. 'She said that when we meet him, we have to ask for a code word. He will say Venus 123 and he also has to give you a half-torn 1000 Ducat note.' I dialled the reception and asked to be connected to Madam Doctor's number. The phone kept ringing. In the meantime, a waiter brought our dinners. I pointed to the patio. The waiter set the dinners and left. I put the phone down and led Amina to the patio and sat close to her. She was still upset. She entwined her legs with mine. We ate in silence. Below us, teeming night lights of Nairobi stretched far into the horizon. 'What are you thinking about?' I asked her. She started to cry. 'Two years. Why didn't you look for me?' she asked.

'Look for you? Amina, you have no idea how much I looked for you. I went everywhere. I checked every hospital.' As I said this, I tried to hold her hand. She spurned it. She was agitated. She came closer and beat on my chest. I let her. She had every right to. What had happened to her was very bad. Suddenly she stood up and ran into the room. I followed her. She picked up her shawl, opened the door, and ran out. I followed her to the end of the corridor. 'Amina, wait . . .come back. It is not safe to go out alone,' I shouted. She disappeared around the corridor. I was afraid to leave Jill alone. I came back to the room, dimmed the lights and sat in a chair facing the door. I waited, hoping that fresh air would calm Amina down. Time ticked on. I meditated: deep breaths, inhale, and exhale. I looked at the clock. It was past midnight. I was getting angry. How childish of her to walk out in a strange city at night? Where could she have gone? I waited. Sleep began to overtake me. I dreamt. I felt vibrations all through my body. I was floating on clouds of happiness. All at once the tempo of the dream changed and I saw six blurry faces floating in my dream. I heard crying of a girl. Suddenly, voices outside in the corridor reeled me back to reality. I looked at my watch. It was 2 a.m. The door creaked open. In the dim light, I saw Amina. She had a Mona Lisa smile on her face. 'You have a nerve . . .' I started to say.

'Shhh,' she said softly, 'you will wake up Jill.' She pulled me up from my chair. I sensed a transformation in her. Had she been drinking? She said softly, 'I ran out angry with you and Madam. I am sorry.'

'Where have you been all this time?' I asked. She ignored me and said. 'What is my future after Jill is gone? I am like a mother to her. Even if you love me, there is no future.'

'Amina . . .' I started to say. She kissed me. 'You are my first love. You have known me, as no one else will. When those animals raped me, I was carrying your child .'

'What?' My head started to spin. 'Yes, I was pregnant with your child for four weeks when those animals raped me and crushed me.' Tears rolled down her cheeks. I held her with a passion. She continued to talk, 'Madam had to abort to save me. You don't know what it means to lose a life that is growing inside you. It was our child, my prince.' She fell silent. Her utterances were like lightning strikes. I mumbled incoherently. 'My child. You pregnant . . . Amina.' She looked up and kissed me. 'I love you...I love you because of your simplicity, your love for music, pictures. But you are still at school.'

'But . . . Amina, you were pregnant . . . I didn't know.' She stepped back and said, 'When I walked out of the room, I was angry. I sat in the dining room to calm down. On the next table was this man. His name is Alfred. When he saw me crying, he asked about my trouble. First, I ignored him, but I had an attraction to him.'

'That is because you are angry and vulnerable. Men take advantage,' I said. She wiped her tears and said, 'It is possible. But one thing led to another and I found that Alfred has been to Jerusha. He knows JCB. We went for a walk. We talked.'

'What are you saying?' I was getting confused.

'What I am saying is that I like this Alfred. I can't say I love him. But I like him. He is thirty-six. He is single and lives in Brazzaville. He has a job, and he wants to marry me.' I became hysterical.

'Marry you? Just like that. Amina, are you out of your mind? You don't know this person from Adam. What if he is a sex slave trader?' Despite my Quantum love for Palita, the knowledge that Amina had carried my child changed everything. I wanted to throw my arms around her and protect her. 'No, Amina. Please. We have to talk to Madam Doctor,' I said in desperation. My hysteria amused her. She said, 'I feel happy, my prince, that you love me. I am doing what is best for both of us. I don't care for Madam. For two years, I was her prisoner. Alfred is waiting outside. Before you meet him, let me explain. He leaves on the six o'clock flight for Brazzaville. And I leave with him.'

'What? In the morning? Leave. What about Jill?'

'Jill is the reason I must leave with Alfred. I can't just hand her over to some German and say goodbye. I would die.'

I met Alfred in the dead of night in the corridor while Amina packed her bag. I was unable to make any judgment of a thirty-six-year-old man taking away a twenty something girl, who could have been the mother of my child, to be his wife. Extremely nervous, I asked, 'How far is Brazzaville'?

'Three-hour flight to Leopoldville and then another hour.'

'Can Amina visit Jerusha?'

'Of course, any time she wishes.

'You will not beat her like how a lot of men do their wives?'

'Of course not.'

'Are you a sex slave trader?' Laughter. 'No.'

I had never faced a more challenging situation. I ran out of questions. With her bag packed, Amina gave me instructions about Jill. 'She likes you and trusts you. Love her, and she will love you back. Feed her well. She likes her hair neatly done. Bath her in the morning.' While she was saying this, she broke down. She walked close to the bed and felt Jill's forehead. 'She still has a temperature. If she wakes up, give her one spoon of that dark medicine. In the morning, give her a tablet from the bottle.'

She paused, took a last look at Jill, hugged me, and left. Alfred carried her small bag. I stood in the corridor and watched them walk away. I wanted to shout and stop her. My mouth was dry. I whimpered like Simba when he was in pain. When Amina and Alfred were halfway through the corridor, I ran and caught hold of Amina's shoulder. She turned; she was still crying. I took all the money from my pocket. 'Here, keep this money as a reserve. If things do not work out, Amina please take the first flight and come home. You have my telephone number. Please phone me.'

'Prince, I don't need money.' I insisted. She kept half and returned me the rest. She joined Alfred. I watched them disappear around the corridor.

Bright sunshine was filtering through the patio door when I woke up. I got out of bed and dialled home. I talked in a low voice. Jeremy informed me that Azul had already left for work. 'Jeremy, have the police been keeping an eye on our house, I mean with no one home?'

'I have not seen any police, but there are lot more army jeeps at commander's home.' I heaved a sigh of relief. 'Has anyone been looking for me?' I asked. Jeremy's answer surprised me. 'Yes, there was a girl and a boy that came yesterday. He had a cast on his hand. The girl kept crying.' I pressed Jeremy to be more specific. He was evasive. I put the phone down. Who could the boy be with a cast on his hand? Who could the girl be that cried as she waited for me? Was it Narika looking for me, or could it be Palita? The phone rang again. I picked it up quickly, not to disturb Jill. The receptionist informed me that a Mr Heinz wanted me to meet him for breakfast at 9 am at Intercontinental Hotel. The time was 8:30 am. I requested the receptionist to arrange a taxi. I wanted to get the sordid Jill exchange done as quickly as possible. I brushed and changed. I wrapped Jill in her pink teddy bear blanket, picked her papers, and rushed out with sleeping Jill on my shoulder to a waiting taxi. Then I remembered that I had left the room without Jill's food and clothes' bags and Mickey. I put Jill in the back seat of the taxi and asked the driver to wait while I fetched the bags from my room. I rushed to the room, scrambled and collected Jill's stuff and rushed back. I was crossing the reception lobby when I heard gunshots outside the hotel. A great commotion erupted in the lobby. There was a stampede from the Garden Restaurant as guests took cover in the lobby. Staff shut the front door and pulled down the shutters. Gunfire continued to be heard outside. I ran to the door. The attendant barred my way. I was hysterical, 'But Jill is in the taxi,' I started to shout. The attendants pulled me behind a counter, 'Brother, it is war. Soldiers will shoot you on sight.'

'But Jill is in the taxi,' I kept saying, in utter panic.

'The taxi is gone,' the attendant replied. Wailing sirens and more gunfire drowned our voices. We crouched on the floor, fearful of stray bullets coming through the glass. I was weak at the knees. I wanted to bang my head on the floor.

We were trapped in the Norfolk lobby. No one knew the reason for the gunfire outside. Everyone in the hotel knew about Jill's story. Two English women comforted me. The manager assured me that she would be safe.

Around ten o'clock, news came that there was an assassination attempt on a senior minister who was attending an early morning interview at VOK Radio Station across from the Hotel. The minister's security men had warded off the attack until reinforcement arrived.

When the hotel doors finally opened, I rushed out looking for the taxi with Jill in it. Most of the area was cordoned off by the paramilitary. There were no taxis in sight. The door attendant told me that at the sound of the first shot, everyone ran away. I spent the next several hours, in futile search for Jill at all possible taxi depots around Nairobi. When I returned to Norfolk the receptionist ran to me. 'Your daughter is here. She is safe. She is in there.' I rushed to the Garden Restaurant and found Jill sitting in the lap of a girl with black framed glasses. Her hair was tied in a pony with a purple ribbon. 'Jill,' I shouted, unable to contain my excitement. I bent down and Jill locked her arms around my neck and clung to me like how a baby monkey clings to her mother. 'My baby, Tam is sorry. Are you okay?' She looked happy. The girl, who had Jill in her lap, looked up. 'Is she your daughter?' she asked. I cuddled Jill and felt her forehead. She had no fever. 'My niece. She is my niece,' I replied.

'What carelessness? Abandoning a child.'

'I did not abandon her. It is a long story. I thank you for caring for her,' I replied.

'Thanking does not help,' the girl replied tersely.

'How did you find her?' I asked. To my surprise, Jill wriggled back in to her lap. I asked the girl if I could sit at the table. 'Yes,' the girl replied. Her face had a classical look as if it was lifted out of a European Renaissance painting. Our art master had shown us a Goya painting that had a similar look. I introduced myself. The girl barely looked up and said, 'I am Mahi.' She continued to play with Jill. Gradually, I learnt from her that when the first shots were fired at VOK, she was just leaving the University. The taxi driver, as he sped, stopped briefly and hurled sleeping Jill at her. Before she could react, the taxi had taken off. Mahi ran in to the Electrical Department with crying Jill. 'She is an adorable and easy-going child,' Mahi said. I inquired if Jill had eaten anything. Mahi ran her hand through Jill's hair and said, 'We were next to the cafeteria so we had no difficulty with food.'

Mahi was blunt and said I was a delinquent. She handed Jill to me and stood up to leave, saying, 'Please, take care of this child.' I was upset that she was leaving without allowing me an opportunity to clear her misunderstanding. When Jill sensed that Mahi was leaving, she began to cry. 'It is okay, Jill,' I tried to console her. Mahi dropped her handbag on the chair and picked Jill up. 'What kind of magic have you weaved on her?' I asked. Jill was happy and stopped crying. Just then the hotel manager came and asked me to accompany him to the reception. Mahi followed me with Jill. At the desk, the manager informed me that due to the VOK attack, government officials and security staff had taken up all vacant rooms in the hotel and since I had only one night's booking he had released my room. This surprised me. 'My booking was for three nights,' I told him. He informed me that there was no instruction to extend the room and that my room payment had not been received as promised. I assured the manager that I would pay the bill and requested him to find me a room in a nearby hotel. He told me that all hotels in the city were fully booked. 'I will arrange a taxi for you to see if some of the smaller guesthouses have availability. Your bags are with the concierge,' he added. In trying to settle my hotel bill Mahi saw me desperately searching my pockets for more money and asked, 'What is the problem?'

'I am short of money. It is a big confusion,' I apologised. Mahi shook her head. 'How did I get entangled with you?'

'I can explain,' I said, trying to hide my embarrassment. She opened her purse and settled my bill. I thanked her and said, 'Please give me your address and I will send you the money, I promise.' She ignored what I said and asked, 'Now where will you go?' I shrugged my shoulder. She continued to shake her head. 'This is impossible. What universe are you from?' We walked to a waiting taxi. A porter loaded my luggage in the taxi. I took Jill from her. In a sudden cat-like motion Mahi jumped into the taxi. 'Don't stand there. Get in. You can't go around with a child, looking for a hotel room, you fool.' She instructed the driver to take us to Easy Guest House.

At the Easy Guest House, I thanked her again and asked for her address. 'Later, now we go for lunch at the Food Alley. Bring a blanket for Jill. It gets chilly in the open.'

During lunch, I tried to clear the bad impression Mahi had of me. She listened to my story and then tapped my head. 'Hello, what is wrong with your grey matter? Have you heard of a fully-grown woman walking away with a stranger in the middle of the night? Or for that matter why did not Jill's mother bring her for examination herself?' Mahi's conclusion shocked me. She thought that I was involved in child smuggling and like a fool had given all my money to Amina. 'If you ask me,' she said, 'I have yet to meet a bigger sentimental fool.'

'I am no fool,' I defended myself. But at the back of my mind, I thought may be Mahi was right. May be Amina was never meant to spend the night with me.

On our way back to Easy Guest House, Mahi asked a question that I had been avoiding. 'When are you handing her over to this German, whoever he is?' I shrugged my shoulder. Mahi changed the subject and said, 'I fly to London tomorrow. I will pay for your room tonight. Would you be able to pay me back?'

'Please give me your address for money transfer?' She handed me a card. I looked at it and asked. 'Where is this Holborn?'

'It is in Central London, close to the BBC office. I don't know any more.'

'What will you do in London?'

'I am writing an Accountancy exam in three months.'

'London will be fun. When I wire the money, shall I phone to confirm?'

'You may. That is if the Interpol has not arrested you for child smuggling,' Mahi replied.

Back in the room I called Heinz's number at the Intercontinental Hotel. Heinz's secretary, Sylvia picked up the phone. I introduced myself and asked her to inform Heinz to come to Easy Guest House, room 10 at three. 'That is in half an hour,' she said.

'Yes, three o'clock at Easy Guest House,' I repeated. I informed Mahi of my decision. She came to my room and helped me fold Jill's blanket and collect and pack all her things. She dressed Jill, who continued to play with Mickey on the bed. I turned my face away from her. Jill realised it. Immediately she said, 'Look, Tam, Mickey is calling you.' I already had a billiard ball forming in my throat. The knock on my door came exactly at three. I answered the door. A middle-aged woman with golden hair faced me. 'Good afternoon, I am Sylvia. Herr Heinz is in the car with the Embassy staff.' I walked out with Sylvia to a parking area and met two Germans standing next to two black Mercedes. One of the Mercedes had a CD (Corp Diplomatique) plate. Heinz, stocky with copious golden hair introduced himself and then introduced me to his companion, who was an attaché with the German Embassy. His name was Herr Josef. I asked Heinz for the half, 1000-Ducate note which he duly produced. Then I asked him for the pass-code. He whispered Venus123 in my ear. I also verified his passport identity. 'Why is Madam Bajaj not answering her phone?' I asked. He shook his head and replied, 'I don't know, even I am waiting for her call.'

I told Heinz to wait and walked back to my room. Mahi and Jill who were running around the room stopped when I entered. 'Tam,' Jill ran to me. I lifted her up. I explained to Mahi that I had verified Heinz's credentials. Then I took a deep breath and said. 'Let's get it done.' I picked up Jill's bags, Mahi carried Jill and we walked out of the room. My abrupt action disturbed Jill. She began to cry and wanted me to carry her. I transferred Jill's bags and papers to Mahi and carried her.

When the Germans saw us coming, two uniformed women came out of the waiting Mercedes. I saw the five of them as the cowboys from *Gunfight at the O.K. Corral*. They started to walk towards us. Jill kept crying and clung to me with greater tenacity. 'It is okay, darling,' I kept saying as I walked towards the Germans. The German posse was now right in front of us. One of the uniformed matrons tried to take Jill from my hand. Jill started to flip about violently, 'It is okay, darling…'

'Tam … Tam,' Jill cried. Her cry plunged daggers in to my heart. The matron wrestled Jill away from my hand saying, *'Herr, es wird leichter sein wenn du sie gehen last,* it will be easier if you let her go.'

'Please, let me carry her to the car,' I said.

'Es muss fruher oder spatter gemacht werden . . . it has to be done sooner or later,' Sylvia said as she pulled me back. I felt hooks tear my heart apart. 'Give her medicines . . . check her temperature . . .infections are dangerous for her . . .'

'Tam . . . Tam,' Jill's cries kept ringing in my ears. I woke up in my room at the Easy Guest House clutching Mickey in my hand. Mahi who was sitting in a chair by my bed was applying cold compress to my head. 'You have been crying. You have a fever.'

'Jill, is she all right?'

'Yes. You almost fainted. You were hysterical. I had to get you to bed.'

'I am sorry. I dragged you into this. Sorry.' I was feeling better. I got out of bed. She asked me, 'Can you handle an outing? It'll be good for you.'

'Yes,' I replied. We walked a short distance to the Agakhan Hospital corner and took a taxi. Mahi asked me a question, 'What was Jill to you that you took it so personally?' I searched my soul. Then I explained to her, 'We all have an atomic frequency. If for example your atomic frequency resonates with mine, we get entangled and I become attached to you. I may even fall in love with you. And, if you part from me, it would tear my heart apart. Do you understand?'

'Sort of.'

'Well, that is what happened between Jill and me and so parting was painful for both of us.' Mahi shook her head and said, 'You have strange ideas.'

The taxi dropped us on Delamere Avenue. Mahi stepped into the East African Airways (EAA) Office. I waited outside, watching the glamour of Nairobi. The evening rush hour was just getting underway. Dapper men and women in elegant dresses were stepping out from their offices, heading to cafes and shops along Delamere Avenue. Suddenly, Mahi thrust an envelope in my hand. 'There, your ticket to Jerusha tomorrow morning for seven.'

'Why are you doing all this?' I asked. She ignored my question and instead said, 'Tuck your shirt in. And don't slouch. It is not the end of the world.' I chuckled, 'Now you see Mahi, your atomic mist is resonating with mine.' Mahi laughed, 'Dream on, you drama queen.' She looked approvingly when I finished tucking my shirt, 'You are useless on your own.' She held my hand and pulled me with her to the Stanley Hotel's Café, where she ordered a creamy hot chocolate for us to share.

I borrowed coins from Mahi and made a phone call home to inform Jeremy to arrange pickup for me from the aerodrome in the morning. When I came back our conversation led to the subject of love and when Mahi heard my profound thesis of Physics-Love she branded me as crazy. The cause of our conversation was a huge colour poster covering the entire side wall of the Woolworth's Building cross the Avenue. When I saw Mahi studying it, I commented, 'It is Sadhana, the new actress in *Mere Mehboob*. Isn't she gorgeous?' Mahi took a sip of the hot chocolate, and replied, 'It is hard for a woman to judge another woman's beauty. She is not bad-looking.' I asked her if she watched Bollywood movies. She laughed and said that she had no time for the jiggery-pokery love plots of Bollywood pictures. Her answer ruffled me. I mean, it surprised me that she did not see the charm of Bollywood pictures. I said to her, 'Oh, poor you! *Mere Mehboob* has a "blind-love" story line. A student falls in love with a girl who is in a *burka*, just by the meeting of their eyes.' Mahi burst out laughing. 'How can there be love without seeing the face?' she asked. When I gave her explanation of Quantum Entanglement which linked people who had not seen one another, Mahi burst out laughing, 'Good Lord! just as I thought, you are not only sentimental, but crazy too. Hello, this kind of love only happens in your Bollywood pictures.'

'Mahi matters of the heart are different. Blind love is a reality. We are all blind lovers.'

'You talk as if you have experienced this,' Mahi commented. I backed off.

Despite my bad experiences since I left Jerusha, the glitter of Nairobi was still dazzling me. But this beatific impression of a paradisiacal Nairobi was about to evaporate. I was to learn that independent Kenya was a pretty kettle of fish. We left Stanley Hotel and were walking towards Indian Bazaar, admiring the architecture of the imposing Khoja Mosque facing us. Half way across Government Road an English Lady ran towards us shouting, 'Get off the road, hurry.' Realizing that we had not understood what she was saying, she grabbed Mahi by the arm and pulled her towards the Traffic Island. Suddenly two policemen appeared from nowhere and punched me and dragged me to the opposite end. 'You, bloody foreigner,' one of them shouted. 'you have no respect for our president.' Confused, I stood peevishly, trying to make sense of what was going on. Government Road was empty of traffic and people were lining both sides of the Road. Soon a motorcade headed by several mounted police with wailing sirens and flashing lights glided down Government Road. Mazee Jomo Kenyatta, the Kikuyu president of the Republic of Kenya was on his way home. I was to learn from the English lady who had pulled Mahi to safety, that this was a daily ritual on Government Road. Anyone seen not paying his or her due respect to the emerging demi-god of Africa was instantly punished.

Mahi realized that I had become withdrawn and despondent after this incident. 'Why don't we go to Pan African Grill for dinner and South African jazz,' she suggested to cheer me up.

Pan African's South African jazz was polished but lacked the rusticity and charm of Gembe jazz. Mahi let down her hair and without her dark framed glasses she looked like Audrey Hepburn. We danced to Miriam Makeba's enchanting voice. When I asked her personal questions, she was matter of fact, 'No need to get inquisitive. No family.' I backed off. When we sat down, I suggested to her, 'Mahi, let us play a game. I will ask you several questions.'

'What for?' she asked.

'It will give me an idea of your personality.'

'Okay, fire your questions.'

'First, let's say that in a storyline for a Bollywood picture there is a cat and I ask you: Do you know of a famous cat with one-carat diamond in its ear?'

'I know of no such cat. Is this for a Bollywood or a Disney picture?'

'Mahi, never mind that. My next question: do you know where to meet a Dr Bartlemann?'

'No? How would I know? May be go to a hospital or look up the telephone directory.'

'This is a good answer, indeed. I would have never thought of that.' It seemed that Mahi was enjoying our little game. She asked, 'Okay, what is your next question?'

'Mahi, if the hero in our story kills a man in self-defence, should he run away to Singapore to escape from the police?'

'What is wrong with your thinking? If the killing is in self-defence, he should try prove his innocence. By running away, he will only prove his guilt.'

'Mahi, a good answer. My next question; if a fat priest predicts clashing Sun and Mars in our hero's horoscope how should the storyline progress?'

'This is an interesting question,' Mahi said as she cut me piece of cake from her dessert plate and lifted the fork to my mouth. I sat relishing the cake, waiting for her answer. She cut a piece a piece of cake for herself and sat back.

'Well?' I asked. Mahi took her time, enjoying the cake. Then she tilted her head sideways, gathered her flowing hair from the back and brought it forward on her shoulder. 'Mahi,' I said, 'stop playing with your hair and answer my question.' A coy smile played on her face. 'The storyline,' she said, 'could go along your favourite Blind-Love theme.'

'How?'

'Let's say the girl in burqa that the hero falls in love with, without seeing her face, I may add, is a girl-friend of a billionaire Sheikh. And when he finds out about the amorous intentions of the hero, he gets his thugs to beat him up. Now that would be a serious clash of Sun and Mars in the horoscope, won't it be?' Seeing my serious face, Mahi added, 'You see, this blind-love is a double edge sword.'

'Mahi,' I said, 'I am amazed by your imagination. Really, I am. Now, I have my last question: Say our hero has a dream in which he sees six blurry faces. He does not know whose faces they are. What meaning could we give to this dream?' Mahi looked at her watch. 'You crazy boy, do you know what time it is? You have an early morning flight. Let's go now.' As we left Pan African, I told Mahi, 'You are opinionated but with a fantastic imagination.'

'How dare you call me opinionated?' she reacted with a passion.

'Mahi, but you did not hear what I wanted to say next. I think you and I could work well as a team in picture stories. I really do.'

'You are a piece of flirt,' she said, 'I am not biting your hook late at night.'

You Touched My Heart

As the Dakota touched down at Jerusha, the cobweb of my old anxieties spread over my heart. Suddenly, the cloud of amnesia lifted from my mind. I had a jarring realisation that I had hidden a dead man in Suwakaki. What if the police were waiting to arrest me? A cold shiver sailed through my spine. The stewardess announced that due to a wedding party occupying the main terminal building, we were to collect our luggage at the bottom of the stairs and use the side gate to exit. Tearful bride send-offs attended by large contingents of family and friends were frequent at Jerusha Aerodrome creating much chaos.

Hot air hit my face as I stepped down from the aeroplane and collected my bag from the bottom of the stairs. Beyond the mirage that simmered at the end of the runway, Garrison Hill with terraces of red-tiled army barracks stood like a mythical mountain. Passing by the terminal building, I paused to see if I recognized anyone from the wedding party. But the glass façade was too misty to tell. The immigration officer stamped my passport. I met our driver at the exit. I was relieved that there were no police cars waiting for me.

At home a lonely Simba jumped up and licked me. I looked around the garden. Jeremy had done a credible job of cleaning it after the havoc of *Giant*. He had propped up the broken branch of the Singapore frangipani, but it looked withered and dead. He was nowhere to be seen. Workers were erecting a marquee in the garden for the Friday feast. I entered a quiet home. Azul had left me a note on the dining table.

Welcome home. The family are stopping in Pala to catch a picture show and will be home after midnight. I will be attending a funeral in the afternoon. Please do not wait for me for dinner. Daddy

I sat at the dining table. I did not like the silence. I got up and loaded the old gramophone with a 78-RPM record. A sad song played while I read Narika's letter, which I had no heart to read before I left for Nairobi.

My dearest, I read love letters that you wrote to that wench who doesn't care for you. She makes fun of you. I cry. Some people want to hurt you. I feel frightened for you. I am in trouble. I am pregnant. Please don't think unkindly of me. Please, please give but half an hour of your time. I will explain all. Please forgive me if you can. I am frightened. Raghuvir follows me. He promises to make me a star of a picture In the Shadow of Kilimanjaro if I go to Bombay. Please help me.

I felt sick to my stomach. I felt lonely. The song playing in the background made me more miserable. Reality tugged at my heart. Rule 2 of murder from *Strangers on a Train,* came to my mind. Murderer always revisits the crime scene. I snapped out of Lata's beguiling lullaby and realised that I had left my torch and a bag with flowers and a vermilion bottle in Suwakaki. I also had to retrieve the leather belt or a rope my attacker used to strangle me to prove my innocence.

Without wasting time, I plunged into Suwakaki and made my way to the bomb shelter, expecting putrefying smell of a rotting body. Instead, muddy, forest aroma greeted me. I had hidden the body against the low wall of the bomb shelter. I walked around it but found no sign of a body. I searched my memory, realising that darkness can be delusional. Doubts flooded my mind. I made another round of the bomb shelter, examining tentacles of the climbers. A few were shrivelled. Did the man not die? I distinctly remember checking his pulse and breathing. He was as dead as can be. Did someone come and take him away? What if he had just fainted and then got up and walked away?

I took deep breaths. If I found my torch around this area, then I would be certain that I hid him in the spot that I thought I did. I walked twenty paces to where I thought I had hit him on his head with the torch in my clenched fist. I searched the area and found it beneath the leaf litter. I picked it up with my handkerchief. I retraced my steps to the tall almond tree cluster looking for the noose my attacker had thrown around my neck. Coiled like a snake, I found a leather belt with a dull silvery buckle. About a yard away, was the vermilion bag. I picked up the bag and the belt.

When reason failed to explain the disappearance of the body, I started to clutch at supernatural explanations. Suwakaki abounded with stories of men dancing with ashes of the newly dead smeared on their bodies and trees simmering in blue mist. May be the disappearance of the dead man had something to do with these myths. I plunged into the depth of Suwakaki, towards the epicentre of this stories – the Suwa mango tree. I followed the overhead high-tension cables. I remember Jeremy saying that the Suwa tree was at the edge of a valley, not too far from an electricity pylon. As I walked, the thick of Suwakaki abruptly opened up to a beautiful natural garden of wild bougainvillea, spider lilies, and violet irises. I veered to my right, climbing an incline beyond which were the towering Suwakaki trees. An electricity pylon stood facing me. The sky was full of thunderclouds. A warm wind picked up, ruffling the garden with a giant surge of energy. The sky opened up and rain poured down. I ran to take cover under the forest canopy. As I approached the trees, fragrance of mango flowers enveloped me. Drenched to the bone, I stopped under the first tree. The air turned cold. I looked up and realised that I was standing under the Suwa tree, subject of all the goblin stories. My realisation was instinctive. I was awed. The girth of the trunk was over two meters. Above me, its thick branches forked upwards and outwards, covered with copious dark foliage that extended several meters around the trunk like a giant umbrella. Suddenly, there was a blinding flash and a simultaneous boom as if a thousand cannons had discharged. A lightning bolt struck the overhead high-voltage cables, splitting into several flashy forks, which jumped from one cable to the other. The flashes continued to run along the high-tension cables, and just above Suwa, the flashes bridged over to the Suwa, lighting it with a thousand minor flashes like a Christmas tree. Every leaf of Suwa turned translucent blue, and silvery flashes jumped from one leaf to the other, from one branch to the other. The lightning energy dissipated and the magic died, leaving darkness in its wake. The reason behind the stories of goblins became clear to me. My scientific mind was working at the speed of lightning. There were certain preferential locations where electrical charges build up during thunderstorms and where lightning strikes were frequent. High-tension cables provide a conducting path for such strikes. It seemed to me that the lightning discharges, which jumped from the high-tension cables to the Suwa, were of low energy not to burn Suwa leaves. I felt lucky that just like the proverbial fall of the apple, which led to the discovery of gravity, the lightning discharge happened the moment I was under Suwa and I saw what I saw. I now knew that there was a scientific basis for the stories of goblins at Suwa. The disappearance of the dead man was not supernatural after all. But it still remained a mystery.

I hurried home and put the crucial evidence from Suwakaki in my rucksack with Palita's clothes. My mind became clear and purposeful. I searched for an ebony box that belonged to Azul which Suleman had given me at Moidin. I wanted to talk to Suleman about it. He had said that it contained something from Japan that belonged to Azul. I found the box in my table drawer. I put it in my pocket and cycled to Vir's hostel. The hostel superintendent informed me that Vir had returned to his village. I cycled to Joger's shop. On the way, I noticed that all the shops along Africa and Zanzibar Road were shut. It was not Sunday. This confused me. I reached Joger's shop just as he was instructing the shop assistant to close his father's shop. He was surprised to see me. 'Where have you been?' he asked.

'In Nairobi, for a few days.'

'Junior, many things have happened while you were away.' Saying this he threw me Tuesday edition of the newspaper. The headline shocked me: 'Double Murder shocks Jerusha.' I skimmed through the story, only picking up the highlights. Late on Friday night after the picture shooting at Old Thompson Hotel, on her way home, according to the story, Savi was lured by Refu to Lake Sand Works. According to the hotel staff, at dawn, Zafur received a call and left the hotel in a hurry. He never returned to the Hotel. The following Monday evening, Zafur's body was found in pieces under a sand conveyor at Lake Sand. Savi's brutalised body was found not too far away, on a sand barge.

I felt faint and a surge of immense sadness engulfed me. I stopped reading and said, 'My goodness! Savi murdered; Zafur murdered .' I felt like vomiting. I put my hand to my mouth and grovelled on the floor to overcome by vertigo. Joger rushed and knelt beside me. Gradually I recovered. I wiped my face and asked, 'Joger, why Savi . . . why Zafur? I had agreed to meet her this coming Saturday at JCB. When dancing with me in the Emerald, she had cried on my shoulder. Who did such horrible things?'

Joger helped me get up and explained, 'Charles, the goon with red teeth is the one who did it. You did not read the full story. He later committed suicide and was found hanging in Lake Sand's office.'

'Charles? Why him?'

'Love and jealousy, that's why. I told you this love business is bad. He was after Savi for a long time. She had spurned him. He had tried to intimidate Zafur in Pala many times before. Finally, with that foxy Refu's help, he played a game and implicated Savi's father in selling stolen merchandise. He was threatening to send him to jail unless Savi broke up with Zafur. She probably cried because Charles was threatening to kill Zafur unless she met him. That is how she went to Lake Sands with Refu, without informing Zafur. There are gaps in the story, but it seems that when she realised her mistake, she managed to phone Zafur before trying to escape. Probably in his desperation to save her, Zafur walked into the den of these killers. After killing Zafur, Charles brutalised Savi and killed her. Then he hanged himself in the Lake Sand office. Police have arrested Refu. He will be hanged for sure.'

When I recovered from my shock I asked Joger the reason why all shops were closed. He hammered me with the news that SB Bajaj, the local tycoon's son and Madam Doctor's husband and another man who was his lover were killed by a train at a rail crossing in Pala. Joger explained that the accident had happened on Monday night and the car they were travelling in was dragged several meters and their bodies were badly mangled and the news did not reach Jerusha until Tuesday. I was puzzled. I asked, 'What has that to do with shops closing?'

'It is SB's funeral just about now and businesses are closed to respect him.' Joger added that Madam Doctor had suffered a massive nervous breakdown and had been flown to Germany, via Nairobi, in an emergency.

'My goodness,' I said aloud. All at once, things began to make sense. Now I understood why Madam Doctor had not answered my calls or had not paid for hotel room as promised. I understood her instruction to Amina to handover Jill to Heinz. Joger looked at my ashen face. 'Junior, do not take it personally. This has been a horrible week. Five deaths in one weekend! It is too much. Let us go to Tembo na Membe to get something to eat and drink.'

This was the second time several lovers had died and Jerusha Circle of Love had turned crimson red. Joger did not know about the additional death in Suwakaki.

We came to an empty Tembo na Membe. Joger brought us fruit juices. His bulging eyes were sad. It seemed that he had a box full of bad news. He told me that Tara had broken up with Ash and was marrying the same boy for whom Nash and I had taken the beating at MIC. In humiliation Ash and his family had gone out of town. Then he told me that Nash had received his British residency vouchers and had left for London in a hurry. I asked, 'Flown to London, just like that?' Joger handed me a glass of juice and answered, 'Yes, no fuss, no goodbyes.' He stopped talking. I felt he was waiting to share something more important. He took out a small booklet and a bundle of papers from a brown bag he had carried with him. 'What is it?' I asked. He handed me the booklet, 'Junior, this has been circulating like a hotcake among the girls.' The booklet had a colourful flowery cover page with a heart sticker in one corner. Its title floored me: Love Poems by Lovesick. I leafed through it and saw my love letters to Palita. This is what Narika was telling me about. Had Henna seen it? I turned to the last page and looked at a black and white photo of me donning an Al Capon hat and a bouquet of flowers in my hand at the European Club badminton tournament. I sat speechless. 'Junior, this society girl told her friends that you were a clown and would do anything for her.' I felt foolish and cheap. Joger kept talking. 'In the end she fell into her own trap. She fell in love with you. Girls desire what other girls love and adore. She realised that you were a gem. She ran away from home and waited with Vir at your house. Vir phoned me, looking for you. He said that Palita was hysterical.' I asked Joger, 'Jeremy mentioned a boy with a cast and a girl. Why did Vir have a cast?'

'Some thugs broke his arm at the temple on *Janmastmi* and took away the letter you had given him for Palita. They beat up the fat priest as well.' I put two and two together. The ruffians who broke Vir's hand and roughed up poor Bhatji must be the same ones who tried to strangle me. Hired killers!

Joger was not done. He waved a wedding invitation in front of me and said, 'Palita's wedding was to take place yesterday, but it had to be postponed because timing was inauspicious. The boy's family returned to Nairobi this morning.'

'Where is she?' I asked in a dejected tone.

'Junior, I don't know and I caution you. These rich mill owners are dangerous. Look how they dealt with Vir and how Ash's and my loves have ended?' I rose above my grief and consoled Joger and said to him, 'What if Harry tried to rape Pari? During *Giant* I had asked you if you were able to forgive her? Where is Pari now?'

'She has been staying at Kit Kat since last week, waiting for my answer,' Joger replied.

'Then go and hug her. Tell her you love her. Love is different than sex.'

I sat starring at the wall while Joger went to refill orange juices. The centre of my soul that was previously stirred by a good song was silent. The shock of Savi and Zafur's brutal murders, the pain of Narika's dismal fate, the suddenness of Amina's departure, Madam Doctor's trickery and manner in which Jill was snatched from my arms, Tara's betrayal of Ash, Nash's departure to UK, and now the shock of Palita's wedding plunged me into a sea of gloom. Suddenly I felt a warm hand rub on my back. I turned and saw Miss Suku standing behind me without her heavy make-up. She came around and sat in my lap. 'Your friend tells me you are sad,' she said, as she caressed me. It was soothing. She held my hand and guided me to her room behind Tembo na Membe where she made me sit on her bed. She unbuttoned my shirt and ran her hand on my chest. I lay down and closed my eyes. When I opened them, Miss Suku was sitting on me, naked, stunningly beautiful in pink light. The imagery of the son of Zeus mounted by the naked moon goddess Selena came to my mind. In the myth, Selena came every night and mounted son of Zeus. Many years ago, Mr O'Leary had told me his desire to be the son of Zeus and be mounted by Selena every night. 'Would you not tire, Mr O'Leary, night after night?' I had asked. 'That's why you need eternal youth of son of Zeus, you silly boy,' he had replied.

I noticed that Miss Suku had only one breast. So the myth was correct. It was of no consequence to me. I put my hands around her and pulled her down beside me. Her warmth blanketed me. The anguish in my heart surged. I began to cry. Miss Suku kissed me and tasted my tears, and we bonded. She understood my pain. 'Miss Suku, you have touched my heart,' I said. She kissed me and said, 'And you have mine.'

We Are Who We Are!

I left Miss Suku's unit. Crying in her warm embrace had done me good, but the billiard ball that had formed in my throat was not easy to melt. Dark clouds crowded the sky. I walked aimlessly on Zanzibar Road. Suddenly there was a blinding flash and rain pelted down again. I ran and took shelter in Old Somero Church. As I fumbled my way in, I banged against a wheelbarrow or some object like that and fell, banging my head against the edge of a pew. What happened next was uncanny. I became unconscious or rather lost my surface consciousness, but underneath it, my mind was fully functional. I slid into dreams similar to the ones I had experienced the night after Nina's fifth birthday and again at Norfolk Hotel when Amina walked out on me. An amphitheatre surfaced on the dream screen of my mind. A mysterious music played in the background whose sweetness was sucking me into a peaceful Void. Suddenly, I heard an enchanting Voice pulling me back from the brink of this Void. 'Wake up,' it said. I continued to slide towards the Void which was like a magnet. 'Wake up,' the mysterious Voice said again, this time more urgently. I arrested my slide towards the Void. The Voice waited until I was more alert. 'Pay attention. Don't get sucked in, rather listen to what your heart has always desired.' There upon the sweet music began to resonate through my soul.

'What music is this?' I asked. The Voice replied, 'It is a preview of God's Symphony which your heart has always desired. I say preview because you do not have the capacity to hear the full orchestra. Only a tiny fraction of the preview that you are enjoying inspires all the music in the world. Enjoy this blessing while you are in this unconscious state. When you awaken, it will fade from your mind. You will have a vague recollection of it and will pine for it all your waking life.'

I felt very disappointed and blurted out, 'That is ridiculous. Why are you teasing me like this?' I looked around to locate the source of the mysterious Voice talking to me. I felt as if it came from the depth of my soul. I cried out, 'Who are you? Where are you?'

I heard laughter. 'Question not that which is beyond your capacity. We are who we are. Think who you are.'

'Who am I?' I asked. The Voice answered, 'You are only real in the imagination of those who are witnesses to your life. Beyond that, your life has no meaning.'

'What rubbish?' I replied.

The Voice laughed a benevolent laughter that reverberated from horizon to horizon. 'Not so rubbish, dear boy. I am unlocking the mystery of your heart. There is one more Circle of Life which whirls in every heart and which determines the essence of its Ego. The happiness and disappointments of the person depend on the glow of this Circle.'

'What Circle is this?' There was a long silence. Then the Voice said, 'It is the Circle of Fading Images. Like a fading photograph, with every successive exit of one in whose mind you are an entity, your own image fades; until a time when you will be a nobody. When your friends shun you, your ego diminishes. You feel most hurt when someone ignores you. In this manner, a time will come when people who you think love you and cherish you will shun you and with that your image will diminish in quadratic proportion. Despite this, people seek love and continue to maintain hopeless relationships so that their lives are witnessed. The satisfaction in the heart is that someone should say, "Yes, I witnessed your life, your hopes, and your disappointments." These words give glow to the Circle of Fading Images.'

What I heard shocked me. I remembered an old photo of Jeff and his friends. Its edges were crumpled and faces in the middle of the photo were all faded. It was very frustrating trying to make out who was who in that picture.

All at once my focus shifted to the Amphitheatre stage where a mist swirled and multiple blurry faces began to dance in a powerful vortex. I cried out, 'End this charade. These faces have no meaning.'

'Sure they have. Look carefully. Theirs are the memories which give you life. These faces sustain your identity. Your joys and miseries are rooted in them.' I strained my eyes. The Celestial Music in the background gathered tempo. Suddenly, I saw Savi's beautiful face just as I had seen it in the Emerald, when she had danced with me. 'Savi,' I called out, trying to touch her. The Voice said, 'You cannot touch her anymore. You danced with her. That was the first validation of your existence in the passport of life. She sensed the sweetness of music in your heart. In that moment, you became one with her. This confirmed her love for Zafur and her resolve to die for her love. You were the catalyst for that transformation. Neither you nor she had any expectations from each other. For an instant, you were two souls happy in the company of one another. You validated each other. It was a magical moment in time which only a few people experience. The hot tears she shed on your shoulder were for safety of her lover who was threatened. Now she is beyond it.' The misty vortex shook violently, and in the blink of an eye, Savi disappeared in its chaos.

The Celestial Music faded and was replaced by a chorus. I saw huge tents. Women in colourful tunics, carrying large mugs, overflowing with frothy beers, were walking hurriedly between benches of revellers. '*Frauline*, Miss, beer for our table,' they were shouting at the top of their voices and singing happy songs. It was the Munich Oktober Beer Fest. Madam Doctor, in a black dress with a plunging neckline was with Heinz at one of the tables. She wore deep red lipstick. A smile played on her face. Perfect! It was like a face lifted from *Lady from Shanghai* poster. Yes, Rita Hayworth was the femme fatale in that suspense picture.

'Why Madam Doctor's face?' I asked. The Voice said, 'She is the temptress. She lusted after you. She tried to tempt you, but you stood firm. Then her temptation turned into a different impulse. She came to your rescue when you needed her. She had many needs and desires of her own. Until she met you, her life was an unfulfilled dream. You were a bridge to that dream, a bridge to the love she thought she had lost forever. Her maternal instinct was searching for means to protect the life that had ensued from her. You were an instrument to that end. You satisfied her needs in a different way. Now she is happy in her being. That is the second stamp of validation in the passport of your existence, the stamp of relationship based on need and want.'

The joviality of Munich Oktober Beer Festival disappeared. The sky changed colour. Beams of white, red, and pink flashed across it. I was in a drama, where the light man was creating moods on a stage. A mansion of vast proportions simmered on horizon. Amina was standing at its diamond-studded door. I experienced the same enchanting joy of love I felt when I sat with her in the Picture House watching *Nagin*. I remembered the warmth of her legs entwined with mine. Picture House's aroma of cigarettes, fried samosas, and fresh orange juice surrounded me. Sweet memories of when I made love to her flooded my mind. The fact that she was pregnant with my child kindled a desire in me to hold her and protect her. Then my memories took me back to the painful episode of her rape, my desperate search for her in Jerusha and Pala, and to the time, in the dead of the night, when she walked out and left me alone with Jill at Norfolk Hotel. 'Amina, Amina . . .' I cried out. The Voice said, 'She is the stamp of selfless love in the passport of your life; not expecting anything from you. She never asked for nor expected your love in return.'

'But, I looked for her. I tried my best to prevent her from leaving,' I said.

'The script of her life was already written. You could not have changed it even if you wanted to. Cherish her simplicity and her dedication. Love her innocence.'

All at once, Old Somero Church turned into a vast playground. I heard Jill's chuckles. My heart danced with joy. 'Jill, where are you? Come to Tam,' I said. I looked up and saw her on the top of a magic slide. 'Tam, look at me! Look at me,' she was shouting, waving her hands in the air. Her golden hair was tied in two ponytails with pink ribbons.

'Darling,' I cried out, 'be careful. Hold on to those handrails.' My joy was short-lived. Old Somero Church turned into a hellish dungeon. I felt someone thrusting a million daggers into my heart, turning and twisting them, shredding my heart into bits. I cried out with excruciating pain. Far away, I heard the crying of a child. I had heard this cry in my nightmares, night after night. Now the crying was much nearer. 'Tam, Tam . . .' I heard Jill. I had goose pimples. A German matron was wrestling her away from my clutch. '*Herr . . . Herr, es wird leichter sein wenn du sie gehen lasst . . .* Let her go. Please let her go.' I was hysterical. 'Jill, it is all right, Tam will look after you .'

The Voice interjected, 'She is the fourth stamp in the passport of your life. She is a symbol of your paternal bond which you will not understand yet. It is a bond no parent is able to break in a million life times. Every parent lives and dies with highs and lows of his or her children. This unbreakable bond is both a blessing and a curse. Not bound to Jill by blood, yet you have experienced this attachment.' Jill's cry continued to echo in my soul.

I was barely hanging on to a bar of sanity on the roller coaster of dreamy emotions when suddenly I saw Narika dancing *Lashya* on a heavenly stage. Her feet hardly touched the stage, yet I felt their weight on my heart. Her steps caused me unspeakable pain. Her graceful hand movements jolted my heart. I had broken her fragile heart. Tears streamed from her closed eyes as she danced. All at once, the music tempo changed. Her face became animated. Terrible drumbeats deafened my ears. Her movements quickened. She began to dance Lord Shiva's destruction dance, *Tandava.* Her moves mutilated my heart. I cried, 'No Narika, please not *Tandava.*'

Distraught, I cried out, 'What is the meaning of this?' The Voice said, 'Ahh . . . it pains you. Look at her face. It mirrors the duality of your guilt and her unrequited love. The destructive cosmic energy of *Tandava* boils in the heart of an unrequited lover. The pain that you feel is your curse. The mythical eagle will peck at your liver every night and in the morning, it will be made wholesome and the cycle will repeat as long as you live. I cried out, 'I don't deserve this curse. I wanted to love her. Circumstances prevented me.'

'Blame circumstances. That is the excuse of every delinquent lover. She pleaded. She cried. She put her life as a wager for your love and all you say is "circumstance". While you suffer the hell of your guilt, her unrequited love is her yellow brick road to heaven. That is the reward of every unrequited lover. Angels will throw flowers at her feet and happiness of paradise will be hers to have. Hers is the fifth stamp in the passport of your life.'

Suddenly a colossal City Light materialised out of thin air. Its dome shimmered like a celestial Taj Mahal. Astonished, I asked, 'What is the meaning of this?' The Voice said, 'The City Light is the temple in your heart where gurgles a fountain of love. The love that you feel is not external to you. It is inside you. Only the stimulus is missing. When it comes, emotions cover it and it turns into a beautiful pearl. That is the City Light – a love oyster.' Behind the City Light, I saw a blurry face. 'What about the Sixth Face?'

'If you have sensed it then know it as the face of Universal Love.' I was in no mood for guessing games. 'Whose face is it?' I cried out. The Voice laughed and said, 'Impetuous boy! True love is not without its challenges.'

'Oh, you heartless Voice, tell me if it is my Quantum Love's face?'

'Quantum Love is a search. Go unravel the secret of Watanabe's paintings.' All at once, there was a loud bang above me. I snapped out of my dream and found myself flat on my back with a throbbing pain in my head. I saw a lightning fireball sailing across Old Somero Church roof. The corrugated sheets above simmered with bluish flashes.

Israeli Spy

I sat on the steps of Old Somero Church, holding my throbbing head. The mysterious Voice had given me a powerful clue. The mystery of the sixth face was locked in Watanabe's paintings. My dilemma was how to unravel the secret in these paintings without Savi? This thought depressed me. I was eager to go to JCB and look at the Watanabe paintings with fresh eyes. While I was wallowing in my misery I heard Joger's voice. He stood in front of me with Luke, the boy soldier, 'Junior, someone saw you run towards the Church, so we came looking for you.' What he told me next was a hammer blow. He told me that Kikuna's men had raided JCB and had looted its cashbox and had found bullets and Israeli military badges in it. They had arrested Azul, saying that he was an Israeli spy. Suleman from Moidin, who was drinking at JCB tried to intervene and the soldiers beat him up and also arrested him. My world fell apart. I became hysterical, 'Where have they taken them?'

'We don't know. It could be MIC,' Joger replied. Fact was that anyone taken by the military to MIC had practically no chance of ever coming back. Joger knew it. I knew it. 'Joger, the Israeli badges were given to me by Gina. They are just toys.'

'Try telling that to the military. But more damning is those bullets.'

'I put those behind the cash box. I collected them from the Hill.'

Joger was agitated. 'I remember. I told you then to throw them away, didn't I? Science had made you blind.' In desperation I asked, 'What do I do?' Luke advised me to talk to Commander Leman. I agreed. 'Friends, meet me here in half an hour,' I told them.

I ran towards home in haste. Close to the YMCA, I saw Gawa Crescent swarming with soldiers. A fleet of strange camouflaged amphibian vehicles most likely from Gama Garrison were blocking the entrance to Gawa Crescent. I broke into a sweat. I hid behind a fence and watched. I hoped that Commander Leman had been tipped off about this. I realised that he had constructed the bomb shelter in Suwakaki for this eventuality. He must be hiding in it. I retreated behind YMCA and ran into Suwakaki from Sycamore Drive. A flock of birds fluttered away. Fumbling my way in the dark, I followed the high-tension cables above to the bomb shelter, found its subterranean door and knocked and waited. Nothing happened. I knocked again. A hatch opened and a shaft of light shone on my face. I said, 'Commander Leman, I want to speak to him.' The hatch closed. After a while, it opened again. Muzzle of a gun was in my face. I recognised the Commander's face in the pale-yellow light. 'Sir, they have arrested Azul at JCB and have taken him somewhere. I need your help, please sir.' Commander Leman whispered, 'I know, son. I am in radio contact. They are held in the MP cells on Garrison Hill. Insurgents control that area. Can you get help from someone who knows how to use guns? Do you know the area around the Hill?'

'Sergeant Luke can help us. He is the one who helped at the barbecue in your garden. I know the Hill.'

'Good. I showed you and Luke how to use the gun one afternoon. A tunnel runs under the fence into the barracks, halfway up the Hill. Luke will know it. A rock stands at its mouth. Find it and wait inside for a bugle call at five and then enter the compound. My men will mount an assault. That will be the best opportunity. Beyond that I cannot help. Run for the MP (Military Police) cells, past the big trash dump, behind officer's mess. Shoot the lock on the cells if you have to and find them. Wait outside.' I waited in the dark. The hatch opened and out fell two assault guns and a Colt, followed by boxes of ammunition. Commander came to the hatch again. 'My men are coming to arrest Kikuna's men who are terrorising my home. Now run.'

I picked up ammunition boxes, tucked the guns under my shirt, and retraced my footsteps to Old Somero. Joger and Luke were waiting for me. I explained to them Commander Leman's instructions. Joger was first to speak, 'Very dangerous.' I looked at Luke, 'Would you help me?' He was quick to answer, 'I owe a lot to you and Azul.' I handed him one of the guns and said, 'Luke, Commander showed us once how this L38 works. I've forgotten. Please show me how.' Luke laughed and said. 'It is simple, just aim and pull the trigger. Keep your hand steady, else the bullets will fly all over.' Joger, who was listening to us, said, 'Junior, count me in. I am coming as well.' I told him that it was not necessary. Joger pointed to his Mini and said, 'Don't be ridiculous. Let's go.'

Garrison Hill

In this way, the memory train that I had been riding brought me to the present, holding a Lee Simpson L38. I realised that the Arrow of Time is always in flight. I am not sure where it would land . . .

In the company of Joger and Luke, I am wading into the dreaded Circle of War and Conflict. My daddy and Mr Suleman are held captive in the Garrison Hill. We are waiting for a bugle call . . .

Who Is the Enemy?

The bugle call comes at exactly five o'clock. As Luke prepares to enter the Garrison Hill compound, I ask him, 'Who is the enemy?'

'Everyone. Shoot to save your life,' he says with a grin and enters the Garrison compound through the tunnel opening. A ferocious gun battle commences in the distance. Joger and I follow Luke who darts past a mound of rotting food waste towards an imposing building. He goes around a wall and waits for us at a side door of the building. He pulls open the door and enters, shuffling his gun from side to side. A few seconds later, he comes to the door and signals us to enter. We follow Luke along a dimly lit corridor. There is a row of cells with half-open doors. We look closely at each cell. There is no sign of Azul or Suleman. My heart sinks. I whisper to Luke, 'Where could they be?'

He points his L38 to the exit door. 'We try the NAAFI, where they lock up drunken soldiers. I was locked up there several times.'

Luke runs ahead, along a thorny hedge. Joger and I follow him closely. The sky is overcast, and it is turning dark. Joger is well ahead of me. Suddenly, two men emerge from the hedge behind Joger. It unnerves me. 'Joger,' I shout. One of the men turns around and runs towards me. Luke's words ring in my ears. 'Everyone is an enemy.' I pull the trigger. Orange blooms flash from my gun accompanied by loud bangs. The gun shakes in my hand. I experience Newton's Law – every action gives rise to an equal and opposite reaction. I tighten my grip and continue pulling the trigger. The man rushing towards me falls a meter from me. I point my gun at the man rushing towards Joger. 'Joger, duck.' The man turns in my direction. I hear bullets zoom past me with malicious zings. I pull my trigger. More orange blooms. My bullets hit him. He slumps on the plum hedge. Shaking with fear, I shout, 'Joger, where are you?' He stands up from behind the hedge like a ghost. 'I am okay.' I run towards him shouting, 'Thank God, Joger, you are safe. I killed men.'

'You did what you needed to,' he says as he waits for me.

Luke rushes to support us. 'That was a close call,' he says. We run to the back of the NAAFI through a passageway, towards a row of low-roofed buildings. Luke seems to know his way and enters a narrow passageway, reeking with stench of urine. I run behind him calling on Imam Ali, *'Nade Ali, help me, Ali.'*

Luke lights a cigarette lighter, which casts a dull glow on a row of cells with grilled doors. We walk hastily along the cells. Luke holds the lighter above his head. In one of the cells, I see Azul and Suleman squatting on the floor. 'Luke, they are here,' I say excitedly. Azul and Suleman are in shock and surprised to see us. Like a professional, Luke signals Azul and Suleman to step back, as he shatters the lock on the grilled door with several shots. He rushes into the cell and says, *'Bwana, kimbiya. Sir,* run fast. Let's get out.'

On our way, back to the tunnel, I hold Azul's hand and keep close to him. My other hand is on my gun. I am ready to fire more rounds if necessary. I keep looking back to make sure Suleman is following us. The gun battle that was distant on the Hill sounds much closer. It is more ferocious. I see the men I have shot, lying face down on the path. I feel sick to my stomach and want to vomit. We move in a tight cluster and keep close to the hedge. The lamp post at the trash dump is casting a dull orange glow around. The tunnel entrance is at its base. Suddenly, several shots ring out from the shadow of the building to our right. 'It is an ambush,' Luke cries. 'run to the tunnel. *Bwana, kimbiya.'* He turns and opens fire to provide cover. Joger snatches my L38 and opens fire to support Luke. 'Run, Junior,' he shouts. Bullets are zinging past us. I clutch Azul's hand, and we crouch behind the rubbish heap. I look back and extend my hand to Suleman. He is struggling to breathe. I let go Azul's hand to pull Suleman. Luke and Joger have pressed their hands on their triggers and blooms of orange are pouring out from their muzzles. Suddenly a shot rings close to us and Suleman drops to the ground.

'Oh no! Suleman, no.' I keel down beside him. The trash heap casts a ghostly shadow on him, hiding his face and body. I cannot see his wound, but he is writhing in pain, gasping for a breath. Azul is turning back. I become hysterical, 'No, Dadd . . . y, don't stop. Run, go.' Azul is approaching us. I let go of Suleman, crawl to Azul, pull him down, and say, 'Daddy, you run to the tunnel.' I return to Suleman. He is limp. I put my hand to his nose. He is not breathing. I whisper in his ear, 'Suleman.' There is no response. I pull him behind the trash heap. In the orange light, his eyes look glassy. I begin to cry. 'He is dead . . . He is dead.' I hear Luke's voice, 'You run. We are outnumbered. Leave him. Run.' I leave Suleman and crawl to Azul who is waiting at the entrance of the tunnel. We enter the tunnel. Joger runs and dives in to the tunnel behind us, while Luke provides cover. We wait for Luke. Suddenly, the gunfire stops. Everything goes quiet. We freeze in fear for Luke. Time stops. Finally, we hear a rustling and Luke wiggles in.

Safely in Joger's Mini, Azul slaps me. 'What do you think you were doing, coming into the compound?' It surprises me. 'Daddy, Commander Leman told me to.'

Joger drives on the deserted Churchill Drive. Azul tells him to drive us to JCB. Past Jerusha Station, Joger leaves the main road and drives over the railway tracks on mud road to Radio Road to avoid possible army road blocks on Africa Street. Suleman's death has miffed us. Through the years, we have grown used to army purges and disappearance of people. We take it in our stride. These things are never discussed in the open. But when someone so familiar as Suleman, who always had a cheerful word to say to me at Moidin's and who came to JCB for a beer once a week and reminisced with Azul about the past, dies, then it causes unbearable sadness in the heart. I put my head on Azul's shoulder. 'Daddy, Suleman is dead . . .'

'He jumped in to protect me. He had no reason to . . . No reason to . . .' Azul's voice shakes. I put my hands on Luke and Joger's shoulders and thank them. I inform Azul about what I have seen near our home and suggest we phone Jeff not to return home with the family. 'Son,' Azul says, 'the Commander had warned me of troubles in the afternoon, so I had phoned Jeff and I told them to head for Kigali.'

'Kigali, but that's Rwanda.'

'Yes, there are direct flights to Brussels. I want them to get out and stay in Europe.'

'Ma, Nina, and everybody?' I asked.

'Yes, everyone.'

Joger stops the Mini at JCB. The street leading to Market Square is deserted. JCB's usual vibrant and lighted front is in darkness. Luke leaves us and runs up the deserted street towards Market Square. Azul rushes to the back of JCB through an alley where a shaft of light shines through a partially open door. Before leaving, Joger clasps my hand, 'Junior, Vir gave this for you. Sorry, I forgot about it.' I point to Kit Kat and ask him if he made contact with Pari since our conversation in the afternoon. He shakes his head. I tell him. 'Joger, carpe diem, cease the day. Things are turning dangerous. Go fetch her and bring her to safety.'

'Thanks,' he mutters. I stand and watch as he drives the short distance to Kit Kat Hotel and stops. Then I run into JCB through the back door. Pedro informs us that the army has imposed a dusk to dawn curfew. Azul is in a strange, focused mood. To me he says, 'You keep to Pumzika and keep the door locked. I want to sort some papers in my office.'

I switch on the table lamp in Pumzika. It is after two years I am entering it. I have missed it. I run a finger over one of the cabinets and find a layer of dust. My mind is a tangled mess. I try to put all the bizarre events out of my mind and focus on the mystery of the sixth face in Watanabe's paintings. Two years ago, on the eve of Gossage Football cup, when I had purchased a colouring set for a recluse from the Recluse Lane, he had promised to paint a Japanese Cherry Blossoms scene for me. I never went back to collect it. He had also told me that he had taken formal training in Hiroshige Painting techniques. Could this recluse help me solve the mystery of the sixth face? I inform Pedro of my intention to go to Recluse Lane. He tries to dissuade me. Seeing my determination, he relents and insist that I return as soon as I can before Azul starts looking for me. I run to Recluse Lane through the back alley and approach a group of addicts playing a three-card game of *Pata Poteya* under a street lamp. I ask them about a painter who painted with brick powder. One of them looks up and says, 'The crazy loner. His shack is along this lane, red one under the lamp.' I walk along and find the red capsule of the type the homeless of Tokyo use. I tap on its hatch. There is no answer. I wait. All at once, a man jumps on me from behind. His stealth unnerves me. 'Caught ya,' he says, 'you thief, stealing my bottles.'

'No, I am not stealing. Don't you remember me?' He scrutinises my face. I scrutinise his face too. In front of me stands a man in his forties, with a clean-shaven face. I do not recognise him. I was expecting a man with a beard and unkempt hair. He shakes his head and says, 'I don't know you.' I remind him that I had given him a colouring box two years ago and that he had promised to paint me a Japanese Cherry Blossom painting. He scratches his head. 'Uh . . . that was a long time ago. You never came. Why are you here?' I tell him about the five Hiroshige paintings that Watanabe painted for JCB. A light goes on in his mind. He says excitedly, 'Watanabe painted only three. He was painting the fourth when things happened at Old Thompson, but I need a drink to think clearly.' I ask the man his name. He says it is Axle. I throw a bait, 'Axle, I will provide you a drink if you accompany me to JCB and tell me about Watanabe.' He is agreeable to my proposal. We walk hurriedly to JCB through back alleys past Market Square. When Axle learns that Azul owns JCB, he asks, 'Is Azul, the Jazzman of Sisia, your father? Is he still with Tiano?'

'Yes, they are together,' I reply.

'What a pair! They had Sisia sizzling with best Jazz outside South Africa.' I cut through the chase and ask him about Watanabe and Miki Kawai story. 'I only know bits here and there,' he replies.

'Axle, please tell me what you know.'

The Land of the Rising Sun

Axle and Azul saw a beautiful rainbow arched over Japan and believed that their pots of gold were hidden at the end of this rainbow in Japan. When they arrived in Tokyo with a foreign trade mission, Japanese trade officials and a part-time Franco-Japanese interpreter, named Miki Kawai, received them. Miki was a nursing student at a College in Kudanshita. During their visits to industries around Tokyo, Miki gravitated towards younger Axle and Azul. In the evenings, she took them to Kabuki Theatre in Ginza and to Edogawa for traditional Japanese dinners. One day when Axle and the rest of the delegation went to visit the Rayon Technology Centre, in which Azul had no interest, Miki invited Azul to the Cheery Blossom Trail at Chi Dori Gafuchi. She was dressed in a flowery Japanese *Yukata,* a more casual form of Kimono, with a Japanese hair make-up which was traditional attire for festive occasions for young Japanese women. It left Azul gasping. 'You look beautiful,' he complimented her. Azul's words were trapping impressionable Miki in a love web. At Chi Dori Gafuchi, Miki spread a Japanese mat under a blooming cherry blossom tree at the edge of Imperial Moat and the two sat eating bento boxes of Sushi, enjoying each other's company. When the wind blew, pink petals rained on them.

Tokyo, the East City of Japan, sitting at the edge of Tokyo Bay, had picturesque Tama River on its western border. Beyond it, the sprawl of Tokyo gave way to hilly Tama Prefecture. Further west stood the snow-capped Mount Fuji, like a monument of heaven. When Axle and Azul saw it from air during their descent in to Tokyo Airport, they were amazed with its beauty, and they both made up their minds to scale it. Several of Hiroshige's famous woodblock paintings showed Mount Fuji from different locations. When the official trade mission business was over, Axle and Azul expressed their desire to Miki to climb Mount Fuji. She was delighted to arrange this for them during the upcoming weekend. Miki, including several other delegates decided to join the expedition. The group commenced their climb from the Fifth Station at Kawa Guchico about a hundred kilometres from Tokyo, at midnight. Their intention was to reach the summit to greet the rising sun. To Axle and Azul's surprise, petit Miki kept pace with the group.

At dawn, they crossed the snowline on their way to the Seventh Station. The climb became steep and slippery. Up above them, the silvery grey peak of Mount Fuiji loomed large. Suddenly Miki slumped on the snow and passed out due to altitude sickness. Azul ran and took her head in his lap, opened a bottle of smelling salts from a first aid box and held it to her nose. She regained consciousness. The group wanted to abort the climb. Azul volunteered to bring Miki back to the Fifth Station so the rest of the party could continue. At lower altitude, Miki's breathing improved, but she suffered from headache and nausea. At the Fifth Station, they checked into a climber's lodge where Miki rested. Azul fed her pumpkin bread with hot soup which revived her.

When it was time for the delegation to return home, Miki was unable to face the grim prospect of Azul, whom she had come to love, leaving. She did not accompany the delegation to the airport to bid farewell as was the custom.

Upon returning home, Azul learnt that the dam project on which he was pinning his hopes to apply Japanese technology was postponed for two years. The investment he had made went sour, and he was forced to take a job in Sisia, running Paradise Hotel.

Miki, deeply in love with Azul, took an assignment with the VSO and came to Jerusha Hospital as a nurse a few weeks after Azul's departure from Japan. It was a hopeless situation, but it was the only way Miki knew to be near Azul. In search of him, she came to Blue Room at JCB and met Watanabe who had recently come from Hakone, Japan, to work on the dam project. With the postponement of the dam project, Watanabe had ample time on his hands and had started to copy-paint selected Hiroshige paintings for JCB. This hard-drinking engineer was a good artist.

At about the same time, another crazy artist by the name of O'Leary, with a thick beard and shoulder-length hair, came to Jerusha. He came from Paris and sat up his easel in Market Square, in imitation of Gauguin, hoping to find his orient on canvass in Jerusha. O'Leary's artistic antics earned him the title of Crazy Drunk. He started teaching art at Jerusha Secondary on a part-time basis. He also gravitated to Blue Room and met Watanabe and Miki. She enjoyed the company of these two crazy artists. O'Leary, a brilliant artist himself, admired the talent of Watanabe and his renditions of the famous Hiroshige paintings in watercolours. The two developed an artistic bond. 'O'Leary san,' Watanabe used to say, 'I am copying Hiroshige, but there is a hidden secret in my paintings.' For many days, O'Leary scrutinised Watanabe's paintings to decipher the secret but was unable to.

With the coming of Miki, the relationship between these two artists took a turn. They became rivals seeking to win the affection of Miki Kawai, who in her turn was burning like a moth for Azul. In this fashion, there was not a love triangle but a love quadrilateral. On the artistic front, O'Leary watched with interest the progress of Watanabe's paintings. As of yet the secret that Watanabe was weaving in his paintings was not apparent to O'Leary.

O'Leary took up a room at Old Thompson and convinced Miki to pose for him. Miki's spending time with O'Leary at Old Thompson began to irritate Watanabe and things came to a head one Saturday afternoon at Old Thomson Hotel during a barbecue hosted by police commissioner,

Mr Pierce. O'Leary, Miki, Watanabe, Azul, Mr Tiano, and Axle along with prominent people of Jerusha were all attending it. Angry with Miki, Watanabe was drinking heavily that afternoon. Crossing the fine line of Japanese etiquette, he started to abuse Miki. She started to cry. 'Leave her alone,' O'Leary pleaded. That made Watanabe even angrier. Azul and Tiano watched in silence. Drunken Watanabe continued his tirade, driving Miki to a breaking point. She snapped. Her reaction angered Watanabe. 'You *haffu* bitch, you are a French slut.' Azul could not take this assault on defenceless Miki any more. He told Watanabe, 'Now, listen, you drunk brute. If you say one word, I will thrash you.'

Watanabe mocked Azul, 'Ehh, you ugly *guaijin,* foreigner, will thrash me, for this *haffu* bitch. Are you sleeping with her too?' Azul lost his cool and hit him. Axle and Mr Tiano intervened. O'Leary took Azul to his suite away from Watanabe. Miki sat crying in Emerald. Tiano and Axle stayed with her and left her alone only for a short time to hear Mr Pierce's speech in the garden. Alone, Miki made her way to O'Leary's suite to join Azul. Inebriated Watanabe followed her. Much later, Watanabe was found stabbed to death at Old Thompson Hotel.

Pieces of a Jigsaw Puzzle

Axle's revelation that Azul was present when Watanabe died shocks me. I ask him, 'Who murdered Watanabe?'

'We will never know. Ask Azul.' Axel adds that, that murky afternoon, Miki was also stabbed. She was moved to the hospital under a cloak of secrecy. Fortunately, her wound was not life-threatening. For me the story raises more questions. 'If Watanabe finished three paintings when he died, who finished the rest?' Axle explains, 'These two artists, Watanabe and O'Leary, rivals in love had an artistic bond. O'Leary understood the essence of Watanabe's genius. He completed Watanabe's fourth unfinished painting that was found in his room at Kit Kat. What is interesting is that besides these four, O'Leary painted one more, making a total of five. These together are the key to the secret Watanabe was weaving in the paintings. Collectively, these are like pieces of a jigsaw puzzle.' As we approach JCB, the clouded sky in the north is glowing orange. This glow is different from the cherry red glow of the slag pour on Murima. Axle says, 'it looks like a forest fire.' We hear wailing sirens of police cars. Axle picks up pace and says, 'Son, we should be indoors.' Then, as if from a sudden recall of past, he says, 'When Tiano took Miki to the hospital, she was pregnant.'

Back at JCB, I guide Axle to Pumzika and quickly go to Blue Room where mostly locals, who were unable to get away before the dusk curfew, are drinking with abandon. Among them I see a bearded foreigner. He rushes to me and asks me if there is any chance of getting to Pala. I explain to him that there are many army check-points along the way and that he is safer at JCB. I see his drooping face and feel sorry for him. I leave him and retrieve the five Watanabe paintings hanging on the wall and rush to Pumzika. I hand these to Axle and plead to him, 'Please, kindly find the secret Watanabe and O'Leary put in these paintings. If there are faces or a face, show it to me.' I walk out and tell Pedro to bring Axle a bottle of best Shiraz wine and a plate of kofta. Then I walk to Wine Garden and read the letter Joger gave me before we parted. It is from Palita.

Dear Lovesick,
Krishna never married his beloved Radha. Whenever Krishna played his magical flute, it threw Radha into a swoon. Likewise, in ecstasy of your love . . .

Suddenly JCB shakes violently followed by a loud bang. A commotion ensues in the courtyard. I rush out, clutching Palita's letter. Pedro says it is real *Na Anza*. Kikuna and Leman's men are fighting in the Market Square. Soon the fighting may spread. Mr Tiano rushes from Blue Room and says to me, 'A phone call for you.' I rush to the front saloon and pick the receiver. 'Hello?' I ask.

'Is that you, drama queen?'

'Mahi . . . are you already in London?'

'No, I am still at Easy Guest House.'

'I will send your money . . . Don't worry . . .'

'It's not the money. I phoned your home but no one answered. Are you all right?' TV is showing army trouble on the streets of Jerusha and Pala. A coup! All flights to London via Pala are cancelled.' I explain to Mahi, 'We have bombardment not too far from where we are. These army purges take a few days to settle. We have a curfew. I am not sure if banks will open tomorrow, but I will get our London agent to get you the money.'

'I said it is not the money. Phone me at Easy Guest House to update me. I will wait,' Mahi shouts. Mahi puts her phone down. Mahi's phone call surprises me. I feel a warm glow for her in my heart. In Nairobi, she supported me through my worst crisis. Like the proverbial Samaritan . . . she fed me when I was hungry . . . I have a good chemistry with her.

The tank bombardment dies down. We are in the eye of the storm. I am eager to learn if Axle has been able to crack the secret of Hiroshige paintings. I want to finish reading Palita's letter. On my way to Pumzika, the bearded foreigner collars me and asks me if the army troubles will end soon because his girlfriend has arrived in Nairobi from London and is anxious to be with her. I explain to him that the army trouble is the big tsunami we had been expecting and that he could phone his girlfriend in Nairobi from the front office.

'I don't have her number,' he strokes his beard and replies.

'What are you doing in Jerusha?' I ask.

'Oh,' he extends his hand to me and says, 'I am sorry I didn't introduce myself. I am Dr Bartlemann.' My jaws drop, 'What? Dr Bartlemann, seriously?'

'Yes. I am attending a physics conference in Nairobi, and I was sightseeing for few days.' Unable to contain my excitement, I ask, 'Dr Bartlemann, tell me about your socks.' My question surprises him. 'What? How do you know about my socks?' Then he bends down and pulls up his trouser bottoms, exposing his socks. I see his right sock is red and the left is green. 'Why are they different colour?' I ask. He smiles. 'Do you know anything about Quantum Physics?' he asks. My eyes light up like hundred watt bulbs. 'A little . . .' Dr Bartlemann says. 'It has a property called Entanglement.' I am about to faint with excitement. 'What has Entanglement to do with red and green socks?' I ask.

Standing at the entrance to Blue Room, clutching Palita's letter, Dr Bartlemann explains that Quantum Physics has two paradoxical properties. The first one is Entanglement. Two entangled objects separated from each other influence the behaviour of each other, even when there is no exchange of information between them. And that is where he says his socks come in. His students at

MIT know that his socks are Entangled and when one is red the other will be influenced and it will be green or some other colour.

'Dr Bartlemann, what has your socks to do with a cat?' I ask.

'A lot. Let me tell you about Schrodinger's Cat.' Excitement grips me. 'Is it a very famous cat?' I ask.

'Yes, very famous since 1935 when an Austrian Physicist, Schrodinger, proposed a mind experiment with this imaginary cat to explain the second Quantum paradox.' I could not believe what I am hearing. A famous cat called Schrodinger's Cat! My silly one-carat dream cat that I have been looking for all this time! Dr Bartlemann explains that Schrodinger took this furry cat with a big one-carat diamond in its ear and put it in a steel box with a very sensitive "trigger loaded" hammer over a pot of poison and a radioactive source. Then he sealed the box. If the radioactive source decays and emits even one atom, it will trip the hammer, break the pot and the poison will kill the cat. The observer on the outside does not know if the radioactive source has decayed and killed the cat. I am totally absorbed by this new information. Dr Bartlemann continues, 'By Quantum Rule, the cat is in two states. There is 50/50 chance that cat is both alive and dead at the same time. In other words, according to Quantum Rule, the cat is in reality in two parallel universes: a universe in which it is dead and a universe in which it is alive. Are you following me so far?'

'Yes, please go on,' I reply.

'So, now we come to the important bit. Until the box is opened, the cat is both alive and dead. Its states are entangled and together they form a "Waveform". Only when we open the steel box, do we know if the cat is alive or dead. It is important to realise that in opening the box, the famous WAVEFORM COLLAPSE happens, that is, *the observer collapses the Waveform. The States of the cat reduce to just one state—either a dead or alive cat.* So since 1935, this famous, diamond-wearing Schrodinger's cat is living in what we call *Quantum Indeterminacy.* No one knows if it is alive or dead! It could be both.'

Eureka! My silly dream cat was not so silly after all. Now I understood the conundrum of its life. How was I to know that this silly dream cat was not living in Jerusha sewers but was hidden in physics textbook and that the answer to my life's enigma was starring me in my face? I am disappointed that in my half knowledge of Quantum Physics, with all the thinking I had done about it, I had failed to understand its key concept, that of *Indeterminacy*. That is what the silly cat told me in no uncertain terms, 'Your love life is as certain as my life!' What a fool I have been! Dr Bartlemann's explanation opens up a crack in my heart. If only I had been informed properly and understood what the silly cat meant, life would have been different. I would not have chased Palita. Narika would not have been destroyed the way she was. I would not have killed a man and would have had a clear idea of where my life was leading.

The bombardment of Market Square resumes. We hear a shrill whizzing of a flying shell and then suddenly there is thunderous boom. JCB shakes violently. A joist above us buckles. Dr Bartlemann pulls me from harm's way from the falling joist. A piece of wood hits my hand. Palita's letter is swept away in the raining mortar debris. "WAVEFORM COLLAPSE," Dr Bartlemann says with a chuckle, pointing to the debris that has consumed Palita's letter. I like his sense of humour. He asks, 'What was the paper in your hand?'

'A letter from my girlfriend . . . about confession of love. I don't even know where she is.' I reply.

'Did you read the letter?'

'No.'

'Ho, ho, ho,' Dr Bartlemann laughs like a Christmas Father. 'Well, now your situation is like Schrodinger's cat. Whatever was in that letter will be forever in a state of indeterminacy. You will never know. You will live in parallel universes, one in which you will be with her and she will love you. In another, she will be separated from you not loving you.'

I leave Dr Bartlemann and run to Pumzika where Axle is hunched over the table looking at the paintings. I am impatient. 'Any luck?' I ask. He replies, 'I am close.' He has arranged the five paintings one over the other. He shuffles them, steps back, and looks at them.

'It is impossible to solve the mystery because in Japan, every person has a personal stamp that is used on official documents in place of a signature. These paintings require a similar Japanese stamp. Where would we find such a stamp and whose stamp?' I remember the small ebony box in my pocket that Suleman had given me. He had specifically asked me not to open it until we met with Azul. I pull it out and give it to Axle. 'Will this work?' I ask. Axle takes the box, opens the lid, and pulls up what appears to be a wooden pen. 'It is a stamp, all right. It might work,' he says. There is a dried ink pad in the box. He takes the wine glass from the table and pours a few drops of wine over the dry pad and watches it soak the pad. He then presses the stamp on to the pad and lifts it up. 'Brilliant. It is a bit faded, but it will do.'

Axle arranges the four paintings diagonally in a rosette, like fan blades, creating a hole in the middle. Then he inserts the fifth below the rosette and adjusts it so that a yellowish-brown cliff face shows through the hole. Then he stamps the cliff face. As he lifts the stamp from the picture, his jaw drops. 'Axle, what is it?' I ask. He is visibly excited. 'Look at this beauty. It worked. This stamp is a technique used in ancient royal courts to establish the identity of the true claimant to the throne.' I am stretching my neck to peek at what Axle has uncovered. Axle continues to mutter, 'It is amazing what Watanabe and O'Leary have accomplished. These two were masters, par excellence.' He then turns around and asks, 'Where did you get this stamp from?'

'Suleman from Moidin gave it to me. He said that it belonged to Azul.' Axle scrapes out a paper cover from the lid of the ebony box. Underneath it is a picture. 'Ahh,' Axle says, 'this explains it. Look at this picture and compare it with the composite of the face from the paintings.' I compare the two. They are similar. Axle comments. 'Look at the mastery of the two artists, Watanabe and O'Leary, born separate but conjoined by thought and artistic symbiosis. This beautiful face belonged to a girl who was in love and pregnant.'

I have my own surprise. Deep in my heart, I was expecting Palita's face to emerge from the painting collage. But never having seen her face, I have no concept of it. The face that I see flabbergasts me. It confuses me. I see Mahi's face; her arched oriental eyes, and high cheekbones. Axle's words come to me in wavelets. 'Son, this is Miki Kawai's face. This must be her stamp.' I verbalise my thoughts, 'How could Palita have Mahi's face? And how could Mahi have the same face as Miki Kawai?'

Axle asks, 'What are you saying?' I am confused. It is too much of a coincidence. A doubt arises in my mind. Could Mahi be Miki Kawai's daughter? I ask Axle, 'You said Miki was pregnant when she was stabbed. Whose baby was she carrying?'

'No one knows, except Azul and O'Leary. And O'Leary would not say anything. After Watanabe's death, he withdrew in a shell, took a few months to finish the paintings, and then disappeared.'

Several questions have been whirling in my mind since I heard Miki Kawai and third man story. The words to these questions now shape up in my mind. Who murdered Watanabe? Is Mahi Miki Kawai's daughter, and is she my father's illegitimate child? There is a glow for Mahi in my heart. Could she be my half-sister? What a twist of fate? I never thought of Azul living in parallel universes. Proof of Quantum Physics right in our own home! If this truth were revealed, it would pulverise our family. Rehmat would be devastated.

Axle says to me, 'Son, you look as if you have seen a ghost.' I fake a smile and tell him about the incident on the night of *Giant* when Mr Ben, the lawyer, had threatened Azul with exposure of Sisia affair. Axle looks sympathetically to me. 'That rascal Ben was always an opportunist. He was my girlfriend's lawyer when together they looted my wealth. Amongst us friends, this Miki saga was known as Sisia Affair.'

I immediately realize that Ben is blackmailing Azul to sell JCB by threatening to expose Miki's story. I ask Axle the question that I have been dreading to ask. 'Was Miki Kawai already pregnant when she came from Japan?' Axle scratches his head and then replies, 'It was so long ago. It is hard to tell.'

The Market Square battle rages on as I grapple with issues of different dimensions. I knock on Azul's door and enter. He is busy sorting papers. He looks up and says, 'Son, I had a call from Jeff from Kigali Airport. They were boarding a flight to Brussels. There was not much time, so I did not call you. Thank God that Yasukuni Shrine picture fell when it did. If it wasn't for the *Majalis* that your mother insisted on, the family would not have gone to Ramji Estate for mangoes for the Friday feast and would have never crossed over to

Kigali. Now they can safely reach Brussels. Even the Ramjis are flying out.' I want to cry. 'When will I see them?'

'Son, hopefully soon.' I fiddle with papers on Azul's desk. He asks, 'Is something the matter?' I come to the point. 'Daddy, who was Miki Kawai?' My question shocks Azul. 'Now is not the time to talk about it.'

'Daddy, I think it is the right time.' He is taken aback by my insistence. 'So be it. It is time I share this burden with someone,' he replies. He bids me to a chair. 'This army trouble could make us refugees and throw us to different corners of the world. I want someone to know the truth.'

Free Love and Such Rubbish

Azul confirms that Miki was in love with him and had indeed followed him to Jerusha but he had not knowingly encouraged her. I ask him a blunt question about Watanabe's murder in Old Thomson. Azul gives me an account of events leading to Watanabe's death. After trying to stab Miki in O'Leary's suite, drunken Watanabe ran out with the bloody skewer in his hand. Not wanting any one to see him, he jumped from the balcony and when he fell, the skewer lodged in his side. He crawled and hid under the patio. He was discovered dead the following Tuesday when both Azul and Tiano had returned to Sisia. The commissioner of Police Mr Pierce was soon to return to London and was expecting a promotion. He did not want the spectre of a murder in the colony to spoil his chance. So he took personal charge of the case and spread a blanket of secrecy over it. Although circumstantial evidence pointed finger at Azul who had punched Watanabe in front of witness, thus establishing a motive, investigation showed that Watanabe had died due to a self-inflicted wound. Commissioner Pierce never took Azul in to custody and went personally to Sisia to question him to avert any publicity.

Watanabe's death frightened Miki, and she followed Azul to Sisia, where she gave birth to a baby girl a few months later. Suffering from postnatal depression, she lost interest in her baby and ventured into the McKenzie Corridor during the malaria outbreak as a nurse, against Tiano and Azul's advice. Later she died from malaria. Her last wish was for Azul to look after her baby. Azul arranged a wet nurse for the baby. Only Tiano and Azul knew about all this.

I ask Azul a direct question, 'Daddy whose baby was Miki carrying?' Azul becomes uneasy. He replies, 'When Miki came from Japan, she was vulnerable and weak. She longed to be with me but that was impossible. O'Leary took advantage of her state. He lured her to Old Thompson Hotel, convincing her to pose for him. That is where she became pregnant. I pleaded with O'Leary to take responsibility for her welfare and marry her. I threatened him. O'Leary was of free spirit and believed in free love and such rubbish. "She can abort," he suggested unashamedly.'

'So daddy, when Miki died who looked after her baby?'

'For some years, a wet nurse took care of her in Sisia. Things got very difficult for me. I was moving back to Jerusha. I had responsibilities at home. I had to do what I had to do. I arranged and moved the child to a nursery at a convent where I have supported her all these years. She has grown up to be a beautiful girl. I had to be careful. I could not even give her my telephone numbers. She always wrote to a private post box, and when she needed to, she contacted Tiano. He arranged money transfers to her and took care of all her needs. I very much wished for her to grow up in a family and all, but it was impossible. She was not an orphan and yet she was one. I was helpless. I went and saw her every couple of months. With age, she became resentful that I did not visit her more often. She thought I had abandoned her. She has no one else in this world. Then she refused to see me altogether. The last I saw her was a year ago.

'What is her name, Daddy?' I ask. Azul gives me her birth certificate. It shows the birth of a Rumico Kawai registered at Bali Hospital in the District of Gisu. I jump up, 'Daddy, you come with me. I want to show you something.' He is surprised. 'What is it?' I guide him to Pumzika. The shelling of Market Square has abated. I know that troops are regrouping and any minute all hell would break loose. Axle is having a glass of wine. When he sees Azul, he recognises him immediately and stands up. 'You, devil Jazzman, Azul? How are you?'

'Is it Axle? Good lord, where have you been?'

'Not too near, not too far. All you my fair-weather friends, not one of you came looking. But I forgive you.'

Axle then shows Azul the secret face that has emerged from the Watanabe paintings. 'Good lord!' Azul exclaims. Axle pats Azul's back and says, 'Just as beautiful as when we first met her in Tokyo. The smile and the hair slide.' Azul shakes his head and says, 'I had heard about a face hidden in these paintings, but I had never suspected it this way. What a genius!'

The rumble of tanks recommences. 'Daddy,' I say, 'yesterday, in Nairobi, I met a girl. Her name is Mahi. She grew up in Broderick Falls. She refused to give me details of her family. She phoned me just few minutes ago. This face looks like hers. Is it too much of a coincidence?' Azul looks puzzled. 'Did this girl say that she was going to London?'

'Yes, Daddy, she helped me a lot in Nairobi. I had run out of money and she paid for my aeroplane ticket.'

'What did she say her last name was?' I pull out Mahi's card. 'Here, Daddy, it says Mahi Trembly.'

'That is her. Mahi is the name by which everyone knows her. Trembly was Miki's French maternal grandfather's name. What a coincidence! And you say you have her telephone number in Nairobi?'

'Yes, this number is hers at Easy Guest House. She just phoned.'

'Phoned you, from Nairobi?' Azul has a look of disbelief on his face. 'What a relief, son! I have been worried about her. She is a rebel. She has refused money I have offered for her London trip. She wants to sit some exam.'

'The Accounting Exam.' Azul continues, 'She refused to talk to me all last year. When I phoned the convent, they said that she had left for London. No contact address.' Commotion in the courtyard disturbs our conversation. Azul and I rush out.

Luke is back and has news that shocks us. He informs us that Commander Leman is dead. We are shocked. Luke explains that Leman was hiding in the forest behind his estate and Kikuna's men smoked him out and shot him in the head. Then they set fire to the forest and all the houses. 'Your house is no more,' he adds. Azul has a look of disbelief. Luke adds that at the Market, Leman's men are retreating and Kikuna has brought tanks on to the streets. We don't believe what we hear. 'Tanks on the street. House burning . . . Daddy, can we go home? Maybe we can save it,' I say.

'There is no home,' Luke says. 'Kikuna's men are surrounding the whole area. It is too dangerous.'

In our little country, we were always worried about *Na Anza*. From what Luke tells us, things have turned much uglier than *Na Anza*. He says that the government in Pala is taken over by Kikuna who has also taken over the country. Our President who is in Arusha is essentially overthrown. He has thrown out the Israelis. He says foreigners are traitors. His men are looting Africa Street. They are hard on foreigners. Luke urges us to leave. Fear grips me. I put my hands around Azul. He says, 'Son, we must leave for Nairobi soon. We cannot leave without Tiano. Gather what you want.' Luke says to Azul. '*Bwana*, most people are rushing towards Pala. The roads to International Airport are jammed and the soldiers are looting everyone. I can arrange escort to Liro and then you must drive on Salisbury Road to the border. Go to Nairobi by road. It is still safe there. The only danger is getting out of Jerusha. We will take side roads to Churchill Roundabout to avoid the checkpoints.'

I rush to Pumzika, pickup three *Nagin* records and the Watanabe paintings, and put them in a box. The sixth face is hidden in the paintings. I want to show it to Mahi. I linger for a minute and run my hand on my music collection. I notice a gift box on the table. I remember Jeff and Salim telling me that they had a surprise waiting for me at Pumzika. I tear open the wrapping and hold in my hand an HMV, mint 78-RPM record. I look at the title:

Film: Be Gunah
Singer: Jaikishan

I scarcely believe what I am holding in my hand. For a good three years, I have searched every corner of East Africa for this record. I read Salim's note.

Dear Brother,

Can never forget Be Gunah for which you were scolded. We searched hard for this record and truth be told, Jeff found it from a shop in Anand, India. It just arrived a few days back. We wanted to surprise you.
Jeff and Salim.

I put the mint record with the rest of *Nagin* records and paintings. Azul comes in and hands me a portfolio of documents. 'These are family records and birth certificates. We may be refugees.' I know exactly what Azul means. In the past several years, we have seen thousands of refugees from Congo, Rwanda, and Southern Sudan streaming through Jerusha. It looks as if it is our turn to go through the same humiliation.

We step out of Pumzika. Axle comes running to Azul when he hears that we are planning to go to Nairobi. He wants to join us and says that he wants to look for a new rainbow in another land. Dr Bartlemann, the physicist asks Azul, 'I am told you all are leaving for Nairobi. Could I ride with you?' Azul agrees. I hurry to the saloon and dial Joger's number. I want to tell him to join the Jeep escort and escape with his family. The phone keeps ringing. I cut the line and dial Easy Guest House in Nairobi. 'Yes,' a sleepy voice answers.

'Could I speak to Mahi Trembly?'

'Connecting.' I wait for what seems like an eternity. My hands are sweaty. The shelling is getting more intense. JCB shakes. I hear a blip, and my phone connects. 'Mahi?' I ask.

'Yes, is that you, drama queen?'

'Stop being funny. Listen, Mahi. The tanks are rolling. We are leaving for Nairobi.'

'Wait, what are you saying?'

'Our house is burning. Intense fighting. Please reserve rooms for us, four. We will be there tomorrow.'

'Tell me more . . .'

'Mahi, later . . . we must leave. They are coming for us. And Mahi listen, before it is too late, we are much closer than you can ever imagine.'

'You fool, don't start that blind love business. Anyway, *Mere Mahboob* is releasing on Saturday. Sadhana, *the actress* will attend the premier. I will buy tickets for us and you could explain how the plot works. I will wait for you.'

Pedro accompanies us to the car with moist eyes. There is no time for lengthy goodbyes. He hugs me and shakes Azul's hand. '*Pole, go* in peace,' he says. Axle volunteers to drive. Dr Bartlemann sits in the front with Axle. I sit next to Azul in the back. Axle drives a short distance to Africa Street where Luke is waiting with two machine-guns-mounted Jeeps. One takes position behind us and the other leads the way. Axle drives behind the Jeep through deserted back roads to Glorious Maternity Home from where our Gawa Crescent comes into view. *Suwakaki* is on fire. The glow that we saw was from this fire. Gawa Crescent is razed to the ground. Flames are dancing about from what remains of our homes. Azul is miffed. I am chocking and squeeze Azul's hand. 'Daddy, what about Simba? Can we look for him?' I say, holding back my tears. Men and boys don't cry. There comes a time when frenzy and whiplash of events shut the sluices of emotions. Heart becomes a stone. In the blink of an eye, the world we knew has ended. In a perverse way, I feel a relief. If the man I thought I had killed was still in *Suwakaki,* it would appear as if he died in violence from Kikuna's men.

Suddenly several shots ring out from snipers hiding in bushes along Sycamore Road. Axle swerves. One bullet hits our headlamp, shattering it. We all become tense and crouch below the windows. Axle barely keeps his head above the steering wheel. Machine guns from our escort Jeeps answer with a spray of bullets. Bhatji's words ring in my mind. 'Only time will tell what clashing Sun and Saturn in your horoscope means.'

I face the full brunt of the turbulence of interference from the Circle of War and Conflict. The lead Jeep gathers speed. Soon we are past Jerusha Aerodrome. The ambers of the burning Gawa Crescent become an orange spec behind us as the looming darkness of Salisbury Road engulfs us and we begin the "crossing of the ocean" to a new beginning.

The End

Glossary

Aalap: Prelude to a vocal Indian Classical composition, usually hummed without words

Abhinaya: Acting (Hindi)

Aji: An endearing word used by Indian man or woman when addressing their spouse.

Arre: An exclamation or a prelude in a sentence in common parlance (Hindi, Gujarati)

Beta: Son (Hindi, Urdu, Gujarati)

Bhor Ki Bela: Morning Hour, a magazine programme on VOK in 1950–1970s (Hindi)

Biryani: Rice cooked with meat and aromatic herbs (Hindi, Urdu, Arabic)

Brindaban: Hindu God Krishna's enchanting gardens

Burka: Face veil worn by Muslim women

Bwana: A respectful address equivalent of Sir (Kiswahili)

Chaat: Fried savouries with tamarind chutney (Hindi)

Chalo Futo: A slang meaning 'get lost' (Hindi, Urdu)

Choghadia: A devotional composition of Khoja Ismailis (Gujarati)

Diwali: Hindu festival of light celebrating the return of God Rama from exile (Hindi, Gujarati)

Deg: A large pot used for cooking in communal feasts (Urdu, Gujarati)

Dongosi: A particular type of sugar cane of East Africa

Falooda: A concoction of milk, rose water, vermicelli chia seed and ice cream (Hindi, Urdu)

Funge Macho: Close your eyes (Kiswahili)

Gayaki: The vocal singing of a musical composition (Hindi)

Ghazal: A form of poetry of Persian origin, prevalent in South East Asia and Middle East

Guaijin: Foreigner (Japanese)

Ginan: A poem of wisdom from Ismaili Tradition of South East Asia

Ghee: Fat extract from milk or clarified butter used in cooking (Urdu, Hindi)

Gopi: A female devotee of Hindu God Krishna

Haraka: Hurry (Kiswhili)

Halwa: A sweetmeat of flour mixed with nuts and flavoured with rose essence and saffron

Hey Prabhu: O god (Hindi, Gujarati)

Hodi: A polite gesture asking if someone is home (Kiswahili)

Janmastmi: Festival to celebrate Hindu God Krishna's birthday

Imam: A Muslim cleric who leads prayer at a mosque.

Irshad: Words of wisdom (Urdu)

Ishq: Love or love desire, used in various combinations to convey the passion and ardour of love. (Urdu, Gujarati, Persian)

Jamuns: Indian dessert of fried dumplings in syrup

Jute ka maar: An insulting gesture of hitting someone with slippers (Urdu)

Kondos: Highway robbers, thieves (Kiswahili)

Lashya: Shiva, the Hindu God's dance in his female form

Le: An exclamation remark in Urdu

Luo: Tribe of Kenya

Mahabharata: Hindu Religious Epic

Majun: Shocking and mocking form of Arabic poetry

Maya: A Hindu religious concept that considers all life and life attachments as illusion

Maha Shay: Esquire (Bengali)

Majalis: A congregational gathering for prayers

Mandap: An Indian wedding stage

Mandazi: African doughnut

Manga: Japanese comic book but erroneously used by the protagonist as erotic magazine

MIC: Military Interrogation Centre

Misra: A word or words around which a verse or verses are written in poetry (Urdu)

Muisi: Thief (Kiswahili)

Mulevi: Drunkard (Kiswahili)

Mushaira: An Urdu poetry symposium

Na Anza: Kiswahili expression for commencement of an event

Nade Ali: A Shia cry of help from Imam Ali

NAAFI: Navy, Army, and Air Force Institutes providing canteens, shops, etc,

Njugu: Groundnuts (Kiswahili)

Nguli: Concoction of fermented yam and millet

Nritya: Dance (Hindi)

NASA: National Aeronautical and Space Administration of USA

OAU: Organization of African Unity

OM: A mystical sound or incantation in Hinduism

Pape: Friend or brother (Punjabi)

Purda: Curtain (Urdu, Hindi)

Paan: Betel nut leaf stuffed with roasted sesame seeds, betel nuts, and other ingredients as an after dinner freshener or as stimulant

Parvana: Moth (Hindi, Urdu)

Puris: Fried Indian tortillas, usually served at breakfast

Raga: In Indian music, *raga* is a tonal framework or basic tune of the composition

Ragotas: Select randomly (Kiswahili)

Raas Leela: An enactment of a mystical dance in which Hindu God Krishna's devotees danced around Krishan while he played magical tunes from his flute

Rampuri: An Indian gravity knife of formidable reputation (Source Wikipedia)

Rotis: Indian bread

Sala Haramzada: Bastard (Urdu)

Samosas: Fried pastry stuffed with spicy meat or vegetables (Hindi)

Sarangi: Indian musical stringed instrument like the violin played with a bow. (Source Wikipedia)

Saraswatichandra: A Gujarati novel of 1950s

Salaam: Greetings of Muslim, meaning peace be to you

Shama: Flame (Urdu, Hindi)

Shyam: Dark. A common name for Indian God Krishan referring to his dark complexion

Shodo: Japanese painting style

Takh de: A slang, meaning deliver the blow (Punjabi)

Tandava: Hindu God Shiva's dance in his male form. Shiva performs the *Tandava* when he dissolves the universe in the never-ending cycle of creation and destruction

Tanpura: An Indian long-necked, plucked stringed instrument

Udhric: An Arabic concept of love in which love is raised to a spiritual height and where in the end the lover dies as a martyr

Uhuru: A Kiswahili word meaning freedom

UN: United Nations

UNESCO: United Nations Educational, Scientific and Cultural Organization

USIS: United States Information Service

Vah vah: A vocal accolade for a performance or accomplishment (Urdu, Hindi, Gujarati)

VOK: Radio service of Kenya Broadcasting Service, Voice of Kenya

VSO: Voluntary Service Overseas

Veena: Indian musical stringed instrument, like the sitar

Wasl: Union. In hands of skilled poets, *Wasl* is used as erotic union. In spiritual usage, it signifies union with the Supreme Deity (Urdu)

Ye lo: An expression of surprise (Bengali)

In Pradhan's debut novel, love, war, destiny, science, and music (especially from movies) flavor the life of a teenager growing up in a Hindu-dominated community in post-colonial Africa.

This story's environment is an exotic, mythical Indian community named Jerusha in eastern Africa during the 1950s and '60s, analogous to similar polyglot outposts in Kenya and South Africa. Narrator Kaku, nicknamed "Einstein" by his peers, is from a cosmopolitan Muslim family. He's perfectly comfortable with the pantheistic culture of Hinduism, African tribes, even Judeo-Christianity. While fascinated by science, the youth draws suggestions of divinity not from religious dogma but from music—be it the metaphorical harmonies of stars and planets, the ghazal songs influenced by the poet Rumi, African-American jazz, or the tunes of Bollywood movies he hears on the radio or on the emotive soundtracks of motion pictures he sees. Kaku comes of age haunted by a vision of a beautiful, phantom girl, whom he sees in his favorite forest. He and his peers' affairs of the heart aren't helped by the socially conservative climate of Jerusha in general and their school in particular, where sex and sex education are a minefield of taboos. Meanwhile, the region is transformed by independence from colonialism, followed by industrialization and, ultimately, all-consuming civil war. Pradhan shows how those upheavals mirror the passion inside the hero, who's stirred by an incurable sense of romance. Comely young females of all types orbit him, but he only seems to want the ones he cannot have, be they an enigmatic nocturnal nymph or a high-caste classmate he convinces himself is his "soulmate." The book often hops boundaries from magical realism to mystical surrealism to science-as-whimsy (including a lovesick dreamer's take on quantum physics and a guest appearance by Schrödinger's cat). Pradhan's singular narrative evokes a mysterious web of fate and chain-reaction equations of human desire and folly. The novel is accessorized by a helpful glossary of its rich, cross-cultural language terms, making for a luminous debut.

A masala banquet of images, nostalgia, and yearnings that won't soon be forgotten – *Kirkus Reviews*

About the Author

My formative years in Uganda were paradisiacal. Amin's racist expulsion changed everything and with that upheaval the world opened up for me. With degrees in engineering from Nairobi and Lehigh University, Pennsylvania, I began a journey that showed me unifying aspects of the world and of one humanity. During my consulting work in Americas, Middle and Far East and Europe it was easy for Mariam and I to live in the cocooned life of Expats, but we decided otherwise and lived as locals, enjoying their cuisines and absorbing their cultures. It contributed to our inner growth. We saw the struggles of local people and shared in their hopes. Far from madding crowds we found treasures of local Sumo wrestling in the suburbs of Tokyo, enchanting Krishna worships at temples in Singapore, sizzling barbecue of fresh-caught Salmon at a local Red Indian encampment in Victoria, Canada and Junaghad Kababs at local a African Tea Shop in Dar-es-Salaam where locals were glad we came. This world view permeates my writing. I have interest in philosophy of the Vedas, Early Judeo-Christianity History and Astrophysics/Cosmology. I currently live in London with my wife, Mariam.